DEATH WALKER

DEATH WALKER

✖ ✖ ✖ ✖

AIMÉE & DAVID THURLO

A Tom Doherty Associates Book
New York

DEATH WALKER

Copyright © 1996 by Aimée & David Thurlo

This book is printed on acid-free paper.

A Forge Book
Published by Tom Doherty Associates, Inc.
175 Fifth Avenue
New York, N.Y. 10010

Forge® is a registered trademark of Tom Doherty Associates, Inc.

Library of Congress Cataloging-in-Publication Data

Thurlo, Aimée
     Death walker : an Ella Clah novel / by Aimée and
     David Thurlo.—1st ed.
          p. c.m.
     "A Tom Doherty Associates book."
     ISBN 0–312–85651–2
     1. Navajo Indians—Fiction. 2. Policewomen—Fiction.
I. Thurlo, David. II. Title.
PS3570.H82D4   1996
813'.54—dc20   95–51556
                                                                    CIP

First Edition: June 1996

Printed in the United States of America

0 9 8 7 6 5 4 3 2 1

To the Taylor staff, past and present, for their support and
encouragement from the very beginning

ACKNOWLEDGMENTS
------ ✖ ✖ ✖ ------

With special thanks to D. R. Garcia for his help and expertise in the field of law enforcement.

AUTHORS' NOTE
———— ✖ ✖ ✖ ————

The rituals described herein have been abbreviated and altered slightly out of respect for the Navajo People.

The psychiatric facility in this work is solely a product of our imagination.

DEATH WALKER

PROLOGUE

———— ✖ ✖ ✖ ————

Kee Dodge looked toward the east as the sun rose above a distant plateau, casting a sunflower glow off the rocks of Red Flint Pass. At this early hour he could still feel the trace of humidity that lingered in the air cooling his skin. In another few hours, it would be gone and only the heat would remain.

He took a deep breath, enjoying the rich scent of piñon that filled the air around him. His class would be meeting here again in the Chuska Mountains, one of the sacred homes of the *Dineh*— the Navajo People. It was a particularly good site for today's lessons of the past. Here an Anglo named Washington and his cavalry had killed several Navajo warriors, and until recently the mapmakers had named the pass for him. But the worm was slowly turning to the advantage of the People. Navajo students had petitioned those in positions of so-called authority, and the place was now to be called Narbona Pass, after the Navajo leader killed there at the hands of Washington's troops.

Though he wasn't in agreement with their insistence on naming the pass after a Navajo who'd died, he was supportive of the sentiments behind it. In another twenty years when people bought new maps, they would at least know the truth.

Dodge took out the prayer sticks, clubs, and the handmade

bow and arrows he'd brought, arranging them carefully on a blanket he'd spread on the ground. Attendance in his classes remained high, counter to the skepticism the college faculty had expressed at first. This new generation of college kids was much more eager to learn than any he'd taught in the past. It was as if they'd suddenly become aware of the incalculable value of their heritage.

For so many years it had been different. Young people had been determined to be just like those outside the *Dineh Tah*, the People's Land. It was good to see this long overdue change.

Dodge emptied the worn cardboard box he'd hauled up the piñon-covered slope. He checked his watch, disliking the concession to Anglo ways that required everything to be ruled by the clock, then started back down to the road. He'd need to review his lesson plans soon in preparation for class, but he'd left his notebook on the seat of his pickup. The morning air was brisk, and a slight breeze blew up the mountain as he made his way carefully downhill.

Kee Dodge reached his truck just as a lone hiker appeared from around the curve of the gravel road. Although it was not unusual for the *Dineh* to walk great distances, this man didn't look like an ordinary hiker, or someone out looking for a missing lamb. His jeans and shirt were too clean and neat, and even his white cross-trainers gleamed with newness.

Dodge exhaled softly, thinking how many times his own truck had broken down on this long stretch. It was almost impossible most times of the year to find anyone to help. Invariably it meant a long walk back to the main highway or on to Lukachukai.

"Pickup broke down, right?" Dodge asked with a rueful smile, disregarding the scowl on the young man's face. "Don't worry, nephew, I've got some tools here. Let's see what we can do."

As Kee Dodge reached over the side of the pickup bed for his toolbox, he heard the young man step up behind him. Before he could turn around, something crashed against his skull. Dodge's world became a bright white flash of pain that quickly faded into a warm black of night. With the taste of betrayal and defeat, Kee Dodge's wind breath left his body forever.

ONE

———— ✖ ✖ ✖ ————

Special Investigator Ella Clah stood in the doorway to her living room, nibbling on a slice of honeydew melon from her brother's garden. It was still early in the morning, but her mother was already helping Valerie Yazzie finish the velveteen wedding outfit Valerie's daughter would wear on her wedding day in less than a week.

Ella's mother looked up and smiled at her. Rose Destea was, like her daughter, taller than most Navajo women, and only a dozen or so pounds heavier than Ella. "Take a break from all that paperwork you brought from the police department and have a decent breakfast. That's not the way to start a morning you're supposed to have off."

Ella shrugged. "There's a lot of work to get done. We've had some major changes in the department. Our new police chief wants things done *his* way. He's determined to recapture the faith people had in us once."

Valerie Yazzie shook her head. The middle-aged Navajo woman wore a perpetual frown that had, through the years, become ingrained in her features. "There were so many we trusted we shouldn't have. It's hard to forget how they betrayed the tribe."

"But the department is clean now, and Big Ed Atcitty is going to make sure it stays that way. He's an excellent leader, and tough, but fair." Ella bit off another piece of the juicy melon and swallowed. "We're just having to do a lot of work fast to put the changes he wants into effect."

"What you find difficult, daughter, is doing things someone else's way," Rose said with a smile. "You've always had definite opinions on how things should be handled."

Ella smiled grudgingly. "Well, I suppose that's true."

Rose turned her attention back to the hem she was pinning. "This is going to be such a lovely wedding dress!"

"You'll be making one for your own daughter before too long," Valerie commented mischievously, nodding toward Ella. "She will want to trade in her gun belt for a cradle board sooner or later."

Ella choked on the piece of melon and reached to the kitchen counter for a napkin. "Don't count on it."

Rose sighed and looked at Valerie. "See how she is? I've just about given up hope." She paused, then with a tiny smile added, "but not quite."

As the telephone rang and interrupted them, Ella gave the phone company a mental high-five. She'd been literally saved by the bell. "I'll take that."

"You might as well," Rose muttered. "It's probably for you. They won't leave you alone, even on your morning off. I never get any calls in my own home anymore."

Ella chose not to comment. It was an old argument. Her mother couldn't understand her dedication to police work and the incredible sense of purpose it gave her. In truth, she found it difficult to explain to anyone. Only another cop could understand that addiction to the incredible highs and lows of the work; the need to restore order to a world that resisted at every turn. Ella walked down the hall to her room, closed the door, and answered the phone.

"Hold for Police Chief Atcitty, please," said the crisp voice of Big Ed's secretary.

Ella sat on the edge of her bed, waiting. More than eight months had passed since she'd resigned from the FBI and moved back to the Rez to stay with her widowed mother. She gazed around her room, lost in memories. Most of what was around her was less than a year old. The fire, months back, had spared the house but ruined everything she'd left behind from her youth. All traces of the girl she'd once been were gone now, and she had more than a decade's worth of new memories and new mementos to replace them. She stared pensively at her framed FBI diploma and gilded marksmanship trophies on the shelf. Last in line was a recent photo showing her being sworn in as a tribal police officer.

Ella was hard pressed to say which of her career achievements filled her with the most un-Navajo-like pride, but she was definitely proud of her new job. It had been created especially for her, here on the Navajo Rez, and it required her own special skills. She was special investigator for the Navajo Police, and answered only to Big Ed. The job gave her the autonomy she'd dreamed of throughout her career, though on the downside, the paperwork load was pretty incredible.

"Shorty, you there?" a familiar gravelly voice asked.

"Yes, Big Ed. What's going down?" Ella was getting used to the nickname Big Ed had given her, although she stood a head taller than her boss and most other Navajo men as well.

Big Ed had been given his nickname because he was shaped like a barrel with arms. Stories around the station claimed Big Ed had never been knocked off his feet by a perp. She believed them.

"I need you to drive over to what we've always called Red Flint Pass, though it's getting yet another name now. Maybe you know it as Washington Pass. A college history class was supposed to meet there. Seems someone murdered Kee Dodge out there before his students arrived."

"Kee Dodge, the historian?"

"Yeah. His students showed up this morning for class and, from what I hear, stumbled upon the body. Get over there and take up the case. I'd like a preliminary report before lunch. I've called the M.E. She'll meet you there along with our crime-scene team. We have a patrol officer in the area already. He'll give you whatever backup you need."

"I'm out the door, Big Ed."

Ella reached for her gun belt and adjusted the pancake holster so that it lay flat against her waist. Beneath a jacket, her weapon barely showed, and that was great for plainclothes work. Fitting her .22 backup pistol inside her custom-made boot strap, she strode out of her room.

"I have to be going now. I'm not sure when I'll be back," Ella called out to her mother, waving to Valerie as she passed through the living room.

"So, what else is new?" Rose said with a sigh. "Just be careful."

"Always."

Ella went to her navy blue unmarked Jeep. It was the perfect vehicle for the kind of rough terrain that comprised most of the Navajo nation. She took the map from the glove compartment and checked the route. It would be a fifty-minute ride at posted speeds, but she could knock a good ten minutes off that in a hurry. She opted for the hurry, knowing that a fresh crime scene would yield the most information.

The drive south on Highway 666 was almost a straight line, but once she turned west at Sheep Springs, Ella had to slow down a bit. Soon the road turned to gravel, and her Jeep left a long, serpentine dust trail as it climbed the mountain road.

When Ella arrived, several vehicles were already parked on both sides of the road. Jimmy Frank, a young but experienced patrolman, was questioning one student. Her gaze then shifted to the half-dozen young adults some distance away, silently awaiting their turn to be questioned. They were dressed casually in jeans, like college students anywhere. Jimmy was going with established procedures, not letting the words of one witness shape another's.

She studied the officer for a moment. Jimmy was in his early thirties, yet he looked so different from the way he had at sixteen, except for the slight belly that pushed against his shirt, hinting at what would come with middle age.

As Ella approached the crime scene, she noted the body was facedown next to the driver's side of a pickup parked about fifteen feet off the road. The students and patrolman were staying as far away from it as possible, although Officer Frank had positioned himself facing the scene so he could ask relevant questions while keeping the crime scene under observation. Logic and cultural beliefs were destined to continue clashing inside them for another generation at least. Ella knew that she would not be the last to have to try and live in two overlapping worlds. Even among the new generation of Navajos, fear of the *chindi* remained, though most would outwardly deny it.

Ella nodded to Jimmy, who continued his interview, keeping the witnesses away from the scene. Walking in a slow, inward spiral around the pickup, Ella studied the ground around the crime scene, making a visual search for evidence. Carefully selecting where she stepped, she finally arrived at the body. There were no recognizable tracks here on the hard ground so close to the road.

As Ella got her first close-up look at the corpse, bile rose to the back of her throat. Blood had begun to cake the gravelly earth beneath the head and neck of the body. The victim's skull had been bludgeoned, and the soft, pulpy matter from within the wound mingled with sharp pieces of bone, giving it the appearance of carelessly ground beef.

Ella forced herself to gulp several deep lungfuls of air, grateful that her sense of smell was the least stimulated by what she saw. She crouched next to the body, forcing herself to think clearly and calmly, relying on her training and the memory that this was not the worst corpse she'd ever seen. Kee lay chest down. From what she could see, he'd been strangled with leather shoelaces, probably after being hit on the head with some kind of tool or club. From the look of the head wound, the strangling had probably been a waste of time.

Although Dodge's back was to her, his face was turned to the right. She noted that his right eye was being held open by an object that had been imbedded in it. It was a piece of something hard and white, discolored at the entry point by blood and aqueous fluid. She leaned closer, trying to figure out what it was, suppressing a shudder.

Ella stared at the object, moving to within a foot of the face.

Though she heard the gasp that came from the students who had turned to watch her, she never looked up. Her gaze was fastened on the object she was now certain was a piece of bone. That was a trademark of skinwalkers, yet something didn't feel right about this. Bone ammunition was their signature, true, but this was too garish. It was almost too flagrant a warning sign.

Relying instinctively on her training to make sense of what she was seeing, Ella mentally categorized the crime as "staged." The killer had spent time trying to leave an obvious impression in the mind of the investigator. The killer could have continued to bash his victim's skull to a pulp, but instead he'd chosen to deliver a coup de grâce through strangulation. Speculating about the object imbedded in the victim's eye, she wondered if perhaps he'd needed to preserve the face to complete the gruesome picture. This crime had definitely been planned in detail.

Next Ella shifted her attention a few feet to her right and carefully studied the pattern drawn on the ground with ashes. It was approximately two feet wide. The ashes appeared to have been trickled through someone's fingers in the manner used for a dry or sand painting. She could make out some figures in the center, but she didn't recognize any of them.

Hearing another vehicle approaching, Ella stood and walked carefully around the truck. As she watched, the medical examiner's wagon pulled up and a middle-aged Navajo woman of ample proportions emerged. Dr. Carolyn Roanhorse slid her large black briefcase off the front seat, then strode briskly toward Ella.

Ella watched Carolyn approach. The woman was in her midfifties and had a cool, businesslike demeanor that Ella liked, although Ella had always suspected it was more a defense than anything else. Carolyn's job as medical examiner had made her a near pariah within the tribe. Few Navajos wished to be around someone who might carry ghost sickness.

Carolyn nodded to Ella in greeting, then followed her to crouch low beside the corpse. She gave the body a quick onceover. "Nasty way to die. Probably took a while."

The statement, typical of Carolyn, also met her official obligation to pronounce the obvious. "What do you make of that object in the victim's eye?" Ella decided to ask.

Carolyn studied it, then glanced up. "The same thing you did, I'll bet."

Ella met Carolyn's gaze. "Okay. Before you get too involved over here, would you mind glancing at this?" Ella pointed to the dry painting.

Carolyn stood up reluctantly and stepped over for a closer look. "That's out of my area of expertise, but I do know only skinwalkers do dry paintings in ashes. Whoever did those figures, however, must be a real beginner," she said bluntly. "I can't even guess what they're supposed to be."

"Yeah," Ella agreed with a wry smile.

Carolyn moved back to the body. "You think this has something to do with the skinwalkers who were involved in your father's murder?"

"Some of them are still at large, so I suppose it's possible, but I'd have to have more proof before I'd reach that conclusion." Ella ran a hand through her shoulder-length black hair, pushing it away from her face. "Personally, I'm hoping this crime has a conventional motivation behind it, like revenge or jealousy. Because if it is skinwalkers, then this is just the beginning."

Carolyn retrieved her tape recorder from the bag. "I'll do my best to get you some answers soon."

Ella's thoughts were racing. She had no wish to battle a resurgence of skinwalkers, Navajo witches. Her mind flashed to the morning she'd seen her father's mutilated body, then on to the final battle she'd barely survived.

A group of skinwalkers, including her police chief father-in-law, had killed him to gain power and protect their interests. In the end, her father-in-law also died, and her cousin Peterson Yazzie, a powerful skinwalker, had been captured and jailed.

She'd learned a lot about herself back then—like the utter reliability of the sense that was now telling her that other crimes would follow this one. Her search for answers would take her down many unexpected roads before the truth was revealed. But, if it was in Ella's power, the human animal responsible for this brutality would be brought to justice.

Ella stepped carefully over to the graveled road, then walked to the small group of students. Officer Frank had them all together now, so he must have finished taking their statements. Ella could see the open distrust in their faces. She wasn't sure if it was because she'd been near the body, or because many in the area still considered her an outsider because of her long absence from the Rez.

Jimmy Frank glanced up, then walked over to meet her halfway. "I've already questioned them, one at a time. Their stories are pretty much the same. They all arrived within ten minutes of the scheduled class time. The victim held his lectures at different sites around the Rez in keeping with each day's subject. Although his knowledge of tribal history wasn't based on formal education, the consensus is that no one knew more about Navajo history than D—the victim. His family had protected and preserved the stories handed down for generations. The Navajo People have lost a great treasure with his death."

"Did anyone witness the crime, see anyone who could have been the perpetrator, or see anyone who wasn't supposed to be here?"

"No. Regina Henderson and Norma Pete were the first to get here. They claim everything was just as we see it now. No cars came their way as they arrived, or passed by since then. The perp must have gone down the other side of the mountain, or left on foot. By the time they discovered the body and backed off, Travis Charley arrived. He stayed here to meet the other students while the girls drove back to Sonostee to call us in."

Ella decided to speak to Regina and Norma while Officer Frank marked off the crime scene with yellow tape. Norma, the smaller and younger of the two girls in their late teens, was crying into a soggy handkerchief. Ella noted that Norma reeked of dime-store perfume. It was better than most smells at a crime scene, however. "I'm sorry that you two had to see this," Ella said sympathetically.

Norma looked up out of red, tear-filled eyes. "It was awful. Now I'm going to have to go to a *hataalii*. I know I'm going to

have dreams about this. I just know it! And what about his"—
she dropped her voice—"you know—*chindi*," she mouthed. "I
don't believe in ghost sickness, but you just never know. I mean
I've heard the stories—"

"Stop it, Norma," Regina said sharply. Nervously she toyed
with the single strand of heishi beads she wore over her denim
blouse. "You're scaring yourself silly. Don't talk about it anymore." She looked up at Ella. "We already told the officer everything we know or saw. Can we go?"

Out of the corner of her eye, Ella saw the white crime-scene
unit's van pulling up. Unlike the resources she'd gotten used to
during her days in the FBI, the tribe's resident crime-scene unit
was composed of only two people and very limited equipment.
Round-faced Sergeant Ralph Tache was the photographer and assistant investigator, and Detective Harry Ute, a cadaverously
thin Navajo with a perpetual glum expression, was the crime-
scene investigator who'd collect most of the evidence.

Ella's gaze shifted back to the students, who all seemed eager
to leave. One of the girls reached down to pick up her bookbag,
set on the ground just outside the yellow tape boundary. Ella saw
her waist-length black hair drape around her, shielding her tear-
streaked face. They were all scared, and so was she, truth be told.
This death would have implications that would carry far beyond
the murder itself. All things were interconnected. That Navajo belief was part of all of them. Evil had surfaced, but now balance
needed to be restored. And that was her job, and her contribu-
tion to the tribe.

As Ella saw the young woman crouch by the bookbag, she noticed a piece of freshly chewed gum on the ground. Someone had
obviously spat it out. "Does that belong to anyone here?" she
asked the group, pointing to the gum.

The students all shook their heads, then glanced at each other
curiously. Finally Ella looked at Officer Frank. The officer pointed
to his mouth. "Still got mine. You can have it." He gave her a
weak smile.

"Make sure one of the team preserves that discarded gum as
evidence," she instructed Jimmy softly, refusing to smile back.

"It may have belonged to the victim, but if it didn't . . ."

Ella allowed her gaze to drift over the students. They shifted nervously and stepped down onto the road, farther away from the yellow tape "fence." Obviously none of them wanted to stay a second longer than was necessary. She couldn't blame them. Ella had learned to shield herself mentally from the horrors of police work but, to them, this was a nightmare or worse.

Ella glanced at Jimmy, who was placing one of the crime team's wire and plastic "flags" near the lump of gum. "You've got a way to contact each of them if needed?" she asked.

Officer Frank nodded. "I know where to find them, and I've taken their statements."

On the outside, she would have asked if he'd recorded all their addresses. But here on the Rez, street addresses weren't always practical. Some of these kids probably lived in areas where the closest mesa was the only identifiable landmark.

"We may need to talk to some of you again later," she told them calmly, "but for now you can go."

The students hurried back to their vehicles, but one of the boys approached Ella. "I saw the ashes on the ground," he said softly. "Is that business starting again? I'd hoped you'd gotten them all last year."

Ella saw the touch of fear in his eyes and knew that whatever she answered now would be carried via gossip all around the Rez. She measured her words carefully. "It's too early to know, but this killer definitely wants to manipulate our conclusions. That's one reason to distrust all these signs he's left behind. We can't take the word of a killer, can we?"

The boy seemed to consider her statement, then finally nodded. "Yes, that makes sense."

"Don't play into his hands by allowing him to use fear against us."

"That's already happened," he said with a shrug. "People will talk about this. That's just the way it is. But they'll only talk in whispers, so maybe gossip won't spread as quickly."

Ella realized he was right. "Will you let the other students know what's going on? Tell them not to give the killer any more publicity or credibility than he's already managed to get."

"I can try," he said doubtfully, then went to his truck.

Ella watched the young man for a moment as he walked away. Maybe he'd be able to influence the others and stop the gossip from spreading like wildfire. At the very least, it had been worth a try.

She shifted her attention to the job at hand and watched Sergeant Tache collect the freshly chewed gum with tweezers. His face was masked in neutrality as if he was trying hard to keep anyone from reading his thoughts. In Tache's case, however, that normally meant he was totally focused on his work. "Get lots of close-ups of that dry painting done in ashes over there. I'm going to need to do some research to figure out what it's supposed to mean, if anything," Ella directed him.

"You've got it," the sergeant answered. "Anything else?"

"I want both of you to go over the area with the usual fine-tooth comb. I want to make sure we don't miss anything that'll help us nail this animal."

Hearing Carolyn clip out a request that sounded more like an order, Ella turned around. Carolyn's tone overcame Officer Frank's reluctance, and he stopped to help her lift the bag containing the corpse into the medical examiner's station wagon. With the body now securely inside, Carolyn slammed and locked the rear doors, then called to Ella.

Ella joined her. "You ready to roll?"

Carolyn nodded. "I'll have a preliminary report for you by tomorrow afternoon. The time of death, maybe this afternoon. We're not exactly backlogged at the moment."

"Thanks. I'll need all the help I can get on this one." Ella met Carolyn's steady gaze. "I've got a feeling we're not exactly going to find the killer's misplaced driver's license around here. But if we can get a lab to test the gum we discovered, and find it was left by the killer instead of the victim, the saliva on it could confirm a suspect's presence at the scene. That, of course, presupposes we have a suspect in mind to compare it to—which we don't, at the moment. Unfortunately, from what I can tell, the killer was really careful not to leave behind anything else we can use. Certainly not the murder weapon, or even footprints."

"Let's see what the victim can tell us. At least there we have something to work with." As Carolyn slipped behind the wheel of the M.E. vehicle, she caught the look Officer Frank gave her. "You know, I was never one to run with the pack, but there are times when the personal isolation of this job really sucks."

"Yeah, I know what you mean."

"At least *you're* starting to gain a little acceptance," Carolyn said.

"No, not really. I may get close, but I'll never be 'in' completely. The department, for one, will never really welcome me with open arms. In a way, I suppose I can understand that."

"You can?" Carolyn's eyebrows dipped.

"Sure. First, I'm former FBI, and second, I'm a woman. Face it, that last part alone would have created problems. Guys, no matter what P.D. they serve in, tend to resent the presence of women. Look at it this way: They put on their badges, and that becomes their trademark. They want the world to believe they're the biggest, baddest guys around, and the crooks should all be shaking in their boots.

"Then they see someone else wearing a badge, only she's prettier to look at, and undoubtedly smells nicer. It sorta smashes the tough-guy image they cherish in their little hearts."

Carolyn laughed out loud. "When you put it that way, I can understand it too." Ignoring the look Officer Frank shot in their direction, Carolyn put the wagon in gear and drove off.

Ella stayed, supervising the team as they gathered evidence, placing everything inside brown paper bags. She finished her sketch of the body and surrounding area, making note of the exact distances at the bottom of the page as the detectives measured and called them out. Later the drawing would be redone to scale. Although they'd have extensive photographic records, photos sometimes gave a distorted view of the scene since measurements weren't included with each photo.

Two hours later, the crime-scene unit packed up their equipment and the scant evidence they'd gathered and headed back to the station. Officer Frank waited as Ella walked outward from the place the body had been in an expanding spiral, searching one last time for anything that might have been missed. Ella couldn't help but notice that the officer was giving her a wide berth.

Jimmy shifted, visibly ill at ease. "If you don't need me anymore, I'll head back to the station and file my report."

Ella nodded, her gaze taking in the area methodically. Absently, she hoped Jimmy was happier with other sorts of crime scenes.

"Are you going to stick around long? There's not much left to do here now."

"I'll be leaving in a few minutes," she answered. "Thanks for your help. You handled everything like the pro I know you are."

Jimmy shrugged, smiled briefly, then went to his unit and drove off.

Ella watched, lost in thought, until his car disappeared from view. An eerie silence suddenly descended over the area. Even the birds were quiet. She suppressed the prickling of her skin that slowly traveled up her arms and neck. Something felt wrong. She shifted her gaze to study everything, missing nothing. That sixth sense most cops developed was working overtime now. The atmosphere of the place had changed, and it was not her imagination. There was a foulness, an inexplicable something, that touched her heart with icy fear.

Ella placed her hand on the butt of her weapon, her body tense, and started moving slowly back toward her Jeep. No threat appeared. Still, she stayed close to the vehicle, knowing the engine block would provide the best cover around.

Then she heard the faint rustle of someone moving slowly through the brush. Her gaze fastened on the piñons to her right. She crouched down on one knee, pistol now in hand, and waited.

The seconds seemed to stretch into eternities, but something told her to stay right where she was. She trusted that instinct; she had learned the hard way. Her eyes trained on the trees ahead, she waited.

Then she heard a faint padding of steps across the dew-hardened top crust of sand. Abruptly a coyote stepped out into the clear and stood watching her, less than twenty yards away.

It was strangely fearless, not knowing she had her gun aimed at its lungs. The creature fixed its strange yellow eyes on her. Then it bared its teeth and growled sharply just once, as if telling her to back off. The sound penetrated her like a needle to the marrow. Her finger moved onto the trigger but she didn't fire.

For a second, both she and the creature stood their ground, the animal not knowing or caring that she held its life under her fingertip. Then, abruptly, the coyote turned and disappeared into the brush.

Ella stood up slowly, sweat pouring down her body. It was only an animal. She shouldn't have let it rattle her. She walked in the direction the coyote had gone, wondering what had brought it here. They usually stayed away from the road, unless there was a dead animal to scavenge upon. She studied its tracks, but only found a few where it had been standing. The animal had walked through the one area of solid sandstone around, making it almost impossible to track him.

She turned around and stared downhill, at the desert floor, which stretched toward distant mountains. Was it skinwalkers, or just nerves? She wasn't sure anymore. Experience had taught her one thing: Out on the Rez things were never quite what they seemed.

TWO

✖ ✖ ✖

Ella drove back north to the station at Shiprock, staying within the speed limit and trying to sort out her thoughts without affecting her driving. Big Ed would be expecting a report from her, and she wanted to review mentally what she'd be telling the top cop.

As her surroundings shifted from piñon woodlands to high-desert terrain, Ella's thoughts kept flashing back to the crime scene. Ignoring the horror of the act itself, she tried to consider the evidence. Most of what they'd found would have to be shipped to the state crime lab in Santa Fe, and processing would take time. Local department facilities were limited to taking fingerprints when booking a suspect and simple blood-typing.

The FBI labs in Washington could do wonders with their state-of-the-art equipment in terms of both speed and accuracy, if she could get them involved.

Almost an hour later she pulled into her parking space beside the station. She still wasn't quite sure whether to tell Big Ed about the coyote. Big Ed was a no-nonsense cop. He had respect for the Navajo culture, but for police work he relied on facts—hard and straight. In her opinion, his biggest flaw was his lack of imagination. He went strictly by the book. Ella suspected it was mostly because he didn't know how to operate any other way and, for routine crimes, the strategy usually paid off.

Ella went directly to the chief's office. After knocking on the open door, she walked in. Detective Harry Ute was already there, relaying the crime team's findings to Big Ed. She nodded a greeting to both men, then sat and listened until Ute was finished.

Then she gave both officers her preliminary report. "That piece of gum," she concluded, "*if* we can link it to a suspect, might end up being our best piece of evidence. I just hope it didn't belong to the victim, or one of those kids."

"What about other prints, on the car, or on the artifacts?" Big Ed asked Ute.

"Everything was literally covered with prints. It's hard to isolate any single set. I can send what we have to the state crime lab in Santa Fe. They have the LP50. They can check what the system has on file against the prints, something like a million on record. If they can get a match-up, then we'd have a suspect with a record, and a starting point for our investigation."

"That search will take a while, even with luck. They're backlogged over there with staff and budget cuts," Ella observed.

Ute shrugged. "We also have our own files to check."

"That gum was fresh. If it belonged to the killer, then we can use it to rule out the students and others we round up along the way. The FBI has tests that could give us a blood type based on the saliva, and some other identifying factors as well. It might help us narrow down the suspect list, once we begin contacting people who knew Dodge."

"I can ask the bureau to cooperate and allow us to use their lab," Big Ed said. "Nobody's faster than they are when they put a rush on things. But that request would have to be filtered through Blalock." He met Ella's gaze. "If you asked him yourself, it might be faster. Blalock and I have had our differences. I know you and FB-Eyes are old friends."

Ella tried not to laugh in her boss's face. Some things never changed. Agent Dwayne Blalock, nicknamed FB-Eyes by Navajos because he had one blue eye and one brown eye, had been assigned to her father's case. He had been more trouble than help, but eventually they had come to terms. Blalock had mellowed some since then, but he was still far from diplomatic. He had no friends among the *Dineh*, her included. That mouth of his was guaranteed to create problems no matter where he went.

"Well, it's not like I'm his favorite person either, but I'll ask." Ella held back the obvious downside that she would hate owing Blalock a favor.

Big Ed grinned, guessing what was on her mind. "Don't worry. He'll need our help sooner or later, and come running for payback. Then we'll cooperate with him, and the slate will be clean."

"Let's hope we don't choke on his request," she said softly. "He's not exactly shy about cutting corners to look good to the bureau."

Big Ed laughed. "You know the FBI way. I have full confidence in you."

Ella said nothing. She appreciated her boss's confidence, but she was being put between a rock and a hard place and she didn't like it. Well, maybe she could tap dance around the issue when she approached Blalock. She'd learned a few tricks herself in the bureau. Of course, most of those tricks were ones Blalock would recognize.

"I'll start looking under rocks for him now," she said with a weak smile.

Ella had already started toward the door when the police chief's secretary came in. She placed a fax in front of Big Ed, then wordlessly turned and walked out.

Ella was in the main hall, buying a can of soda from the machine, when Big Ed yelled for her to come back. "I think your prayers were just answered," he said with a tight-lipped smile as she reappeared in his doorway. "You may be able to *exchange* favors." He handed her the fax. "He's asked specifically for your help. You've had training in hostage situations."

"No more than anyone else in the bureau," she said with a shrug. "But what I *do* have is firsthand experience in that kind of situation *as* a hostage," she said, remembering that terrible day a year ago in California. "You've heard about that." Ella had been eating supper at an L.A. diner when a disturbed young man had entered, armed to the teeth with pistols and explosives. Ella managed to kill the perp, but not before he had seriously wounded several people.

"Well, he's got a crisis in Farmington. The perp's a Navajo man. He tried to grab his own kid from his Anglo ex-wife after beating her up, but the police showed up before he could get away." Big Ed handed her the fax. "The address is on there."

Ella glanced down at it. "This is outside our jurisdiction. Is that going to be a problem?"

"Cooperation between the Farmington police, the bureau, and our department is officially encouraged nowadays. You might still find egos that'll be bruised, but this job comes at their request. Get your tail moving."

"Will do."

Turning toward the door, Ella nearly collided with Big Ed's secretary. The look on the woman's face was enough to keep Ella in the room.

"Now what?" Big Ed grumbled, then looked down at the note she'd handed him. "Oh, shit." He stood immediately and reached for his cap. "Gotta go."

"What's wrong?" Ella asked, trying to read the note upside down.

"See for yourself," the chief mumbled, handing her the message as he stepped past her out into the hall.

Ella read the note. "Bus accident at Sheep Springs. Many passengers trapped in wreckage. All available rescue units in route. Fatality rate high."

She placed the note back on the desk. The accident had occurred at the turnoff that led to Crystal—*and* to Red Flint Pass. There was nothing she could do to help, unfortunately, so it was time to get to her own assignment. Perhaps she could make a difference in Farmington.

Ella strode out of the building to her unit. Placing the bubble on top, she raced east down the highway out of Shiprock with lights flashing and siren wailing.

As she drove, Ella considered the chances of there being a connection between Dodge's murder and the accident. It was very unlikely. The two events had occurred several hours apart. The only link, sadly, would be if curiosity had increased traffic in the area. But curiosity would have come mainly from non-Navajos. The *Dineh* wouldn't seek out a murder location. Still, it was possible that the disharmony created by the murder would be blamed for the disaster and, if so, the fear that would be engendered would certainly complicate things.

Ella radioed ahead, letting Blalock know she was on her way and giving him an ETA. She wasn't eager to face another hostage situation, and hoped privately that this one would be resolved peacefully by the time she arrived. Her last one had left a blood-soaked trail that still haunted her nightmares, and this time there was a child involved. That thought and its implications made her heart turn to ice. She gripped the wheel tightly, her knuckles turning white under the strain.

Forcing her fears aside, she took a deep breath and let it out again. She was an expertly trained detective, an ex-FBI agent who had resigned despite the enticement of a promotion. Fear would work for her, sharpening her instincts and fine-tuning her senses. And this was certainly the type of situation where a woman officer excelled. Men tended to be too confrontational when they dealt with other men, especially in this part of the country.

Before long, with the reservation far behind her, she reached the busy streets of Farmington, heading toward the community college area above Twentieth Street. As she reached a residential district she saw a roadblock ahead. Red flashing lights seemed to fill the tiny street, flanked on both sides by inexpensive tract housing. Residents had been evacuated and were being contained behind a police barrier at each end of the lane, where they waited anxiously for something to happen.

Four units were positioned around the front of the house in a half circle, shielding the group of officers who crouched behind them. One glance let her know that snipers were in position on roofs across the street and in an adjacent house.

She passed through the first barrier, badge in hand. Blalock, tall, brown-haired, and well dressed in a gray suit, was behind the center police unit. He was talking on a portable phone to the hostage-taker, asking the man to surrender.

Ella made her way to where he stood. "I'm here," she said as he put the phone down in disgust.

"About time, too. What the hell took you so long?"

"The Navajo police helicopter was having the rubber bands rewound, so I had to drive. Counting the seconds, were you?"

"Cut the crap. Here's the situation. The guy's name is Tony Zahnes, born and raised on the Rez, apparently. That's why I had you called in. You can establish a rapport better than I ever could."

"I remember going to school with someone by that name. Give me everything you've got on him."

"He married Jenny Wilson, an elementary school teacher from Farmington, ten years ago. They've lived apart for the last three years and finally divorced six months ago. He's an alcoholic, and was judged an unfit father, so the courts awarded sole custody of their little girl to the mother. Zahnes apparently went on a binge, broke into his ex-wife's home, slapped the woman around, and tried to take the kid back. Before he could get the kid's stuff and leave for the Rez, one of the neighbors spotted him through the kitchen window. He knocked the kid's mother in the head with the butt of what she says is a big automatic pistol, maybe a .45 caliber, then left her bleeding in the kitchen."

"So the wife is still in there?" Ella asked.

"No. The neighbor pulled her out when the husband took the girl into the other room. Then she called us."

"Where's Jenny Wilson now?"

"She's at the hospital by now. She fought like crazy not to leave her kid, but the paramedics insisted."

"Tell me about the child. What's her name, and how old is she?"

"Her name's Lisa, and she's seven."

"Did you shut off all the utilities in the house?"

"Right away, and we had the phone company put a lockout on the phone. We're the only ones who can talk to him now. It's just too bad it isn't winter. Nothing like the cold to hurry up negotiations."

"What about food?"

"Jenny told us that today was grocery day, but she hadn't gone to the store yet. The fridge and the cupboards are nearly empty."

"Good. That'll give us some bargaining power."

"Word of warning, Ella. He's convinced the girl is his ticket out, and he really wants his kid back. He's not thinking too straight either. He's been drinking, but he's not so drunk that he's going to be easy to fool."

"You want me to take over negotiations now?"

"Yes, your common background with this guy should give us an edge."

Ella nodded, picked up the phone, and identified herself by name as a police officer. "Didn't you go to school with me at Shiprock High? It's been a long time, but your name is really familiar. Come outside so we can talk, and get to see each other again. No one will harm you."

"No. Lisa's *my* kid. She belongs with me and with our People. She needs to grow up like a Navajo. She needs her father."

"But right now you're jeopardizing her life. That's not what you want for her, is it?" Ella countered, keeping her tone calm.

"The cops won't hurt her?" Tony scoffed, his speech slightly slurred.

"Not on purpose, no, but do you really want to take chances with her safety?"

Silence followed for several minutes. "Are you there?" Ella asked.

"Yeah. You say you're Navajo and that I should trust you. But I can't even see you. I remember Ella Destea from school, and then hearing about her after she became Ella Clah. But that woman wouldn't hide from one of the *Dineh*. If you're who you say you are, come over and talk to me. My daughter needs some food too. You can bring her and me some hamburgers. And some fries."

"Release Lisa first."

"No. But if you don't come in, I'll kill her and myself."

Ella heard the deadly intent in his voice. She had no doubt that he'd carry out his promise. "All right. Let me get the food, then I'm coming in."

"Unarmed. I read about what you did in L.A."

"All right."

Blalock elbowed her hard in the ribs. "Are you nuts? If anything happens to you, the bureau will barbecue my butt. He's talking murder/suicide. You know what that means. He's hoping to make it easier on himself by goading you into killing him."

"No. He's scared. I remember exactly who he is now. Tony was only a year ahead of me in high school, and not a macho type. What he's looking for is a way out for himself and his kid."

While an officer raced to the fast food place down at the corner, Ella unbuckled her holster and handed Blalock her weapon. "Keep this for me."

"You got a backup?"

"In my boot."

"Stay sharp. I don't want you coming back out of there in a body bag," he snapped.

"You and me both. And think of all the reports you'd have to do by yourself."

He rolled his eyes and started to answer when the uniformed officer returned with the bag of food.

"Here I go," Ella said, stepping around the squad car into the open, hands out in front of her. "I'm coming in now." She spoke loudly enough so he could hear from the house.

"Stop!" The one word reverberated in the silence of the street. She froze in her tracks. "What's the problem?"

"Take off your boots, and leave them there in the street."

Ella felt her heart lodge in her throat. She hadn't counted on this. But many guys on the Rez carried knives in their boots, and Tony was apparently not taking chances. She sat down in the street and slipped her boots off.

"I knew this wasn't a good idea," she heard Blalock whisper

from behind the unit. "Try to get him in front of the window or door. Our snipers need a line of sight."

"I'll do my best." Ella stood up in stockinged feet, feeling almost naked without her backup pistol. "Okay. I'm coming in now, Tony," she yelled.

Ella approached carefully, watching for signs of movement in the house. There'd be no room for mistakes now. As she stepped up to the front door, she heard footsteps, and a little girl about four feet tall with dark brown eyes and waist-length black hair opened the door.

Ella smiled and handed Lisa the bag of food, then followed her in. The second she was through the door, Ella's gaze shifted to her captor. "Hi. I'm here."

"I remember you from high school, and I also heard what you did against the skinwalkers. You're my best hope now."

She studied Tony carefully. His black hair was worn long in a ponytail fastened at the base of his neck, in keeping with tradition. He wore well-worn denim jeans made for work, not style, and a long-sleeved workshirt. Since Tony's speech was completely clear, she concluded that he wasn't as drunk as he'd led everyone to believe. That meant she had a better chance of reasoning with him. "You're trapped in here, and they're not going to let you walk away. You've got to trust me. Step outside with me. Give yourself up. That's your only chance."

Tony kept the forty-five auto pointed directly at Ella's chest. "I just want my daughter. There's nothing wrong with that."

Ella looked over at the little girl, who had curled up in a fetal position on the easy chair. "You'll lose her one way or another if you continue this. Look at her. She's terrified of you. Put a stop to this now, for her sake and yours."

Zahnes's gun wavered for a moment, but the uncertainty passed, and once again determination set his jaw. "She doesn't understand, that's all. She'll be fine once we leave here. I'll take her to the Rez with me, way back, and no one will find us there."

"And then what'll you do? Lisa will need food and a place to live, water, and medical care. And is she going to give up school to hide out with you? Think man! What kind of future can you give her if you'll always have to stay on the run?"

He shook his head, dismissing her point. "I'll take care of those things. I'm offering her a chance to learn about who and what she is. It's better for her than staying with her mother. Jenny hates the *Dineh* and everything connected to us. That's why she divorced me. And now she wants to make Lisa forget she's Navajo. That's not right. If you understand the *Dineh* and you value what we are, then you know why I have to do this."

"No. There are other ways for her to learn about the People. If you force her to leave her mother, Lisa will hate everything associated with the tribe."

Zahnes looked at Lisa, then back at Ella. "You're wrong. Someday she'll thank me. Now I want you to go out there and get a car for us. A Jeep, maybe. And if I see we're being followed, I'll kill Lisa and myself."

Ella looked straight into the man's eyes. He wasn't bluffing, and she didn't have to be a cop to know that. "You've come all this way just to make sure your daughter gets only the best, but now you're willing to take her life? Think of what you're doing!"

She knew the anxiety their words would create in the little girl, but right now Ella's concern was to save all their lives. She couldn't shift her attention away from Tony to speak to Lisa. Training and experience had taught Ella the danger of that.

"Lisa would be better off dead."

"Really? Look at her! You're the one who's causing her all that suffering." The little girl had withdrawn and wouldn't look up at either of them. She was curled in a tight ball, oblivious to everything around her. "She has a life now, and she needs her mother. If you love her, you can't take those things from her."

"You don't understand. Without me around, she'll grow up thinking our people are all nothing. That's how her mother feels."

"That problem is really between you and your wife. Why are you involving your daughter? She's the innocent victim here. Give her a future, or at least the chance of one. Despite your intentions, what you're doing is taking things away from her, not adding what she needs. That's selfishness, not love."

"She's my kid. I love her." His voice broke, but he cleared his throat quickly in an effort to cover it up.

"If you love her, let her leave. Look at what you're doing. There's no way out of this for you, not without paying some kind of price. The worst part is that you're going to take her down with you. You know what? You don't deserve a daughter like her. You don't deserve anything as long as you go on putting yourself first. The best you can do now is face what you've done, and let her go. Give her a chance."

Ella saw the flicker of anger in his eyes, and for a second she thought he was going to shoot her. Then he glanced at his daughter. "Take Lisa out of here," he snapped, looking at Ella. "Go on. Move!"

Ella went quickly to the little girl's side, but the child huddled even deeper into the cushions of the chair. Without hesitation, she scooped the girl into her arms and opened the door.

She'd just stepped clear of the porch when she heard a click that made her blood turn to ice. Ella set the child down, urging her forward with a push. "Run!"

When the girl hesitated, Ella shoved her into the arms of a SWAT-team member, who had run over from the side of the house. Lifting the child in his arms, he ran behind the line of vehicles.

Ella turned and stepped back onto the front porch. As she entered the house again, she saw Tony bring the barrel of the gun up to his mouth.

"No, don't!" she yelled, lunging forward.

A deafening roar shook the walls of the house. The air seemed to turn crimson as Ella collided with Tony, knocking him backward. The massive slug that had exploded his skull plastered tissue and blood on the walls in a horrific spiderweb pattern.

Ella sat back on her legs in despair as the SWAT unit came storming through the door. She tried to get to her feet and out of the way, but no part of her body seemed to work right. Her legs had turned to rubber, and her vision was blurry. She couldn't hear clearly either. No matter how hard she tried, she couldn't make out what anyone was saying through the incredible ringing in her ears.

Then she felt a pair of hands under her arms tugging her up, and as her eyes focused, Ella saw Blalock. She knew his lips were moving, forming words, but nothing made sense.

"What happened?"

She could read the question on his lips, but the reality of what she'd done slammed into her with such force, it knocked the air out of her. "Mistake," she managed.

"You got the kid out alive, you did okay. You'll get a commendation for this."

Ella felt ill. It was like déjà vu. Another hostage situation, another incredible fiasco, and he wanted to give her another medal.

"I'm going to need you to answer some questions," Blalock continued. "Are you up to it?"

Her vision had cleared, but the sight before her, and the smell of gunpowder and blood, almost made her choke. "Get me outside," she whispered in a shaky voice.

He took her arm and propelled her toward the vehicles. "You talked to the kidnapper, then he let you leave with the kid. What happened? You were at the door, then suddenly you turned around and went back in."

"I heard him pull the hammer back, and that's when I knew what he was about to do." She swallowed, determined not to fall apart. "I blew it. I didn't stay in control. I was concentrating so hard on getting him to let the kid go, I wasn't reading his signals. I was more afraid of what could happen to the little girl."

"You did what you had to do. As far as I'm concerned you handled it like a trouper."

Ella felt sick to her stomach and her hands were shaking, but she didn't want Blalock to see her losing control. She had to get hold of her emotions before she fell apart.

Blalock must have read her expression, because he abruptly changed the conversation. "By the way, earlier when I requested you, your chief said you'd be glad to assist. He was so cooperative, I think he already has some payback in mind. Any idea what he wants?" He took Ella's boots and holster from a police officer and handed them to her.

She tried to push down the emotions that were tearing at her insides as she reattached her holster and then fumbled with her boots. She would concentrate on the murder of Kee Dodge. She had to. She could still do some good there. "The bureau's lab could really help out the tribe right now. We need your fancy equipment and some fast answers."

"You've got it," Blalock answered. "I'll make the arrangements. The Albuquerque bureau office uses the Albuquerque lab, so we'll deal through them. It should be faster than going all the way to Washington." He lapsed into a thoughtful silence. "Is this connected to Dodge's murder? I heard about that from one of my contacts. It's supposed to be a little on the weird side."

"Yeah, you can say that."

"Like last summer?" he asked, knowing she'd need no clarification.

"I don't know. It's much too early to tell for sure."

"But you have a gut feeling about it, don't you?" he observed.

"It's only a guess," Ella shrugged, then continued. "The killer took special care to leave some unmistakable clues," she explained. "It was very carefully staged and planned. On the basis of that, I'm willing to bet that he wants attention focused on him."

"A serial killer?"

"Maybe, but this isn't going to run any textbook course."

"Nothing on the reservation ever does," Blalock muttered. "I better finish up here."

Ella watched him leave, then signed a report one of the Farmington policemen handed her. It was time for her to go. She caught a glimpse of the body bag being hauled out and practically ran to her Jeep, where she was at least partially shielded from view. She gripped the wheel tightly, trying to get her hands to stop shaking, but she was not wholly successful.

She'd blown it, dammit. She should have been able to talk him down. It shouldn't have ended like this.

Once again, Ella felt the contents of her stomach rise to her throat. She swallowed hard. She had to get herself under control. The more she tried to push away the darkness of her world, the stronger it seemed to get. She shook free of the thought. She needed to concentrate on what she *had* accomplished. She'd saved a little girl's life as well as her own. She had controlled the hostage-taker's actions at least that much. No one would hold her responsible for what had happened. And she couldn't hold herself completely accountable for the actions of another either.

Logically it made sense, but, inside, she felt as if her chest had been locked in a vise. She started her vehicle, assuring Blalock she was fine with a wave of her hand. She had work to do, and it was time to get back to it.

THREE

✖ ✖ ✖

Ella threaded her way carefully through Farmington and soon was back on the highway, heading west. She wanted to talk to Kee Dodge's family. She knew he had a wife and a daughter. They'd be reluctant to speak of the dead this soon after the murder, and might even refuse to speak to her, but she had to try.

As Ella came around the Hogback, she picked up the mike, asking for a 10-20 on Mrs. Dodge's home. After getting the location, she made a brief radio report on the outcome of her work for Blalock while en route. Dodge's home was in a farming area on the flood plain alongside the San Juan River, a twenty-minute drive northwest of Shiprock.

The road leading to the tiny wood-framed house was nothing more than two deep furrows cut between fields of melons. She slowed down, shifting to a lower gear to avoid getting trapped in the damp soil. She saw a sheep corral first, then spotted a girl about sixteen tending several newborn lambs. The girl's long black hair was braided in a single strand that hung down her back, almost to the pockets of her jeans. She was wearing a red and silver Shiprock Chieftains T-shirt.

Ella parked next to the corral and identified herself.

The girl introduced herself as Cindi Dodge and nodded, not

surprised. "My mom said someone would come by. We got the news from an uncle who works for the tribal police. He came by to tell us."

The girl's expression was taut. There was a touch of fear in her eyes. She refused to meet Ella's gaze, and her own darted continually back to the sheep. Still, Ella sensed an uneasiness in the young girl that transcended a natural distrust of the police. Navajos, particularly, the younger ones, were taught it was rude to meet someone's gaze. Ella had been raised the same way. "Where can I find your mother?"

Cindi led the way wordlessly to the house. As they approached, a short Navajo woman wearing a traditional multicolored long skirt and a bright red blouse came out to meet them.

"I'm Ernestine. I've been expecting you." The woman nodded, but didn't invite Ella inside. Instead she gestured toward two metal chairs that were placed in the shade of the partially enclosed *portal*.

Ella took one chair as Ernestine Dodge seated herself in the other. Her daughter stood silently by the door, watching. Ella waited a polite moment, then spoke. "I need to ask you some questions about your husband."

Ernestine nodded once. "There's nothing I can tell you, only that I believe this is part of the trouble your family brought down on us. Your father stirred up all that evil because of his church and many were killed. Bad things always follow you, too, it seems. Just this morning after you went to where my husband was killed, a whole busload of our people were hurt right on the same road you'd drive on to get there."

The statement had the impact of a physical blow. Although Ella knew it shouldn't have taken her completely by surprise, the bluntness of Ernestine's words was a shock. "Surely you don't think that either me or my family is to blame for what has happened."

Ernestine shrugged. "Your family attracts trouble. That's all I know."

Ella remained quiet, refusing to give in to anger or to sorrow over her father's death. Her gaze drifted to the loom that had

been set up at the other end of the porch, and then to the basketball goal on the old telephone pole by the fence. At long last
she was ready to speak again. "The tragedies today had nothing
to do with one another, or with my family," she said calmly.

"I may be wrong about the bus wreck, but I was told about
the condition of my husband's body. He had no enemies. How
else can it be explained?"

"I don't know yet, but I will," Ella replied simply. "Had anyone threatened him, or had he been in an argument with anyone
lately?"

"No."

Cindi Dodge moved closer to her mother. "Well, he had been
fighting with Stubby, Mr. Todacheene, over the water, remember? Daddy said Stubby took more than his share from the irrigation ditch, and everyone else was being shortchanged."

Ernestine scowled at her daughter. "That's not a reason to kill
a man like your father."

"Why don't you let me decide that," Ella answered, then
shifted her gaze to Cindi. "Did you overhear any of these arguments?"

Cindi shrugged. "Everyone did. Just ask around. But Stubby
does pick fights. He likes annoying other people. At least that's
what Dad always said."

"It's true," Ernestine admitted. "But it still means nothing.
Clyde Todacheene wouldn't harm anyone."

"What about your husband's students? Did he mention any
who gave him trouble, or who were behaving strangely?"

"No. In fact, he was pleased that they were so interested in
the old ways and in learning what he had to teach. It wasn't always that way, you know. This interest in our past is something
new among the young people."

"Would you be willing to take a look through his things and
inside his truck, and tell us if anything is missing? I'd like to rule
out robbery as a motive."

Ernestine looked horrified. "You know better than to ask me
that. His truck was part of him, and the *chindi* . . ."

Ella exhaled softly. "How about if I give you a list of what he had with him inside the vehicle. Will you tell me if you notice the absence of anything?"

Ernestine took a deep breath. "All right."

Ella walked to her vehicle and radioed in. After receiving and writing down the list Detective Ute gave her, she returned to the porch. She sat down and handed it to Ernestine.

The woman studied it for a long time. "If something is missing, I don't know what it could be."

"There was no money in his wallet. Do you know how much he had with him?"

Ernestine shook her head. "I don't think he had any. I remember him asking me yesterday if I could stop by the bank because he was out of cash. He used the last he had to buy gas. Only I forgot. I intended to do it today."

Ernestine handed Cindi the list. Cindi studied it then, shaking her head, and handed it back to Ella. "Everything seems okay to me."

Ella studied their faces. They were not trying to conceal anything, but neither seemed the type to really notice minute details. The hem on Ernestine's skirt was partially torn, and the scarf that Cindi had used to tie back her hair was practically falling off, but the girl hadn't noticed.

"Dad was a good teacher," Cindi put in, "but he was never really organized. He could have had almost anything with him. We wouldn't know something was missing until we went looking for it."

Ernestine nodded in agreement. "She's right."

The older woman paused for a long time, but Ella sensed she had more to say. She waited patiently, not disturbing the silence. At long last, Ernestine spoke. "Knowledge will die with him, and the *Dineh* will lose part of their history forever. This shouldn't have happened. Do you think you'll catch the person who did this?"

"Yes. I won't give up until I do. Count on that."

When Ernestine stood and walked to the house, Ella knew she'd get nothing further from her today. She'd been lucky to get as much cooperation as she had. Cindi, meanwhile, grabbed a worn basketball from inside the screen door and went to shoot baskets.

Ella returned to her vehicle, thoughts racing through her mind. It was clear that her family would come under personal attack again unless she found answers fast. What had come as a surprise was how quickly the suggestion had arisen that the bus accident was somehow related to the crime. The Navajo People were superstitious, and connections between these closely timed events were not unexpected, but she had hoped not to confront it during her investigation just yet. Tense and apprehensive, she quickly decided her next move.

Ella checked her watch as she headed down the highway toward the PHS hospital. It had been about seven hours since they'd found the body. Maybe Carolyn would have something preliminary for her by now.

Thirty minutes later, Ella parked by the rear doors and went downstairs to the morgue. An Anglo lab technician was sitting at her desk typing, dictaphone earphones on.

As Ella approached the desk, the woman looked up. "Dr. Roanhorse said you'd probably be by," she said, recognizing Ella. "The doctor said for you just to go in. She's checking tissue samples, but she wants to talk to you."

Ella braced herself as she went through the doors. The last time she'd been here, it had been to view her father's body. Her skin turned as cold as ice as she stepped inside. Tile floors with a drain in the middle just accentuated the dreadful feel of the place.

Carolyn glanced up and turned the tape recorder off. "I thought you'd be showing up here soon."

"Have you discovered anything so far that I should know about?"

"Well, he'd been dead for about an hour when I checked the body at the scene. That puts the time of death around seven A.M. Also, the bone imbedded in the victim's eye isn't a human bone," Carolyn said slowly. "And it was inserted after the victim had already died."

"Wait. Back up a bit. Don't skinwalkers use human bone?"

"That's what I've always thought, but maybe you should verify that with your brother."

Despite herself, Ella glanced down at the table. The corpse had been covered with a sheet, but the dented outline of the head was visible through the drape, reminding her of the brutality of the crime. "So, we may be dealing with a skinwalker wannabe."

"That's my guess, too. But there was that painting done in ashes . . ." She let the sentence hang.

"I'll take photos of it to Clifford. As a *hataalii* he'll be able to tell us what it's supposed to mean, if anyone can."

"I'll keep working. But Ella—this isn't like before. The people who worked on your father's body were experts in the Navajo Way. This is something else—amateurish, for lack of a more appropriate term. It's like someone wants to make you think a skinwalker did it. Maybe they want to bring up memories that'll confuse your thinking."

Determination shot through Ella like a bolt of electricity. "It won't work."

Carolyn glanced back down at the body beneath the sheet. "I'll let you know the moment I finalize my report."

Leaving Carolyn to her work, Ella walked out to the parking lot. She'd pick up the photographs from the crime scene if they were available, then head over to Clifford's. If their family was going to come under attack again, the sooner her brother knew what was going on the better things would be.

Ella drove directly to the station. As she parked in the small parking lot, she noted that Tache's vehicle was one of those that remained. She was almost sure that Tache had developed the photos by now. He was one of the most efficient and hardworking cops around.

It was near dusk, that time in between light and dark when shadows stretched almost to the horizon. Shifts had changed, and the office staff was long gone. Nerves stretched taut, she left her vehicle, automatically searching the area with the vigilance of a cop about to come under fire.

She walked directly to the back of the building where her

small office was located. It had been Sergeant Peterson Yazzie's once, but now it held only a small desk with computer, her file cabinets, and a few mementos of her past. She'd hung her UNM diploma on one wall, and a shooting trophy she'd won during her days at the bureau was on a file cabinet. It was stark and utilitarian, but she was finally home. Her accomplishments in the outside world weren't as important to her as that one fact.

Ella sat back in her chair organizing her thoughts. As her gaze fell on the desk drawer, she felt a prickle of uneasiness. The drawer had been left partially open. She always shut things all the way, part of her predilection for order.

Ella pulled out the drawer slowly and carefully. It slid easily, and the contents didn't appear to have been touched. Of course, anyone could have come in searching for a pencil, or a paper clip, or any of half a dozen other things. She glanced down at the little box of clips. The lid was shut, just as she'd left it, and all of her pens and pencils seemed to be there.

Perhaps the person who'd been in her desk had left something behind instead. Ella thought for a moment, trying to remember the last time someone at the station had borrowed something of hers. Scanning the drawer, she noticed nothing new among the supplies.

She reached underneath the drawer, running her fingers back and forth, remembering the time Blalock had bugged her mother's home. Not feeling anything fastened there, she pulled the drawer out completely and set it on her desk.

Ella got down on her knees and looked into the open cavity where the drawer had been, running her hand over it. She really wasn't sure if she was being paranoid or just cautious, but after the murder she wasn't about to get complacent about anything.

As she got to her feet, Ella noticed a thin, tan-colored, rectangular outline about an inch wide and four inches long on the back of the drawer. Touching the spot, her fingers detected the sticky residue left by a piece of masking tape. The residue was tacky enough to have been recent.

She stood and surveyed the rest of the room. Something had

been taped behind the drawer, out of sight. She considered the possibility that the previous tenant, Peterson Yazzie, had hidden something there.

Playing a hunch, Ella stretched to the right and looked down into the trash can beside the desk. Beside a few wadded-up balls of paper, a discarded piece of masking tape rested in the bottom. Taking a pair of tweezers from the desk drawer, she retrieved the tape and studied it. There was an imprint etched into the sticky side. Ella recognized the pattern. It was the outline of a key. Now she knew why the intruder had come.

Turning the tape back and forth, she tried to guess what the key unlocked. It wasn't a house key; it was the wrong shape. The impression was long and relatively narrow, like that of a key used on a safety deposit box or a car. Perhaps lab experts could enhance the impression using laser technology and give her more information.

Ella carefully placed the tape into an empty computer disk box and placed a rubber band around it to hold the flap shut. Labeling and initialing the box, she placed it into a manila mail pouch. This had to be sent out for analysis tomorrow. Only Peterson Yazzie or one of his skinwalker cohorts would have known about the key and been able to retrieve it right under the nose of the department.

Ella looked around, wondering what else had been touched, or tampered with. She searched the entire office methodically, going through every drawer, including underneath and behind each piece of equipment or furniture. Nothing seemed missing or out of place. Finally all that was left to search was the closet. She opened the door and glanced inside, but what she saw made her jump back instinctively, reaching for her pistol.

Slowly Ella relaxed and returned the handgun to its holster. The small rattlesnake coiled on the floor of the closet was missing its head, and the smell told her it had been dead for hours.

Hearing footsteps coming down the hall, Ella turned around. Tache stopped at her door, holding a manila folder in his hand. "What in the heck is that?" He stared at the snake with obvious distaste.

"A present," Ella said in clipped tones. "Will you go and make sure all the evidence taken from the murder scene is secure?"

"I can assure you it is. It's all kept in a vault, and any attempt to open it would be obvious."

"Check anyway."

Ella picked up the dead reptile with the mop handle, locked the door, and walked to the Dumpster outside. Snakes were said to be messengers, but the only message this one carried was the sign of death. By the time she returned, Tache was standing just outside her door, waiting.

"Everything's accounted for," he said.

"Good." She unlocked the door, went back inside, and handed him the envelope. "See if the experts can track down what kind of key this is."

"I'll make sure Ute gets it," he assured her.

"And lock your offices from now on." She glanced at the folder in his hand. "Do you have something for me?"

He nodded. "I developed the shots of the crime scene. I had a feeling you'd want to see them."

"That's why I came back," she admitted. "Thanks for expediting this. I especially need the shots of that dry painting done in ashes."

He handed the file to her. "They're in here along with the others. By the way, I took a real close look at it. I'm no expert, but I've studied our ways and I didn't recognize any of the figures. Of course, that may just mean the killer's a lousy artist."

"Or the figures may not be traditional. I'm planning to look into it tonight."

"Will you let me know what you find out? I'm really curious."

She nodded once. "Have we had any press nosing around yet? With the murder, then that bus accident, I expect a lot of traffic. But the reporters really shouldn't get some of these details, especially the tribal newspapers. I want to release a prepared statement for them, and keep the details under wraps. I'm afraid people will panic, and that's the last thing we need."

"Word has already started to spread. My cousin called earlier and wanted to know if the rumors that skinwalkers were behind the murder were true. Everyone's scared. They think that evil is gaining strength now with one of our teachers dead. To many, that also explains the bus accident. The way I figure it, it's just a matter of time before the press shows up demanding answers we don't have."

"Okay, thanks for the warning. I better get to work on that release right away."

"I have some books on dry paintings in my cubicle. You want me to bring them to you? I didn't really have time to study them all, but you might be able to find some matches and decipher out what those figures mean."

"I'd appreciate that a lot, if you don't mind."

"I'll be back in a minute."

Ella sat down in front of her computer and began to draft a statement. Before long Tache returned holding two large volumes.

"These are out-of-print books that some anthropologists compiled many years back," he said. "For generations our people relied solely on the spoken word and much has been lost. These are practically invaluable now."

"I'll take care of them, don't worry." Ella took them from him carefully and returned to her desk.

Ella ceased work on the press release and began to look through the books. She was scarcely aware of the passage of time as she pored over the drawings. She searched methodically for similarities, taking into account the lesser skill of whoever had done the figures in ashes at the crime scene.

It was completely dark outside by the time she finally stood up and stretched. There was no way around it. She'd given it her best shot, but none of the drawings in the book appeared to be even remotely like the figures in the ash dry painting. With reluctance, she picked out the close-up photos and stuck them inside a large manila envelope. Getting nonauthorized personnel involved in a case went against her training, but she needed her brother's help now.

When Ella walked across the building to the side entrance,

only the dispatcher and a couple of evening-shift officers were still around.

As she stepped out the door, a flicker of movement caught her attention. A figure was walking between the few cars that were still parked outside. Halting in the shadows, Ella watched for several moments. The person was holding something under his arm as he went from car to car, peeking inside. Ella slipped back inside and called out to the dispatcher sitting at the other end of the hall.

"Find another officer and have him join me in the parking lot. Someone's sneaking around out there and I'm going to take a look."

Leaving the envelope with the photos propped against the wall, Ella went back out noiselessly, intending to stalk the stalker. It was a man; she was virtually certain of that from the way he walked. He was wearing a cowboy hat and that, coupled with the darkness, made it impossible for her to discern any details of his features. She inched closer, trying to get a better look at what he was holding. It wasn't a gun. It was shaped like a small shoe box, or a loaf of bread.

As the figure came out into the open briefly, the parking lot floodlight illuminated what it was that he carried. It appeared to be several sticks of dynamite bound together. Suddenly the figure ducked down, disappearing from her view.

Certain she'd been spotted, Ella moved in quickly, gun in hand. She checked underneath the cars as she moved. Her quarry's feet would be visible from that angle, and she could use them to get a fix on where he was heading.

Suddenly a flash of light from the building caught her attention. She saw two armed officers step out quickly and duck behind cover.

As she shifted her gaze back to the cars, she caught another flicker of movement and saw the figure dash away from the parking lot. One of the officers still standing near the doors yelled for him to stop and aimed a powerful flashlight in his direction.

The elusive figure picked up speed instead, and Ella heard the thump of something hitting the pavement. The officers took off after him as Ella scrambled over to where the man had been to see what he'd dropped. Her breath caught in her throat as her worst suspicions were realized. Between two cars was the bundle of dynamite, held together with electrical tape. A digital timer was connected to the primer and a flashlight battery with wires. She carefully lifted it so she could read the timer in the glare of the floodlight and was startled to see it was counting down. It had fifteen seconds to go.

"Bomb!" Ella yelled, in case any officers were still close by.

Holding her breath, she grabbed her folding pocketknife. With no time to decide if the bomb was booby-trapped, Ella quickly slashed the wires leading to the battery. The timer went blank.

Feeling shaky all over, she leaned against the nearest car. This shouldn't have happened, not here on the Rez. This was a big-city-type crime. She stared at the disabled bomb still in her hand, then set it down gingerly, trying not to disturb it any more than necessary.

Hearing footsteps rushing up from behind her, she spun around and steadied her weapon against the hood of the car. The two Navajo cops stopped in their tracks.

"Sorry," she muttered. "Did you get him?" She moved toward them, motioning for them to keep their distance from the bomb, while keeping it in sight.

"No. He knows the terrain around here really well. Even in the dark, at a run, he chose the shortest way back to the road. He had a pickup waiting." The sergeant was talking to her, but his eyes were on the bomb.

"License plate?" she prodded.

"Too dark to make out."

"Make and color?"

"Ford, late 1980s, tan color or close, and covered in dust."

"Just like practically every other vehicle around here."

"Yeah," the sergeant answered.

The patrol officer's gaze shifted from Ella to the bomb. "What do you think he was aiming for? The station?"

Ella hesitated. "No. He was going through the vehicles here.

I guess he was searching for one in particular."

"Whose Jeep is this?" the patrol officer asked, gesturing to the one beside Ella.

"Mine." Not giving them time to engage in any more speculations, she said, "I'll stay here. Go call whoever handles ordnance disposal and get them over here."

An hour later, the bomb had been checked, photographed, and disassembled. Ella finished her report to Big Ed recommending security cameras be set up in the hallways leading to their offices and the evidence room. She'd also completed the carefully worded press release. With the bus accident, which had resulted in four deaths, the murder might get less attention, which would serve her purposes. For now she'd keep the bone found in the victim's eye a secret. The students probably had not taken a close enough look to have spotted it. Maybe later it would become her ace in the hole.

Ella sat back in her chair. She stared absently at a fly buzzing around the room. A moment later it landed on her shoulder. She stared at it, lost in thought. In ritual, Big Fly was said to have knowledge of many things and places, since he was free to travel everywhere. He was said to warn and inform Holy Man.

She stared at the iridescent green insect, remembering the way of the *Dineh* and trying to reconcile herself to her own past as part of the tribe. Skinwalkers, although they had been with the *Dineh* since the beginning of time, represented an evil that had no place in the present. It was up to her to use all the modern police techniques at her disposal to bring them, or whoever wanted to impersonate them, to justice.

Ella brushed the fly off and stood. She'd combine knowledge with experience and bring both to bear on this case. She'd solve it, relying on logic to guard her against superstitious fears.

She picked up the press release and the envelope she'd retrieved with the photographs of the dry painting and walked out. Locking the door, she strode down the hall, her thoughts racing. Tache had spread the word, and all the offices were closed and locked. Crimes steeped in lore and tradition evoked deeply rooted fears, but it was no different anywhere else. People on the outside laughed when they read their horoscopes, or saw a black cat cross their path, but some part of them wondered. What the *bilagáana* world feared went by different names, that's all.

She'd nearly passed the evidence room when, almost as an afterthought, she decided to go in for one last look. Fishing the keys out of her pocket, she unlocked the door and went inside. Harry Ute had tagged most of the evidence for delivery to the FBI tomorrow, and she'd added the bomb to the shipment. There was nothing new here, but something continued to nag at her. She stared at the pouch containing the evidence from the ash painting and saw the small attached note Harry had left for the techs. Although the particles were minuscule, he was almost certain that what had looked like ashes had actually been nothing more than ground-up charcoal briquets. The discovery made a bell ring in Ella's head, and questions leaped to the foreground of her mind.

Ten minutes later, Ella was racing down the nearly deserted highway toward her brother's home. Clifford had been accepted and welcomed by the tribe after last year's trouble. In fact, in the eyes of some, he was a hero. Public sentiment had shifted in his favor since it had been learned that he'd successfully battled the skinwalkers and had protected the tribe as well as his family. She envied his new status, wondering if the same would ever be true for her.

As she passed the Chapter House, she noticed there was only a small gathering of teenagers hanging around outside the entrance. The well-publicized accident today had cost many Navajos a loved one. Maybe this explained the uncharacteristically poor turnout. A country-western band was playing inside, and she caught the rhythmic thumps of ground-shaking bass. Both the Anglo and Navajo culture had staked their footholds. But unlike gatherings of young people on the outside, there was no liquor on the Rez to complicate teen activities, at least officially.

After another thirty minutes, Ella slowed to take the turnoff that would lead to Clifford's. He and his wife Loretta were going to have another child, but the pregnancy so far had been troubled. Loretta was constantly ill, and had taken several falls. In Ella's opinion, the death of their first child still weighed too heavily on them. Their son had died during Clifford's fight with the skinwalkers, one of many casualties.

Her brother had been doing a Blackening Song to purify the land when Loretta had unexpectedly gone into labor. She'd delivered the child stillborn. In those days, Ella hadn't really believed that the two incidents were related, but she'd learned a few things since then.

The porch light up ahead flickered through the gloom of night as she turned down the well-worn path to her brother's home. The small adobe structure had a new addition to it, built in preparation for the family they hoped to have.

She parked a polite distance from the front door and waited with the headlights on to be invited in. She didn't have to wait long. Loretta came to the front door and waved, recognizing Ella's vehicle even in the dim light that came from the porch.

Ella grabbed the file with the photos, then went inside.

Loretta led the way to the kitchen, offering Ella some stew and fry bread. The tantalizing aroma made Ella's mouth water, and suddenly realizing she had skipped lunch and dinner, she found herself unable to decline. It was more than her appetite though; she needed the familiarity and the normalcy of food just as badly as the nourishment. "I'm still working, but I'd love some."

Loretta smiled. "Sister-in-law, work or not, you have to eat. How can you ever attract a man of your own if you're just skin and bones?"

Ella grinned back, knowing that the comment was Loretta's way of teasing her, more than an actual observation. "I don't want to attract any men. I want to intimidate the bad guys. And I can do that best by being a lean, mean, fighting machine."

Loretta laughed. "Not exactly the way I'd describe you, though I'm sure it's the way you love to see yourself. In my opinion, you're too thin. You're lean from lack of eating, and if you keep skipping meals you'll be too weak to be a fighting machine."

Ella looked greedily at the food Loretta placed before her. At least some fences had been mended. There had been a time when her sister-in-law and she hadn't had much to say to each other. "I gather my brother isn't home?"

"He'll be back in a little bit. He went over to see Betty Natoni. She still lives alone in that hogan out near Dry Wash. Betty said that she'd been struck by a whirlwind and hadn't been feeling well. She wanted your brother to do a Wind Chant."

Ella nodded. Betty was in her eighties, a proud woman who adhered to the old ways. She would no more go to the PHS hospital than she would move out of the hogan she'd lived in since she was a child.

Ella ate her mutton stew, lost in thought. There had been a time when she would have claimed it was foolish to turn down the progress that had come to the People from the outside. Now, she wasn't so sure. She still resisted clinging only to the old ways, but she had also learned that there was much to be said for them.

To walk in beauty, to find harmony—that carried a value all its own. Nowadays most people agreed that one's mental state affected health. Navajos had been saying that since long before Columbus was even born. Progress wasn't as easy to define as Ella had once believed.

Loretta recognized the roar of a pickup's engine and went to the window saying, "Here's my husband now."

Loretta met Clifford at the front door. "I'm glad you're home," she said.

"It took longer than I expected," Clifford said softly.

Ella came out of the kitchen, bowl still in hand. She could see the weariness etched on her brother's face as he took off his denim jacket and placed it on a big hook beside the door. "Hi," she said, greeting him with a wave of her spoon.

Clifford looked past Loretta and smiled at her. "Good, I see you're finally eating something that isn't smothered in ketchup. But it's Friday night. Why aren't you out with one of the men from the tribe?"

Ella rolled her eyes. "I'm working."

His eyes clouded for an instant. Then as if sharing his wife's concern, he forced a thin smile. "You're *always* working."

"Just like you," Ella countered with a smile.

"Good point," he agreed.

"Can I talk to you for a few minutes? I need your help figuring something out."

Loretta took the empty bowl from Ella's hands. "You two go ahead," she said gesturing to the sofa. "I'll be in the kitchen making some coffee."

As soon as Loretta was out of view, Clifford gave her a worried glance. "I'm glad you didn't say anything to Loretta. I don't want her worried. I've been hearing gossip about the murder then that accident all day. Is it true? Are they back?"

There was no need for Clifford to explain who "they" were. Ella could see the touch of fear that made Clifford's eyes narrow, accentuating the patchwork of tiny lines that framed them. "That's what I want you to tell me. I don't know what's going on, brother, but I think we're being manipulated."

She recounted what she knew about the murder of Kee Dodge, carefully avoiding mentioning the victim's name. "I brought you photos of the dry painting. I've tried researching those figures, but I couldn't find anything even close."

"You're certain about the ashes?"

"The killer used powdered charcoal."

"Charcoal?" His eyebrows knitted together. "Let me see the photos."

Ella retrieved the file she'd brought. "Here they are, from a variety of angles."

Clifford studied the photos carefully, laying them out side by side on the coffee table. Silence stretched out for a long time, but Ella was careful not to interrupt. Finally, after what seemed an eternity to her, Clifford glanced up. "These are just poorly done stick figures. I have no idea who or what they're supposed to represent, if anything." He paused thoughtfully. "And something else. Skinwalkers use ashes to create their dry paintings, not ground-up charcoal. And normally their goal would be to depict the person or people they intend to kill. There's nothing in these pictures that resembles the murdered man."

"So these figures could represent a future target?"

"Yeah, but they seem more like some wild combination of the Holy People and plant life." He shrugged. "Were you able to make anything more out of it?"

She shook her head. "No. That's why I brought the photos to you."

He sat back on the sofa and regarded her for a very long time. "The ones we fought before would have shown more skill at dry painting, and they would have known what materials to use. Someone wants to mislead you."

She nodded slowly. "I thought that too."

"But, just to be sure, may I make a suggestion?" Seeing her nod, he continued. "Talk to Leonard Haske. He has been a *hataalii* for over forty years. He's in this part of the Rez now, visiting his daughter who just had a baby."

"Do you think he'll help me? No one wants to answer these kinds of questions," Ella said slowly, "particularly when I'm the one who asks them."

Clifford took a deep breath. "He'll answer you because the safety of the tribe is at stake. But you're right in saying he would prefer not to speak of these things. Face it, it's a subject any of us would rather avoid."

"If you asked him, would he talk more freely with you? The tribe accepts you, but the same can't be said for me. To most, I'm still an outsider."

"You're wrong," he said quietly. "What you're sensing is the natural reaction most people have to police officers. You *do* belong here."

"Yes, I do," she agreed, "but no one forgets that I chose to leave, and that I turned my back on all of our teachings."

Clifford shrugged. "What you tried to do was foolish. You could never run away from who and what you are. Our family has certain abilities, and those would follow you anywhere, whether or not you acknowledged them. Your gift is your remarkable intuition, and look how it continues to help you."

Ella pursed her lips, suppressing the urge to deny Clifford's comment. He insisted her investigative successes had a supernatural source, while she still preferred to think of her intuition as particularly sharp powers of observation, an instinct honed and developed to perfection by her training as a cop. But some things weren't worth arguing about. "I wish I could get people to trust me."

"Things would be easier for you, true. But, little sister, if you have to work hard for it, you'll appreciate it more when it happens. That's part of your nature."

Ella smiled. "You may have a point."

Work finished, Ella stayed for a cup of coffee and a generous helping of local gossip from Loretta. When she left, her brother gave her a map of how to find Haske's daughter's home. There were others she had to talk to, but it was already too late tonight. It was time to go home. She'd get an early start tomorrow and tackle everything fresh then.

Moonlight covered the desert in a silver-gray mantle. It looked peaceful enough, but something still made her restless. There was trouble brewing that went beyond Kee Dodge's murder. A ripple of fear was already reaching out through the tribe. So many deaths in such a short time—the murder then the bus accident—would feed the growing disharmony and foster chaos among them. The beliefs that sustained the People could also work against them now.

She thought of Leonard Haske. She'd only met the *hataalii* once, about fifteen years ago, but she'd never forgotten him. The man's piercing gaze, the power and presence that held those around him in thrall, had left an indelible mark on her. She remembered being in awe of him, thinking that nothing could ever stand up to the power of that Singer's song. The tribe needed men like him now more than ever.

Across the reservation a shadow moved stealthily through the dark. It was late, but night was his ally. He was a silent hunter in search of prey. He moved swiftly and silently through the desert, like a coyote, or better yet, a wolf. He spoke in low tones to himself, with the ease of someone who had always found himself his own best audience.

This was his time; he was finally coming into his own. He felt powerfully alive, more animal than man. He could feel the fire in his belly nourishing him even as it slowly consumed him from within.

The moon edged out from behind the clouds, and the desert came alive with the song of its night children. He crawled toward the edge of the mesa and watched the hogan below. The Singer was preparing a sand painting by lantern light. Perhaps it was for himself. He could smell the man's fear, and the power it gave him electrified every cell in his body.

He saw the *hataalii* look up, studying the area around him. He knew the old man could sense the threat against him, though he couldn't do anything about it.

He drew power from the Singer's concerns, and felt his own strength grow. He was the invincible hunter who roamed the night. Darkness—that time which heralded the symbolic death of each day, defeating the light. Now it allowed him to view with impunity the life he would take. He threw his head back, but resisted the scream that built inside him. The need to complete the kill thrummed through his body. But he would wait. He would do things right.

He crept away silently, feeling the hunger in his belly, the need to kill pulsing and growing stronger with each beat of his heart.

Soon. He would do it soon.

FOUR

✖ ✖ ✖

Ella woke up slowly, but it was still dark. Turning, she checked the clock on her nightstand. It was only five A.M., but sleep had eluded her all night long. Images of the hostage-taker's distorted face and bloodless lips accusing her of failure had haunted her nightmares.

She sat up, tossed the sheet and light quilt back, and went to the window. As a cop, crazy nightmares came with the territory. But until now, she'd never questioned her ability to cope with them. Cockiness, it seemed, was another of the casualties of experience.

Ella pulled on a pair of jeans and a chambray work shirt, then walked barefoot into the kitchen. She wasn't hungry, but she poured herself a bowl of cereal anyway, needing the comfort of routine. As she opened the carton of milk, she could feel her hands shaking, a leftover from the horrific play of images that had filled her nightmares.

Remembering Tony's ghastly death, Ella gave up on the food and sat at the kitchen table, staring at her hands. She'd considered getting out of law enforcement dozens of times, but being a cop was all that gave her life here on the Rez purpose and definition. The truth was she needed the job far more than it needed her.

With an exasperated sigh, she stood up, went to her room, and finished getting dressed. The sun was rising, and her mother would be up soon. Deciding she might as well get an early start, Ella adjusted her pancake holster, making sure it fit securely at her waist, then checked her spare clips before returning them to her pockets. She then examined her boot holster and the backup pistol there. There were two rounds in the derringer, and it had taken both of them the last time she'd needed it.

For a moment she felt like a knight-errant getting ready to do battle. She smiled, liking the mental image. Sometimes harsh realities needed a touch of soft fantasy to make them easier to bear.

Ella started toward the front door. Today she'd visit Dodge's neighbors first. By the time she made a stop at the Totah Café for coffee and finished the drive out to that farm, it would be morning and a decent time to call. After that, she'd go see Haske.

Ella went to her Jeep, checked the tires and oil, then began the journey. Touching base with the dispatcher as she drove through Shiprock, she learned that all the evidence pouches were slated to be sent by courier to the crime lab in Albuquerque, and would be given top priority by request of the FBI—Blalock had kept his promise to put a rush on it. They would have some preliminary results by the end of the day, with luck.

As the miles stretched behind her, she felt an unfamiliar restlessness nagging at her. Normally these long drives helped sort out her thoughts, but right now the delays created by the incredibly long distances she had to travel to interview people grated on her nerves. She recognized the symptoms of post-stress syndrome even in herself. She'd lived through too many partial victories this past year to be immune to the strain.

Ella forced her thoughts onto the tack she wanted to take when she spoke to Dodge's neighbors. She knew getting them to talk to her freely and openly wouldn't be easy.

It was eight in the morning by the time she reached Elsie Billey's home. The seventy-year-old woman had lived in a modest cinder block house right off the irrigation ditch as far back as anyone could remember. When her only son had been killed in Vietnam, everyone had thought Elsie would die too. Her grief had been great, but everyone had underestimated the strength of the elderly woman who had already buried two husbands.

Ella parked near the front door and waited, but she didn't have to wait long. Elsie came to the front door, wearing a long skirt and a bright red long-sleeved blouse. Recognizing Ella, she waved.

Ella left the vehicle and walked to the door, stopping on the wooden steps. "It's good to see you. It's been too long."

Elsie nodded, concern in her eyes adding to the serious look on her wrinkled face. "Bad things are happening again. I heard about that accident where all those people were killed, and about the murder of my neighbor. I figured the police would be by soon."

"That's why I'm here. You've been a friend of my family's for years. I'm hoping that you'll also see me as a friend."

"Your mother's clan and mine are related," Elsie said, reaching up absently to touch the large silver and turquoise squash blossom around her neck. "We belong to the Deer People, and you to the God People. We're all Red Soil People." She gestured inside, then offered Ella a chair. "What do you need from me?"

"Information. Your neighbor must have made some bad enemies."

Elsie shook her head. "No, that's not true. I would have heard if that had been so."

"Maybe I should look for someone who was giving his family trouble?" Ella asked, trying to find another way to open the doors to the information she was certain Elsie had.

"Oh, you've heard about his argument with Stubby over the irrigation water." Elsie shook her head and shrugged. "That's just Stubby's way. Besides, both those old men liked to argue. It gave them something to do."

Ella sat back and regarded the elderly woman for several long seconds. Her hair was tied back in a bun at the base of her neck, but several strands had worked loose and hung down in errant locks. "If you were me, where would you start looking?" Ella asked directly.

A flicker of something undefinable crossed Elsie's eyes. "Gossip travels too quickly here. Whatever I say could do much harm."

"Gossip has already traveled," Ella insisted. "The sooner I find answers, the quicker things can go back to the way they should be."

Elsie walked to the stove, turned on the butane burner under an old kettle, and added spoonfuls of instant coffee to a pair of white mugs.

Ella watched her work, allowing the silence to stretch out. She wanted to prod for answers—the quiet preyed on her nerves—but to insist now would have the opposite effect. Finally Elsie joined her at the table, placing a mug of the steaming liquid in front of Ella.

"Have you learned yet about my neighbor's daughter? She is causing her mother much heartache. She's a stubborn, spoiled child." Elsie added at least five spoonfuls of sugar to her own mug before taking a swallow.

Ella remembered Cindi Dodge. She'd been more outspoken than her mother, but that's all she knew so far. "Tell me more about the girl."

"Her boyfriend is Steven Nez."

Ella searched her mind. The name sounded familiar. But the man she connected to the name was married and about twice Cindi's age. "You don't mean Sally's husband, do you?"

"Yes, that's exactly who I mean. Steven Nez would show up at Cindi's house every afternoon when both her parents were at work. One day, the girl's father came home and found Steven there. He hauled Steven out by the back of his shirt and threw him into the truck. He told Steven that if he ever caught him around his daughter again, he'd get a seat full of buckshot. Then Cindi started seeing another boy, one her own age who had moved here from Fort Wingate. I heard Steven was jealous."

She shrugged. "Steven blamed Cindi's father for everything. You see, Sally found out, too, and kicked him out of the house, so now he's lost everything."

"Thanks for your help. I'll keep it confidential, don't worry."

"Steven is a worthless man, but I don't think he would murder anyone," Elsie added slowly. "I just can't understand why anyone who knew my neighbor would do such a thing."

Elsie knew more about people than anyone else Ella could think of. She spent most of her time alone, and passed the days walking around the area, watching her neighbors. Sometimes they called the station to complain about her looking over their fences, or standing by their gates. "Was Kee Dodge ever said to associate with skinwalkers? Or have you ever heard any talk about him being a skinwalker?"

Elsie's face drew taut, and the lines that framed her weather-roughened face deepened. "It is time for you to go." She stood up. "That is not a subject ever to be discussed in this house."

Ella realized her mistake and tried desperately to recover ground. "I'm working on behalf of the tribe. It's for their sake I'm asking. I know there is danger speaking of these things, but for the sake of the People, won't you talk to me?"

Elsie's eyes narrowed. "You have dishonored the name of one who is dead. I have nothing else to say to you."

Ella stood up, realizing that in her own way Elsie had answered the question. If Ella had dishonored Kee Dodge by linking him with skinwalkers, then that must mean that Dodge hadn't been suspected of being a Navajo Wolf.

Ella returned to her vehicle. Unfortunately, the next three houses she visited proved to be a complete waste of time. Either the inhabitants knew nothing or they were unwilling to talk to her. Finally she headed back down the highway. It was time to pay Leonard Haske a visit.

She picked up her mike and reported in. Although the signal kept breaking up, the transmission was still clear enough to be understood. Carolyn Roanhorse and Big Ed had both asked to see her.

Since Carolyn's office was on the way to the station, Ella opted to stop there first. Forty minutes later she found Carolyn at her desk, sipping a diet cola and eating a sugar-glazed doughnut.

Ella smiled. "Diet Coke doesn't cut the calories of the dough-nut," she teased, "no matter what you may have read in your medical journals."

"But it does wonders for the guilt," Carolyn retorted easily. "Want a doughnut?" She gestured to the box on the table behind her.

Ella took one of the "smart pills," a term she'd picked up for pastries among some of the Navajo cops, mainly to be sociable. "Heard you wanted to see me."

Carolyn handed her a copy of the autopsy report. "The bone inserted in the victim's eye came from a cat."

Ella skimmed over the report. There was nothing else new there.

"Notice that there's no mutilation of the body, like before, ex-cept for the eye," Carolyn said slowly, clearing her throat.

Ella knew precisely which "before" Carolyn was referring to. When skinwalkers had murdered Ella's father, their deadly sig-nature had been left on the corpse for all to see.

"I'm nearly convinced this has nothing to do with skinwalk-ers," Ella confessed. "I'm hoping it's an isolated incident and the killer was hoping to throw us off the trail by leading us on a wild-goose chase." Ella stood up and took the autopsy report from the desk. "I'll be talking to you soon. For now, I better get my hind end over to the station. Big Ed wants to meet with me."

"Yeah, I heard that from my cousin who works for the de-partment. The chief has a surprise for you."

Ella smiled. It was hard to keep any secrets on the Rez. Every-one had too many relatives. "Care to give me a hint?"

"Your life may get easier—or not."

"Gee, thanks," Ella said, and laughed seeing the mischievous look on Carolyn's face. The woman had a penchant for riddles. "I guess I'll be going then."

Ella returned to her vehicle and drove down the valley to the station. She wanted to find out if anything new had turned up on the case. It was much too early for a report from the bureau, but she could still hope.

As she walked through the side doors, she heard the clamor

of voices coming from the back of the building, and some laughter. The Navajo radio station was playing over the loudspeaker. Ella walked down the hall, noting with satisfaction that a surveillance camera had been set up. It was not obvious, but the field of view ensured complete coverage of the hallway. She was glad Big Ed had agreed with her recommendation. As she reached her office, she saw that someone had left a copy of the Farmington paper on the floor by her door. Picking it up, she unlocked the door and walked inside. The hostage/suicide situation and the bus accident were twin headlines on the front page. A brief account further down the page promised details on the Dodge murder.

"Great, you're back." She heard Big Ed's unmistakable voice behind her. "I've got good news for you."

Ella turned around and saw Justine Goodluck, her second cousin, wearing a Navajo police badge clipped to the belt of her slacks. She stood next to Big Ed with a proud smile. "This is your new assistant," he said obviously pleased. "We scraped some additional money together for this year's budget. Based on the importance of the crimes you handle and recent events, the council thought we should use it to give you an assistant. Justine has been a patrol officer with the department for two years, as you probably know, and has attended special classes to further her qualifications. She's now a fully qualified lab technician, and we're putting together a small lab for her on the premises. Having Justine assigned to you exclusively means Detective Ute will have more time to work on other things. He's overworked as it is.

"Justine can conduct most of our routine testing with the equipment she's been given, so you can have more immediate results. The budget requires her to wear more than one hat in order to warrant the position, so she'll also be doing investigative work with you, under your supervision, and will assist you in gathering evidence. I also briefed her on our added security measures, and the need to keep everything locked."

Ella smiled at Justine, who was barely five foot two and a hundred pounds. She looked like she should still be in high school.

Her cousin had been the youngest of seven children, and the one everyone had overlooked. Her older sisters and brothers had all excelled, either in athletics or academics. Justine had been the one whose talents had never been particularly strong in either direction. "I knew you were interested in law enforcement, but . . ."

"Cousin, when I was in high school I kept hearing about you, and all you were accomplishing with your life. When I started looking around for a career, I knew I wanted to go into law enforcement, like you, so I joined the tribal police. I've been taking all the courses that were available to me, and have just returned from a forensics class at the FBI Academy. I want to be able to serve the tribe like you have."

Ella smiled, surprised by the admiration that shone in Justine's eyes.

"Well, I'll leave you two to work. Justine has already started reviewing the case, so I know you'll have things to discuss."

As soon as they were alone, Justine grinned at Ella. "Yeah, I know what you're thinking. I'm too young, or just not as experienced as you'd like. But I'm going to be the best thing that ever happened to you."

Ella burst out laughing at the young woman's confidence and bravado. She could see herself in Justine. She'd been a lot like that at the start of her career. "I have no doubt that you're good at your job. Many apply to be cops on the Rez, and openings are few. Only a handful actually make it."

"Once I make up my mind, I always carry through. Besides, it's just like you told me many years back, before you joined the FBI. You said that anyone who was willing to work hard could make a dream come true."

"*Many, many years?*" Ella stared at Justine in surprise. "I don't even remember saying that, though it sounds like something I would have said."

"I never forgot it."

Ella nodded slowly. "Be aware of one thing, cousin. I'm glad to have a helper, but the cases I get are usually the ones nobody else ever wants."

"I know. That's why you need me. Now let me show you

what I've been doing, and why I'm going to be the best assistant you've ever had."

Ella chuckled. "You're the *only* assistant I've ever had."

"Well, that should make things even easier," her cousin answered. Justine placed several files she'd held tucked beneath one arm on the desk. "I've studied the evidence and run a check for you on the prints we found. No one with a record left any latents on"—Justine lowered her voice to a whisper as she mentioned the victim's name—"on Kee Dodge's truck or belongings."

Justine's voice returned to a normal level as she continued. "I did a comparison check on all the vehicle tracks and footprints found at the site too. Most were linked to the students who'd driven there and walked around. But there is one set of footprints that didn't match. They were made by Nike cross-trainers. It's a very common brand, but around the Rez most men wear boots. From the imprint and size, nine, my guess puts the suspect at about five foot seven, weighing about 155 to 160 pounds."

"I'm impressed."

"Good. That's what I was trying for. And I've got more." Justine checked her notes on the second file. "The leather shoelaces used to strangle the victim were a common brand, found at most groceries or drugstores in our area. I know NCIC may have a report on similar M.O.s, but I'm really not sure how to access that."

Ella smiled. "I intend to check that now that I've got Carolyn's autopsy report."

"I've also got one piece of information that came from the Albuquerque crime lab, via the FBI."

"They faxed something?" Ella glanced around her desk.

"No, I called the agent in Farmington, knowing he'd put a rush on things for us. The crime lab began tests with the saliva on the gum almost immediately upon receipt. I took a chance, figuring they might have answers they could give us verbally before anyone got around to writing the report."

"Good thinking!"

"Their tests are very hopeful, according to Agent Blalock. The blood type doesn't give us much because it's type O, the most common. We can rule out the victim, however; his blood type was AB. But the saliva in the gum is from what they call a secretor. That's an individual whose body fluids, like his blood, can be grouped. According to experts, sixty to eighty percent of the population are secretors. So we have a good chance of establishing that the gum was chewed by a particular individual. All we need is a suspect to get a comparison sample from. Until then, however, it's just one more report."

"Let me check some data banks and see if I can find a similar M.O. on murder victims in the Four Corners area," Ella said, switching on her computer. "If it works, we may get a lead."

"You don't sound hopeful."

Ella shrugged. "I don't think we're going to find any easy answers on this case. This killer is too organized." Ella cleared her throat. "The best I can hope for is to find a loose trail, or another slip-up, like the gum, that could lead to Dodge's murderer. Many killers have long histories of brushes with the law. Prior convictions, especially ones like aggravated assault, could point us in the right direction."

"I'll help you look through the files and data banks."

Justine's enthusiasm again reminded Ella of herself at that age. She'd been eager to change the world back at the start of her career. Nowadays she was satisfied with making a good collar that would stand up in court. "Okay, let's both get busy."

With Justine working her own leads from the computer in her lab, Ella accessed state computers. She mentally reviewed what she knew as she searched for any leads. The killer lived in the area, she was sure of it. He had stalked Kee Dodge, then struck at a time well in advance of the start of the class, knowing the road to that class site was not well traveled. He'd known there was no need to rush, as evidenced by the time he spent creating the charcoal dry painting. He'd imbedded the bone in the victim's eye, and had taken care to remove any evidence that might incriminate him, like the weapon he'd used to initially strike down the victim. Everything had been considered, except the gum.

Perhaps it was time to take a closer look at Dodge's students. In this type of killing, where everything had been meticulously planned, the murderer often enjoyed playing with the police by getting involved and acting helpful. That egotism pointed to the weakness that would eventually bring him down.

She called Justine into her office.

"It's time to track down Steven Nez," Ella said. "See if there's a listing in the phone book."

"No need. I know where he and Sally live. It's in Shiprock, just west of the high school."

"He's not living there any longer, but maybe Sally can tell us where to find him." Ella hadn't forgotten what Elsie Billey had told her.

Following Justine's directions, Ella drove past several alfalfa fields, then saw a single trailer parked just east of some low hills. Two small children were playing tag outside, while a jeans-clad woman in her mid-thirties hung up laundry. "That's Sally," Justine confirmed.

The woman turned and glowered as Ella opened the car door and stepped out of the vehicle calling out that she needed to speak to Steven Nez.

"He's not here. You're wasting your time," Sally snapped.

"I'd like to ask you a few questions," Ella said clearly, not approaching, but instead holding out her badge.

"I can't help you. I kicked Steven out. He doesn't live here anymore." Sally's gaze shifted to Justine as she too stepped out of the vehicle. In a flash, the annoyance on Sally's face turned to rage. "*You!* How dare you come to my home!"

Sally spun around and unsnapped the chain that anchored an enormous mutt to her clothesline pole. "Sic 'em, boy!"

The bear-sized chow cross, suddenly free, ran directly at them. Ella and Justine froze, knowing that running was the worst thing to attempt. The dog stopped a dozen feet away and growled menacingly. "Good boy," Ella encouraged. "Aren't you a brave dog!"

After fifteen seconds or so, the dog's tail started wagging, and he came up and licked Ella's outstretched hand.

"You worthless mutt!" Sally yelled. The dog turned, lowered

his ears meekly, then walked over and lay down in the shade with an old bone.

Ella walked cautiously toward Sally Nez, one eye still on the dog. When Justine followed, Sally rushed toward her.

"How dare you come with *her* to my house!" Sally yelled. Ella glanced at Justine for an answer, but saw only confusion on her cousin's face. "Calm down, Mrs. Nez. We just wanted to ask you a few questions, and what you're doing now is just going to send you before a judge." Ella brought out her handcuffs so Sally could see them.

"No. Please, don't do that," she said wearily. "If you arrest me, there won't be anyone here to take care of my kids."

Ella felt defiance ebb from Sally Nez and defeat set in. The two children, neither old enough for the first grade, huddled on the steps of the trailer, staring at them fearfully. "We didn't come here to arrest you, or anyone else. Why did you set your dog on us?"

"Because you brought *her* to our home! My children don't need to see the girl my husband wanted to abandon them for!" Sally glared at Justine.

"You mean *me?*" Justine was surprised. "I'm a police officer, and I've been out of state for the last eight weeks!" She gestured down to the badge she'd clipped to her belt. "I would barely recognize your husband. We've never even met."

Sally blinked. "You're not Cindi Dodge? Janet Frazier showed me the photo in the yearbook, and you look just like her." Sally's gaze remained distrustful.

Justine gave the woman a bewildered look, then produced her photo ID. "Honest. I'm Justine Goodluck. I'm twenty-two years old, not some high school kid."

Sally's face crumpled. "I'm really sorry. I thought you were her, looking so young and all. You don't have any idea how hard it is being married to Steven. He's good-looking, likes to go dancing, and attracts a lot of girls. He tells them all kinds of stories about how I don't do this, or do too much of that. Pretty soon they end up feeling sorry for him and agree to meet him. The younger ones particularly. After a few times, they end up coming here to tell me I'm no good, and to beg me to let him go." She scoffed. "*Let* him go? I finally had to kick him out."

Now that Sally had mentioned it, Justine did look a lot like Dodge's daughter. Ella put away the cuffs. It had been a reasonable mistake, and she'd get far more from this woman by showing some sign of goodwill than any other way.

Sally gave her a grateful smile. "Thanks. Now tell me how I can help you. I figure you're here because of the murder." She turned and waved to her children, letting them know everything was all right. Immediately they resumed their game of tag. "Steven didn't do it, you know, though from what others told me, he hated the old man for messing up his little romance."

"Did he speak to you about Cindi's father?"

"No. But then again, we never talked much. For the past few years all our conversations have been short, like his paychecks. I've always known he made more than he brought home."

"Where does he work?"

"He had been working in Farmington for Sherman Construction, laying sheetrock. But he had an argument with his boss and got fired about a week ago."

"Tell me about Steven. Does he become violent when he's angry?"

"Steven?" Sally looked surprised. "No, not at all. Even when he drinks too much, all he does is fall asleep. He's a tomcat, that's for sure, but he's never even spanked the kids."

"Where could he be found now?"

Sally shrugged. "I'm not sure. I know he isn't at his mother's—she wouldn't have him. She doesn't like what he's been doing to me and the kids. My guess is he's probably at his brother's. They're two of a kind. Joe drinks too much, and lives way out near Teece Nos Pos."

"Thanks, Sally. If Steven comes back, will you give us a call?"

"Sure. Are you going to arrest him?"

"No. I just want to ask him a few questions."

"Oh. That's too bad."

Her disappointment was so evident that Ella struggled hard to suppress a smile. "But if he breaks the law we won't be as easy on him as we were on you."

Sally smiled. "Then I'll just hope like crazy he puts up a fight."

"Will you be okay?" Ella asked, her glance shifting to the kids.

"Yeah. It's easier, really, with Steven gone. He was just one more kid I had to look after. My mother's coming to stay with us, too, so I can go to night school. I want to become a midwife. I figured others, like you, have made it on your own. There's no reason why I can't do the same."

Ella was quiet and thoughtful as she walked back to the car with Justine.

"Is something wrong, boss?"

Ella smiled at her title. The only "staff" she'd ever had was a contagious bacterium. "You know, I could really empathize with what Sally's going through. There was a time when my biggest dream consisted of marrying a handsome man and having his children. But then life stepped in. It forced me to see that there were all kinds of options open to me."

Justine shrugged. "My career is important to me, but I think the drive to find a good mate and have children is instinctive."

Ella glanced at Justine. "You're still so young. Thinking of marriage yourself?"

"Not yet. I love my work too much, and I don't want to hassle with divided loyalties. Those usually make a mess out of a cop's personal life."

"Police work does tend to be all consuming, that's true. It's hard to find a mate who can understand and live with the demands it makes."

"Also, let's face it, we really don't meet that great a selection of men. In this line of work, we're mostly around bad guys or other cops."

Ella laughed out loud. "And neither of us wants to get involved with a crook, or a man who does what we do for a living."

"In a nutshell," Justine agreed with a grin.

Ella entered the station's parking lot and pulled up next to Justine's vehicle. "It's time for us to split up. I want you to track down Kee Dodge's students. His classes were open to anyone who wanted to audit them and were held all over the Rez, so it may take a while. Officer Jimmy Frank has the addresses of the students who came to the last class. Find out from those students who else regularly attended his lectures, and start interviewing those people. I particularly want to know about anyone at all he might have had problems with. We have progressives around here who believe that to look to the past is to embrace it. See if any of them ever disrupted Dodge's classes. I recommend you try to talk to Professor Wilson Joe. He's a good friend and could be a lot of help. We went through a lot together last year. You can trust Wilson."

"It is going to take a long time to track everyone down, even with help."

"Then you better get started," Ella said. "And one other thing: See if anyone remembers hearing about a cat disappearing in the past few days, or being found dead."

"A cat, huh?" Justine looked at her strangely. Then nodded with sudden understanding. "Oh, right. A cat, of course."

Glancing in her rearview mirror as she pulled back onto the road, Ella saw Justine walk over to her patrol unit. While Justine took care of the other leads, she'd finally track down Stubby Todacheene and Leonard Haske.

FIVE

✖ ✖ ✖

Ella knew where Todacheene lived; his farm was downriver a half mile or so from Kee Dodge's. As she drove past the victim's farm, she could see Cindi off in the distance with her basketball, practicing. It was over ninety degrees outside, yet the girl was shooting free throws. Ella could see one of the reasons why Shiprock kids played basketball so well. There wasn't much else for them to do besides farm chores.

The Todacheene house was quite small, a square gray-stuccoed wood-frame house set under a stand of cottonwood trees. A large, well-tended vegetable garden was next to the dirt track, and farther down were fields of alfalfa that needed cutting. Nobody was in sight around the house, but Ella could see an old green Ford pickup parked by the end of the vegetable patch. Nearby, a tall, skinny Navajo man in his fifties was working with a hoe, cutting weeds beside a small ditch.

Ella parked at the end of the dirt trail so the man could see her and waited. He looked over after a few minutes, then stood up straight and waved. She got out and walked around the garden, approaching from the side.

As Ella got close, the man stopped his work and leaned on his hoe. "You're Big Ed's detective, aren't you? The one they call L.A. Woman?"

Ella nodded, managing a smile. That nickname had stuck, despite the fact she'd resigned her FBI post in Los Angeles months ago. She stopped and appraised the man. She wasn't sure if he was scowling at her, or merely squinting in the bright daylight. The blue bandanna he wore kept the hair from his eyes, but did little to protect him from the blazing sun.

"People call me Stubby, from when I was a fat little kid," Todacheene muttered. "I wondered when you'd come asking about my water-hog neighbor. Not a day went by that he didn't open the gates to flood one of his fields. Did you know half of his crops rotted away each year from all that soaking? You'd think he'd consider our needs, but no, he never did. I guess now, with that lazy daughter of his left to do the watering, I'll finally get my share from the big ditch. She's never been much use around the farm, if you ask me."

"Then you didn't get along with your neighbor?" Ella managed to get a sentence in as Stubby stopped to take a breath. She got the feeling he was trying to make her think he was an old grouch.

"Get along with that old mule?" Stubby turned and looked toward the Dodge home, and his voice trailed off. When he turned back, his eyes were old and sad. "Not when it came to water, I suppose. But he was a good man, and asked us over whenever they butchered a sheep, or baked a basket of corn, or brought in the melons. I suppose I always got all the water we needed. I guess I liked him most because he liked to argue too. We liked disliking each other, if you know what I mean." Mist formed in Stubby's eyes, and Ella suspected this time he was quite sincere.

"Would you mind if I asked where you were the morning he died?" Ella had to know, despite the possibility of upsetting Todacheene even more.

Stubby shrugged, and his voice was uneven at first. "That's the kind of question you get the big bucks for asking, I guess. No need to think about it. I was watering my upper field. When he was gone teaching, I had a chance to get enough flow to irrigate even there. You can ask my other neighbor. He helped me open the gate by the river."

"Thank you for your time, sir." Ella nodded. "I'll leave for now. May I come back later if I think of any more questions?"

Stubby shrugged and began cutting weeds again. "You know where I'll be. Here, or a few yards farther down the row. Come back if you want."

Ella turned and walked back around the garden to her car, noting the melons and squash growing larger by the moment in the New Mexico sun. All it took was decent soil and a bit of water to meet the needs of the People, she decided.

It took Ella over two hours to reach the stretch of reservation that led to Haske's daughter's home. It was in a new traditionalist's community that had sprung up in the middle of nowhere, just off the main highway.

As she approached the cluster of houses, she noted that a large number of them had beehive ovens in the back. Many traditionalists preferred to bake bread the old way. Quite a few had hogans nearby, too, for religious purposes.

Ella continued to study the area as she drove up. A large sheep pen filled the air with the familiar fragrance of animals and dung. Two women, one old and the other young, probably mother and daughter, were busy washing wool from freshly sheared sheep. For a moment, it felt as if she'd stepped back in time. Yet there was a serenity here that drew her. She was slowly becoming aware of her increasing affinity toward the old ways, although she'd never thought of herself as a traditionalist. Certainly cops, though many were conservative, didn't generally fit that description.

She followed the directions her brother had given her and went to the last house facing the mesa. A large collie lay on the front porch and scarcely looked up as she parked. A young woman cradling an infant looked out the window.

Ella stepped out of the vehicle and leaned against the door, clipping her police ID badge to her shirt pocket so there would be no question as to her identity. The Jeep, of course, had no official markings. Tucking the file with the photos under one arm, she waited.

Several moments later, a young girl—about eight—came out to meet her. "I was sent to get you, police officer lady. Will you come around back to the hogan with me?"

Ella smiled at the little girl. Her hair hung loose almost to her waist, and she had large red lips that suggested she'd eaten a popsicle in her recent past. She wore old jeans with an elastic waistband and a large Washington Redskins T-shirt that probably belonged to her brother.

Even here, in this traditionalists' enclave, the old and the new were always side by side. She followed the girl around the house. Leonard Haske was just outside the hogan on his hands and knees, crushing some herbs in a shallow bowl. She watched him in silence, knowing he'd speak to her when he was ready.

He finally glanced up. "What can I do for you?"

"I need some information, uncle. My brother suggested I come to you."

Haske picked up the bowl with the herb mixture and carried it inside the hogan, gesturing for her to follow. As they stepped through the blanket-covered doorway, Ella saw him touch the leather medicine pouch at his waist. A beaded ear of corn was woven at its center. Words memorized long ago came back to her reminding her that corn was the gift of life.

Haske took a pinch of the contents of the pouch and scattered it inside the hogan. He then placed several other substances he'd collected into a bowl and burned them. Soon a pleasant smell permeated the hogan. "This is done to keep evil away while you and I speak."

Ella nodded slowly. Reaching inside the large envelope, she pulled out the photos she'd brought. "Do these mean anything to you?"

Haske studied them carefully, then finally shook his head. "This was not done by a *hataalii*. If anything, it's the work of a blasphemous fool." He sat back and closed his eyes.

Ella waited, uncertain if she was being dismissed. She was acutely aware of each minute that ticked by, but she remained still.

Finally Haske opened his eyes and looked at her. "Do you feel it?"

His gaze was oddly penetrating, and Ella had to force herself not to look away. "Feel what, uncle?"

"Close your eyes, and allow everything that surrounds you to touch you. Don't be afraid. You're safe here," he assured her.

Ella did as he asked, wondering what he expected from her. As she quieted her senses and forced herself to relax, she felt an odd stirring that made her flesh prickle. It was a unique sensation, like electricity running in waves over her skin. The second she opened her eyes, it disappeared.

Haske smiled and nodded. "So what I've heard about you is true. You do have the gift."

She wasn't sure what to answer. The sensations that had coursed through her had probably been attributable to that odd incense. "I'm a good cop, uncle, and I've learned a lot about people. Believe me when I tell you that I'll fight whatever disrupts the harmony of the *Dineh*," she answered.

Haske's eyebrows knitted together. "You don't accept it? I would have thought . . ." He shook his head, then shrugged. "No matter. It's yours to use or not. Now tell me how I can help you."

"Do you know who might have wanted to kill the man who taught stories of our people's past?" she asked directly. Then, seeing the startled expression on Haske's face, she chided herself for bluntness. At least she'd remembered not to use the name of a dead man in Haske's home. "I'm sorry to bring such talk here, to this place"—she gestured around the hogan—"but in truth, I can't think of a safer place."

Haske's expression relaxed somewhat. "The herbs and the protection that surround us here are as real as the gun you wear at your waist," Haske answered.

Ella tugged at her cotton windbreaker, making sure it covered her weapon. She felt self-conscious wearing it here, but she had no choice. Regulations were regulations.

Haske took a long, slow, deep breath. "Trouble has come to our people again. You felt it when you attuned yourself to your hidden senses a moment ago. There's an imbalance, as if the evil is waiting, and growing as it does. The death of the elder triggered disharmony like a wave across a lake. Those people on the bus felt its force and even that man in Farmington. We are all in danger now."

Haske's words were making her skin crawl. She tried to shake off the feeling. "Have you heard of any skinwalker activity, uncle?"

"No. But there is danger surrounding us, and it is close at hand. It's pressing around you and me right now."

"Do you think someone is after you?" she asked, prodding for clearer answers.

Haske shrugged. "I'm not worried about myself. I'm ready to join my ancestors when it's my time. But you still have much to learn and much to do." He paused. "Your brother helped my wife many years ago when she was ill and I wasn't here. Out of respect to him, I will sing a blessing over you."

He began the words of a chant. The song filled the hogan with a feeling of power so strong it became an almost tangible presence. It was as if the elements were amassing themselves protectively around them. As the last note faded, he released a pinch of corn pollen into the air. "May your trail be in pollen," he concluded.

Ella thanked him, knowing that there was no higher blessing. Pollen increased individual power, and it cleared the path of danger. Pollen signified sustenance, light, and life.

Ella returned to her Jeep with a smile on her face. It was a ceremony she'd seen performed hundreds of times, yet it still made her feel refreshed, renewed somehow.

She started to drive toward the station, but then changed her mind and took the turnoff leading home. She'd stop there for dinner, then go back to work.

Shortly after seven, Ella walked inside her home, scratching Dog as he got up to greet her. She called out to her mom, and received an answer from out back. Rose was gathering a freshly washed bedspread from the clothesline.

"I'll be inside in a minute," Rose answered. "A letter arrived for you today. It's on the kitchen table."

Ella saw the envelope and picked it up, noting there was no return address. Always wary, she tore it open carefully and pulled a note from inside. As she read the message, her knees buckled, and she dropped heavily onto the chair behind her.

"What's wrong?" Rose asked as she came through the back door. "You look as if you don't feel well." Looking down at the letter Ella held in her hands, she added, "Bad news?"

"You could say that. It's from Peterson Yazzie."

"Hasn't he been confined to a psychiatric hospital?"

"Yes, but he's claiming responsibility for Kee Dodge's murder and the bus accident. He warns that even from there, his reach is deadly."

SIX

Ella studied the letter, knowing with every instinct she possessed that it was genuine.

"We have not finished with you yet, dear Ella," Peterson wrote. "Our signs are everywhere for you to read—from the death of the old man, to those fools in the bus on the highway. Our reach is deadly, you know that now. No matter where you go, you are not safe. You can keep no secrets from me. Even your most private files hidden inside your office are available to me whenever I wish. You are outmatched, cousin. You'll come to regret the day you returned to the reservation."

Peterson Yazzie's handwriting was quite familiar to her, and as she read each word, it was as if they were being spoken aloud in his voice.

Whether or not he actually was responsible for Dodge's murder was another matter entirely. People like Yazzie banked on fear, using it as a tool so often it became second nature to them.

"That man is capable of many things," Rose said quietly. Leaning against the kitchen counter, she studied Ella's expression.

"He's crafty, all right," Ella answered, "and he's got one heck of an intelligence network."

"Remember his past reputation makes it easy for him to intimidate people and get what he wants."

Ella looked up at her mother. She didn't want to discuss the details. Peterson's claim that his people could enter her office whenever they wished annoyed her, particularly because it had been true once. But what bothered her most was Peterson's mention of "signs" left at the crime scene. No details of the ash painting or the bone fragment had been in her press release. Yet it was almost as if he knew. She knew for certain that no unauthorized person had entered her office since the time when the key had been removed and a message left.

She looked at the date stamped on the envelope. It had been mailed yesterday. Of course by now news had traveled from the student witnesses to their friends and relatives. Still, his oblique reference to that painting unsettled her.

"What else does he say?" Rose prodded gently.

"He's goading me, but that doesn't bother me. What does is that he seems to be in possession of information he shouldn't have." Ella lapsed into silence, afraid she'd said too much and raised questions in her mother's mind. She didn't want to worry her, and learning about the ash painting would certainly do just that.

"Not knowing is worse," Rose said softly. "What are you keeping from me?"

Ella smiled. She'd forgotten how easily her mom could read her thoughts. Ella gestured down at the paper on the table. "You can read it."

Rose's face contorted with a brief flash of anger, then with effort she schooled her features into stillness again. "He manipulates well. Now I understand why you have to work so hard to maintain your temper." Rose sat down on the chair across from her daughter. "These signs—more skinwalker activity?"

Ella told her mother about the charcoal dry painting, and what she'd found out. "If Peterson's still behind bars, and his activities can be accounted for, then that'll prove that this is only a skillful bluff. It's very possible he wrote this just to get attention."

"That could very well be," Rose admitted. "Let's face it. He would certainly know how to do a proper ash painting, and so would his followers. It's part of their training. Precise details

play an important part in their rituals, as in ours, and any skinwalker would pay more attention to that than the killer did."

Ella stood up. "I'm going to contact Big Ed." Ella dialed and
after a few minutes managed to reach her boss's pager. She was
grateful when the return call came only a few moments later. Ella
gave Big Ed a full report, then waited as he considered his reply.

"I don't like this," Big Ed finally said. "I'm going to call the
psychiatric hospital. A request from me personally will get us a
faster response. I'll demand an official accounting of all his movements, even if it entails talking to every nurse and guard."

"On another, hopefully unrelated, matter. Do you know how
that bus accident happened?" Ella asked.

"Survivors say the driver swerved to avoid hitting some
sheep in the road. He lost control," Big Ed replied, then paused.
"What do you mean, 'hopefully'?"

"Some of the people I've spoken to claim that the murder was
just a trigger for a series of disasters. I was just thinking out
loud," Ella explained.

"Well, they're wrong. We have enough on our hands already.
I'll get back to you."

As Ella hung up the telephone, she saw her mother by the
stove preparing their favorite dinner dish, a Navajo taco. The
aroma of the freshly fried sopaipilla filled with beans, chiles, and
meat permeated the air, making her mouth water.

Rose sprinkled some shredded cheddar cheese over the
steaming food and placed it on the table before her daughter.

Ella's eyes widened. "I hope this is for both of us, mother."
The sopaipilla was huge, flaky, and golden, brimming over with
a cheesy pinto bean mixture that spilled all the way to the rim of
the plate.

"It's for you, and I expect you to eat every last bite of it. You're
going to need your strength."

"If I eat all this, I won't be able to fit behind my steering
wheel!" she protested with a laugh. "Come on, split it with me."

With a martyred sigh, Rose picked up another plate. She divided the portions, stubbornly leaving sixty percent of the food
for Ella. "I worry about you," Rose said. "I can't help you catch

criminals, but at least I can make sure you're well fed and healthy. Don't deny me that."

The simplicity of the statement and the strong emotions behind it made a warm rush of affection course through Ella. For a moment, she could see herself in her mother, and her mother in her. The need to provide comfort, to be needed, was very much a part of them both.

Ella observed the way her mother held her fork, and for a moment was entranced by how similar their hands were. The bond that held them as mother and daughter was stronger now that they were both widows. Recognizing and sharing each other's pain had drawn them together in a way good times never could have.

The telephone rang just as Ella finished her last bite. She walked to the counter and picked up the kitchen extension.

"Yazzie's been under almost constant supervision," Big Ed informed her. "He most definitely has *not* left the facility at any time. They are just as worried about a homicidal ex-cop as we are."

"What about telephone calls?"

"He talks to his lawyer, of course, and those conversations are privileged, but that's about it. I spoke with my cousin's wife who works there, and she said that the staff is intimidated by him, and so are the other patients. She claims that weird things are always happening around Yazzie. It got so bad that Administration was forced to hire more guards to keep everyone calm."

"Weird how? This is a mental facility, right? You would expect things to be a little, well, different."

"I asked her that too. She said that one of the nurses had lost an earring and for days had everyone looking for it. Peterson handed it to her one morning when she was there with the orderlies taking his vital signs for a routine checkup. She swears she'd never been in his room before, and the duty logs back that up. And Peterson had been confined to his room that whole week after throwing a tray at an orderly. Of course there are many possible explanations, but things like that unnerve those who've heard rumors of his . . . powers."

"So basically it's quite possible he intimidated someone into carrying a letter out for him," Ella concluded.

"That's about it, and likewise for him to have heard something he could use as a basis for his reference to the ash painting. Gossip travels at lightning speed."

"I'd like to go over there first thing tomorrow to see what else I can find out."

"I'd recommend it, then get back to me. Anything new on the murder so far?"

"Not yet."

After dinner, Ella sat in the living room with her mother. Ella had been trying to learn to knit and was starting with a basic sweater, but the results were far from stellar. She ripped out the last three rows, noticing she'd made a mistake in the pattern. Maybe she just wasn't cut out for domestic things.

Still, it was something to do for now. Inactivity bothered her. The letter had disturbed her more than she dared let on. She planned on staying close to the house tonight. Although she doubted anyone would openly attack her home, lessons of the past were hard to forget and dangerous to ignore. She thought for a moment about Dog, out chasing rabbits and reconfirming his territory. He'd bark if anyone approached.

"I'm glad you're home tonight," Rose said, spinning wool on her wheel.

"Are you worried, Mom? I really don't think . . ."

Rose shook her head. "No. It's just nice to have you here, and not working on reports for once."

"It's good to be home." Ella glanced at her knitting and finally put it down. "But I've made an amazing discovery. If I had to knit for a living, I'd starve."

Rose laughed. "You're too impatient, that's all. You expect to be an expert in two days."

"Mom, there is such a thing as aptitude." She held up a wavy section supposed to be bottom ribbing. "This isn't going to be my thing."

"You have to find yourself a hobby, daughter. Something to occupy you besides your work."

"I agree, but I'm now sure it isn't going to involve yarn or thread." Ella walked to her desk and retrieved the cleaning kit for her gun from the drawer. Unloading and clearing the chamber of her pistol, she began working on the slide with a soft cloth.

Rose sighed. "There *has* to be something I can interest you in!"

"I have to clean and oil the action, Mom, and I might as well do it now, unless it'll bother you."

Rose sighed. "No. Go ahead."

An uneasy calm descended as they each worked at their respective tasks. Rose had turned on a Navajo-language radio station, and Ella kept her ears tuned for the news. There was mercifully little coverage on the bus accident and Dodge's murder, and only a little more on yesterday's kidnapping and suicide in Farmington. At least for now.

Ella finished cleaning her weapon, loaded it again, then carefully placed it back in the holster. It was nearly ten, and she was tired.

She walked to one of the darkened windows in the kitchen and looked outside. The moon was full, illuminating the ground clearly. Everything looked calm and peaceful. She closed her eyes as she had at Haske's hogan and tried to draw strength from the desert itself. A vague prickle of fear seeped through her instead.

She was just too keyed up, that was all. She needed to get some sleep. The problem was she doubted she'd be successful at that tonight.

As she turned, Ella saw her mother standing there with a glass of herbal tea. "It will help you relax. I know that letter upset you."

Ella took the tea. "I'll take the note into the office tomorrow first thing. Maybe Justine can lift a print or two, and we'll find out who Yazzie's got helping him."

Rose nodded slowly. "I'm glad your cousin is working with you. At times like these, it's good to have family around you." Ella met her mother's eyes. "You're expecting the worst?" "I feel the disharmony all these troubles have brought to us. I'm trying to prepare," Rose answered frankly, then returned to the spinning wheel in the living room.

Shortly after daybreak Ella dropped the letter on Justine's desk with her instructions. By seven, she was on her way to the psychiatric facility on the other side of Farmington, on the Bloomfield highway.

Throughout the drive she could feel her tension mounting. Peterson was a master at mind games, and he had learned to intimidate others while still a cop. Manipulating the hospital staff was something that would appeal enormously to him. What would positively delight him, however, was knowing he'd put one over on her. The thought angered Ella. She would find his accomplice and end this new charade of his.

Peterson, despite his cunning, had always underestimated her, and that had led to his downfall before. His own colossal ego would never even consider the possibility that they were evenly matched.

Ella arrived forty-five minutes later at the Hilltop Psychiatric Hospital, which was located on a barren knoll overlooking the banks of the San Juan River two miles away. Ella noted with satisfaction that the two-story building was constructed more like a jail than a hospital. Windows were missing from the ground floor entirely, and those on the second floor were too small to allow an adult to exit. Razor-wire topped tall inner and outer fences, and guards at the gates made unauthorized visits or departures unlikely.

When an armed security guard escorted her through the locked entrance, Ella noted the quiet efficiency of the place and approved.

After identifying herself, Ella was ushered to Dr. Ray Kring's office by an orderly. As director of the facility, Kring had acquired a reputation for keeping things running smoothly.

Ella's news concerning the letter took the salt-and-pepper-haired Anglo by complete surprise.

"I cannot imagine who would have mailed that for him. The only letters he's ever written are to his attorney. I see the sealed envelopes myself. I've made it a point to know everything that concerns *that* patient."

"I'm not here to blame anyone, Dr. Kring, but I do think this matter warrants looking into."

"Yes, of course. Let me show you the security we maintain around Yazzie. I don't take anything for granted when it comes to any of our patients. We've increased the number of armed guards on each shift to four, and there are twice that number of trained orderlies on hand."

"Has Yazzie had any visitors lately?"

"Only his lawyer." Dr. Kring stood, and Ella noted how tall the doctor was. At five foot ten, she wasn't used to looking up at women or men on the Rez.

"How about friends or relatives?"

"Friends—*him?*" Kring strode to the door, holding it open as she passed through. "I don't believe he's capable of that." He stopped by his secretary's desk and glanced at a record book she handed him. "Perfect. He's in the exercise yard right now. You can see for yourself." Seeing the puzzled look she gave the log book, he added, "I require a record of where Yazzie is being held at all times."

The precaution made her stomach tighten. She could sense their fear, and in her own experience with Peterson, knew it was justified. Kring led the way down a long, well-lit hall, then up the stairs. Along one wall were several tiny windows. A Navajo guard stood at one, watching below.

Kring gestured for her to join him. "Yazzie can't see you through this glass. It's one-way."

Ella stepped up and looked down at the interior exercise yard below. The presence of one guard for each inmate, and the doughnut shape of the hospital, made even that area high security. She located Peterson Yazzie a second later sitting on one of the concrete benches as two other maximum-security patient-inmates played a game of basketball. Peterson's face was neutral, and he made no move to join the game, though she knew he was particularly fond of the sport.

Ella noticed how neither of the players would look in Peterson's direction, even when they had to go near him to retrieve the ball. "They're scared of him, aren't they?"

"Terrified is more like it," Kring answered. "He played once, and neither man would guard him close or try to block his shots. Yazzie got really mad. Then, two days later, both guys started coming down with the flu. Of course the story got around that he'd caused the illness. Some continue to argue the guy's just a con artist, but I notice it's never within earshot of Yazzie."

The guard watching from the next window cleared his throat. "If you don't mind an opinion . . ."

Ella glanced at the Navajo man. "Please, go ahead."

"I know that man from the Rez, and after being assigned to watch him, I've learned what makes him tick. He's a born actor. He's aware of the stories about him, and he plays to his audience. He doesn't want to be approachable; he remains more a mystery this way."

"So you think it's all a good act?" Ella pressed.

"No, not at all. It took more than that to accomplish the things he did on the Rez. What I'm saying is that he's very intuitive about people. He knows how to manipulate situations that are already there so that people end up believing and doing exactly what he wants them to."

Ella nodded slowly, then shifted her gaze down to the yard. To her surprise, Peterson Yazzie was looking up. He seemed to be staring at her, but that was impossible. This was one-way glass. Her breath caught in her throat when he smiled and waved.

The eye contact was direct. It wasn't a matter of looking in her direction; he was looking straight at her. "He knows I'm here." She snapped her head around and looked at Kring.

Kring shrugged. "Not by seeing through this, he doesn't. And you didn't give us any advance warning you were coming. He may be doing this because he knows a fourth guard is always watching from here."

Logical, but Peterson had looked *at* her, not in the direction of the guard next to the window. Her body prickled with unease. He *knew*. She was as certain of that as she was of her own name. She tried to recall who else she had seen on the way upstairs. The orderly, Kring's secretary, and perhaps one or two doctors and nurses in the hall.

"Who's spoken to him in the past fifteen minutes?" She glanced at the guard.

"No one, and he's been out there with three guards and two other inmates for a half hour now. You've seen for yourself. Nobody goes close to him."

Still, somebody had signaled him, somehow. There was an explanation if she had the time to find it.

"He has only one confidant, his lawyer," the guard assured her. "And if you ask me, that guy's scared shitless of him too." He cleared his throat. "Pardon my language."

Ella considered the information as she accompanied Kring back to his office. "When's the last time Yazzie's lawyer was here?"

Kring stopped by the secretary's desk and picked up the log for Peterson again. He flipped to a section near the back and handed the notebook to Ella. "I've had my secretary note the dates of each contact he's had with his attorney, including letters Yazzie mailed out to him."

Ella studied the list. A letter had preceded the bombing attempt at the station by three days. "Do you happen to have his lawyer's address handy?"

Kring returned with Ella to his office, flipped through an address file on his desk, then copied the information onto a sheet of notepaper. "Here you go. His name is Bruce Cohen and he lives in Farmington. I've only got his office address and number, but you shouldn't have any trouble tracking him down."

Ella went back to her car. The memory of Peterson's soulless stare as he looked directly into her eyes still made her skin crawl. It was all trickery, of course, but there was no doubt the man was a master of deception.

Ella picked up the radio mike and reported in. Justine was

away from the station reinterviewing students and would be out of touch most of the morning and early afternoon. The area of the Rez she'd be in made reliable radio communications nearly impossible.

Ella gave Big Ed a sketchy report, then racked the mike. As she continued on to Farmington, she speculated on what approach to take with Peterson's attorney. She'd met Bruce Cohen during the trial. He was young and inexperienced, but a very hard worker. He'd also been the only public defender willing to take Peterson's case without being coerced.

When Ella walked into the public defender's office twenty minutes later, she realized just how overworked Cohen was. His desk was a foot deep in file folders, and other records were stacked in a cardboard box on the floor.

He glanced up through red-rimmed eyes that looked like road maps to hell. "Make it fast, Special Investigator Clah. I've got two defenses to put together for preliminary hearings this afternoon."

Ella pulled up a wooden chair from against the wall and sat across the desk from him. "You know why I'm here." She decided to make him assume she knew more than she actually did.

Cohen cleared his throat and broke eye contact. "I have no idea," he lied badly. "And I'm much too busy to play games."

Ella leaned back, deliberately allowing a stretch of silence to fill the air. "Peterson Yazzie, your client, is getting into more legal trouble, Counselor. This comes at a time when he's already been charged with almost every major offense on the books. And you may have the opportunity to share in that—but not as his attorney."

"Is this a threat of some sort?" Cohen challenged with a bravado that he couldn't quite carry.

"Counselor, look at the facts. Your client has very little contact with the outside. You're it, actually. So let's talk about the letters."

"If you're censoring my client's mail without due process—"

"Not yet, but I could arrange for him not to be given any writing materials at all."

"What letters are you referring to? What was in them?"

"I received an interesting letter from Peterson, Counselor, which someone was kind enough to mail out for him." Ella then decided to do some bluffing of her own. "We were able to lift one fingerprint. It's not Peterson's. I think it's yours. You might find it tricky to explain to the review boards, not to mention the courts, why you're smuggling threatening letters out for your client."

Bruce Cohen leaned back in his chair, and for a tiny moment she knew what he'd look like as an old man. "You don't know what I'm dealing with here. This isn't an ordinary client."

"What I know is that you're scared to death of him."

"You would be too, if you had any brain cells at all," Cohen snapped. "Yazzie's a monster. He's not like you and me. Hell, he's not like anyone at all. He belongs in that institution. His freedom is virtually nonexistent, yet he can still make things happen on the outside."

"Like what?"

Cohen stood. "Yazzie is insane, but he's not stupid. Far from it."

"Has he threatened you?"

"Me, personally?" Cohen shook his head. "Yazzie wouldn't touch me. He wants me to file an appeal."

Ella felt a dozen questions rush through her mind as she considered his reply. "Your family?"

Cohen walked to the window, looked around, then returned to his desk. "It's not what he says, but what he lets me know indirectly." He shrugged. "I'm starting to sound as loony as he is."

"No. Not to me. Remember, I know him too. I was the one who put him behind bars."

Cohen gave her a long, thoughtful look. "You have no legal right to stop my client's mail. We both know that. If you push it, you'll lose."

"If your client wins, neither one of us does."

Cohen's eyes narrowed as the message struck home. "What would you have me do? Stop mailing his letters? You have no idea what you're asking."

Ella acknowledged the admission with a nod. "I don't want

you to stop doing anything. I want to continue getting the letters he sends me." If Yazzie was really tied to the murder somehow, it could provide her with information on the case. "What I need from you is information. Who else is he sending things to?"

"So far, no one."

"Next time he asks you to mail something, I want you to let me know."

"All right," he conceded. "Now, if you don't mind, I've got work to do."

Ella returned to her car and started the drive back to the reservation. She felt genuinely sorry for Cohen. He was in way over his head with the likes of Yazzie.

Twenty minutes later, she approached the turnoff that led to her home. Ella decided to stop and make sure everything was all right there. She wasn't expecting trouble, really, but it would give her one less thing to worry about. As she went up the road, her gaze darted around the sagebrush and junipers, searching for any sign of threat. Everything seemed normal and quiet, but she couldn't help but remember Haske's warning.

When she finally pulled up in front of her home, she saw Dog asleep on the porch, belly up, and her brother's pickup parked by the kitchen door. She was glad Clifford lived nearby and that he visited often. It reassured her to know that her mother was seldom as alone as the terrain around the house seemed to indicate.

Ella opened the front screen door a moment later. She heard her mother and brother in the kitchen and went to join them. Rose glanced up as Ella came in, and smiled. "I wasn't expecting you home so early."

"I can't stay. I was on my way to see Big Ed and thought I'd pop in and see if there was anything you needed." She shot Clifford an inquiring glance. His calm expression told her nothing was wrong.

"Your brother came for the same reason," Rose commented absently, and Clifford finally smiled. "You two aren't worried about me, are you? There's no need to be. They will never attack *my* home again."

There was no hesitation or doubt in Rose's tone. Although she knew her mother's intuitions could be trusted implicitly, Ella didn't feel comfortable dismissing a possible threat so quickly. "We always worry about you, Mom, just like you do about us." Rose nodded. "Well, that's what family's for. We care too much to do otherwise." She poured both her children a glass of her special herbal tea. "I'm going to spin some more wool. You two visit. You really don't spend enough time with each other."

Ella waited until her mother was out of the room before saying anything to Clifford. "I'm glad you're here."

"Trouble?" He looked in her eyes questioningly.

She told him about her unnerving experience with Peterson at the hospital facility. "I honestly believe he knew I was there."

"I don't doubt that he did. He used to be a cop. He knows how to search out the little signs, just like you do. Maybe he heard the sound of your Jeep coming up the road, or your voice through a vent. Also, you've got to remember that he does have one big advantage over you. As a skinwalker, he knows all about misdirection. Peterson can use tricks you've never thought of."

"That may be so, but I'm a better-trained cop than he ever was. I can still throw him a surprise or two." She saw the skepticism on her brother's face, but decided to ignore it. "Keep an ear out for Peterson's buddies. If any of our people are still in league with him, I need to know who they are. You can bet they're going to take any opportunity to spread as much fear as possible, linking the bus accident to the murder, and all of that to the power of the skinwalkers. In the meantime, I'm going to request additional patrols around Cohen's home and office. Nothing obvious, just a way of making sure his family's not being physically threatened. I have a bad feeling about that."

"Peterson is capable of anything. Nothing he could ever stoop to would surprise me."

Her brother stood and walked to the door. "I've got to go see a patient across the Rez. Be careful and take care of yourself," he said.

After he'd left, Ella, too, got under way. She was certain that Cohen's fear of Peterson was real, but how far would Cohen go to maintain the safety of his family? Although she doubted Cohen would do anything more than mail a few letters for Peterson, she wasn't really sure. The minute she got back to the station, she'd do a background search on the man.

As she headed down the highway, Ella got a radio call from Justine. Patty Ben was having a group of women over, to demonstrate native dyes that could be used to tint wool. With summer starting and sheep-shearing season at its height, this community class was bound to attract women from all over the reservation.

"I thought you might like to come," Justine said. "We could meet there and I can bring you up to date after we get a chance to mingle and hear what people are saying."

Ella noted the directions to Patty's. "I'll be there in thirty."

Gossip was a favorite pastime on the Rez, and what better place than a gathering like that. As they worked, the women would talk. Ella could learn the latest news, people's fears or concerns, and all the while enlarge her circle of contacts. Certain that was Justine's strategy, she found herself looking forward to the meeting.

Ella drove east out of Shiprock and turned onto the dirt track leading to the Ben residence. She noted the many vehicle tracks that had recently disturbed the wide ruts. Half a dozen or more cars and pickups would be there already.

The first thing Ella saw as the road led her down off a bluff was an empty sheep corral. The thick woolly *churro* sheep had been sheared close and now wandered about, grazing on the thin desert grasses. Women sat in the shade of a windbreak made out of cottonwood branches and brush while Patty dipped samples of wool into vats filled with indigo, red, and yellow dyes.

Ella walked around, staying toward the back, and saw Justine. Her young cousin was taking an active part, taking notes about the composition and preparation of the dyes.

Uncertain what kind of reception she'd get, Ella kept a low profile. When Patty's demonstration concluded and everyone gathered for refreshments, Ella was glad to see the women welcomed her.

Patty came up to her and handed her some of the dry, freshly tinted blue wool. "Will you take this to your mother? She was interested in this new dye."

As Ella agreed, two more women joined them. They were both dressed in jeans and cotton blouses, though one was in her twenties and the other in her fifties. Although they said little, they seemed to stay near Ella expectantly.

"What do you think of our class?" the younger asked. Her tone indicated she was only making polite conversation, but the light of curiosity in her eyes told far more.

Ella smiled politely. "I think it must be wonderful to make such beautiful things," she said, gesturing to a woven shawl Patty had draped over a chair for all to see.

Another woman, about Justine's age, came up to join them. She was dressed more traditionally in a long skirt and a bright red cotton blouse. "I want to learn all this. Doing things faster isn't necessarily better. I mean, we can all buy wool, but it's just not the same."

The eldest of them shook her head. "It doesn't have to be all one way or the other. There's a place for both." She then glanced at Ella. "Tell us, what brought you here today? Is it the trouble we've all heard about?"

"Partly," Ella admitted, "but I'm also interested in learning about the old ways. All of this," she waved to the sheep and the wools, "is part of what I am too. It feels good to reconnect to it."

"Understandable." Patty nodded, glancing at the others. "But we all know that your duty to protect the tribe never stops. You work all the time. So I hope you don't mind my bringing this up. We all have families we want to keep safe. Tell us what we can do to help you and ourselves."

The offer touched Ella deeply, filling her with a special warmth. Their implied trust and acceptance were two things she needed in her life right now. Having these women who were active and scattered all over the Rez listening for trouble was an asset she couldn't afford to turn down. "Stay alert to potential trouble. Keep your eyes open and listen. We're all taught to walk in beauty and seek harmony. When you sense someone who upsets that, come to me. I'll take it from there."

"Do you think this will all be over soon?" one of the young women asked.

Ella considered her reply carefully. "I don't want any of you to be overly concerned. Anyone who commits crimes against our people will be brought to justice."

"White man's justice?" one elderly woman challenged.

"And our own. No one has the right to take the life of another member of this tribe," Ella answered. "That's not our way."

The woman nodded somberly.

Silence stretched out among them. Finally Ella broke the tension by openly admiring a deep russet dyed wool.

The next hour was far more pleasant. The women were eager to teach. Ella found she enjoyed the process of mixing the dyes and coloring the wool. Timing and technique were everything, and that suited the perfectionist in her.

As they worked, Ella felt the warmth of being part of the group. The acceptance she'd found among the women was strangely fulfilling. She hadn't experienced that kind of closeness outside law enforcement before.

After a while, Ella reluctantly returned to the car, Justine at her side. "This was an excellent idea," Ella said. "What better place to build contacts than among those who take classes to learn traditional skills?"

Justine gave her a slightly embarrassed smile. "Well, to be honest, that wasn't the whole reason I asked you to meet me here."

"Oh?"

"Your mother called my mother and mentioned you desperately needed a hobby. They twisted my arm."

Ella blinked, then laughed. Sometimes in the seriousness of her job, she forgot that there was another side to life on the reservation. "Well, thanks for confessing. I've got to admit, this was one of the most enjoyable undercover operations I've ever been drafted into."

SEVEN

—— ✕ ✕ ✕ ——

A short time later, Ella joined Justine at the Totah Café off the main highway in Shiprock. As Justine consumed a thick slice of freshly baked peach pie, Ella studied the report her new assistant had completed.

"I tracked down everything I could on that bomb," Justine said. "The serial numbers show the dynamite came from a batch that was stolen from a construction site on the Rez a year ago."

"I remember. No sticks were recovered, but we suspected most, if not all, were used by the skinwalkers to blow up their tunnels beneath the old church last year." Ella's gaze grew distant and unfocused as her memory flashed back to those dark hours. "So this came from that batch. Interesting."

Justine finished her pie. "I've also tracked down the digital timer. The device came from the Circuit Shop in Farmington. The label was still attached. It must have been stolen from their inventory. Their computer bookkeeping shows no sales of that model within the last three months."

"Good basic detective work," Ella commented.

Justine hesitated. "I could have done it faster, but I *have* been tracking down students from the victim's classes, as you asked," she said a bit defensively.

"Anything new turn up?" Ella asked.

"Not at all. I tracked down a student who'd missed class that day, but he didn't know anything. He's been at home with a respiratory problem the last two weeks. I also checked with the students who were there, but I got the same story they gave in their statements. I wasn't able to find Professor Joe, as you suggested. He didn't have any classes today."

"I need you to do something else for me. Run a check on Bruce Cohen from the Farmington public defender's office. I want as much as you can get."

"Consider it done."

Ella sipped her iced tea. "Now I've got to fill you in on what's been happening." She told Justine about the letter and her visit to the Hilltop Psychiatric Hospital.

"It wouldn't have been hard for Peterson to know about the ash painting," Justine said quietly, her eyes big as saucers. "Even my brothers knew by this morning."

"So it's traveled that fast, has it?" Ella mused.

"He's one scary guy trying to jerk your leash."

"There's one bit of evidence that really disturbs me. What you've uncovered on that bomb tells us that one of Peterson's skinwalker buddies is responsible for that incident."

"Yeah," Justine admitted. "But I find it hard to believe the would-be bomber and the murderer are the same person. The two crimes are vastly different."

"Yeah, I agree. It's too bad, really, because we at least know *something* about the killer from the evidence we have. Everything we know about criminals suggests the killer is a man. He's probably an average-height Navajo and wears size nine Nike cross-trainers. That suggests he's young, and either interested in learning about the old ways or maybe someone with a beef against Kee Dodge. He may live in a place where burning wood isn't practical, like an upstairs apartment, so he chose ready-made charcoal." Ella paused, seeing that Justine was writing down everything she was saying in a notebook.

When Justine looked up again, Ella continued. "His actions were premeditated, organized, and he staged everything. He doesn't know much about witchcraft imagery, but he does know they work with ashes instead of using natural pigments. That's still a pretty thin profile, however," Ella concluded. "We just don't have enough to go on yet. We've got to keep digging."

Justine nodded. "I've been asking about missing cats, but no luck so far. Cats wander off. It's part of their nature."

"Have you heard of any roadkills?" Ella ventured.

"Checked that too. Mostly dogs and lots of little critters. It's summer."

They paid the tab, then walked out to the parking lot. "I still need to establish a contact at the community college," Justine said. "I have to find someone who's around the students, or at least knows a lot of them."

"Go back and track down Wilson Joe. He's your best source out of my generation. I also think it's a good idea for you to develop your own sources. Because of your age, you're more likely to get people to talk to you freely."

"Yes, but with reservations," Justine said cautiously. "I've taken a lot of courses, but nothing traditional. And a lot of people around here know I'm a cop." She weighed the matter for a moment. "Maybe I should approach this a little differently. Let me see what I can come up with."

Ella watched Justine get into one of the department's unmarked vehicles. Justine would do well. She was tenacious and had very good instincts for police work.

Moments later, Ella was on her way to Wilson Joe's office at the college. The semester would end in a few weeks, and with finals just around the corner, almost every student she saw would either be in a rush to class or desperately hitting the books.

As she parked her vehicle and walked across the newly erected campus branch, she could feel tension in the air. Students sat in small, subdued groups, and they looked up anxiously whenever anyone approached. There were few smiles, just a wariness that had little to do with finals.

It wasn't what she'd expected at all. Students had obviously reacted strongly to the death of their professor and the other deaths that had claimed the lives of tribal members. Snippets of conversations she heard as she passed confirmed their fear. They were worried about an evil they could all feel, yet one that remained out of their grasp. Even here, in this enclave of progressive thinking, beliefs held for centuries made them dread the disharmony that had given evil the power to take the lives of those who'd walked in peace among them. It was as if a darkness had fallen over them, and strange sounds could be heard just outside the door.

Ella approached the southernmost of four hexagonal hogan-shaped concrete-and-stone buildings, one at each compass point. Going in the entrance, each of the doorways facing east according to custom, Ella walked around a circular corridor to Wilson's small office. Two young Navajo women were standing in his doorway. She saw the admiration in their eyes as they listened to Wilson explain some assignment.

Silently she watched him go about his business. He was a born teacher as well as a handsome, intelligent man. Wilson needed the stability of his job as much as she needed the adrenaline rush and excitement of hers. In all the basic ways they were as different as night and day. Despite her mother's hopes, Ella wondered if anything beyond friendship could ever develop between them.

Wilson smiled at Ella as his students finally left, and gestured for her to come in. "I figured you'd be by today. Rumors are flying all over the campus, and the kids are all pretty grim about what happened to their teacher as well as the bus accident. Half of them believe the two incidents are linked and that the tide of events has turned against the People. The others aren't sure what to think."

Ella took a seat beside a pine desk equipped with a computer and printer. "I noticed the atmosphere on my way here. What's the latest gossip about the professor's murder? Are fingers being pointed in any particular direction?"

"Not from what I've heard. The most common theory is that the killer isn't really a skinwalker."

"You're kidding." The accuracy of the gossip took her by surprise. "How did they come to that conclusion?"

"Kids who saw the crime scene say that there are things off

the mark, though that's as specific as it gets." He gave her a long look. "I did hear one theory that makes sense." Wilson steepled his fingers beneath his chin. "Some think that although you took care of the initial wave of skinwalkers, their children and relatives were left behind and now want revenge. They may not know the details of skinwalker magic, but they're willing to improvise and learn as they go."

Ella considered it. "It's an interesting thought."

"How are you coping with the fallout from that kidnapping thing in Farmington, Ella? I suppose you got roped into that in the first place because you're Navajo." Wilson's voice softened.

She nodded. "It turned out so badly, yet I did my best." Ella tried to sound philosophical. She didn't want sympathy, although she knew Wilson's concern was genuine. "To be honest, I try not to think about it now. There's a killer out there somewhere and that's where my energy must go."

"I hear you, and you're right." Wilson looked at his watch. "Oops. I've got a class to teach. Why don't you walk with me?" He rose from behind his desk and gathered up his notes.

Ella waited for Wilson to lock up his office, then matched his strides to an identical building directly north, about two hundred yards away.

"If you hear any gossip I might find interesting about the killer or a resurgence of skinwalkers, let me know," Ella said.

"Is the suspect you're searching for one of our students?" he asked, looking around to make sure no one was close enough to hear.

"I don't know, but that's certainly one possibility."

"Don't be cagey with me," he said softly. "I deserve your full trust."

Ella realized that he was right. He'd stood by her when the going had been deadly, and had never even thought of walking away. "I really don't have much to go on. But I will tell you that Peterson Yazzie wrote me a letter. He claims to be behind the murder and even hints at a connection with the bus accident."

Wilson stopped and put his hand lightly on her arm. "Do you believe him?"

"I don't know. That man's a born liar, but he gives me the creeps. I've never been able to psych him out."

"Right now, I suspect he's doing a number on you," Wilson said, watching her expression speculatively.

"He's trying," Ella admitted grudgingly. "Now tell me about the kinds of students the traditional courses are attracting."

"That's a difficult evaluation to make. I can't narrow it down to any particular set of kids. What I find most interesting is that although the numbers are never large, there's always a steady interest."

"Anyone opposed to these classes, or overly interested?"

"I'll ask around. In the meantime, why don't you audit one yourself? There's an old *hataalii*, Leonard Haske, giving an open lecture near the site where the skinwalker problems culminated. It'll be held in the canyon right behind where the church now stands. It's going to start in an hour or so."

"By the church?" Ella's voice rose slightly.

"He chose the spot. He's teaching about balance and harmony, and the role of a *hataalii* in finding the pattern and helping restore it."

"He should have picked a lake, or a shrine. Not that place."

"Maybe. But that's where he'll be."

"Thanks." Ella said a quick good-bye, then hurried to her vehicle. The old man was tempting fate. Yet she couldn't deny it was a perfect chance for her to watch from hiding and study the ones who came to the lecture. There was plenty of cover around that area and she would be providing protection for Haske as well.

As she drove to the church, Ella found herself appreciating the opportunity more and more. She parked in the new church's parking lot, then climbed around the base of the hill. She stayed low, searching for the best vantage point. Almost instinctively, she searched for signs that someone else might have already beaten her to the punch.

Ella moved almost silently, selecting the best cover the rocky ground provided. Her gaze was ever vigilant, but she was certain she was alone.

Hearing the cars beginning to arrive below, she moved closer to the gathering, hoping for the best possible look at the proceedings. Dissatisfied, she edged further downhill. She wanted to study the faces of those around Haske, rather than the *hataalii* himself. From hiding, she'd have the advantage of a fly on the wall. People would react naturally if they didn't know they were being watched by a cop.

After a few minutes of moving about, she settled down in the middle of a thick outgrowth of silvery green sage. She watched Haske, with his herb mixture bowls before him, sitting on a blanket facing the group of five students. Their ages ranged from early twenties to late forties, and that disparity surprised her.

Ella recognized Duncan James, the oldest person at the lecture not counting the Singer. If memory served her, he'd been interested in becoming a *hataalii* himself once, but something hadn't worked out. She couldn't remember what. Nowadays, James owned a garage in Shiprock. It surprised her to see him take time off during the day to be here. She made a mental note to talk to him about it later.

One face in the crowd made her smile. Justine was right there, next to a young man maybe a year or two younger than she. He was dressed in tan slacks, and had his hair cut short, almost shaved around his ears, in a style currently popular among Anglo youths. Although the student's attention was ostensibly on Haske, his body language, like his proximity to Justine, spoke of a thinly veiled interest in her.

Ella's eyes drifted to the two remaining young women. Ella recognized both. Irma Betone and Louella Francisco were both aspiring teachers. Like their mothers, they wanted to teach at Shiprock schools.

Ella studied every expression except Justine's, but no one in the group appeared to harbor anything more sinister than curiosity or interest. As Haske continued his presentation, Ella kept her eyes peeled for new arrivals, but no one else showed up.

Almost ninety minutes later the class broke up, and Haske expressed his pleasure that they had listened so well. Ella saw Justine leave with the young man. As the others drove off in their vehicles, Ella remained where she was. Kee Dodge had been killed in a remote area like this one. She watched over Haske as he gathered his bowls and herbs and carefully packed them into a box.

Ella had intended to remain where she was but then, unexpectedly, Haske glanced up. His gaze seemed to find her, despite the thick grasses that had kept her from discovery.

"Why don't you come down now?" he said calmly. "We can talk again, and perhaps you can tell me why you've been hiding."

There was no way Haske could have known it was she, though he must have caught her movement when she selected that particular spot. This was the second time something like this had happened to her. She began to wonder if perhaps she had suffocating body odor, or halitosis that traveled for miles.

"I had a feeling you might come back," Haske continued, "once you knew that my students often include those from the college."

With her pride stinging, Ella stood up, brushed off her jeans, and stepped out into the open.

Haske smiled at her. "All hunters spook their game every once in a while. Don't look so disappointed. I'm always aware of my surroundings. It's second nature to a *hataalii*."

Ella approached him curiously. "How could you have possibly known it was me?"

"I didn't know who or what was there at first. But I saw two birds fly away from that area and not return. I considered the possibility that an animal was wandering about. Only then, as the breeze blew toward me, I smelled that delightful perfume you wear."

"I don't wear perfume, uncle," Ella protested.

"Soap, then. It reminds me of wildflowers. It's very light. But I remembered it from when you came to my hogan."

Ella nodded. "My shampoo." At least this was an explanation she could understand and accept. In the city no one would have been able to discern that subtle essence, but out here things were different. Some people, particularly the older ones, were highly attuned to scents.

"Now tell me what you were trying to accomplish. You could have joined us, you know. Everyone is welcome."

"I wanted to observe your students without them knowing," she answered, although now she was wondering how effective she'd been.

Haske began loading things into the back of his old truck. "I suppose that means you've found nothing new to help you on your case."

"Not enough to help me get the murderer," she admitted.

He expelled his breath in a weary sigh. "As the time passes, the danger to the *Dineh* and especially to you and your family becomes more acute. Are you aware of that?"

"In what way do you mean?"

"Your list of enemies is growing. There's already been talk that your family attracts disharmony and evil."

"That's outrageous! We fight it."

"There is some truth to what they're saying." Haske raised one hand, stemming her protests. "To find harmony there must be balance. That requires the darkness as well as the light. Of course that's a philosophical viewpoint, and not the way they meant it at all."

"Please, help me stop talk like that before it creates a severe problem."

"You can count on that, despite the fact that a problem already exists. But I also want you to promise to stop shadowing *my* movements. I am a *hataalii*. I am as capable of taking care of myself as you are. I don't carry a gun, but my ways can be effective, particularly when dealing with our own people."

"It may not be skinwalkers, uncle. I tell you that in confidence because you need to be aware that the threat facing the tribe may be different from what it appears to be."

Haske nodded slowly. "The face of the threat may be different, but the fear it feeds on is the same."

Ella searched his eyes, trying to figure out what he knew and how much he simply guessed at. Despite her training, she was unable to read the old man. Haske exuded power and confidence, but even those were no match against a cold blade, or a bullet. "Overconfidence can be fatal, uncle. I don't mean any disrespect; it's only a warning for your benefit."

Haske nodded. "I tell you again not to worry about me. Your concern should be focused inward. You are the one in the most danger. The ones you hunt will also hunt you. I only have myself and my patients to worry about. There are many who are depending on you. Your attention is constantly being diverted, and that makes you vulnerable."

"You have a point. But, like you, I also have my training, and my abilities." Ella smiled at him. "I'll make a deal with you. You watch your back and I'll watch mine."

Haske chuckled. "That's a done deal."

Ella went back to her vehicle, this time walking down the trail that the other cars had followed. Haske's charisma was every bit as strong now as it had been in his younger days. In fact, maybe it was even more so. His ability to blend inner strength with gentleness of spirit made him appear completely indomitable. She thought of her brother. Clifford also exuded power and confidence, but he masked his own gentleness, not yet recognizing it as a strength. She wondered if her brother would ever possess the presence that came so effortlessly to Haske.

As Ella slipped behind the wheel, she heard her radio crackle alive with static. She picked up the mike and acknowledged the call.

"Bruce Cohen from the public defender's office wants you to call him as soon as possible," the dispatcher informed her.

"Give me the number." She jotted it down as the dispatcher read it over the air. "Ten-four."

Ella picked up her cellular and telephoned Cohen. After a moment, Cohen came on the line.

"I think we should meet. I'd like to discuss a few privileges my client would like extended to him as soon as possible," Cohen said in a taut voice.

There was an unmistakable tension in his tone that told Ella he was worried about something.

"Name the place and the time," Ella said.

"How about at Danny's? I can be there in forty minutes. Will that be a problem for you?"

Ella was certain the edge in Cohen's tone indicated fear, but she couldn't figure out what was behind it. "I'll be there."

"Okay," Cohen said, then hung up.

Ella replaced the receiver, lost in thought. This didn't have the feel of a trap, but something was definitely up. She decided to get to Danny's early and take a good look around before the meeting. Under the circumstances, a little caution couldn't hurt.

EIGHT

— ✖ ✖ ✖ —

Danny's coffee shop, off the reservation and just a block off East Main in Farmington, was a popular eatery among the locals. It reminded Ella of a little place she'd frequented back in L.A. The sudden memory of her last visit there speeded up her heartbeat, and she made a mental note to be extremely alert.

She watched the entrance doors for several minutes, paying particular attention to anyone who seemed to be wandering by, or hanging about. Finally Cohen arrived, parked by the side, and went in without looking her way. He was alone and seemed nervous, as if afraid someone might see him there.

Ella left her vehicle. Unable to detect any signs of trouble, she stepped through the side door. Cohen saw her almost immediately and hurried to meet her.

"Come on. I don't want to dally," he said. "I'm in the corner booth."

"What's the matter?" Ella asked, sliding in and facing the room.

"You weren't followed, were you? I'm sure I wasn't."

"No, and I checked out the area before I came in. What's up?"

Cohen shifted nervously in his seat. "I'm taking one hell of a chance talking to you. Maybe this was a mistake."

"It probably will be, unless you tell me what's going on."

Cohen's gaze darted around and sweat began to bead near his hairline. "Shit. This is getting too weird for me. I'm just a public defender trying to do a job. I don't need this extra crap."

"If you tell me what's going on, I'll do my best to help you," Ella insisted quietly. "You came this far. Now take it all the way."

A waitress older than Ella's mother came up and placed glasses of water in front of them. Declining the laminated menus, Ella and Cohen ordered iced teas.

Cohen took a long shuddering breath. "I had a message from Yazzie today. There's a new letter he wants me to mail."

Ella gave him a quizzical look. There had to be more to it than that. Cohen looked ready to bolt. "And?"

"He also told me to check with your brother, and see what happens to the families of those who cross him." He wiped the perspiration from his forehead. "When I looked into it, I found out that your sister-in-law lost a child last year. We only found out two days ago that my wife is pregnant. No one knew. *No one.* But I don't need a sworn statement to know what he meant."

"It may have been nothing more than an accurate shot in the dark," she said, not really believing it herself.

"Give me a break. He knows Rachel is pregnant. That's all there is to it. I'm a logical man. I'm willing to concede he could have had someone look through our trash and find the home pregnancy kit. But if he did that, then he could conceivably do a lot of other things too." Cohen bit the inside of his cheek and looked around furtively. "This guy's spark plugs aren't all firing, but he's smarter than hell. Is it possible he's also found out I talked with you?"

"No," she said flatly, "but I might as well tell you, he's very good at mind games. He'll probe, and if he spots the slightest weakness he'll zero in on that. He'll watch your every reaction for answers. Unless you're careful, you'll be giving him all he needs to get leverage over you." Ella sipped the iced tea the waitress had brought.

"I take pride in my work as a public defender, but this Yazzie is some piece of work." He spat out the words as if they left a sour taste in his mouth. "I'll be damned if I'm going to let this psychopath threaten my family."

Even the macho pride in his words couldn't disguise his fear. And if she could sense it, Ella had no doubt that Peterson already had. "Don't try to brazen it out with Yazzie. You'll be better off letting him see you're scared. Allow him to think you wouldn't cross him for the world and that he's got you precisely where he wants you. His ego wants to believe that anyway."

Cohen regarded her carefully. "Well put. The fact I'm scared to death shows, right, no matter how I try to hide it?"

"It's natural to be frightened of someone like Yazzie."

Cohen shifted nervously in his seat, making the vinyl crackle in protest. "Listen, just in case we're being watched, I want you to give me something to take back to my client."

"What's he asking for?"

"He wants a radio in his room to listen to the Navajo radio station. When I spoke to Dr. Kring, he said he'd have to ask your boss first. Yazzie told me to talk to you directly. He said you understood him better and I was to remind you that you needed him. Something about harmony, and the light needing the dark."

The words, so close to what Haske had told her, made her skin crawl. Yet there was no way he could have known about the conversation. He was just utilizing their beliefs and hoping to strike a nerve. "Tell him we've met, and that I'll consider a trade. I know what he wants. Now tell him I want the name of whoever had access to the cache of explosives stolen from the construction site."

"You're kidding. Just like that?"

"Sure. He wants something from me. Now let's see what he's willing to trade for it."

"Well, he hasn't tried to choke anyone in the last few days," Cohen snapped back. "Does that count?"

"What are you talking about?"

"I thought you'd heard." Cohen shrugged. "Just a minor detail. He grabbed a nurse and tried to strangle her when she brought him a capsule instead of a pill for his headache. He said she was trying to poison him."

"What happened?"

"Not much. He let her go even before the orderlies had a chance to do anything. I think Yazzie did it as a power play, just to prove he could. The woman later told the director that Yazzie could have killed her, but had chosen to release her instead." He shrugged. "Kring won't let women into his room anymore, not even for a second."

Ella nodded slowly. Yazzie never ceased to amaze her. "I don't blame him."

Cohen reached under the table and slid something over to her. "The letter Yazzie wanted me to mail is inside that paper bag. Take it and do whatever you want with it, but make sure it's mailed by the end of today." He stood up and threw two dollars on the table. "I'll tell Yazzie what you said."

She watched him walk out. Cohen seemed to have recaptured some of his courage. Of course, once he was face-to-face with Yazzie, there was no telling how long it would last.

Ella felt the bag beneath the table just as the waitress returned to make sure everything was all right. Ella ordered a slice of pecan pie and received it almost immediately. She sat there for a while and sipped her tea, watching. Assured no one was paying undue attention, she asked the waitress for a doggie bag for the pie. Quickly paying her bill, Ella took both bags with her out to her vehicle.

Ella decided against making a report to Big Ed just yet. Instead she drove to the PHS hospital and went directly to Carolyn's office. She wasn't there, but Ella located the medical investigator a few minutes later in her lab.

"I brought you a piece of pecan pie, your favorite," Ella said placing it before Carolyn.

"A bribe, right?" Carolyn's eyes narrowed with suspicion.

"Am I really that transparent?" Ella gasped with feigned shock.

Carolyn said nothing.

"Okay, so it's a tiny bribe. I need you to do something for me, and keep it to yourself." She brought out the bag containing the letter. "I want to know what this letter says. Can you X-ray or fluoroscope it?"

"You'd probably have better luck steaming it open."

"That might show and I don't want to risk it."

"How about if we hold it up next to our X-ray viewing screens?" Carolyn suggested. The envelope looks pretty thin."

"That's an idea. Let's give it a shot."

Carolyn glanced down at the envelope. "Can I touch it?"

"Sure. I know who wrote it, and who has handled it already." Ella saw the question in the other woman's eyes. "Yazzie."

Carolyn studied the name and address on the envelope. "A post office box in Farmington won't tell you much. Do you have any idea who Barbara Sanchez is?"

"Not a clue. I could try to get a court order to force a street address from the postal authorities, but the name and address would probably be phony. I don't think Yazzie would be stupid enough to leave us with any trail we can follow."

"Which is why you want a look at the contents. Let's see what we can do."

Carolyn took the envelope over to the viewing screen, turned the lights on, then slipped the envelope under the top clip. Words stood out clearly, but because the paper inside was folded, some of the lines were upside down and backward. "I'll read out the letters, and you write them down," she told Ella. "It'll take a while to make some of them out, so have a seat."

Ella found a tall lab stool and wrote each symbol down in her notebook as Carolyn called it out. As long as that letter made it to the Farmington post office before five, she'd be okay. Despite knowing she was not pressed for time, waiting to see what the message contained was more difficult than she'd expected. She held back trying to read what she'd written, concentrating solely on Carolyn's voice.

Finally Carolyn announced that it was the end of the message. Ella began assembling the letters into words and then the few sentences. When she was done, Ella read the message aloud.

"Here it is: 'Possessor for secret into Navajos. Rug made great preserve hidden finally. As more have work perfect copy.' That's the message."

"What the hell is that supposed to mean?" Carolyn looked at Ella. "It sounds like one of those textbooks that attempt to translate Navajo phrases into literal English."

"It's a code of some sort, but I have no idea how to decipher it. I'm going to pass it to one of the FBI cryptographers, but it'll be days, or weeks, before I get an answer. Even then, there's no guarantee they'll be able to break it."

"If you find out who Barbara Sanchez is, maybe it'll give you an idea of how best to pursue this."

Ella removed the letter from the clip. "That's exactly what I was thinking. It's out of my jurisdiction, but I'll set up a very discreet stakeout by the Farmington post office." Ella smiled, seeing Carolyn run a finger around the edges of the pie and then stick it in her mouth. "Enjoy. And thanks for your help."

Ella walked out to her Jeep. First she needed to get hold of Justine to let her know the new plan of action. Then she would mail the letter and set up surveillance with Justine at the post office. Maybe they'd get a break and one of them would spot and be able to identify the person who'd rented the box. It would be another day before the letter reached the box, but "Barbara Sanchez" might check the box every day.

Ella was able to get through to Justine a short time later. Her assistant was on her way in from the college, so the transmission was clear.

"Meet with me at Luther's Self-Serve. I want to get some snacks, then you and I are going to a stakeout."

"Ten-four," Justine replied.

Ella drove slowly to Luther's, knowing her assistant was at least fifteen minutes behind her. She used the time to devise a plan. Four to six in the afternoon would mean a rush of people at the post office. She'd need an extra pair of eyes just to make sure she didn't miss Yazzie's contact. Together with Justine, however, she was certain they'd be able to succeed. It was all in the timing and positioning. If Barbara Sanchez didn't show up today,

Justine and Ella would set up shifts to cover the post office from opening to closing tomorrow.

Ella arrived some time later at the gas station. After a moment of hesitation she gave in to temptation and walked inside to prowl the rows of candy bars and snacks. By the time Justine arrived, Ella had a paper bag full of assorted chips and candy. Justine eyed her stash with raised eyebrows. "I didn't know you were a junk food junkie. Or are we in for a long haul?"

"I don't know, but we have to stay alert, and in the bureau I learned how a sugar rush can work for you."

"Who are we after?"

"Get in. I'll give you the details on the way."

At around four that afternoon, the post office experienced the beginning of the evening rush. Justine had taken a position inside, but to avoid being obvious she continued to walk around. Most of the people came in, checked their box for mail, and left quickly. No one paid any attention to Justine, except for an occasional man who sneaked a once-over.

Ella had asked the postmaster for a favor. By pretending to sort mail behind the counter, she had a clear view of box 2687. If anyone approached, she'd have a clear look, then be able to slip out the loading dock, to back up Justine if that became necessary or, preferably, simply to tail the suspect. Without a court order, and out of her jurisdiction, there was nothing more she could do legally to find out the identity of whoever had rented the box. The postmaster had let her stake it out, but wouldn't let her see the records without a warrant.

People came and left, but no one tried to open the box. Ella had observed a postal worker place a junk-mail letter in the box facedown, so she knew the user hadn't just peeked in at an empty box and left. Unofficially she'd learned that no one had any recollection of the person who had that particular box, but that meant nothing. There were hundreds of boxes in that station, though it was only a branch.

After the service counter of the post office closed, the front door remained open until ten. Justine remained inside, pretending to be reading a letter, but Ella moved to her Jeep, watching from outside. The narrow, but long, rectangular window on the side of the adobe-style building still allowed her to see the box and any people inside.

At ten, the door was finally locked for the night. Justine came out to join Ella. Leaning back in the seat, she rubbed her feet. "We try again tomorrow?"

"Yeah. What's on your schedule?" Ella asked, tossing an empty candy wrapper into the backseat.

"I've tracked down several adults who have audited the victim's other classes. I've interviewed most of the ones I've found, but I still have zip. Tomorrow I'm going to talk to Betty Lott, who's just out of high school. Furman Brownhat, one of the students I met at the community college, suggested I talk to her. He said that she attends quite a few of the free lectures. I know Anna Lott, her mom. She's a nurse at the PHS, and thinks our medicine men are a bunch of primitive quacks. Anna went to school off the Rez and thinks a lot like the Anglos do."

"Yeah, I know that family." Ella nodded. "One time Anna's mom, Rita Mae, called in my brother to do a Sing for her. Anna refused to let him in the house. There were a lot of bad feelings because Anna ended up taking Betty and moving away from home."

"That's why I can't figure out what Betty's doing attending those lectures, with her mom so set against traditional healing."

"She may be rebelling. This sounds more like a family squabble than a plot. Don't read too much into it, okay?"

"I'm not. I just figured that it's worth looking into. But I've had the dickens of a time tracking her down. Betty's supposed to be living with Anna in a trailer home near the community college, but she's never there, and neither is Anna. Betty's not a regular student, so I'm going to try and catch her before she goes to work at the bookstore."

"Sounds like a plan. I'll take the morning shift. You can relieve me after lunch. We'll pull four-hour shifts throughout the day. The letter will be there by lunchtime, and if the person's expecting it, then they'll be there sometime tomorrow for sure."

"I did a background check on Cohen like you asked. He's never even had a traffic ticket. He's squeaky clean. I also asked around about him. He's a regular Boy Scout. There's nothing even remotely shady about him."

"Thanks." Ella considered the information. It confirmed her own feelings about the man. No surprises there.

When they arrived back at Luther's gas station, Ella parked beside Justine's vehicle. "What will you be doing now?" Justine asked. "Are there any reports I can help you with tonight?"

"You're not quitting?"

"After six candy bars? No way. I figured I'd go back to my desk and catch up on paperwork."

"Forget it. We'll both have to get an early start tomorrow. Let's call it a day and pretend we have private lives to go to," Ella teased.

Justine laughed. "You sound like my mother. And your mother when she talks to my mother."

"Well, it's the truth. We're both addicted to our jobs." After Justine waved good-bye, Ella started along the highway in the direction of home. The Southern Fried Chicken was upwind from the station, and the aroma of food filled the air. Ella decided to stop for a box of chicken before the place closed. Frustration always made her hungry, and this case was making her ravenous.

Several minutes later, box of chicken in hand, Ella went back to her Jeep. She was starting to pull back out onto the highway when Justine's car went past. A pickup was following close behind her, although traffic was light at this late hour.

A shudder of uneasiness coursed down Ella's spine. Chiding herself for being overly cautious, she started to pull out to follow Justine.

Suddenly her radio came to life, and Justine's voice came over the air. "Boss, I think I've got myself a tail. There's this pickup that's been behind me for a while. How far toward home are you?"

"I'm still in the area. As a matter of fact I'm about a half mile behind you. I'm just pulling out of Southern Fried."

"Funny, I was about to go there myself, but then I realized I might have company."

"Ready to see if this is anything more than a coincidence?" Ella asked.

"You bet."

"Then take the turnoff leading to Fred Benally's place. Nobody goes down that road except family and visitors since it's so bad it rattles your teeth. There's lots of big arroyos that cross the road. We can ambush the guy in one of them."

"Got it."

"I'll close the gap in a while. But I'm going to go without lights once I reach the dirt road," Ella said.

Ella saw Justine's taillights as she turned, then the pickup behind her pulled off and stopped on the shoulder of the highway. Ella pulled off too, killing her lights, and waited. After hesitating there for several long moments, the driver proceeded to follow Justine.

"He's still following," Ella said. "When you reach the first arroyo, stop almost at the bottom. We'll trap him where he can't turn around."

"Got any ID on the pickup?"

"Can't read the license plate, not without coming up close and blowing this."

Five minutes later, Justine radioed back. "I'm at the bottom of the arroyo, and in position. My vehicle will be facing him as he comes down over the top. I'm going to flip my headlights on at max the second I see him. What's his ETA, and yours?"

"You should be seeing him in another thirty seconds or so. I'm about two hundred yards behind him. Get ready."

A moment later, Ella saw Justine's lights come on. She flipped hers on as well, and activated the red flasher she'd placed on the dashboard. "Get out with your hands up," Ella ordered through the loudspeaker.

Through the glare, Ella could see that Justine had her pistol at the ready, bracing it over the open door of her car. "Out of the car. Now!" Ella repeated.

A young man came out, hands held high. "It's just me!" came the voice. "What's going on?"

"Put your hands on the car, and don't move." Ella approached cautiously. As he turned toward her, the lights from her car illuminated his face. She'd seen him before somewhere.

Justine holstered her handgun. "Furman, what the hell are you doing here?"

He had a weak grin on his face. "I stopped for gas at Luther's and saw your car there. Someone mentioned that you'd be back for it later, so I went to buy some chicken. I was hoping to talk you into sharing some with me when you returned. But when I got back I saw you pulling out. I followed, hoping to catch you. Look for yourself," he gestured to the front seat. "I even bought some corn on the cob. You told me you liked it, remember?"

Justine nodded, looking pained. "Furman Brownhat, meet Special Investigator Ella Clah." Justine gave Ella an embarrassed look and put her gun away. "I did say that," she assured Ella. "We met earlier and attended one of the classes."

Ella remembered that Furman was the young man she'd seen with Justine at Haske's lecture. "Why did you follow her up this deserted road?"

Furman shifted from one leg to the other nervously. "I was planning to flag her down. I thought I was showing a little creativity and, with luck, she might appreciate that."

Ella bit her lip, trying desperately not to smile. "Well, in that case, I suggest next time you get a little less creative. Right now you both better get back on the main road. This place is perfect for ruining a tire or an oil pan."

"I'll wait for you back on the turnoff," Justine told Furman, then gave Ella an apologetic look.

As Furman got back into his pickup, Justine met Ella's gaze. "I had *no* idea. I'm sorry about this."

"He's your contact, I gather."

"You bet. He knows a lot of people, and he attends the classes. He's the one who told me about Betty Lott."

"Then go handle your source. I'm going home."

"I should have figured it was nothing," Justine mumbled.

"No," Ella answered quickly. "We're working a very dangerous case. Better to take the chance of looking foolish than to end up dead."

"Got it, boss."

Her voice was stern. "I mean it. Don't take any chances. And I will expect you to cover me just like I did you. If we make a mistake, let it be on the side of caution."

As Ella pulled out onto the highway several minutes later, she saw Justine park next to Furman's pickup. For a brief moment she envied her assistant. Justine was young, and at least for now wasn't encumbered by the emotional baggage that years in law enforcement imprinted on a cop.

Ella stared into the darkness beyond the range of her headlights. She tried to shake free of the strange mood that had come over her. She had no real reason to complain about her life. She liked being single. There was a lot to be said for answering to no one but herself.

Yet every now and then she longed for someone special in her life. She wanted to recapture the thrill of dating someone she cared about, that crazy kaleidoscope of emotions she hadn't felt since high school. But maybe at thirty-four, she'd seen too much of human nature to feel totally carefree around another person. Fear and distrust would eventually undermine her. Some things, like innocence, came only once in a lifetime.

Ella arrived home and parked near the kitchen door. The lights were on inside, and she could see Rose putting away dishes. Ella climbed out of the Jeep slowly. No matter what else happened in her life, there was always a sense of continuity about coming home. It reconnected her to the past while giving her strength to face the future.

Rose met her at the door. "You look as if you've had a difficult day."

"Yes," she answered, not feeling up to elaborating.

Rose seemed to sense it. "There's some green chile stew I can heat up."

Ella shook her head. "No. I have a box of chicken I left on the car seat. I'd love some of your tea to go with it, though."

A few minutes later, as she sat across the table from her mother, Ella noticed how Rose had a habit of stirring her tea though she never put sugar in it. Ella glanced down at herself and saw she too was stirring, though she hadn't added anything to it either. Continuity. It made her wonder what kind of daughter she would have had, or might have still.

Ella shook free of the thought. She tended to get overly philosophical when she was dead on her feet. "Do you mind if we don't talk much tonight? I need time to just lay back and think."

Rose smiled. "When I was much younger, and trying to figure something out, I used to take dinner into my room, turn the lights off, and sit in the window, eating alone by moonlight."

Ella smiled. "That's just what I want to do tonight."

Rose handed Ella the half-eaten plate of chicken from the table and the glass of tea. "Go then. If you decide to talk, I'll be around."

Continuity. Some links went so deep nothing could ever destroy them. Even time, with the enormous power it wielded, could not stand against them. If anything, it strengthened them even more.

NINE

✖ ✖ ✖

The next morning, Ella stopped by the office to fax the strange message she'd intercepted from Peterson over to the FBI. Once finished, she drove to the Farmington post office. She arrived shortly before eight. She saw the postmaster come out and unlock the lobby doors. Cup of coffee in her hand, Ella went inside.

As the hours passed, her restlessness grew. She had checked as the postal clerks sorted and put away the mail, and the letter was already in the mailbox. Despite the morning crowd, no one drew near that particular box. Ella wondered if she'd been compromised somehow, but that didn't seem likely. No one had given her even a passing glance.

Ella met Justine outside on the loading dock shortly after twelve. Although Ella hadn't really done anything except stake out the box, she felt more tired than if she'd run a marathon. "If you see anyone getting that letter, get hold of me on the radio and make sure you follow them."

"Where will you be?"

"I'm going back to talk to Duncan James."

Justine nodded. "I remember he was at Haske's lecture. I know he was a wannabe Singer who never really followed through with it. Have you learned something more about him?"

"I haven't got a thing on him, not even a gut feeling. All I know is that he's interested in the past, and he attends the free lectures. What interests me is why he never pursued being a Singer. I'm also wondering if he's thinking about going into it now because of the gossip about skinwalkers and things getting out of balance. It's only a fishing expedition, but who knows? It might lead someplace."

"Then I hope it turns out better than my visit with Betty Lott."

"Did you manage to find her?"

"Oh yeah, for all the good it did me. Seems Betty disagrees with everything her mother has to say about any given subject. I think she's interested in our traditional ways mostly because Anna hates them. There's such animosity between those two!"

"It happens that way sometimes between mothers and daughters. They can be too alike, or not alike enough. Either of those can cause trouble."

Justine nodded. "Bottom line though was that I came up empty. I just don't think Betty knows anything we can use. I certainly hope you have better luck than I've had when you talk to James. We're running out of leads."

"No, not really. I still have to check back with Bruce Cohen. Yazzie may have decided to trade. Plan on being here at the post office all day if I get hung up, okay? If you need someone to relieve you, call me. I'll pass the request on to Big Ed myself."

"I won't need anyone. I've been on stakeouts before. I can handle this."

Ella nodded. "Just don't let boredom make you complacent. And stay in touch with me."

"Will do, boss."

As Ella drove back to the Rez, she speculated on the best way to approach Duncan James. There was no way to tell how he felt about her family. She'd have to sound him out, and go slowly. There were so few leads in this case, she had to stir up the waters whenever possible to see what came to the surface.

Forty minutes later, she arrived at James's garage, just outside Shiprock. James did good business here, catering to travelers going through the Four Corners area in every direction. She parked where she wouldn't block any of his service bays and walked inside.

The high-pitched sound of an air hammer seemed to echo back at her with incredible intensity. She went to the man crouched in front of a tire he'd just lifted down from a car on a rack. "I'm a police officer. My name is Ella Clah. Are you the owner?"

"That's me, Duncan James," he answered, and turned around. "What can I do for you?" His eyes narrowed as they settled on her. "I know who you are. You let Tony shoot himself right in front of his little girl. What brings you *here?*"

The unexpected backlash from the hostage situation struck her like a slap in the face. With effort, she decided to let the vicious remark pass. "At the moment, I'm tracking down anyone who ever attended the lectures our recent murder victim gave." Since Ella wasn't really sure if James had attended those or not, she waited without elaborating.

"Yeah, I went to a few. So what?"

"No problem. I've heard about you, that's all. Since you've got a little more life experience than the students who normally go to them, I was hoping you could help us."

"What do you need?" James regarded her thoughtfully.

"You've been to some of the lectures. Did anyone there ever strike you as a troublemaker or seem clearly out of place?"

James considered it. "The kids, for the most part, never seem to belong at those lectures, if you want the truth. They just don't show the right attitude. They wear their new jeans, and shirts with somebody else's name on them. They listen to country music before class, after class, and sometimes during it. They want to learn, but they don't really want to commit to anything."

"What about you? This is a pretty modern, high-tech operation," she said waving around at the garage and its collection of hydraulic tools and computerized analyzers. "Yet I heard there was a time you wanted to be a Singer."

"I did, then I realized it would take years and years, and I had to find a way to make a living to support my kids."

"Do you regret your decision now?"

He considered it in silence for a long time. "I'm not sure. Sometimes I'd say yes but, you know, the most you can do is master some Songs. And even that takes a long time. Being a mechanic is more practical." James shrugged. "I don't know, maybe it's like looking back and thinking of the girl you left behind. There's always a little bit of regret for what might have been."

"As a gas station owner, you see almost everyone sooner or later. You hear a lot of talk most of us never would. Do you know if the victim had any enemies?"

He rubbed his jaw. "I know about Steven Nez. He was going out with the dead man's daughter, and he already has a wife."

"Do you think he could have been the killer?"

"No, but that's the closest the old man ever got to having an enemy, as far as I know." James wiped his oily hands on a rag. "Now I have a question for you. I've heard the rumors that skinwalkers are active again," he said, his voice barely audible. "Many think the *Dineh* are in for some rough times. I've given it some thought, too, but there's something that doesn't add up to me. If skinwalkers are becoming active, wouldn't you and your brother be the logical targets? Why pick on an old man like the historian?" He looked at her thoughtfully. "The only answer that makes sense to me is that the murder was carried out to incite you, and the choice of a victim was more or less random."

Ella considered the implications. James had brought up a good point that hadn't occurred to her. Up to now, she hadn't considered the possibility that the murder had been a way to get her involved, knowing her position in the tribal police. "Call me, anytime, day or night, if you hear anything," she said, handing him her card.

"No answer to my question?"

"I don't have one. I'll have to think about it."

"You do that," he muttered.

As Ella walked back to her vehicle, her mind was racing. She'd suspected that the elaborate staging at the murder scene had been done to divert her from the true motive of the crime. But maybe her theory had been too simplistic. Perhaps it was a little bit of both. The killer had wanted to confuse and distract her, but at the same time, he'd wanted to make sure she was involved. Maybe the staging had been the killer's way of challenging her. That sounded like Peterson Yazzie again. As an ex-cop he certainly would have all the knowledge needed to direct and misdirect at the same time.

As she drove back to Farmington, intending to relieve Justine, Ella received a radio call. The dispatcher informed her that Peterson Yazzie was asking for a visit. "He won't talk to anyone but you," the dispatcher added. "Dr. Kring wants to know how soon you can get there. He needs to speak with you too."

"Concerning what?"

"The doctor wouldn't say."

"Okay, I'm on my way. Tell him to expect me. 'Four?"

"Ten-four."

Ella racked the mike. To assume that Peterson was about to hand over the name of the person behind the bomb incident just didn't sound right. Something more was going on. That would also explain Kring's eagerness to see her.

Ella felt tension coiling all through her body. She had no desire to meet Peterson face-to-face again, but her fear was ridiculous under the circumstances. Although Peterson had tried to kill her before with a shotgun, at the psychiatric hospital he was unarmed. She'd handled tougher men hand-to-hand while making arrests, and there'd be plenty of orderlies around if things got rough. She'd be in no danger whatsoever.

Despite the logic of it, Ella felt her hands grow clammy with sweat. She picked up the mike and radioed Justine. A moment later, the line secure, she got an update on the stakeout.

"If you need me there, I can delay this meeting," Ella said.

"No. Nothing's happening here. In fact, the parking lot is almost empty right now. Business won't pick up again until the work crowd starts heading home."

"All right. I'll come and relieve you as soon as possible."

"No rush. If one of us has to pay Yazzie a visit, then I'm glad it's you. You have far more experience with him than I do, and I have a feeling I'd be hopelessly outmatched. He scares the bejeezus out of me, to be honest."

Ella bit back the obvious reply. He scared the bejeezus out of her too. Crazy people had a way of doing that. Normal rules and constraints didn't apply to them, so their behavior was always unpredictable. With Yazzie it was all that and more. "He's not an easy one to deal with. But he's just a man," she replied staunchly. "Of course, he *does* have a few more tricks up his sleeve than an ordinary crook."

There was a pause at the other end. "He's dangerous. Don't kid yourself."

There was something so sobering about Justine's tone. Ella felt her stomach clench. "Yeah, well, I'll keep it in mind. Ten-four."

As she drove toward the hospital, she tried to psych herself up for that meeting. The last time Peterson had spoken to her was the day she'd taken him into custody. He'd given her a brief warning. She could still see him in her mind's eye mouthing the words "we're not finished with you." As time had gone by, Ella had viewed it as just another threat from a disturbed felon. Now she wasn't so sure.

A short time later, Ella was escorted through the last security door in the hospital lobby, and up to Dr. Kring's office.

The tall Anglo was pacing behind his desk as she walked in. His gray eyes were framed by lines of tension. "I'm glad you're here. We're having major problems with Yazzie. He's increasingly hostile, and is making the lives of my staff miserable. None of the methods I use on my other patients work with him. I was hoping you could give me some insights on how to deal with him. I don't believe in this skinwalker stuff, but I'm willing to use his own beliefs to control him. Is there any way to neutralize his supposed powers?"

"No, not really. I mean there are complex ceremonies, but they're meant to restore harmony and undo any harm the skinwalker has caused. Peterson wouldn't be touched by it. Even if you brought in a Singer, Peterson would be up to his old tricks the second he left."

Kring's hands clenched into fists, then slowly unclenched. "He's undermining the morale of my staff, and I've only got the best, most professional people around."

"What's going on now?"

"He's insisting on having his personal radio. He wants to listen to the Navajo station. Initially I said no. Then, from what I understand, he asked his lawyer to contact you."

"Cohen did, but when I spoke to him, I agreed to put in a good word with you only if Peterson gave me the name of someone I'm looking for."

Kring nodded slowly. "Okay. I understand what's happening. Either he doesn't want to give you the name or he doesn't have one. But he's determined to get me to agree to the damn radio, and he's hedging his bets."

"How?"

"He's playing tricks. If I find his accomplice, I'll barbecue his butt, then make sure he never gets a job like this again."

"What's going on?"

"When I confined Yazzie to his room, he promised to make things difficult for everyone else too." He gestured toward the wall. "Then the electric power in this institution started going off and on at random. I've had two electricians out here, and nobody can explain it. It isn't happening anywhere else in the area, just at this institution. They've checked the wiring, but so far they've found nothing."

Ella shrugged. "He's definitely using this problem of yours, but he may not be responsible for it."

"You think that hadn't occurred to me? But let me tell you what happened last night. The electricians had been here and the lights were on again. I was about to go home when I learned that Yazzie had asked to telephone his lawyer. I went to talk to him myself. I told him he'd have to wait until morning. His behavior didn't warrant any special favors."

"What happened then?"

"He was furious with me. I could see it on his face. Then he went to the light switch. Two orderlies stepped toward him and he stopped. He stared and stared at the switch. I finally got up to leave. By the time I stepped into the hall, we were in total darkness again. I could hear him laughing inside his room."

"He wants you to think his powers can even affect electricity. The timing was pure luck."

"Yes, but he knows how to milk it, and he's got half of my staff ready to quit. I want things back to normal. I'm sick and tired of all his games. I'm ready to give Yazzie a battery-powered radio just as long as he behaves. We don't allow electrical cords in a patient's room because they could use them to hang themselves or choke someone. Do you have any objections?"

"To a radio, yes. A tape player would be much better. But don't give him anything yet. Let me talk to him first."

"I'll have him brought to one of the secure conference rooms. And I'll have two of our orderlies standing by just outside, watching through the glass."

"Good."

Ten minutes later, after leaving both her handguns locked in Kring's desk, Ella was face-to-face with her worst nightmare. Peterson's eyes were flint hard, but his expression was amicable. "Oh, I'm so pleased to see you again, cousin!"

Ella nodded once. "Seems you've been creating quite a ruckus around here."

He opened his palms in a self-deprecating gesture. "In my own small way, I do try to keep things from getting too boring."

"You're doing an admirable job. I commend you."

"High praise from a worthy adversary. So how is your life nowadays? I understand that you have my old office. Does it remind you of me?"

"No. I've changed everything except the desk. It's almost as if you were never there, really," she said casually.

"I'm sorry to hear that. I would have liked to think that you missed me. I do miss you and your family. We used to be so close."

Ella knew that she must not lose her temper. Although it was taking every shred of will power she possessed, she forced a smile. "They were fond of you too. But then again, that's what made you such an effective criminal. Of course your moments of success are over for good, now. The victory was clearly ours."

Peterson's eyes flashed with anger, but in a heartbeat his poise returned and there was only calm reflected there. "There are many battles yet to be fought," he answered simply. "I understand, in fact, that you've requested my help. A name?"

Ella felt her heart drumming against her ribs. Maybe to keep her off balance, he would go ahead and give her a name. "An even trade. Something useful for something useful."

Peterson gave her a slow, easy smile. "I'm very surprised that you didn't find what you needed long before now. The key to your success was there within your reach for quite some time."

Ella remembered the break-in at her office, and knew he was referring to the missing key. "Speak plainly," she snapped, determined not to reveal what she knew.

"You don't really expect me to just hand you a name, do you? My, shall we say, associates, wouldn't exactly approve of such a thing. Besides, where's the sport? Instead of a name, how about if I give you a color? Think blue." He smiled as if inordinately pleased with himself. "Now, about my radio. Please, nothing with earphones. They give me a headache. I'll need a supply of new batteries too. Any good brand will do. Use your own judgment there."

"What radio? You haven't given me anything."

"I've given you everything you need to know," Yazzie said indignantly. "Don't tell me you're going to welch on our deal. Don't you think you can figure it out?"

"*When* I do, you'll get a tape player, but no radio."

"What is it with you, L.A. Woman? Do you lose your nerve around me? Or was it after that man ate a bullet in front of you in Farmington?"

She stood up slowly, resisting the urge to reach across the table and rip out his jugular with her thumbnail. "If you hadn't spoken in riddles, then you wouldn't have as long to wait."

"How about giving me a radio with only one set of batteries? If, by the time they wear out, you still haven't got what you want, then we'll both have nothing."

Ella held his eyes, refusing to look away. He was taunting her. To not give him something was to de facto admit that she lacked the confidence to match wits with him. "You'll get a tape player with old batteries, and whatever music the people here can dig up."

He chuckled softly. "Once you puzzle it out, I'm sure you'll see just how wonderfully helpful I've been. Perhaps then you'll come back and pay me another visit. I get lonely without my old friends."

"We'll see."

She saw him gazing at some spot behind her, and turning slightly, she followed his gaze to the wall switch. She glanced back at him, and he smiled benignly. She forced herself not to flinch. He had the look one would expect to see from someone who enjoyed pulling the legs off lizards.

"All my love to your mom, Ella," he said as she left the room.

Ella stopped by Kring's office and gave him a brief report. "Make sure he gets something with batteries that have been used for a while. I don't trust him."

Ella strode out to her vehicle, lost in thought. Mind games. Peterson Yazzie excelled at those. The clue he'd given her about the color blue could mean almost anything. It was the type of clue that would only mean something *after* she found her own answers. Damn him.

Ella tried to tell herself that it was just police work, that it had nothing to do with pride. But the game had changed. She not only had to deal with skinwalkers who had singled her family out for their revenge, but with the People's strong belief that more harm would befall the tribe until the balance was restored. And there was a killer to bring to justice. Was it all connected? She hoped no more would die before she made the final move.

TEN

✖ ✖ ✖

Ella arrived at the Farmington post office just outside the Rez shortly after seven. She parked across the street and walked inside.

Justine was walking around the lobby, pretending to sort through mail in her hand, glancing only casually at those who entered. Ella gave her a nod, and met her by the self-serve desk next to the postal scale.

"I've been here all of today. No one's opened that box. I don't think my cover's blown either. No one's paid attention to me at all, except for a cute guy who tried to strike up a conversation. Either this isn't a pressing letter, or the recipient has no idea it's coming."

"That's not only possible, it's likely. From what Dr. Kring told me, Yazzie doesn't talk to anyone except Bruce Cohen, his lawyer."

"So this stakeout could go on for several more days."

"No, not really. We don't have the manpower to invest on it. I figure we'll do another full day, then we'll have to pull back unless Big Ed gives us some backup."

Ella shifted so she could see the entrance doors. "Why don't you go home, have dinner, then come back tomorrow? I'll finish tonight's watch."

"I can stay . . ."

"You've done more than your share already today. I'll take over. Go home, get some rest, and we'll meet at the office tomorrow at seven A.M. We need some time to catch each other up on the case." Ella picked out some discarded envelopes from the trash. These would add to her cover.

"See you tomorrow then."

Ella watched Justine walk out of the post office, her assistant blinking in the direct sunlight. She could tell Justine was beat. Sometimes lengthy stakeouts punctuated by nothing but boredom turned out to be the hardest ones to handle.

Ella strolled around the lobby keeping several empty envelopes in her hand as she pretended to walk to one box, then another, as patrons entered or exited.

For an hour, nothing happened. Even the walk-in traffic began to trickle to practically nothing. The janitor came, swept the floor and emptied the trash cans, then left. Noticing that a broom had been left out, and needing to stay busy, Ella picked it up and pretended to be part of the cleaning crew.

Ten minutes later, restless, and almost certain that once again she'd wasted their time, Ella stopped sweeping and glanced around. The post office lobby was completely empty. She was putting the broom back when an Indian man wearing a baseball cap and a blue windbreaker ambled up slowly to the section she was watching. Ella moved to one side, trying to figure out if he was going to the right box. His back was to her and he was blocking her view. She strolled toward him casually just as he opened the door and extracted the letter.

Ella stopped, not wanting to alert him, but something about her actions must have spooked the man. He turned and raced out the door.

"Police officer! Stop!" she ordered, but the man never slowed.

Ella was only a few yards behind him when she saw him jump inside an old Chevy and take off down the street. It took Ella less than ten seconds to reach her Jeep. He wouldn't be able to get far. Requesting backup from the Farmington police and giving a general description of the car, she weaved through the early evening traffic. She kept her eyes glued on the speeding vehicle ahead. No way he was eluding her.

Ella saw the Chevy turn into an alley behind some old four-story businesses facing Main Street. She pressed down on the accelerator, anxious to keep him in sight. It was just a matter of time before he was intercepted by the Farmington police or she forced him to pull over. Either way, this jerk wasn't getting away.

As Ella entered the alley, she felt a prickling over her skin that warned her of trouble. Her cop instincts began working overtime. Her gaze darted everywhere, searching beyond the illuminated area of her headlights with her searchlight to see around the Dumpsters.

Slowly she drove on a little farther. Suddenly the Chevy shot out from behind a trash-filled Dumpster, blocking her way. The barrel of a shotgun appeared from the backseat window behind the driver.

Ella slammed on the brakes, whipping the Jeep to the left to put the engine block between her and the threat. She ducked down just as the windshield exploded into a waterfall of cubed glass. The shotgun continued its thunderous blasts, striking the front end and passenger doors with hammering blows. Ella, on the floorboard, threw open her door to slip out.

Suddenly the new blast of a rifle was added to the shotgun fire, and a bullet ricocheted off the pavement beneath the car. Her left front tire exploded, and the car sagged on the driver's side. The rifle sounded again, and she realized that the other front tire was now history. Her vehicle was being ripped apart!

Ears ringing from the noise, she hugged the transmission hump and called for help again on the radio. "Ten-eighty-three. Shots fired, in the alley between Broadway and Main. Cross street is Auburn. Officer needs help!"

Ella kept her head low as she dove out the door, then crouched low behind the flattened front tire as another shotgun blast shattered glass above her. Her vehicle was disabled, and there were two well-armed assailants out there, gunning for her. There was no way she was going to let them just walk up and blow her away while she was cowering on the floorboard of the car.

Nine-millimeter handgun in hand, she felt inside her jacket pocket for the two extra clips. She had plenty of ammo, but her pistol was outgunned against the firepower of a shotgun and high-powered rifle.

A deadly silence fell and seconds crept by with agonizing slowness. She resisted the temptation to take a look. They were probably waiting, their sights trained, trigger fingers ready, hoping she'd do just that. Instead, she listened, ready to nail them when they tried to move in.

Another thirty seconds elapsed. She heard sirens wailing in the distance. There was no sweeter sound. Her odds were looking better. Gathering her courage, she moved to the rear of her Jeep and peered out, looking from underneath. To her surprise, the Chevy was gone. She cursed loudly. They must have taken advantage of the covering fire that had kept her head down and ears ringing, and slipped out of the alley. They were long gone.

Ella stood up as two patrol vehicles shot into the alley. She held up her badge immediately and ran toward the lead car. Giving the officers a fast description, she watched them race away after her attackers. She didn't hold much hope that they'd catch them now. Those two guys had been prepared for trouble.

Ella accepted a ride back to the Farmington police station. After she filled out a report and made a telephone call to bring Big Ed into the picture, Justine arrived, ready to take Ella back to the Rez.

As Ella rode back with her assistant, her thoughts continually drifted to Yazzie, and she cursed the day he was born. Lately, all the wins had been his. "My car's going to be in the shop for days, so I'll be using my own pickup unless Big Ed finds me a loaner. After my conversation with him tonight, that may take awhile."

"Yeah, when he called me at home and asked me to pick you up, he sounded really ticked off."

"He doesn't like surprises. I should have filled him in on what we were doing at that post office. But he hates to have someone in charge report every action they take. He likes his people to take the initiative. And the fact is, until now, I really had nothing concrete to report."

"What's changed? The suspects got away."

Ella told Justine about her meeting with Yazzie. "I've been thinking about what he told me. He said I had the key I needed already. What if he meant it literally, and was referring to the key that was taken from beneath my—his—old desk? He may not know one of his followers had removed it recently. Peterson also said something about *blue*. I have no idea what that suggested. Let's see if anything's come back on that imprint."

"I remember inheriting that from Harry Ute." Justine nodded. "I'll check if it's in any of the reports that have come in via fax."

"Let's go back to the office then. My meeting with Big Ed is tomorrow first thing." Ella braced herself for a very long evening.

Forty minutes later, they sat in Ella's office. No report on the key had come in from the lab. "If it wasn't one A.M., I'd call the labs."

"Shall we call it a night? I don't see what else we can do." Justine yawned.

Ella pursed her lips. "I'm going to call Blalock."

"At this hour? What for? He won't know what the labs have."

"Maybe he can goose someone on duty at the Albuquerque office, and they'll get back to me tomorrow morning. I owe old FB-Eyes a wake-up call or two anyway, after what he put me through last year." Ella gave Justine an evil smile, then picked up the phone. Blalock wasn't thrilled to hear from her, but he seemed alert enough to take action. "I'll get back to you," he said.

Ten minutes later, Ella's phone rang. She had it in her hand instantly. "Hello, Dwayne. What's the word?"

Blalock was almost upbeat, considering the time. "I got ahold of the agent on duty in Albuquerque, Ella. The crime-scene unit is out in the field right now, working a suspicious death on one of the local pueblos. When they go back to the labs, one of them will check and see what they have so far on that key of yours and fax you a preliminary. I gave them your fax number there."

"Thanks. I appreciate it."

"Good. Now can I get some sleep, or do you have any other crimes you'd like me to solve for you before sunrise?" Blalock mumbled.

"Get your beauty rest, guy. You need it." Ella hung up the phone, a smile on her face.

"So what now?"

"We wait until it comes in. If there's any chance it's something we can move on before morning, I'd like to know about it. I have to find answers soon. Fear of what's to come is translating into restlessness now, but the longer this is drawn out, the more dangerous things will get."

Justine nodded. "One of my brothers works for the tribal council. I understand that the tribal president is going to be increasing pressure on the department. The families of the victims, including the ones who died in the bus accident, have gone directly to him. We'll be getting that backlash soon." Justine stopped abruptly. "But you didn't hear that from me, okay?"

Ella nodded. "I appreciate the advance warning."

"Let's go to my office. The fax machine is there, and we can try to get some sleep while we wait," Justine suggested. "The ringing phone will wake us up the second the fax comes through."

"I suppose we can try sleeping in the chairs there," Ella said slowly.

"I have a two-man sleeping bag in the back of my vehicle," Justine said. "It belongs to my brother and his wife, but they won't mind. If we lay it out, neither one of us will have to sleep on the floor."

"Sounds good to me," Ella answered.

Ten minutes later, Ella lay down on the soft, down-filled sleeping bag. It felt wonderful beneath her, despite the tile floor underneath. She closed her eyes, intending to will herself to relax, but there was no effort involved. Without even being aware of it, she drifted off to sleep.

The next sound she heard was the fax machine phone ringing, then the feed of paper coming through. Ella was up in a second, reading the report as it came in. "They suspect it came from the trunk of a Ford sedan made between 1958 and 1963. If my memory serves, Peterson used to drive an old Ford Thunderbird, and it was blue. I wonder what happened to it?"

Justine yawned. "A car that age is probably falling apart by now. We could try old Ralph Ben's place. That salvage yard of his has practically everything. Maybe Yazzie ended up selling it to him for parts."

"It's worth checking up on. Though whatever might have been hidden in that car is probably long gone, it still could give us some clues. We'll head over there at sunup," Ella said glancing at her watch. "That'll be about two hours from now. If they've hidden something in his old car, then for whatever reason they've chosen to call attention to it now. I'm eager to find out why, and what it is."

"Well, until then, we might as well go back to sleep. I'll set my watch alarm."

"All right. We'll grab all the sleep we can, then get going."

The next sound she heard was the electronic beep of Justine's wristwatch alarm. Ella opened her eyes slowly and reluctantly. Taking a deep breath, she realized slowly where she was, and why.

"Wake up, cousin. Time to get going," she said, nudging Justine.

Justine's eyes blinked open and she sighed. "I don't want it to be morning yet."

"You can quit early tonight. For now, we've got to get over there."

Fifteen minutes later, they were on the highway. Ella rolled down the window, allowing the cold morning air to hit their faces and force them awake.

"Why don't we stop and get some coffee someplace?"

Ella was tempted to say no, but without sleep and food, they weren't going to be much good to anyone or the case.

As the sun peered over the Four Corners power plant far to

the east, Justine pulled into Millie's, an all-night coffee shop next to the highway.

After consuming two coffees and a half-dozen honey-glazed doughnuts, they got back on the road. Ralph Ben's business had originally been an auto repair shop. He'd done a good job, and cheaply, so his services were much in demand. Often, however, the clunkers people brought to him were beyond repair. As the years passed, the land around his home had become a graveyard for cars nobody wanted.

The Ben family eventually had turned it into a salvage yard. It was nothing more than a rolling stretch of rocky soil and arroyos the Ben family had asked the tribe to allocate to them. Still, it was a profitable sideline. People came here searching for old parts no one could order anymore.

"I'll be willing to bet that Old Man Ben will be able to tell us exactly where any old Ford Thunderbirds are," Justine said.

"Even so, that's no guarantee we'll find the right one there." Ella glanced at her watch. "Big Ed will be at the office at eight-thirty. That gives us a little over two hours to get this done."

"Well, at least you found out something about the key. That's certainly positive information you can tell the chief."

"I'd also like to give him the name of a suspect linked to the attempted bombing."

"Why are you so worried about this Farmington thing? I mean, granted, your Jeep was all shot up, and it'll cost a bundle to repair, but you were able to flush out some of Peterson's band and still keep from being shot in their ambush."

"When Big Ed came on as police chief, I know he had implicit faith in my abilities, and in the training I'd received in the bureau. I'd hate to see that faith eroded, particularly now. I've had my share of opposition from the community, and there are those who would like to see me off the force. So it's important to me that Big Ed knows that my instincts and abilities can be trusted. Otherwise, next time I need for him to let me handle things my own way, he may not be so inclined, considering the politics of his job. I work better when I don't have to keep checking in every time I make a decision."

Justine nodded slowly. "I can understand that. And from everything I've heard, Big Ed has a long memory. You don't get a lot of chances with him if he thinks you've messed up."

Thanks to Justine's penchant for speed, they arrived at Ben's Salvage ten minutes later.

"Park near the front of his house, then let's see if he notices we're here," Ella instructed. "It's still awful early in the morning."

Justine followed the suggestion. "How long do you want to wait? He may not even be up."

"If he's not, then we'll start looking around the yard for Peterson's old car. There's no fence here. I don't think he'll mind."

"Probably not," Justine agreed.

Ella caught a flicker of movement from around the side of the house. Ralph Ben, dressed in jeans and an old work shirt, was walking toward his front porch. "It looks like he's been up for a while. Morning prayers maybe," Ella commented, seeing the pollen bag tied to his belt.

Ella opened the car door and stepped out to stand beside the car. She saw Ralph look their way, then wave, inviting them to join him.

"You two are up early," he said as they reached the porch. "I haven't seen any cops around here for a long time. What brings you to my place?"

Ella studied his expression. "Tell me, when was the last time you saw cops here, Uncle?" She used the title not to denote kinship, but out of respect, as was customary on the reservation when addressing an old person.

He smiled. "Oh, close to a year ago, I think. Peterson came by. But then, he's not a cop anymore, so maybe that doesn't count."

Ella nodded. "Tell me about Peterson's visit, Uncle. Why was he here?"

His eyebrows knitted together. "I'm not sure. Let's see . . ." He stared across the salvage yard absently. "Sergeant Yazzie was looking for a part. No, wait, that's not it. He was looking for that old Ford Thunderbird he used to own. I tried to tell him that it was no longer worth fixing up, but he wanted to check it over anyway." He shrugged. "Peterson wasn't the kind of man I'd ever argue with."

"So, did he find the car?"

"Yeah, it's still here, a sixty-two T-bird. It's one of those from after they started getting big. He must have believed me after all about it not being worth fixing up. He just looked it over. Then he left, and that was the last time I saw him." Ben gestured toward the north end of the yard. "Funny thing though. About two weeks ago, someone else came by. He was interested in that car, too, but then I guess he came to his senses. It runs, but I'd be willing to bet that you couldn't get more than a few miles down the road without it overheating. The transmission is bad too."

"Who was this man who came by, Uncle?"

Ralph shrugged. "I know almost everyone around here, but this fellow wasn't familiar. He was Navajo, but he sure didn't talk much. I tried to get him interested in some other cars I have for sale, but he wasn't listening. Kept turning away when I spoke. Rude, for a Navajo."

"Tell me everything he did, from the time he arrived."

"He walked over to the T-bird right away, carrying a big wooden toolbox. Looked it over, listened to the engine, lifted the hood and trunk stuff, then just stood there for the longest time. Really strange fellow. I finally decided to leave him out there, thinking that the hot sun would help him make up his mind."

"And?"

"I went back inside the house where it was cooler. I looked out the window every so often, and he'd be just standing there. Sometimes he'd open the trunk or hood again, then look inside, tinkering with his tools. Finally he came over. He left some money and told me it was a deposit. He told me to make everybody keep their hands off of it until he returned with the rest of the money. As far as I'm concerned, that doesn't apply to cops."

"Can you show us where the T-bird is, Uncle?" Ella asked.

"Sure. Let me find the keys first." Ralph went back into the house and came out again a few minutes later. "Here's the ignition key and the trunk key."

Ralph led the way across an area filled with rusting car parts, old tires, and junkers that would have needed a miracle to run. Ella heard movement under an old pickup chassis as they passed by.

"Mind the snakes," he said.

Ella minded. Snakes had a place, but out here one was likely to run into rattlers, and she'd seen the damage those could do. She had no desire to test the theory that their fangs wouldn't penetrate boot leather.

Finally they arrived at a faded blue Ford Thunderbird. It was the longer, heavy version, not like that red sporty one she used to see on a TV show. She studied it, noting the elements had been kind to the car and remembering Peterson's single, grudging clue.

The car looked operable, if shiny chrome mattered. Ella could feel Justine's eyes on her as she walked around it then crouched by the rear tires. After a moment, Ella stretched out and studied the underside of the car. Nothing appeared to have been disturbed there.

"Do you want me to open the trunk?" Justine asked as Ella got to her feet.

"No, don't disturb anything. Something doesn't feel right here." Ella glanced at Ralph. "The man that looked at this car, did he focus his attention on one part of the car more than another?"

"I couldn't say," Ralph replied with a shrug. "I got tired of watching." As a pickup trailing blue smoke approached, Ralph shielded his eyes from the sun and peered over at the newcomer. "That's a customer now. I'm supposed to fix Hubert Franklin's truck this morning. I don't know how much good I'll do—that pickup needs a new engine—but I told him I'd try." The ancient pickup rattled to a stop near the front of Ben's house. "If you don't need me here, I better get to work."

"We'll take care of ourselves, thanks," Ella assured him. As the old man walked out of hearing range, she glanced at Justine. "Good. I was hoping he wouldn't stick around."

"What's up? Did you see something that bothered you?"

"No, but something's fishy. Think about it. The key and this car are linked to Peterson. Nothing about him, or connected to him, can be trusted. I want to make sure of what I'm doing, or not doing, from here on."

"You think they'd booby-trap this car? If I'm reading you right, that's what you're worried about."

"Sure. It's something he'd do almost instinctively. Trickery is in his nature." Ella glanced into the rear seat of the car. "And he did lead me to this vehicle. Considering we know it has been tampered with lately, we need to go slowly with this."

"So how do you propose we go about opening the trunk?"

Ella took her time studying the back door, and making sure there were no wires connected to either the handle or the door itself. "I'm thinking of checking out the interior first, and under the seats. Then if I don't find anything suspicious, we'll drill a very small hole in the trunk and take a peek."

"I've got just the tool that will let us have a real clear look. It's a small laparoscope. You can look through keyholes, under doors, and so forth. Real spy gear."

Ella nodded in approval. "Excellent." As she slid into the rear seat of the car, she looked around carefully, checking under the front seats first.

Justine leaned inside and crouched by the open door. "Maybe we should lift out the rear seat. We could get to the trunk through the back panel."

"No, don't touch it." Ella tried to move the cushion slightly to check for wires. She found none, but was still uneasy. "If we continue using common sense, we'll be following the steps Yazzie would expect someone to take." She shook her head. "We have to do something unpredictable. Let's drill that hole through the top of the trunk right now, instead. Once we take a look, we'll have a better idea."

"We could call Sam Pete."

Ella shook her head. Sam Pete was their bomb squad, but his role had always been to disarm and dispose of ordnance, not search for it. If they found a bomb, then they could call him. "Let's not bring anyone else in, until we have more to go on than Yazzie's puzzles."

"I'll go borrow a drill."

"Tell Ralph we'll reimburse him for the damage."

"To this clunker? What damage?"

"Just tell him."

"Okay, okay."

While Justine walked back, Ella sat on her heels and studied the backseat. Nothing could be trusted. If she kept that firmly in mind, she'd be fine. She stepped out of the vehicle as Justine approached with a big, battery-powered drill and a metal box Ella figured contained the laparoscope.

"This drill isn't as powerful as one of those extension-cord jobs, but he put in a new, especially hard bit for us. Ralph said it'll go through that sheet metal like it's butter."

"Good." Ella took the drill from Justine's hands. "I'll start this. Just in case, why don't you wait behind that row of cars?"

"No way. You might need my help."

"Definitely a possibility," Ella conceded, stepping forward and picking a spot on the trunk where she hoped there were no metal braces underneath.

She worked the drill slowly, concentrating on creating a big enough hole before the battery ran down. "I don't know what's going to piss me off more—finding out he's really booby-trapped this, or finding out he hasn't," Ella joked cynically.

"Let me finish that for you." Justine looked around Ella's arm for a closer look.

"I've just got a little to go," Ella answered, then a moment later the drill bit broke through, slipping forward and speeding up to a whine. Ella worked the bit back out, then shut off the drill and set it down on the ground. "Now get out the laparoscope."

Justine inserted the optical fiber tip carefully into the hole, and they both looked at the small viewing screen.

Ella was first to speak. "There's our dynamite. It's been booby-trapped to the trunk door with a blasting cap. Had we used the key, it would have been the last thing we would have done."

"I hate to bring this up," Justine said slowly, "but we really have no way of knowing in what condition that stash has been kept. I don't know much about explosives and detonators, but I do know they have a tendency to become unstable with age and under harsh conditions. If there ever was a time to call in some backup, I think this is it."

"Yeah, we're in perfect agreement. Call Sam Pete."

"Oh, and while I'm at it, are you aware of the time? We're going to be late meeting Big Ed."

Ella glanced at her watch. It was eight already. She groaned. One more thing she'd have to explain. Well, maybe the progress she'd made on the bombing attempt would be enough to offset her absence at a meeting and her bullet-ridden Jeep.

ELEVEN

—— ✖ ✖ ✖ ——

Two hours later, Ella sat on the tailgate of an old Dodge pickup. Big Ed was next to her, watching Sam Pete work about a hundred yards away. "The Jeep we gave you was brand-new. Now it could be proudly parked in any row of this salvage yard."

Ella said nothing, mostly because she had a feeling that anything she could say right now would be precisely the wrong thing.

"I've looked over our inventory for another vehicle, but we don't have a large number of cars on hand."

"Do you want me to share with Justine?"

"No, that won't be necessary. But the vehicle that'll be assigned to you is several years old. It's low mileage though. Harry takes care of all our cars, and he tells me it runs like a charm."

"Thanks. I appreciate getting another unit quickly."

"Don't thank me. I got the order to give you one from a higher authority, and I don't mean God. I, personally, wanted to let you sweat for a while."

Ella kept silent. Something was really bugging Big Ed, and she had a good idea what it was. She figured that sooner or later he'd get around to it. It was better not to press.

"From now on, I want you to fill me in daily on your plans,

in writing or orally, *before* you get started. I realize that I've always encouraged autonomy from my department heads, but this case is different. I have to report to the tribal president myself now. And I *never* want to hear from an outside source, like the Farmington Police, what one of mine is doing. Clear?"

"Crystal," she answered. "No problem."

"The tribal council is getting nervous. There is a lot of political pressure to solve the murder, and to get Peterson's people taken care of once and for all. When politicians call me on the carpet about what my department's doing, I like to have ready answers, you get me?"

"Yes, sir."

"Getting results, that's the most important thing now. I don't want you or any of our people hurt. That'll just feed into the belief that the evil in our land is getting stronger and heighten the fear that's been just beneath the surface among the *Dineh*. But I don't care if you destroy half the vehicles in the department as long as you put this case to rest."

Sam Pete extracted the case of dynamite from the trunk of the Ford. After placing it inside an armored box, he waved to them. "I'm taking this a few miles out into the desert, away from any possibility of breaking windows, then I'm going to blow it up. I've got lot numbers and photos for you, but this stuff's unstable and even transporting it that far is risky. We can't keep it."

"Go ahead," Big Ed yelled back.

"Yazzie has answers," Ella said. "I'm going back to that hospital and wring them out of him."

Big Ed gave her a long, thoughtful look. "If you think that you can force anything out of that man, you're wasting everybody's time. You're smarter than that, aren't you?"

The words stung, but she knew he was right. "I'd like to shut him up and wipe that superior smile off his face."

"Understandable, but don't let him lose interest in the game he's playing with you. If that happens, he'll shut down completely, and you'll lose a possible source of future information. Just remember, he set you up with this bomb. Everything he did or has done was to lead you here, to open that trunk. Blowing you and anyone else unlucky enough to be near you into pieces was part of his plan. Stay one step ahead of him—always."

As Big Ed walked away, Ella found Justine busy searching the interior of the Thunderbird. "We'll get this car towed to the impound yard," Ella said. "Then you and I are going to go over it with a fine-toothed comb. I want fibers, fingerprints, hair samples, dirt, anything that will lead me to the Navajo who booby-trapped it."

"We can check and see who has experience with explosives too."

"Yeah, just remember it doesn't take a genius to make a bomb like this. All they need is one of those how-to-make-a-bomb manuals," Ella said. "We should check people who worked construction or mining and feel comfortable around dynamite."

"That list may be lengthy," Justine warned. "A lot of the *Dineh* have worked the mines."

"Maybe once we've gone over the car, we'll be able to narrow it down. The man who made the bomb might have been sloppy. He figured most of the vehicle was going up in smoke."

As Justine went to call in for a tow truck, Ella met Ralph Ben. "It seems this got a lot more complicated than either of us expected," she commented.

Ralph shrugged. "That's okay by me. I still get paid for that old clunker, and no one got hurt here, including me."

"I'd like for you to try and remember back. I need to know everything you can recall about that man who came to see the car."

"I didn't recognize him. I already told you that."

"I bet there are things you noticed without even being aware of it. Let's go over to your porch to talk. It'll be more comfortable for both of us out of the sun."

Ella walked back to the house with him. It was still early, but the temperature was already climbing. At least clouds were amassing to the west. It might rain later on this afternoon. That would help cool things off again.

"Was he as tall as I am?" Ella asked Ralph as he sat down on one of the old metal folding chairs.

"No, he was more like Big Ed, but not as fat."

Ella tried not to smile. She could imagine what her boss would have said if he'd heard that.

"My age, maybe?"

He considered it. "He was wearing a cowboy hat, and dark glasses. I really couldn't tell you how old he was." He paused. "But he stood straight, and walked like a young man."

"Good. Think back. What color was his hat? Black?"

"No, brown. And he had long hair. I remember it stuck out around the hat," Ralph nodded.

"Excellent. Did he look like someone who makes his living working indoors, or outside?"

"His hands weren't like a workingman's. I remember thinking that. He also wasn't wearing any rings. He had a gold watch though, on his left wrist. Looked expensive, with one of those metal bands. Not leather."

"Did he have a western belt buckle, like yours?" Ella smiled.

"Yes, he did. I recall it was gold, like his watch. And his boots were shiny. I forget the color, black or brown. Not those snake-skin kind." Ralph smiled, pleased with himself.

"I knew you could do it! Keep thinking about it, and if you remember anything more, give me a call," she said, handing Ralph her card.

Justine came up and cleared her throat. "Do you have a moment?"

Something in Justine's tone made Ella's flesh prickle. Something was wrong. She was suddenly very tired of surprises.

Ella led Justine away from the porch. She could feel her young cousin's growing tension. When she was certain they were out of Ralph Ben's hearing range, she stopped. "What's going on?"

"I've got bad news. The *hataalii*, Leonard Haske, was just found dead."

It took a few seconds for the news to register over the sudden numbing of her brain. "You don't mean from natural causes, do you?" Ella observed, her voice uneven.

"No. He was murdered, and it's some sort of ritualistic thing, from the preliminary report I just got."

"Where?"

"Near the Shiprock itself. I'm not sure about this, but I think it's at his family's shrine. He was supposed to meet with someone he was training to take over for him someday, Vernon Kelewood. Do you know him?"

"Vaguely."

As Justine started her vehicle, Ella placed the bubble on top of the car and switched on the siren. "Step on it. The way the clouds are building, I'm almost certain it's going to rain this afternoon."

The irony of such a crime occurring near Shiprock, Tse' Bit'a'i' to the *Dineh*, passed through Ella's mind. The dark igneous rock, once the throat of a volcano, stood over 1,450 feet above the floor of the desert. The massive geologic feature figured prominently in Navajo ceremonial lore.

In one story Monster Slayer hid on the mighty rock and killed two enormous bird-creatures who had been preying on the People. Later, he turned the babies of the creatures into the eagle and the owl.

Shiprock itself had once been considered sacred too. Part of the Enemyway ceremony, which included rituals for protection and power, was performed near the rock. But when a Sierra Club climbing party profaned it in 1939, it could no longer be used in sacred rites. Ella wondered if the killer, or killers, knew this.

They arrived forty minutes later. The trip would have taken closer to an hour if Justine hadn't practically floored the accelerator until they left the main road. Ella glanced at the police officer who was standing alone at the scene, his back to the high volcanic wall or dike that projected from the desert floor. The massive structure was one of three ancient lava flows extending from the volcanic neck of Shiprock like collapsed tripod legs. Officer Winston Atcitty looked as if he would have rather been anywhere else on earth than there.

Ella stepped out of Justine's car, her gaze taking in the scene. As she walked closer, she saw that Haske's body lay facedown near a cairn of rocks, halfway up the slope to the dike. This was, in turn, about fifteen yards from the dirt track that passed as a road. Blood stained the ground around the body, having seeped from its back and legs. "Who found him?" she asked the officer.

"His apprentice, Vernon Kelewood. He's with the family right now. The daughter took it badly."

Ella nodded. "Did you call in the crime-scene unit?"

Officer Atcitty nodded. "They're on the way."

Ella glanced back and saw that Justine was already busy taking measurements and sketching out the crime scene. "Stay here until we're finished. I'll be needing you to help us canvass the crime scene for evidence."

As a breeze blew across the mesa, Ella gazed at the southeastern horizon. With luck, it wouldn't rain for at least four more hours. But a breeze was coming up, and that meant evidence could be obscured or lost. "Work as fast as you can," she told Justine as she approached the body.

Ella crouched near the crudely sewn suede-cloth medicine pouch that lay near the victim's right hand. Herbs of a type she didn't readily recognize had been scattered about. She picked up a tiny piece of leaf and sniffed it. There was no scent she could make out.

Justine handed her an evidence bag. "We better get those secure right away, or the wind will carry them everywhere."

Ella studied the medicine pouch, mentally comparing it to the one she remembered Haske carrying. "This isn't his, or if it is, it's a new one. The one I saw him with had an ear of corn done in beadwork in its center. It was leather, and much better made."

Justine pointed to the man's waist. "Like that one?"

Ella moved closer, saw the large deerskin pouch partially beneath Haske's side, and nodded. "So what's this other one doing here?" she mused, glancing back at it. "I think we better ask Vernon."

"There's no gunshot or stab wound, but it looks like someone smashed part of his skull and neck," Justine said. "His legs are at a strange angle, too. I'll bet they're broken. I'll be interested in Carolyn's findings," she said, mostly to herself.

"There's no sign of a struggle, so either he didn't put up a fight or the body was moved."

"It's bad business," Justine commented. "A *hataalii* maybe killed by another." She gestured to the extra medicine pouch. "At least that's what the killer wanted us to think."

Ella studied faint tracks and a trail of dark clumps on the ground that could be blood. She noted there were only two sets of footprints. One obviously had come from the victim. The other, she surmised, were probably Kelewood's. She'd confirm that later.

"Someone spread sand over these marks and drops of blood. And take a look at the back of his shirt. There are small paint chips clinging to it. My guess is he was struck by a car, and then dragged here."

Ella went to the road, searching for clues there. Someone had taken his time, because all tire tracks had been removed. Yet Haske's truck was still parked there, and its tracks led back up the road a ways. They disappeared where they had been mixed up with the killer's vehicle. A few scattered clumps of blood and sand were at the edge of the area where the tracks had been swept away.

"I think he was struck by the killer's vehicle right here. Then the body was dragged over to the shrine, and the extra pouch was placed by his hand. Then the killer wiped out his tracks as he went back to the road," Ella told Justine.

As Justine studied the evidence, Ella went directly to the car. She had to verify Peterson Yazzie's whereabouts. A quick check confirmed that he was still at the psychiatric facility, locked in his room.

Ella walked back to Justine. "You take care of things here. Officer Atcitty will help you out, and Tache and Ute should be arriving soon. I'll take your vehicle and go talk to Vernon Kelewood. I also have to speak to the victim's wife and family. I'll be back as soon as possible."

Ella drove down the road to the house where Haske had been living. Recriminations pounded in her brain. She should have done more to protect him, despite Haske's annoyance at the prospect. Her instincts had clearly warned her that he could be in danger.

She thought of his family and the sorrow they now had to bear. Her heart went out to them. She knew what it was like to face such a loss. To make matters even worse, his daughter had just had a baby. That child would never know its grandfather. Anger began to build inside her, and she fought against it, wanting to keep her thinking clear and focused. For the second time in as many weeks, the life of a man who had so much to give to others had tragically ended. She wondered what the death would do to the tribe. Fear could spread like wildfire now. The balance between good and evil had suffered another blow.

When Ella pulled up at the house, Vernon Kelewood came out. Ella parked the vehicle and got out as Vernon approached. Although he had been training to take Haske's place someday, Ella could tell at a glance that he had little of the charisma his mentor had possessed. His head was bowed and his shoulders slumped as he walked, like a man defeated.

"I knew you would come here. I waited."

"Tell me what you know, and what you saw today."

"I went up there to meet the *hataalii*. He told me yesterday to come at sunrise and plan on staying all day. I was to begin learning certain Songs of Blessing. He warned me that there was danger to everyone on the reservation. He told me that he'd warned you too."

She saw the accusation in his gaze and forced herself not to flinch. "What else did he say? Did he mention being afraid of anyone in particular?"

"He was afraid for the People, not himself. The *hataalii* was aware of the danger we all are facing. He spent his life benefiting others, yet when he needed help no one was there. Now he's gone, and we are without his protection."

Once again Ella heard an accusation in his tone. Refusing to allow herself to be distracted, she focused on the questions she needed to ask. "Tell me exactly what you saw when you arrived at the scene."

"I saw his pickup but not him, so I called out. He didn't answer so I went looking for him." He stared at the ground for a long moment. "I found him by the cairn of rocks. That's his shrine."

"Who else knew you would be meeting him there?"

"It was no secret. We'd both been at a Chapter House meeting last night, and I know we talked about it then. He mentioned to the others there how important it was to keep to the old ways in these troubled times. He complained that the younger ones didn't respect things like their own family shrines. There was even graffiti spray-painted in places that were holy to the *Dineh*."

"Had your teacher ever mentioned taking on other apprentices?"

Vernon considered it. "I know he felt that we needed more Singers, and he was willing to teach. As far as I know though, no one had approached him. Learning to be a Singer takes dedication and a lot of hard work. Just one of the Songs can take years to memorize. Rituals leave no room for mistakes. They've got to be done exactly right."

"Was your teacher satisfied with your progress?" She knew Navajos were always reluctant to speak on behalf of others, but she figured she had to ask.

Vernon hesitated for several long moments. "I can't say for sure, but I will tell you this: A few months ago Duncan James came to talk to him. You know that he's always wanted to be a Singer, but with his family and all, he just never went after it." Vernon paused, and looked at the empty hogan. "Duncan asked to become an apprentice. I heard my teacher tell him he was much too busy with me, that I had showed remarkable progress, and he didn't want to divert his attention."

Ella considered what Kelewood had said. "*Have* you shown remarkable progress?"

Vernon gave her a sheepish smile. "Yes, and no. He was satisfied with what I'd learned so far, but he never felt I was particularly bright or gifted. I think my teacher didn't feel Duncan was suited to become a Singer, and used me as an excuse to refuse him." Kelewood took a deep breath, then let it out again with an audible sigh. "But I really don't know for sure. All I'm doing is guessing."

"Thanks, I appreciate the help you've given me."

As she turned to walk back to Justine's car, she heard running footsteps. Ella turned around and saw a young woman rushing toward her.

The woman stopped in front of Ella, facing her squarely. Her hair was tied back in a traditional bun at the nape of her neck, and her black eyes shone with tears. "You knew there was danger. My father even did a Song over you for protection. But you did nothing to stop this." Her voice cracked but she continued. "He came here to see his grandchildren, and now he's gone. His death is on your hands."

"I did offer him protection, but he wouldn't allow me to do anything that would interfere with his duties as *hataalii*."

"He was stubborn. You should have insisted! My father paid with his life for your incompetence." Tears streamed down her face. "Your family only brings sorrow and misery. I wish you'd all just leave!" She turned and ran back to the house.

Ella watched Haske's daughter for a moment. She'd spoken out of grief, but the words were still hard to take. Ella was tired of having her family take the blame for every bad thing that happened. These murders had nothing to do with them! Yet she also knew the futility of trying to defend herself against an accusation like that.

Frustrated, Ella went back to the car. She'd return to the crime scene and help out there. Then, after Haske's family had had a bit more time to adjust, she'd return.

Ella drove back to Haske's shrine. She went around Officer Atcitty, who was studying vehicle tracks. Up ahead, she saw Carolyn was examining the body. Justine was helping Tache and Ute, making sure nothing was missed.

Ella went directly to Carolyn. "Anything noteworthy that you can tell me right now?"

"The killer left us his signature. Once again he's marked the victim with a bone. This time I found it lodged inside the Singer's mouth."

"Human?"

"I doubt it. Probably cat again."

"Cause of death?"

"A crushing blow to the skull. He was struck by a car, too, just prior to the lethal blow. From the level of impact on his body, I'm sure his assailant was driving a car rather than a truck. The main contact area was his spine, so I can tell you he wasn't facing the vehicle when it made contact. Death wasn't instantaneous. He was still alive when he was dragged over here. Blood flowed from the lacerated skin around the spine, and soaked the ground. Had he been dead, there would have been no blood flow."

"Thanks, Carolyn." Ella left her and went up to Justine. "Have you got anything for me?"

"Not yet," Justine reported. "Any theories on what went down here?"

Ella thought about it for a minute before answering. "The killer must have known the victim was coming here, or else followed him. Either way, it was premeditated. The victim undoubtedly heard the vehicle, and hadn't been afraid of its approach because he stayed on the road. Possibly he recognized the driver or the car and didn't feel threatened. Or maybe the car slowed down, as if to stop, then sped up at the last second. Either way, by the time the *hataalii* realized the driver's intentions, it was too late."

"You think it was the same person who killed the historian?" Justine asked.

"Probably. Carolyn found a bone in his mouth."

"But nothing else matches. There's no ash painting here, just that medicine pouch in his hand," Justine said. "You think it's a copycat killer?"

"No. I never mentioned the bone in the press release. It's the same killer, I'm certain of it. What we must do now is trace everything the Singer did during the last twenty-four hours of his life."

"Yeah, the 24/24 rule. The two most important things in an investigation are the last twenty-four hours of a victim's life, and whatever clues we find within twenty-four hours after the body's discovered." Justine's tone was pensive.

"The Singer's wife has been dead for years, but I want you to talk to his daughter. You may get more from her than I could. And ask about the extra medicine pouch," Ella added. "I'm going to put out an APB on the killer's car. We know it must have sustained visible damage. Then I'm going to start calling every garage and body repair place in the county."

Ella radioed in, requesting that patrol officers check out any car with recent front-end damage, and blood or cloth fibers adhering to it. The message would also be passed along to every law enforcement agency in the area.

Finished, she racked the mike. Ella glanced around, trying to decide what to do next, and saw Carolyn place the body in what had been dubbed the "croaker sack." She then signaled Atcitty to help her carry it into the wagon. For a moment, Ella felt sorry for Carolyn and for herself. They were both doing jobs that needed to be done, but no one seemed particularly appreciative of it.

"I'll have results as soon as possible," Carolyn said as she approached.

"Thanks," Ella replied.

"Do you think this will be the end of the killings?"

"Unfortunately, no. I wish I was making faster progress, but so far the most likely suspect is safely in custody. I'm going to pay him a visit next. If he knows something, I've got to squeeze it out of him one way or another."

Ella approached Justine as soon as Carolyn drove away. "Justine. I want you to take the evidence we have back to the lab and start looking it over. Try to identify the contents of that medicine pouch. If the herbs inside came from a certain area, that'll give us a starting point. I'll continue using your car. You can ride back in the crime-scene van."

"Okay, boss. I'll get right on it."

"In the meantime, I've alerted patrol units, and I'm going to walk around the community below, where Haske was staying. Maybe I'll get something useful from some of the residents," Ella added.

"That's a tight-knit area of conservatives," Justine warned. "I've heard my older sister talk about it. It's not going to be easy to get them to open up to you."

"I've got to try."

Ella drove back down to the community, left Justine's car parked near one of the mailboxes, then strolled around. Two women were hanging laundry. They'd been speaking in hushed tones, but as Ella approached, they suddenly lapsed into silence.

Ella held up her gold shield. "Excuse me, ladies, but I'd like to ask you some questions."

"We don't know anything," the older one said.

Ella studied the woman. She was in her late fifties, with more salt than pepper in her hair. There was something indomitable about her expression. It would have been easier to crack a piñon nut open with a straw than to get her to divulge anything.

"You probably heard what happened to the *hataalii* this morning," Ella continued. "I'm going to need help to track down the killer. Will you help me?" Ella had decided that the direct approach was her best chance here.

"How can we tell you what we don't know?" the younger one countered. Her hair was fastened tightly in the traditional way, and her belly was swollen in the last trimester of pregnancy. "I was hoping he would be around when my child was born. Now there is no one."

"There are other Singers," Ella said gently.

"Not like our friend. I've known him all my life, and *no one* is his equal," she answered staunchly.

The veiled reference to her brother was unmistakable, but Ella chose to let it pass. "Then you understand why I must find whoever did this. Did the Singer have any enemies?"

"No, of course not," the younger one said.

The elder woman finished hanging up a pillowcase. "That's not quite true. A Singer makes enemies; we all do. Sometimes patients don't get well, sometimes he turns men aside who want to learn to become healers." She shrugged. "There are many possibilities."

"Are you referring to anyone in particular?" Ella persisted.

"You are the detective. Go find out," the older woman said curtly, then turned and went inside her home.

Ella decided to canvass the street. She walked up a well-worn path that doubled as a sidewalk and saw a Navajo woman in her mid-thirties working in a small vegetable garden.

The woman saw her approach and stood up. "You've come to ask about my neighbor," she said wearily. "You can ask while I work. I still have weeds to pull before the ground dries up again."

Ella walked across a section of desert grass that made up the front yard. "I need to know more about him—who visited him recently, anyone he argued with, anyone who visited him often, whom he visited. Any information you can give me will be appreciated."

The woman nodded. "I'm Lois Mike. Do you remember me? I was a year behind you in school. My last name was Pioche then."

Ella wanted to say yes, but at the moment, the best she could do was associate the name with the family. "I remember your brother, Billy. He could really play basketball."

"Yeah, he graduated the same year you did." She continued to weed the little patch filled with tomatoes, snap beans, and summer squash. "Things were simpler then, weren't they?"

"In a lot of ways," Ella admitted. "Will you tell me about the Singer? How did others here see him?"

"We wanted him to stay. He understood us so well. We figured that now that Rosemary had her son, the Singer would want to be around to see him grow up. We really had great hopes he'd move here."

"Where's his home?"

"Near the Wood Spring trading post."

Ella glanced at the empty streets. No one would come out until she left. "It's a close-knit community, isn't it?"

"Very."

"But you've really set yourselves apart here," Ella commented.

"That's what Rosemary's father didn't like about us at first.

He thought there were too many divisions among the *Dineh* already." Lois shrugged. "But we started winning him over. It's true we prefer traditional ways, but we're no different here than if we lived in the new housing areas in Shiprock." She paused. "Eventually he started to see that too. I think he was seriously considering moving here."

"Did you happen to see him yesterday?"

"Off and on. He spent most of the day in the hogan preparing herbs. He was getting ready to do a Sing for Betty Poyer. She hasn't been feeling so good lately. Vernon was right there, too, helping him with the herbs and making prayer sticks."

"Can you think of anyone who might have done this to him?"

Lois grew serious. "A Singer like my neighbor has many friends. His enemies are those who are also enemies of the tribe."

Ella understood the reference to skinwalkers. "Have you heard any gossip about anyone in particular, maybe someone who lives in this area?"

"If we had someone like that around us, he would have been driven out," she said flatly. "Our community wouldn't have allowed it to continue. We listen to what is going on in our world. Everybody knows about the historian and his eye, and now about the *hataalii* and what happened to him. It's spoken about in whispers, but people know. That's why they're afraid. More bad things will happen now, like the bus accident. You can count on it. People sometimes say that fear of the unknown is the greatest fear of all. But in this case they're wrong. It's what they know that terrifies them most." She glanced around. "Now you better go before I end up in trouble with my neighbors."

"One last thing. If someone's vehicle, a car, suddenly turns up missing, will you call me?"

"Sure. I'll get hold of you, one way or another."

Ella walked back to Justine's car, checking out the vehicles she passed. Once again, she was faced with a man who had many friends and few enemies, a man who was nonetheless dead.

TWELVE

✖ ✖ ✖

It was midafternoon by the time Ella entered the station. Stopping briefly by the front desk, she picked up the keys to her "new" police car then continued down the hall. Justine was coming out of the lab, newspaper in hand, as she walked by.

"Anything new?" Ella asked, handing Justine's car keys back to her.

"Big Ed is now doing the press releases himself," she said, accompanying Ella to her office. "He wants you to concentrate solely on the case. Also, Carolyn . . . Dr. Roanhorse called. It's a cat bone again. She thought you'd want to know as soon as possible."

"Anything else?"

"Carolyn sent over the victim's clothing and I managed to get pieces of the grille and another tiny piece I'm sure came from a turn-signal light. I sent it to the lab, and they'll get back to us. There wasn't much to work with, so they warned it would take some time."

"Great. At least that's something."

"We are getting answers, though admittedly we've had to work for each little piece. We are now pretty sure that both victims were killed by the same man," Justine said.

"And that he may be targeting authorities on Navajo culture. Get me a list of known authorities in every area of our culture as soon as possible. Wilson Joe may be able to help you compile it."

"You'll have it. When it's ready, do you want me to put those people under protective surveillance?"

"We don't have the manpower. What we have to do is warn them of the danger, ask them to keep a close lookout, and make sure they know to call us at the first hint of trouble. Of course if anyone has been threatened, or feels they're in immediate danger, we'll place them in protective custody right away."

"I'll get started on that. Meanwhile you might want to take a look at the tribal newspaper." Justine placed it on Ella's desk. "Check the headlines, then the editorial page."

Ella glanced down at the front page briefly. Another disaster of sorts made the top story. "COAL MINE TO SHUT DOWN. HUNDREDS WILL LOSE JOBS." Ella felt her flesh prickle. This story came on the heels of the *hataalii*'s death. Fear would hold the People in a tight grip now.

No arguments supporting logic would matter. Some would claim that evil was methodically destroying the tribe from within. In a way, it was true. Belief and fear had always been her most dangerous adversaries. Struggling against the heaviness of spirit that weighed on her shoulders, she turned to the editorial page.

A long letter written by Walter Billey suggested that Ella's brother, Clifford, could be involved in the murder of Kee Dodge, and might be indirectly responsible for the bus accident the same day in the same area. Billey then hinted that other troubles would follow unless the entire Destea family, including Ella, was driven off the reservation.

"I've checked on the author of that letter," Justine said, walking back inside Ella's office. "There is no one in the records by the name of Walter Billey. There's a Warren, and two Wesleys, but that's it. The name is as phony as the charges."

"You sure? No distant relatives of the Billey clan?"

"I tripled-checked it. Trust me."

Ella nodded, lost in thought, as Justine dropped off the daily report for Ella's signature and left the office. Ella's thoughts were racing. The writer had obviously expressed the sentiments of at least a few people in the area. He'd probably just been too afraid of retaliation to use his own name. Personally she hoped the gossip monger got a sunburn on his tongue while spreading his lies.

Ella picked up the list of phone messages Justine had collected for her. Bruce Cohen had called three times. She picked up the phone and dialed his number.

"I've been trying to get hold of you, Detective Clah. Where have you been?" Bruce demanded.

"You'll hear about it soon enough on the news. That's my concern anyway. If you needed me right away, you should have said it was an emergency. The dispatcher always knows where to reach me."

There was a long pause. "It's not an emergency, just something I thought you should know. Peterson asked me to mail two letters yesterday. One went to the tribal paper, the other went to you."

Ella cursed herself for not checking her telephone messages yesterday afternoon, but things had been so hectic. "Do you know anything about their contents?"

"No. All I can tell you is that they were in plain white legal-sized envelopes. But the one that went to the paper can't be very private."

"I'll look into it. Thanks for letting me know. How are you holding up?"

"I tried the tactic you suggested with my client, and so far it's worked. The creep likes having people who worry about what he might do to them. There have been no further threats."

"There probably won't be any more, unless he feels you're getting too complacent or cocky."

"I wish I'd never heard of this case," Cohen muttered.

"We have something in common then." As Ella hung up the receiver, she felt genuine sympathy for the man. He was stuck trying to protect his family, forced to deal with a dangerous killer whose legal rights he was also sworn to protect. But Yazzie had underestimated the strength of family ties. Perhaps not ever having experienced that love was his biggest weakness.

Ella checked in with tribal patrol units, county law enforcement agencies, and body shops, hoping they'd found the vehicle used as a murder weapon, but there was still no trace of it. She was sitting back in her chair, sorting her thoughts, when Clifford walked in.

"Hi, Special Investigator Lady. I was driving back home and since I had to go by your office, I thought I'd pay you a visit.'

"Then this is the first time ever," Ella smiled. "What's really on your mind?"

Clifford gave her a quick half smile, then his face grew serious. "I've been thinking about that day when I told you to seek out the old Singer. Now he's dead."

"I know," she said sadly. "The backlash already started too. There's talk that our family brings trouble and is responsible, directly or indirectly, for the tribe's problems. The next thing you know, they'll claim we're responsible for the coal mines' closing down."

Clifford nodded. "Evil brings evil. All things are connected. What people don't realize is that our family weighs in the scale for good. We are needed more than ever if balance is to be restored."

Ella knew that her brother was referring to more than the fact that they were honest people who fought on the side of right. His beliefs centered on the special abilities—gifts, some said—that they both possessed. But her intuition was based mostly on logic and training. Not wanting to argue, she let the matter drop.

"Your instincts tell you the murders are going to continue?"

She exhaled softly. "Unless I catch the killer, they will."

"Do you have any leads?"

"Not usable ones. So far, everything points to Peterson, and he's in custody. He knows something though. I'm going to have to try and get some more information from him."

"He'll give you enough to keep you coming back, but never enough to solve the crimes," Clifford warned.

"So far that's been the way it is. Any idea how I can trick him into making a mistake?"

"I don't think there is a way. Remember that although we

both know a great deal about him, he also knows about us. And he has one advantage: he doesn't care what happens to anyone else. To him, your desire to catch the killer before he strikes again makes you vulnerable. It also makes you susceptible to his deceptions."

"Susceptible how?" Ella prodded, her gaze thoughtful.

"The more time you spend with him, the more opportunities he'll have to manipulate you. Soon he'll get you used to making concessions in exchange for information. Nothing will happen abruptly, little sister, but he's counting on a slow progression that will give him the opportunity he wants to strike back hard."

"He's already tried, and failed." Ella told him quickly about the bomb in the car. "I can deal with him eye-to-eye," Ella assured him. "Now let's change the subject for a moment, brother. Do you know Walter Billey?"

Clifford gave her a puzzled look. "I think you have the name wrong. There's a Warren and a Wesley. Which one are you interested in?"

"Neither." Ella passed the newspaper across the desk toward him. "Have you read this little gem?"

Clifford scanned it, but his expression remained calm. "There is no Walter Billey. This phony letter was meant to stir up trouble. The newspaper publisher should know better than to print this without verifying the source."

"That's why I'm going to go talk to the newspaper editor. I believe there's a good chance that this came from Peterson."

"How can he get a letter out? Aren't there restrictions on him?"

Ella explained. "The thing is, I don't want to put a stop to it. He may know something."

"Then the progression I warned you about has already begun." Without further word, Clifford walked out of her office.

Ella considered what her brother had said. He didn't understand. She would use Peterson, not the other way around. She'd be on her guard.

Ella closed her office door and went down the hallway scarcely looking at the other officers along the way. Ella stopped by Justine's lab and peered inside. "I'm going to the newspaper office in Window Rock. I'll be back in a couple of hours or so."

"Do you need me to go with you?" Justine glanced up from the microscope.

"No, you can probably do more good here."

Justine rubbed her eyes. "Don't count on it. I got zip on the herbs in the medicine pouch. They're mostly weeds with no use that I've been able to discern. At least if it had been tree leaves, I could have considered the possibility that they had come from a tree struck by lightning—that makes sense and has a recognized use. Bits of pollen, soil, water—all those are tokens of power. But the stuff in this pouch was probably just grabbed off the ground as filler. I think there's even potpourri in here, but I'm still checking that out."

"Another non-lead," Ella muttered. "If they want us to believe in the validity of the clues they leave, why do they make such basic mistakes?"

"I've given this some thought. What if it's not meant to mislead anyone except the general public? The perp may be counting on the gossip that flows naturally after each crime. Someone sees a medicine pouch, they tell someone else. But police findings aren't necessarily made public. The public may never know that it's not a genuine medicine bundle. That may be precisely what our killer's counting on."

Ella considered Justine's theory. "That's Peterson Yazzie's type of game. I feel him in this. Yet logic tells me that all he's doing is trying to get some attention, and the extent of his involvement could be limited to his imagination. Meanwhile, how are you coming with the evidence?"

"I'll have a better handle on things by the time you get back. I'm going to be running the fingerprints I've lifted from the vehicles next. Some PD's in our area have Descriptor Index files in their data banks. I can describe both murders, and if there's a similar MO, then some of the data bases will supply me with fingerprints I may be able to link to the crime we're investigating. It's a long shot, sure, but I figure it can't hurt."

"Keep up the good work," Ella encouraged. "I'll take care

of the footwork while you track down things from your end."

Ella went out to the parking lot and located her vehicle, a four-year-old generic Ford sedan, in gray. At least it had the proper equipment, and air-conditioning.

Ella started up the unfamiliar vehicle, discovered the air conditioner really did work, and forced herself to concentrate on the facts they had on the case. Speculation on the extent of Peterson Yazzie's involvement was distracting her from the main path of the investigation, she knew. Someone had murdered two of the tribe's best cultural resources. That was the heart of the investigation. She had to let her instincts take command and let the killer lead her back to Yazzie, if he was indeed part of all this.

Fifty minutes later, she pulled into the parking area of the newspaper's Window Rock office. She walked inside, identified herself, then asked to see the editor-in-chief.

Jaime Beyale stepped out of the adjacent office and gestured for Ella to come inside. "Ella! I haven't seen you in a good fifteen years." The woman smiled. "Of course you may remember me twenty pounds thinner."

Ella grinned. "Jaime. You were the editor of the *Tomahawk*, our school paper, and now you're the editor of the *Dineh Times*. Seems fitting."

"Somehow I remember you as more of a homebody," Jaime observed, "not as one of the People's top cops."

"Back then I was a lot more domestic," Ella agreed. "But life has a way of changing you."

"Is it the editorial letter we printed that brings you here? It's our policy never to print a letter unless we verify the source. But there was a slip-up. I had a call from Warren Billey because he wanted to know if there is some relative he didn't know about."

"Is that possible?"

"You tell me," Jaime answered and slid a plain white envelope across the desk for Ella to see.

Ella saw the Farmington postmark, and the handwriting. "I think I know who wrote this, and it wasn't anyone in the Billey clan. Mind if I take it and check for fingerprints?"

"Not if you tell me what's going on. Trade?"

Ella paused, considering the newspaper woman's request. "Will you keep it under wraps for now?"

"If you'll give me the rest of the story first, as soon as it breaks," Jaime said.

"You've got yourself a deal," Ella agreed. "I visited Peterson Yazzie a few days ago. I have reason to believe that he wrote this, hoping the paper would print it after confusing the similar names."

"Yazzie, why? I thought he was out of the picture now. Isn't he?"

"He's supposed to be getting psychiatric care, if that's what you mean."

"So now he's trying to stir things up again?"

"I think that's part of his plan."

"Well, that certainly explains the tone of the letter. I don't think Peterson hates anyone as much as he hates your family."

"Does Peterson Yazzie have any friends here on the Rez who you know about?"

"Not any who would stand up and be counted," Jaime answered.

"Will you double-check any more letters that come in on this vein? I mean, if they're legit, then it's your call on what to do, but it's the bogus ones that I don't think either of us needs."

"You've got that right. Our newspaper's reputation is on the line here. I'd like to print an editorial, challenging this impostor to come forward under his or her own name. That would, in a way, invalidate the impact of the letter we printed."

Ella considered it, then shook her head. "It might stir up more questions and keep the issue alive. That would only give Peterson more publicity in the long run. I'd rather you just let it drop for now."

"All right. I'd hate to give Yazzie any more power and influence than he already has. There's a lot of bad things happening to the People right now, and we can't give him credit for that too."

As Ella walked to her car, she had a good feeling about trusting Jaime. She hadn't disclosed any information that could jeopardize the investigation, but she sensed she had made a valuable ally.

As she started back, her radio crackled to life, and she heard her code coming through the air. When Ella picked up the mike and acknowledged the message, Justine's voice came through clearly.

"Boss, I just found out something I think you need to know. My second cousin Leroy Johnson is the postmaster at the Shiprock office. I was talking to him on the phone during my break, and he told me that the Singer's family has taken the death harder than we expected. His daughter is taking her new baby and moving to Fort Defiance to be with her 'little mother,' you know, her mother's sister. She left a change of address with him."

Ella thanked her assistant. "I'll go over there now. Maybe I can talk them into staying until the case is closed."

Ella went past the station and continued toward the remote community. It took her only half an hour at top speed, but by the time she arrived, the house was empty. Ella left the vehicle and glanced at the small sheep pen. All the animals were gone too. Ella walked to the house and peered inside the window. The curtains had been taken down, and outlines remained on the wall where pictures had been.

Lois Mike saw her and came out. "They left this morning. The water in their well had dropped so low the pump wouldn't draw up any water. They had to fill their jugs from my house. They took the sheep in the back of a pickup. They're not coming back."

"Where did they go?" Ella wanted to confirm what she'd heard earlier, and if possible, nail down an address.

"Rosemary said that she was going to stay with her 'little mother' in Fort Defiance. She said she hated living here now. With the hogan there, all she could think of was her dad. She feels responsible, you know."

"Why?"

"She thinks that if she hadn't let you see her dad the day you came over, he might still be alive. She said she should have made sure you never got within a mile of him."

"She can't believe that!"

"She's not the only one who thinks like that around here," Lois said, gesturing at the neighborhood. "They know you and I went to school together. They said if you came back, I should ask you to stay away from all of us. The water in their wells is dropping, too, and they think it's part of the trouble."

"How do *you* feel?" Ella asked pointedly.

Lois shrugged. "I know you and your family are okay. But I've got to live here. These are my neighbors."

Ella shook her head. "I'm sorry about the water problem. It's not related to anything except a dry summer. And I can't make a promise to stay away. I'm in the middle of an investigation."

"I told them you'd say that," Lois answered. "But you won't find the killer here. Whoever did that came from somewhere else. I know all these people."

"Do you have any idea how often a cop hears those same words? Many times the killer turns out to be someone from across the street who seems perfectly normal in front of his neighbors. You watch the news, don't you?"

"Yes, and I understand what you're saying, but it's not anyone in this community. What you're talking about happens in places where the neighbors don't really know each other, except maybe when they pass one another on the way to a mailbox. It's different for us here. Everyone knows everyone else, and the wives talk a lot among themselves. I know each time Janet has a fight with her husband and what they argue about. I know when Betty's boy colics and when Mary Ann's husband comes home drunk. There are no secrets here."

Ella knew there was a certain amount of truth in what Lois was saying, but she also knew that secrets could be kept from husbands, wives, and neighbors for a lifetime.

Ella returned to her car, acutely aware that almost everyone here was avoiding her. They were staying inside as if she had the plague.

Ella drove directly to the Shiprock post office. She wanted to look up Leroy Johnson. Thirty minutes later, as she walked inside, she noted that the lobby was virtually empty. Good. She wanted to ask a favor, and the fewer people who knew she had even come here, the better it would be.

Ella found Leroy behind the counter. Although she hadn't seen him for ages, there was no need to introduce herself.

"I've been postmaster here for the last twenty years," he said with a kind smile. "There are few people I don't know."

She studied his salt-and-pepper hair, tied back in traditional style, and his weathered and lined face. He was thin, but at fifty looked as fit as most twenty-year-olds. "I need a favor, Uncle," she said quietly. "I want you to keep an eye out for any personal mail that comes to me, particularly anything without a return address. Instead of sending it with the regular carrier, will you keep it here and call me?"

Leroy nodded. "Are you trying to protect your mother from some unpleasantness? I read that letter in the paper," he added.

"She's been through enough," Ella answered without really doing so.

He nodded slowly. "You can count on me."

"I really appreciate it." She paused, clearing her throat. "One more thing, Uncle. Will you keep your ears open to any discussions or gossip about the elders in our community? I'm interested in anything at all that affects them, or is about them."

He nodded slowly. "I'll do my best to help you." He gazed at a poster on the wall showing the latest Rock-and-Roll Legend stamp. "There's a lot of talk about the murders, and of the other things that have been happening, of course. Many think that the death of the historian and now the *hataalii* are tied to other things, like the bus wreck and the coal miners losing their jobs. Our people know everything is interdependent and some are getting scared. Even the wells are starting to dry up, I hear."

Ella nodded. "I've heard that too. Fear is contagious, and the *Dineh* do talk. Have you heard of anyone being attacked or threatened?"

"I did hear something about one of our stargazers, but that was several months ago."

"What happened?"

"Someone jumped her," Leroy answered. "She said that some guy tried to choke her right outside her hogan and she barely managed to break loose and lock herself inside a shed."

"Did she report it to the police?"

"I don't know. But I remember that what scared her most was that she didn't recognize the man."

"She saw him?"

"A glance, nothing more, but Naomi Zah is pretty sharp. If she didn't recognize him, it's nobody from around here. She's lived on the eastern Rez as far back as anyone can remember. Everyone knows her, or has heard of her, and she knows everyone."

Ella had met Naomi Zah years ago, and she had to agree with Leroy's assessment on all counts. "Thanks. I'll look this up on our records."

"I don't think you're going to find much. I remember someone saying that the cops assumed it had been her husband and didn't spend too much time investigating it. Raymond has a tendency to drink too much. I got that third- or fourth-hand though, so I'm not sure how accurate it is."

"I can take it from there. Thanks for the tip."

"Do you think it's connected to the murders?"

"Probably not, but it's worth looking into. Who knows? She may end up providing a clue no one's even thought of yet."

"Well, she is a stargazer . . ." Leroy let his voice trail off.

Ella returned to her vehicle, her thoughts racing. She'd wanted to find a trail, and now finally she had something she could follow up on.

Ella picked up the mike and checked in. Justine was ready to be patched through. "Carolyn Roanhorse wanted me to tell you she has some preliminary autopsy results."

"Thanks. Anything else?" she asked, hoping Justine had discovered something new from the evidence.

"Not a thing. Sorry."

"In that case, I'm going to stop by Carolyn's now."

"I'll be here when you return."

"Ten-four." She racked the mike. Ella wanted to talk to Carolyn personally. Carolyn wouldn't include theories or guesses she'd arrived at through a subjective process in her report. Face-to-face, however, she'd be far more likely to do just that.

As Ella pressed down on the accelerator, her heart began pumping fast. She couldn't believe that the recent bad news was only the beginning of some great darkness about to fall upon the Navajo People, but there was something in the air that was making her nervous. It was almost like those ultrasound frequencies that were out of hearing range, yet nonetheless had tangible effects. Maybe it was just a cop's gut feeling, but she suddenly felt scared witless of what was yet to come.

Ella drove through Shiprock thinking it seemed hotter and drier than usual, even for this time of year. The weeds on the school grounds were the only forms of life flourishing. She had a feeling the few puffy clouds in the sky today would produce no rain. That's the way it had been lately. The lowering of the water table shouldn't have been any great surprise, but it was frightening nonetheless. She remembered dry summers when the sun-parched ground yielded nothing for cattle to graze on, and only the smell of dust and scorched grass filled the air.

Ella pulled into the hospital parking area a short time later and went directly to Carolyn's office. There was no secretary sitting by the desk, so she opened the double doors and glanced inside the autopsy room.

Carolyn sat on one of the gurneys eating a chocolate bar. A body lay on the next wheeled cart over, covered with a sheet.

Ella blinked. "Jeez, don't you want to take your break outside and eat that someplace more pleasant?"

Carolyn stared at the chocolate bar in her hand, then shrugged. "It's cool and pleasant enough in here, and very quiet. In fact, around these folks"—she gestured toward the body behind her, and the refrigerated wall unit that housed others—"I never feel guilty about the calories. They remind me life's short, and we might as well enjoy all of it."

"There's a morbid thought," Ella said.

"It's a morbid job."

Ella tried to appear relaxed, but this room gave her the creeps. "You got something for me?"

"You bet. I've verified from the wounds that someone in a car struck down the Singer. Only then, as if to make sure, he also bashed in the back of his skull with a blunt object. He seems to want them helpless before he finishes them off. Or maybe he likes the actual kill to be up close and personal."

"We've got a real charmer, don't we?" Ella muttered cynically. "But why implicate skinwalkers on his first victim, then *hataaliis* with the second? What's he trying to do?"

"Make you suspect everyone? Or turn everyone against everyone else? These murders have certainly created some anxiety among the public."

"Interesting theory. I hope you're wrong."

"So do I, if you want to know the truth." She glanced at her watch. "Hey, I'm starving. This candy bar is the only thing I've eaten all day. How about we go out and get a bite to eat someplace else? I could use a change in company," she admitted, wheeling the gurney with the corpse toward a storage locker.

"Let's go. My treat."

Nighttime settled over the barren desert. Miles away, a silent figure studied the crude recording studio inside the portable Language Arts department's building. He needed another kill. Soon. Waves of heat washed through him, accentuating his hunger despite the cool breeze. It was dark now, and it would remain that way for many hours. He liked this strategy better than striking at dawn, especially so close to houses and people. The last old man had almost dodged in time, and he had barely managed to get him with the car. The quack had paid for it though, with a terminal headache. Night was better. They would never see him coming.

He could feel his body throbbing in sync with his pulse. He had changed. He was no longer ordinary, someone nobody ever gave a second glance. He was a force now, one that they couldn't defeat. He had the powers of a demon within him, he could feel it. Everyone was afraid now, unable to sleep thinking they would be next. And only he knew who it would be.

He selected the victims carefully, and struck when they least expected it. Like now. She entered the room alone and sat behind a console. Tonight, she'd be his. It was right. He felt excitement wash through him. He was on the hunt.

He started to move in when he heard the sound of an approaching car. No. It couldn't be. She was supposed to be alone tonight, like every other time he'd watched.

Then he saw it was a police car. Seething with anger, he watched the uniformed officer emerge. The winds carried the patrolman's voice to him, warning her, his victim, about him. He wanted to howl in frustration.

Slowly he gathered strength from the night. He knew all the ones he had selected. His enemies wouldn't be able to stop him. Nothing could stand against him for long.

THIRTEEN

─────── ✖ ✖ ✖ ───────

The following morning shortly after seven, Ella unlocked her door and stepped inside her office. Justine appeared seconds later, papers in hand.

"You've been here working already?" Ella commented, surprised. "Nobody used to beat me to work in the morning." Ella tried to suppress a yawn.

"You wanted me to give you a list of elders who might be considered cultural experts. I've compiled one, but it's lengthy. There are dozens and dozens of people all across the reservation who might be described that way."

"But how many in this area?"

"Seven, depending on how you define them."

"We need to warn them right away."

Justine nodded. "Already done. I contacted the officers who patrol their areas and asked them to speak to the people. They'll also be on the alert, and keep a watch out for trouble."

"Okay, good. Take me through your list."

"Naomi Zah, a stargazer, along with your mother and brother are the first ones that came to mind. Then there's Sadie Morgan. She's recording an audio dictionary in Navajo. And Herman Cloud, who is a friend of your family's *and* mine."

Ella nodded, remembering how helpful Cloud had been

when she'd been alone in front of the police station, engaged in a battle for her life against the skinwalkers.

"Then there's Victor Charlie. He's an expert on plants that can be used as forage and for grazing by animals on the reservation. His father used to be the foremost authority, but everyone knows that he passed all his knowledge to his son before he died. Charlie knows how to find the best grazing spots, has maps on the location of water holes, and often teaches herders about plants that can be used as medicine for the animals."

"His name sounds familiar," Ella mused.

"He's also the cartoonist for the paper. He's quite a character but, unlike his family, his heart isn't in herding. His love is creating those funny little characters he uses to poke fun at everything."

Ella nodded, remembering who the man was. "Has any of them requested protective custody?"

"No, just the opposite. They insist they can take care of themselves and that they're in no danger."

Ella nodded, not surprised. "Some of them can, but others . . ."

"I know, but really, with our manpower situation we're not in a position to insist, unless you can get Big Ed to borrow some officers from other parts of the Rez."

"Not likely, until we have more to go on. We've got to start making some real progress to find this killer." Ella filled Justine in on what she'd found out about Naomi Zah. "Can you get me more information on that incident involving her?"

"Let me see what I can find." Justine sat at the computer terminal and called up the case history. "It looks like what Leroy told you was pretty accurate. Her report was dismissed for lack of leads and evidence. The investigating officer, Joseph Neskahi, believed that it was probably her husband wanting to put a scare into her."

"Or not," Ella concluded. "Have you ever met Naomi?"

"Not personally, but I hear she's difficult at times. If she doesn't know you, you'd be better off finding someone to take you up there and introduce you."

"Thanks for the tip."

"Have you managed to get anywhere on the fingerprint search?"

"Absolutely nowhere on the vehicles. The prints I found on those were from the victims and their families. There were a few other smudged prints here and there, but those didn't have enough points to be much use. We'd never get them admitted as evidence against anyone. We did, however, get a partial on the envelope sent to the newspaper. It matches Peterson Yazzie's. He tried to handle it on the edges, obviously, but there was a thumbprint on the back of the note itself, when he folded the paper. He was the writer too. It matched up letter for letter with a handwriting sample of Peterson's I pulled from his old files."

"That's no surprise, but thanks for making it official. I'm going to follow up on Naomi Zah this morning. I'll check with Wilson Joe first and see if he knows her personally. If he does, then I'll get him to introduce me."

"I'm going to have coffee with Furman Brownhat. He's been telling me all he knows about the students who attend the special lectures. I'm doing a background search now on Irma Betone and Louella Francisco. Both are studying to be teachers and they went to all of the historian's lectures. Furman told me that sometimes they'd really challenge him with some tough questions. I understand that they also tried to do a paper on the *hataalii,* but he wouldn't give them the time of day."

"How friendly are you getting with this Furman?" Ella asked pointedly.

"Don't worry. I've already checked up on him. He's okay, but to answer your question, it's strictly business as far as I'm concerned."

"Good, because I'd hate to think of you getting involved with someone who could be considered a potential suspect."

"*Involved?* No chance. I'm getting quite a bit of information from him, and maintaining that contact does require a certain level of friendliness, but that's all there is to it."

"Okay, humor me for a moment. Tell me about the background check you did on him."

"He tells people that his father was killed in a hunting accident, but he confided in me that it was just a cover story he made up. Apparently his dad committed suicide, and you know how rare that is on the Rez. Our files here confirm Furman's story. I asked him why he felt the need to hide the truth, since he wasn't to blame for his father's actions."

"What did he say to that?"

"He was quiet at first, embarrassed, I think. But then he told me that he hates to see the pity on people's faces. I could understand that, you know? It would bother me a lot if I was in his shoes."

Ella considered it. "Okay," she said at last. "Just be careful around him. It's easy to get too involved with people on a case, and that means your objectivity is slowly eroded."

"I'm a professional. You never have to worry about me. I know what my duty is," Justine said crisply.

Ella smiled. "I know you do. It's just that I've been there. I know how difficult it is to play the game you're being forced into."

Justine exhaled softly. "It is difficult, but I can handle myself." She walked to the door. "See you later."

Ella watched Justine leave. No matter how much Justine denied it, Ella could tell that Furman had struck a sympathetic cord. There had been deep concern in Justine's voice as she described Furman's background.

Justine was a professional, but she was also human. Cynicism and toughness came with age and experience, and Justine had neither to back her up. Whether her young cousin knew it or not, she was very vulnerable.

Setting aside those concerns, Ella walked out to her car and drove to the college. There was business far more pressing to occupy her thoughts right now. She had to find the right way to approach Naomi Zah. If anyone could help her, she was confident Wilson could. When she'd first returned to the Rez after her father's murder, Wilson had been her best friend and ally. She owed him a lot, and now she was once again going to him for help. Somehow, it felt right.

Ella parked in the college lot, then walked to the hexagonal building where Wilson's office was. She knocked on the open door of his cubbyhole and was rewarded by a genuine smile of welcome.

"Hey, it's good to see you! You never come around anymore."

"There's been a lot going on, as you've no doubt heard."

His expression grew somber. "Yeah, gossip's all over the campus. Two murders already." He shook his head slowly. "Then there are traffic deaths, coal mines closing, wells going dry. But the talk is confusing, as always. Some blame skinwalkers. Others say a Singer has gone bad."

Ella rolled her eyes. Even that had somehow leaked out. She needed to find a way to keep a lid on all pertinent information. If all the details got out, the killer could change his strategy and make things even more difficult for them. "We don't know anything for sure. The signs point in a variety of conflicting directions. They're meant to confuse and raise the anxiety level of the public. At that, they succeed admirably."

"You've got to hurry and catch whoever's doing this. I don't like the talk I've been hearing about you and your family, and how you are bringing disaster upon the tribe."

She took a deep breath, then let it out slowly. "It's a mess, and I am trying to clean it up. That's why I'm here. Do you know Naomi Zah?"

Wilson nodded slowly. "If you need to question her, I better warn you that it's going to be tough. She's had problems with your brother. They don't see eye to eye on things. Singers sometimes use stargazers to ascertain the nature of an illness. Your brother treated a relative of Naomi's once, but he didn't ask her to come and help. The woman recovered, but Naomi never forgave Clifford for not calling her. Your brother tried to explain that he didn't want to burden Naomi with such a long journey. It would have been a day's travel for her and it was during our rainy season. But Naomi felt she'd been insulted."

"I have to talk to her. Will you help by introducing me?"

"I can take you out there now if you want. She's always home. But after that, I can't guarantee anything."

"Fair enough."

Wilson offered to take his own vehicle, but Ella declined. She had a radio in hers, and there was no way she was going out to a remote area without it.

"Do you think Naomi's in danger?" Wilson asked as the miles stretched out between them and Shiprock.

"I don't know, but it's possible. Naomi may have a lead, and that's why I have to speak with her. If I don't start getting answers soon, I'm afraid other people will die."

"I'll do my best to help you, but if you tell her honestly what you just told me, you won't have a problem. Naomi takes her work as a stargazer very seriously. Her life is dedicated to helping others who need her." He paused. "You know, one of the things she does is find people and items that have been lost. I don't know if that ability of hers can help you track down the killer, but if she offers to use it to help you, say yes. You can judge the validity of what she finds later."

"You sound like you believe in it, or her," Ella said.

"She's done some remarkable things. My grandmother went to her once. She'd spent months searching for a ring her mother had given her. I remember Naomi told her to look in the vegetable garden, and that's where she found it, between the rows of squash and carrots."

"If Naomi knew they'd searched the house, it wouldn't take a giant leap to conclude it was outside. Almost everyone has some kind of garden out here. It's brilliant logic coupled with a lot of luck." Ella's tone was skeptical.

"*I'd* say so too if this had been an isolated instance, but I've heard too many stories about her." Wilson crossed his arms and shrugged.

"All I need from Mrs. Zah is a description of someone. If she gives me that much, I'll consider it a win."

"A description of whom?"

Ella shook her head. "Sorry. This is one thing I can't share with you. It's a matter of duty, not of trust. I hope you can understand."

Wilson nodded. "But I don't like it."

"I know. You're an old friend, and I don't want to annoy you, but this isn't my secret to divulge."

A lengthy silence stretched out between them as Ella drove rapidly down the asphalt. Finally Wilson pointed to a dirt road ahead on the left that cut across a sagebrush- and juniper-covered lowland. "Her son-in-law cleared that path with a bulldozer, then hauled in some gravel. It was almost impassable in winter before that. Just follow it straight to the hogan."

Several minutes later, Ella parked in front of a large hogan, well hidden among the low trees. A thin red and black blanket covered the entrance, stirring gently in the morning breeze. A short distance away was a sturdy wooden storage shed.

They didn't have to wait long before Naomi Zah came to the entrance and waved them inside. It was quiet out here, and Ella knew she must have heard the car a mile away. Ella's gaze rested on Naomi. She was a wiry, strong-looking woman in her early sixties.

"I'll introduce you and try to break the ice," Wilson whispered as they walked up to the hogan's entrance.

"I'll need to talk to her alone. Is that going to present a problem?"

"Not to me, but it might to her. If it's not going well, do you want me to stick around?"

Ella considered it. "I need answers from her, so we'll play it any way she wants."

Wilson led the way up and introduced Naomi to Ella.

"I need your help, please," Ella said. "I'm investigating the deaths of two of our people."

Naomi bowed her head once. "Then you are here officially?" she asked Ella.

"Yes."

Wilson cleared his throat. "And that's why it would be better, providing you agree, for you two to talk alone. Is that all right with you?" Wilson asked.

Naomi's gaze was skeptical as it fell on Ella. "The policeman who came here before thought I was either lying, or just a foolish old woman. Are you prepared to take my word?"

"I wouldn't be here if I wasn't," Ella answered.

"Then I will speak to you alone." She led the way inside, and both women sat on a blanket beside a small potbelly stove. The stovepipe extended out through the smoke hole in the center of the hogan's roof. "Now tell me what it is I can do for you."

"I need you to remember everything you can about the assault."

"Why do you want to know now? It's old news."

"It was an unexplained act of violence, like the recent murders. I'm trying to follow up on anything that might point me to the killer."

Naomi nodded slowly. "Yes, that makes sense. I can't find the killer for you stargazing. I've tried that already. But maybe I can remember something useful to you, even though this happened several months ago." She took a slow, deep breath. "He frightened me. To come here, to my home, and then try to harm me . . ." She shook her head slowly. "It doesn't happen, or I should say it never used to happen, here."

Ella braced herself for some comment about her family bringing trouble, but none came.

"That night I'd gone outside the hogan to look around. I was worried about my husband," Naomi continued. "He had left to go to the store in town, but he still wasn't back. Our truck is old, and it was a cold night. I grabbed my blankets and decided to go to the top of the mesa and see if I could see him. I was only a few feet away when someone came up behind me."

"You turned around?"

"I never had a chance. He was on me like a hawk. I wasn't expecting trouble, so the first thought I had was that my husband had returned and was playing a trick on me."

"When did you realize you were in trouble?"

"As soon as he tightened his hold, I realized it wasn't Raymond. This man was about the same size as my husband, but thinner and stronger. I remember the scent on his clothes. It smelled funny."

"Can you describe the scent?"

She hesitated. "A little like whiskey, but it wasn't liquor. It was strong and unpleasant."

"Did you ever see his face?"

"Yes, but it was nothing more than a glimpse. I was fighting for my life! His arm was around my neck, and he kept tightening it."

"Show me how?"

Naomi stood and faced away from Ella. Taking Ella's arm, she brought it around her neck. Ella completed the choke hold. "Like that?" Ella asked.

"Exactly."

A move learned in police training. Though it had been outlawed in several counties, it appeared on TV shows regularly. "How did you get free?"

"I tried kicking him, but he just laughed. I had one hand loose, so I reached up behind me hoping to get to his eyes, but grabbed the top of a stocking cap instead. I couldn't do anything else, so I yanked it down over his face so he couldn't see. He had to ease his hold to pull it back up, and that's when I got away from him. I think he expected an old woman to be weaker," she chuckled.

"What happened then?"

"I ran inside the shed and held the door shut. I had my ax right beside me."

"Did he try to force the door open?"

"No. He heard Raymond's truck coming up the road and ran away. I never saw him again, and I've waited. I loaded our shotgun. He won't take me by surprise again."

Ella saw the determination in Naomi's face. "I believe you. Now tell me what he looked like."

"It was dark, but he was Navajo. His hair was long, like a warrior's, coming down to his shoulders. His face was narrow, and he had hairs on his face, like he was trying to grow a beard. Silly thing for a Navajo to do."

"If you saw him again, would you recognize him?"

Naomi considered it. "I think so."

"One more thing," Ella remembered. "Did you notice what type of shoes he had on? Were they boots, sneakers, or what?"

"Sorry, I didn't. He could have been barefoot for all I know."

"All right." Ella stood up from the blanket. "I really appreciate your help. Would you look at some photographs for me if I come back?"

Naomi nodded. "If you will do something for me."

"What do you need?"

"Need? Nothing, but I'd like you to talk to Officer Joseph Neskahi. Tell him I was telling the truth."

"I will do that," Ella assured her.

Ella walked back out to the car where Wilson was waiting. "Thanks for helping me today. It went well."

"I guess Naomi was pleased that one of Clifford's family came to her. I think in her mind it balanced the scales."

"Yes, there's that, but I also think she was glad for a chance to help protect the tribe."

Ella took Wilson back to the college. As she drove, her mind wandered to Naomi and what she'd learned. There had to be a way to track down the man responsible, even now. The scent she'd detected was a clue, but so far it pointed nowhere. Could it have been alcohol after all, or maybe a paint solvent? Or perhaps even cheap cologne?

"I heard that an officer came to speak to one of our teachers, Sadie Morgan. She's a good friend of mine. Is she in danger?" Wilson asked as they approached the campus.

"She may be," Ella admitted. "It's not a good idea for her to be alone."

"Thanks for telling me. I know she likes to work late, and she can be extremely stubborn. I'll see to it that she gets some company."

"I hope she took the warning seriously."

"She did, but Sadie's also convinced that she's safe. Like many people she owns her own rifle, and she can use it. She's keeping it with her when she's working late."

Ella felt her stomach tighten. People on the reservation were raised around shotguns and rifles. They weren't careless with them, but fear had a way of making a trigger finger itchy. "Tell her to be careful anyway. Too many things can go wrong."

"She knows enough to take care picking a target, and she's a good shot."

"That's all good, but being armed won't help if she's caught off guard."

Wilson nodded. "You mean it may be someone she knows or trusts."

"That's one possibility." Ella parked her car in the college lot. "If she's your friend, talk to her. Her best defense is to avoid making herself into a target."

She was working her way out of the parking lot when a student walking by waved at her. It was Justine's contact, Furman Brownhat. Ella stopped and rolled down the window. "Hello. How are your classes going?"

"As well as could be expected, I suppose, considering what's been happening around Shiprock lately." Furman sounded a bit uneasy, but for now Ella was willing to attribute it to the circumstances of their last meeting.

"What's the talk among the students you deal with? Are they worried about the murders?" Ella wanted to get the pulse of some of the students. If they were as concerned as their parents, the community was indeed in trouble.

"It's that, all right. And all the other disasters that seem to be hitting the Navajos. Some of the kids will have to leave at semester because their fathers or brothers will be out of work since the mine is closing. Do you think it's all connected, like some are saying? Will bad things continue to happen?"

"I hope not, but I am doing all I can to nail this killer. The other things—well, they're beyond my ability to prevent, or fix."

A car behind Ella honked and she realized she was blocking the way. "Gotta go. Talk to you later."

"Sure. Say hi to Justine for me, okay?" Furman stepped back and waved again as Ella drove past.

Moments later, Ella was on her way to the station. Picking up her mike, she checked on Justine's whereabouts and asked to be patched through. Justine seemed eager to meet as soon as possible. After agreeing to rendezvous at the Totah Café, Ella racked the mike. Justine was on the trail of something. Ella could tell from the change in her assistant's tone. Curious, she pressed a little harder on the accelerator.

Twenty minutes later, they met at the coffee shop. Justine was already sitting at a table that faced the room, waiting with coffee and two slices of pecan pie. "You've got to try this pie, boss. It's excellent."

Ella smiled as she sat down. Taking a bite, she found her assistant was right. "Do you have something for me *besides* the best pie around?" she teased.

"Well, I asked Vernon Kelewood to check the list of items his teacher had with him when he died. He did, and noticed something was missing." Justine's voice rose slightly.

"According to Kelewood, his teacher always carried a special piece of abalone shell in his medicine pouch. It was supposed to have special healing powers." Justine shifted, leaning forward conspiratorially. "The shell was not there—not in the pouch, and not in the area. We did a thorough grid search the other day, even raked through the sand in several places. Had it been there, we would have found it," Justine assured her.

"You think the killer took it with him," Ella concluded, nodding slowly. "It's very possible."

"And guess what else I found out. The historian was missing a page from his notebook. Our killer is taking souvenirs from his victims," Justine said.

"Or maybe he views them more as trophies," Ella answered. "Anything else?"

"Well, nothing as intriguing as what I've just told you. I did complete a background search on all the people who attended the historian's lectures. Not everyone has an alibi—in fact few do—but none of them has a criminal record. I'm now checking to see who may have a connection to both victims. Oh, and one last thing: I did find out that the Singer was approached by the college to teach classes on traditional Navajo medicine."

"What was his answer?" Ella asked.

"He refused to teach just anyone to become a Singer. He insisted that wasn't the way it was done. But he would teach classes *about* Singers. He would tell about their lifestyle, what was expected, how difficult the training was, and why some chose to follow that life path anyway."

"Was the fact he'd been asked common knowledge?"

Justine hesitated. "Everyone in administration knew. One of the secretaries said that she was asked to do a course description of it for the fall catalog."

Ella considered everything she'd learned. "I sure wish that the trail to the killer was a little more clear cut. All these bits and pieces still don't map it out enough." She exhaled softly. "The next thing I'm going to do is bring mug books over to Naomi's and see if she recognizes anyone." Ella paused. "I sure wish we had a police artist available. Ever since we got that computer graphics program that allows us to generate sketches of suspects, we haven't kept anyone on the payroll. It does a great job with Anglos, but that program has a hard time creating images of Navajos."

"I have a friend who'd help. He'd stay quiet about it too."

"Who?"

"Victor Charlie."

"You want me to go to a cartoonist?"

"He does caricatures and portraits too," Justine said. "He sketches well, and fast. He's got the skill, believe me."

Ella considered Justine's suggestion. "Do you think he'd agree to go with us to Mrs. Zah's hogan? I think this would work better if we brought him to her, rather than the other way around."

"I can ask." Justine shrugged.

"Good. You take care of that while I go find Officer Joseph Neskahi." Ella dropped a few bills on the table. "Let's get busy."

FOURTEEN

✗ ✗ ✗

As the road stretched out before her, Ella planned her meeting with Neskahi carefully. The request she wanted to make was going to be tough on him, but she needed his cooperation. Her dealings with Naomi Zah would become easier if she could get Neskahi to do things her way. Yet this wasn't something she could ever order him to do.

Ella went through the dispatcher and got a location on Officer Neskahi. After being patched through, she arranged to meet him back at the station.

Thirty minutes later, Ella was in her office, waiting. The areas the tribal cops patroled were vast, and backups were not always possible. She knew of the long hours and dangers the officers faced constantly, and wouldn't have second-guessed any of them under normal circumstances. But she had no choice now.

Officer Joseph Neskahi came through her office door just as she closed the folder on the report he'd filed.

"You wanted to see me, Investigator Clah?"

Joseph Neskahi was a young but experienced officer with a lot of energy. He was built like a safe—square, hard, all planes and sharp angles. "Have a seat, Joseph," Ella invited him.

He sat down stiffly and stared at her. "Is there a problem in my patrol area, or with one of my reports?" He glanced down at the folder on her desk.

"No, I just need some information from you. The matter came up as I was conducting our two homicide investigations. I've been tracking down every lead, though there are precious few of them."

Neskahi nodded and seemed to relax a little. "I've heard about the killings. What has that to do with me?"

"You investigated the assault on Naomi Zah a few months ago. Tell me what you remember about it."

He shook his head somberly. "I took Mrs. Zah's statement, but there was no physical evidence except the bruises on her neck. By the time we were called in, there were no footprints or vehicle marks, nothing we could follow up on. The wind had covered everything by then. The only thing I had was her description of the suspect, and it was much too general. I was looking for a young Navajo with long hair and a scraggly beard who smelled funny. I checked with local mechanics and painters, even a guy who sprayed houses for bugs. I didn't get anywhere. I went to see her after that. I told her that she hadn't given me much to work with, and that there was nothing more I could do. She got angry, but I couldn't change the facts."

"Any gut feelings about it?"

"At the time, the only thing I could figure was that she was trying to find a way to get Raymond Zah to stay home. From what I'd heard, he had a habit of going off on his own for several days at a time, drinking. It was still winter, and I think she was worried about him. If you've been out to that hogan, you know it's in the middle of nowhere. He's the only company she has out there."

"But now you're not so sure?"

"We don't have violent crimes out here very often. The murders put a new perspective on that case."

"She had the impression that you thought she was lying."

He shook his head. "No, I told her that she should have called us in sooner. Mrs. Zah didn't report the crime until the next day, when she went to town. By that time, the trail was gone."

"It would help me out a lot right now if you'd stop by there and talk to her. Can you do that?"

"Talk to her about what? I was right. There was no physical evidence."

"Oh, I know you were right. But I need her to cooperate with me, and she's not going to do that easily if she thinks we didn't do all we could to protect her before. Maybe you can reassure her that you never doubted her word, that kind of thing."

"I *did* increase my patrols in her area," he said slowly. "Maybe it would help if I told her that."

"Have you maintained those extra patrols?"

"No. I stopped a while back, when there was no other trouble."

"Start again."

"Do you think she's a target of a killer? Do you think he's the one who attacked her before?"

"I don't know, and that's precisely my point."

"Okay. I'll go talk to Mrs. Zah this afternoon. Maybe she'll calm down a little when she hears I kept an eye on her before."

"Point out that you'll be around again," Ella suggested, "so if anything happens she should call in immediately."

"Problem is she has no phone out there. I don't think she has the money for a two-way radio either."

"We'll provide her with a CB radio, then. Get the one the Hit-and-Run officer used on that truck driver case. Take it there and show her how to operate it."

"On whose authority?" Neskahi asked, his eyes narrowing.

"Sign it out in my name. I can authorize this as part of our on-going investigation. I'll tell Big Ed just as soon as I see him, since he wants to be kept current."

"Bringing her that phone should certainly help me smooth her things over with her," he conceded.

"Do me a favor, will you? Tell her that I'll be by later to talk to her."

"Sure thing."

As Neskahi left her office, Ella stared at the sheet of paper before her. Today she had dropped a note by Big Ed's office to fill him in on her plans. Now she had to update him on current and future action. She began listing her next moves when Justine came in.

"I managed to get hold of Victor, our artist. He wants to cooperate, but his truck won't start." Justine chuckled. "When you see his truck, you won't be surprised."

"So he wants us to pick him up and take him to Naomi's?" Ella asked, and saw Justine nod. "That's not a bad idea. I was going to suggest it anyway. I'd like to speak with him first to brief him on what we need to know."

"Do you want me to take you both? My unit is a lot newer than that old interagency car you've been saddled with. Victor lives in an area that's crisscrossed with sandy arroyos and big boulders. You never know what's right underneath the surface. But I've been there before so I can pick my way through."

"If anything else happens to whatever vehicle I'm in, yours or mine, Big Ed's going to have my hide pinned to his wall. How confident are you we won't get stuck or rip out an oil pan?"

Justine bit her bottom lip pensively. "The odds with me at the wheel are in our favor, but there are no guarantees. The reason Victor's truck is a mess is because of where he lives."

Ella sighed. "We'll go at a snail's pace then, and walk in part of the way if we have to. I *don't* want to have to explain why our two-officer section has lost another vehicle."

"Clear. I'll drive *very* carefully."

Ella took five minutes to finish updating her report for Big Ed and then dropped it off at his office. They were under way moments later. Justine made good speed on the highway, but twenty minutes later she turned off, heading down a dirt road that quickly became more like two wagon ruts. She downshifted, then inched along slowly.

"At least there's no way we're going to get stuck here. The ground is as hard as asphalt. Is this part of the old Santa Fe Trail?" Ella joked.

"The terrain will change soon. We still have to cross a big, dry arroyo."

"This guy's really young. Why the heck does he live out here so far from everything?"

"You'd have to know Victor to understand. He's a bit on the eccentric side. He used to live in Shiprock, but people would drop by during the day. Since he works at home, the interruptions began to affect his concentration. He decided that the simplest answer was to move someplace where no one who wasn't extremely motivated would want to drop by. One of his uncles gave him some sheep and helped him set up a prefab house out on a little mesa. He's got a generator for electricity and he heats with LP gas. Almost no one visits so he's totally happy out here."

As they approached a wide, dry-looking wash, Ella loosened her seat belt and peered ahead. "No way. We'll get stuck in that sand, and we'll have to send for help. Can we walk from here?"

Justine pulled to a stop. "We could, but it's about a mile of rough hiking."

Ella considered the heat. It was nearly noon. "Have you driven across this before?"

"Yeah, sorta. I got over halfway before I sunk. I had to get Victor to tow me out. Today that wouldn't be possible."

Ella took a deep breath and muttered a curse. "We'll walk."

It took them thirty minutes of hiking, then a rugged uphill climb to finally get to the top of the mesa. Through weeds and brambles, Ella could see a small structure in a clearing below them. The house stood amidst sand and rocks, a solitary outpost against the beaten earth. A bit farther away, she could see an empty sheep pen. In a low spot of the mesa were about fifty sheep munching on the dry grasses and brush.

"At least it's downhill from here," Ella commented.

"You've seen his sheep. Did I tell you about Toad Dog?" Justine smiled.

"What is that? Some sort of fable?"

"No, it's his dog. Toad Dog looks after the sheep, but that isn't how he got his name. He likes to play with toads, but never kills them, though I'm sure some of them have died of fright. TD—that's what he's called for short—is about the size of a small pony, and all hair. He's Victor's buddy, so try not to say anything against him even if he drools on your pant leg. He's been known to back people up against a tree if they misbehave."

"Wonderful," Ella answered sarcastically. Is there anything else you might have neglected to tell me?"

Justine shook her head. "No, not that I can think of offhand."

As they descended the hillside, Ella heard something rustling through the cluster of stunted junipers to her left. Expecting a sheep, she jumped when a huge black beast appeared. It looked like a bear, but they usually didn't come down from the mountains during years when the forage was good.

Justine knelt down on the ground and reached out her arms. "Hiya TD, did you come to show us the way in?"

Ella blinked. Whatever it was, it looked much too big for a dog. This beast was huge, and its hair stood out like a cross between a porcupine and a chow. "*What* kind of dog is it supposed to be?"

"Nobody's sure. Victor found him on the side of the road when he was a puppy. You could hold him in one hand, Victor says. Then he just grew and grew. And became this," Justine said, standing up and giving the dusty animal one last pat on the head.

TD walked over to Ella, sniffed her knee, then jumped up on his hind legs and gave Ella a hearty lick on the face.

"Oh, gross!" Ella stepped back, wiping her face.

TD growled low, annoyed.

"TD gets upset when people aren't friendly," Justine warned. "If I were you, I'd get down to his level and pet him. Otherwise, TD will act funny around you, and Victor might decide there's something about you that can't be trusted."

Ella crouched on the ground and petted the dog. The animal seemed instantly mollified, eager to accept her gesture of friendship with another hearty lick. "Okay, guy, I haven't been kissed this enthusiastically in months. Give me a break, okay?"

Justine burst out laughing. "Come on, TD. Let's go see Victor!"

As they started down the hill, Ella wiped her face. "It's not just spit, it's slimy. Good grief!"

"But he likes you, which means Victor will too. What's a little slime in view of that?"

"Yeah, you say that because he didn't get you in the face," Ella grumbled.

Five minutes later, as they approached the house, Victor came outside and waved. "I sent TD to find you. I see he was successful! I was afraid that you'd get stuck in the arroyo. My uncle got trapped in there a few days ago and my dad had to come haul him out. I should have warned you before you set out."

Ella breathed a sigh of relief, glad she'd insisted on walking. "We parked on the other side and walked."

Victor nodded heartily. "Excellent idea."

Ella studied their host. His hair was buzz-cut short, military style. There was no other military precision about his appearance, however. His T-shirt was threadbare, and the slogan that had once been on it was impossible to read. His jeans were frayed at the hems and a pocket was hanging half unsewn.

"Come in. If you walked here, you're probably thirsty. I've got some cold soft drinks."

"I'd like that," Ella admitted, wiping the perspiration from her brow.

The low-roofed house was cool, shaded by four piñon trees that had grown to nearly twenty feet tall. The living room was decorated with realistic-looking caricatures of Navajo and Anglo politicians and cartoon strips. All were signed by Victor. His furniture consisted of an old stuffed sofa and three red beanbag chairs. A small TV sat in the corner on a homemade bookshelf. As they went into the kitchen, Ella saw a small stove, refrigerator, and single sink. The dinette set was a folding card table and four matching folding chairs. Victor invited them to sit down.

He went to a refrigerator, snatched the drinks quickly, and closed the fridge door. "I've got to get stuff in and out fast. I'm running low on the liquified petroleum gas that powers my fridge."

He handed them each a cola, then sat across from them petting TD, who seemed to adore resting his head on Victor's knee. "I understand you want me to play police artist," he said.

"It's no game. I need your help," Ella admitted. "If you can help Naomi Zah by turning the description she gives you into a portrait, then maybe we'll have an image of the suspect we need to search for."

"You are aware that I specialize in cartoons and caricatures, right?"

Ella nodded. "Justine assured me you can handle this and now I see why. I took a look at some of your sketches as we came through the living room. I've seen most of those people, and what you do is very realistic."

He nodded. "I'm fast, too, and Naomi should feel comfortable with me. I've known her all my life."

"That's great. It's a bonus I hadn't even counted on," Ella admitted.

"But I can only work from what she gives me. I can jog her memory by giving her several face shapes and that type of thing, but it's going to be up to her and the accuracy of her memory in the long run." He grabbed a backpack, stuck a handful of pencils and sketch pads inside, and slipped the bag over his shoulder.

Ella finished the last of her cola. "Thanks a million for the soft drink. I really needed it. It's hot out there, as you're about to find out."

He nodded. "That's okay. It's a small price for living out here." He turned toward the dog. "TD, watch the sheep!" Victor opened the back door, and the dog bounded out eagerly.

"You leave him here to watch the sheep?" Ella wondered aloud.

"Sure. He is very responsible. I've never even had a lamb hurt when it's just been him here alone with them. He takes his work very seriously."

Ella tried to keep her sigh of relief from becoming audible. TD would have been a pain on a car trip. With Justine driving, she knew the dog would have been all over her.

They were on their way twenty-five minutes later.

"TD seems to like you and Justine," Victor said proudly. "He's a wonderful judge of character, too, you know."

"He's a nice dog," Ella said, grateful that there was only one of him to bathe her with a gooey tongue.

"Can I ask you why you just didn't take mug shots over to Naomi?" Victor's question interrupted Ella's mental drift and brought her back to the business at hand. "Seems to me that would have been easier."

"I do have a mug shot book with me, but before Naomi starts to look at hundreds of faces, I'd rather you worked with her. Then it'll still be clear in her mind. Afterward we'll see if we can match the person she saw to a known felon."

Victor nodded. "I've got some ideas on how to jog her memory even more. I'll have her describe this guy by comparing him to people we both know."

"Good idea."

"I'll be able to get a sketch that you can work from, if anyone can. We all want to catch this guy, particularly people like me who live in a secluded place."

"Do you have a phone, or a radio?" Ella asked.

"I've got a CB radio setup, and I've also got a cellular. And I've got TD. If anything approaches, he lets me know in plenty of time."

"He sleeps inside or out?"

"Outside, right on the porch, so he can watch the sheep and me."

"Good. If you ever sense trouble, you give us a call immediately. We'll handle it."

"I think you mean what's left of him after TD gets his teeth into him," he chuckled. "He's not nice to strangers who come up unannounced. And my shotgun is even more unfriendly."

Ella felt that funny tightening in her stomach. "You know how to use it, and practice with it often?"

"I've been around rifles and shotguns since I was seven. I usually hit what I aim for, whether it's a rabbit or wild turkey. If I couldn't, I'd have grown awful tired of mutton stew by now."

"Just be careful what you shoot, please?" Ella asked.

"I always am," he answered, then lapsed into silence.

Ella wondered if she'd offended him, but the thought of people, ordinary citizens, so ready for an armed response made her jittery. Unfortunately, there was nothing she could do to stop them until the case was closed, and that might not be any time soon.

FIFTEEN

——— ✖ ✖ ✖ ———

Ella sat near the door of the hogan, hoping a breeze would stir. The skies had turned into a maze of gray clouds that were ripped every few seconds by bright flashes of lightning. Thunder in the distance rumbled constantly, like distant artillery, and the increased humidity made the air feel sticky. Yet, despite all that, no rain appeared. Although the land was dry and rain was needed, Ella hoped it would hold off a while longer. If it didn't, she had a feeling getting Victor back to his home today would be all but impossible.

Ella watched quietly as Victor prodded Naomi's memory with all the finesse of the best police artists she'd worked with. He sketched with painstaking attention to detail, erasing and modifying any feature Naomi felt wasn't quite right. Although Ella still hadn't looked at their sketch for fear of interrupting Naomi's train of thought, she could sense that a clear impression would be the result.

Ella stood up and joined Justine just outside the hogan doorway. "Do you think it's another false alarm, or will the rain really get to the ground this time?" Ella asked quietly, smelling the ozone in the air.

"It'll rain, and it'll come down in sheets. Let's just hope it's after we take Victor home."

"If not, the department can put him up at a motel, or take him to a relative's house."

Ella heard movement inside the hogan and turned to look around. Naomi held the sketch Victor had drawn. "This is just like I remember him." She waved at Ella to come back inside. "Take a look."

Naomi placed it on top of the CB Ella knew Officer Neskahi had brought. Naomi had said nothing about it so far, and to avoid distracting her from the task at hand, neither had Ella.

Ella studied the sketch of the shaggy-haired man and the stringy, ineffective beard. It was no one she knew, but the sketch was detailed enough to work with. She glanced at Justine, who was looking at the drawing too.

"Not too many Navajos try to grow a beard, and you can see why." Justine shrugged. "If I've seen him before, I can't place him."

"Now we can look at all those pictures you brought," Naomi said.

Ella nodded to Justine, who produced several thick volumes. "I'm going to drive Victor back home while Justine takes you through these, then I'll come back," Ella said.

Victor picked up his things. "Good idea. Once it rains I'll have to hike in, and that can take a long time. Normally it wouldn't matter, but the sheep may need tending in the storm and I have some sketches I have to finish by the end of the day tomorrow. I really don't want to lose time walking back home from the main highway."

"I'm curious," Ella said as they walked to the car. "How do you get by when you're snowed in and you have to get something to the paper?"

Victor shrugged. "They send someone to the turnoff, and I hike out there. As long as I have enough time, I can usually meet them. It's not that big a hassle."

As Ella drove Victor home, she decided to bring up the possibility of keeping him on call for the department. "Would you be willing to work with us again, if the need arose?"

"No problem."

"We'll pay you a fee comparable to what you get at the paper. I'll make sure of it."

"Yeah, but this time I did it as a favor to Justine, okay? She tutored me in high school when I was a freshman and sophomore. I don't think I could have passed my math or science classes without her help. She didn't get paid for it either; it was all volunteer work through the Honor Society."

"So you're even now. But if there is a next time, you'll be paid, okay?"

"Sounds good to me. I can always use some more money for supplies and things. I've been saving up, hoping to get a phone line in. Then I could fax my 'toons on bad weather days."

"Then it's settled."

As Ella reached his turnoff, she noted that the clouds had begun to dissipate, once again without rain. "I can take you all the way up to the arroyo."

"That's great."

As they drove on, Ella glanced around. There wasn't another sign of civilization in sight. "Do you ever miss living in Shiprock?"

Victor shook his head. "Here, I have my animals, and TD can run around all he wants." He unbuckled his seat belt as she stopped by the dry wash. "The only noisy neighbor is an occasional bleating lamb." He opened the passenger's door and got out. "See you around."

Ella watched him hurry across the sandy arroyo. She remembered life in the various cities where she had worked with the FBI. Although people had been all around her, she'd never felt more lonely than she had during those days. She'd drowned herself in her work as a way to avoid the loneliness. Even if she'd lived out here by herself, with only the mesas as neighbors, she'd never suffer from the isolation she'd felt back then. The Colorado Plateau, as inhospitable as it seemed at times, was home.

As Ella returned to the highway, she used her cellular to call Clifford. She wanted to show him Victor's sketch as soon as possible.

Loretta answered the phone. "He's not here, but if you need him right away, go to where the Singer's body was found."

"Of course," Ella muttered. She should have known her brother would have been asked to purify ground that had been tainted by death.

Ella glanced at her watch, then had the dispatcher relay a message to Justine on the CB they'd provided for Naomi. She was going to be delayed a bit.

Ella drove uphill to the volcanic dike south of Shiprock, then parked on the dirt road and proceeded on foot toward the shrine. Her brother would be somewhere up ahead, and she didn't want to disturb any Blessing rite he might have started.

She found him several moments later, laying out a dry painting that he would use after sundown. He glanced up, hearing her, and gave her a thin smile. "What brings you here? This land is not yet purified."

"Have I disturbed you?"

"No, I'm just getting things ready for tonight. I'll begin then."

She took out Victor's sketch and showed it to him. "Do you recognize this man?"

He studied it for a long time. "I don't know this person. But he looks young. Is this the killer?"

"Possibly. At this point I have no clear answers. The trail on this case leads in conflicting directions."

"Yes, I'm aware that one of the killings points to skinwalkers, and the other to a Singer." He stared off in the direction of the Carrizo mountains to the northwest. "I've been giving this some thought. This could certainly be the work of one of Peterson's skinwalkers. They specialize in misleading others."

"I realize that too. That's why I haven't neglected that angle. Peterson would know all about criminal profiling, and the evaluation of evidence. If he's behind this, even remotely, he'd make sure we were getting conflicting signals. Thinking he's outsmarting us would appeal to his ego."

"Have you noticed, too, that the ones killed are the people most likely to know how to combat Navajo witches?"

"Yes, they were both experts in our culture," Ella said. She gazed downhill toward the San Juan valley, where the town of Shiprock lay. "The killer is close by, I can feel it. He's within my reach, if only I can identify him."

"Keep trusting your gift, little sister. It will never lead you astray, no matter how confusing the evidence may get."

"All cops rely on instinct. Since mine, as you know, is extremely sharp, I'd be a fool not to trust it," she answered softly.

He nodded in approval. "Maybe you're finally ready to accept a little present I've been keeping for you, just waiting for the right time."

Ella looked at Clifford quizzically. "Now you've got me curious."

He reached inside the medicine pouch attached to his belt. "This was given to me years ago by a medicine man from another tribe. I want you to have it now. It's a hunting fetish that will heighten your awareness."

Ella expected a mountain lion, or perhaps a sharp-eyed eagle. She stared at the small carving in her brother's palm, puzzled. "I'm not sure I know what it is," Ella said, taking it and studying it more closely.

"It's a badger. The powers associated with the animal the fetish represents are magnified in the human who 'feeds' and cares for it. Badgers are skillful fighters, and generally give an account of themselves all out of proportion to their size. The qualities associated with a badger, and those who carry its fetish, are courage, tenacity, and self-confidence."

Ella grinned. "Badgers are phenomenal diggers too. Maybe that'll work hand in paw with the cop in me."

Clifford shook his head. "No, don't joke about it. It's a gift that can be very special, if you let it be."

"It already is, because you gave it to me. I'll carry it with me always," Ella said, placing it in her jacket pocket.

"Find answers soon," he warned. "I don't like the way fear is spreading among our people. And if the pattern continues, those who can carry on our ways will soon disappear. Then our people will be as helpless as they were during the Civil War, when we were prisoners at Bosque Redondo. Evil will have claimed a victory over us. This time, however, the damage will be permanent. We may end up losing all our culture. We have very few left who know the old ways."

She nodded slowly. "I'm aware of *all* the dangers, including those that come from moving too fast."

"Do you want me to go with you next time you see Peterson? I may be able to spot something, an inconsistency, a trick, that you may not see."

Ella considered his offer. "No. I don't want to pull any surprises on him just yet. He underestimates me, and as long as he does, that gives me an advantage."

Clifford shrugged. "My presence would put him on his guard instantly, that's true enough," he agreed. "He and I have too much past history of fighting each other." He pursed his lips and gazed at her thoughtfully. "But, then again, so have you. Do you realize that?"

"Yes, but Peterson still sees me as your little sister. He thinks of me as a threat, sure, but a manageable one."

"Then that is his weakness, and the only card you'll have against him. But it won't last. Each little victory you have will make him wiser."

"I'm aware of that," Ella admitted.

"If he is involved, do you think the victims are ones he's chosen?" Clifford asked.

"I don't think so. If they were, then you would have been the first to die, brother."

"You're absolutely right about that. Peterson wouldn't have passed up a chance, and no one has threatened me in any way."

"I will catch whoever's committing these murders but, in the meantime, watch after Loretta and yourself, okay? I think you are in danger from the one who killed the others."

Leaving Clifford to finish his ritual preparations, she walked down to where she'd parked. A vague uneasiness kept her alert. She made a visual search of the immediate area, but nothing seemed out of place. Slipping behind the wheel, she attuned herself to that special sixth sense that had kept her in one piece throughout the years. Slowly she forced herself to relax. No, she wasn't in any immediate danger here, nor was her brother. Her restlessness was too unfocused, more a feeling of impending danger than an imminent one.

Hating the annoying, spine-chilling sensation that seemed to have become her familiar companion, she started the engine and put the car in gear. It was time to pick up Justine.

Ella finally arrived back at Naomi Zah's late in the afternoon. She'd had precious little to eat, and her stomach growled in protest. As she stopped in front of the hogan, Justine stepped out of the six-sided log structure. She had the mug books in hand, and looked tired as she came to the car.

"What happened?" Ella asked, getting out and tossing the keys to Justine.

"Naomi's gone. Her nephew came by on horseback, ponying a mare. They left together. Her sister isn't feeling well. The nephew asked Naomi to come tell her what's wrong so a Singer can do the appropriate Sing. Naomi said that she'd be back tonight. We'll have to bring the mug books back then so she can finish looking them over."

"All right. In the meantime you and I have work. It's past time for a strategy meeting. We can do that during the drive back."

Ella organized her thoughts as Justine headed for the highway. "Why do you think the first two victims were targeted?" she asked.

"They had great expertise; we already decided that."

Ella shook her head. "No, I mean why those particular men? There are others."

"He probably decided to pick at random from those who fit his criteria. My guess is those were the most available."

Ella considered it. "Plausible theory. The first murder gave the killer all possible advantage. His victim had no reason to expect trouble. The next target he selected was one who'd been aware of the first killing, but felt his capabilities would be more than a match for the perp. His overconfidence gave the killer the advantage again."

"Agreed."

"Now, let's analyze the style of murder, not the method. In both cases the victim was incapacitated first, *then* killed. During the last few minutes of the victim's life, the murderer is in full control."

"Are you saying that's his signature? His need to have the victims helpless before he finishes them?"

"That and the bone. If I'm correct about this, no matter how he changes his M.O., that signature will remain the same in future victims. And with this individual, there *will* be more victims until we put a stop to him."

Ella thought for a moment, then continued. "So let's see what else we can put together about this guy. He's into power—power over his victims at least. He wants total control before finalizing the kill. He strikes very early in the morning, so he could have a job he has to go to later, or maybe a class. I'd be willing to bet, since he knows the victims' schedules, he's watched them for a while before attacking. I think he would enjoy the power of knowing who the next to die is, and that it's all in his hands. He's probably thrilled that so many people are afraid now."

Justine shuddered. "Great. We've got a sociopath who gets off on having the power over life and death. He's so proud of himself he even collects trophies."

"Let's review our physical profile of the killer. He's male, young, and relatively strong; we saw that from the strangulation of Dodge. The neck was nearly severed by the leather shoelace. But he's not an overpowering guy. He used a club to knock out the first victim, and a car on the Singer, who was bigger and stronger. He's almost certainly Navajo, or would pass for one. Anglos still are easily noticed and remembered around here. He fits the category of an organized killer, so right there, we know even more things about him."

"Like what? I'm not really up on this behavioral science stuff. I've been trained to examine mostly physical evidence."

"The organized offender likes the hunt. He's predatory. His background will often show that as a kid he was truant from school, and he stocked up an impressive list of suspensions. He lives by the code that rules are meant to be broken, and he'll have spent time coming up with ways to get away with as much as possible."

"That describes a lot of kids nowadays, even around here."

"That's true, but the rest of the pattern will help narrow down the search. As an adult he probably has had trouble keeping a job. He also has a really tough time taking criticism. He won't have a steady girlfriend, unless he feels he's in total control of her. But the one glaring trait that will mark who and what he is will also make him harder to catch. This guy's going to be a chronic liar, and accomplished at it. He'll also be incapable of feeling guilt, so he'd probably be able to beat a lie-detector test."

"Just talking about this guy gives me the creeps," Justine admitted. "It could be anyone. He's hiding behind a mask, and that means he's got an incredible chance to study his victims in perfect safety."

"Power. He craves it. And if he's a skinwalker wannabe, that whole scene feeds his fantasies. The powerful Navajo Wolf. He stalks, he kills. But he stays in the shadows. He likes the thrill of that on-the-edge existence."

"I think he's playing a game with us by doing things like, leaving the ash painting and the medicine pouch."

"He's testing us, and himself," Ella answered.

Ella had Justine pull into the diner a few miles from the station, and they ordered a couple of sandwiches to go. "I don't want to take a formal dinner break, but you look as if you need something to eat as badly as I do."

Justine agreed, "I'm famished."

As the women ate chicken sandwiches in the car, Justine drove them on to the station.

"How's the search for evidence coming along?" Ella asked as they continued down the highway. "Anything new?"

"I've checked everywhere, from car washes to dealerships, searching for the car that struck the Singer. Nobody's come in with a vehicle showing front-end damage that would be consistent with having struck down a man. I even checked the car washes thinking that, at the very least, the killer would want to make sure he removed all traces of blood."

"He may have taken care of that with a hose at his home."

"True."

Ella waited until Justine parked, then handed her the folder with Victor's sketch. "Make as many copies of this as possible, and circulate them among law enforcement personnel only. I want everyone on the lookout, but I don't want the suspect to know we have an idea what he looks like. He might decide to change his appearance, if he hasn't already." Ella left Justine's vehicle and walked to her own. "I'll see you tomorrow."

"What are you going to be doing?"

"While you're working on the evidence here, I'm going back to Naomi Zah's to wait for her."

Justine nodded. "Okay, boss. I think I'll start by checking to see if there's been a fax from the bureau."

Ella pulled back out onto the highway. She was tired, but she had to go back to Naomi's if there was even the remotest chance of the stargazer identifying one of the mug shots. She picked up the mike and asked the dispatcher to raise Officer Neskahi and have him meet her on TAC two on the radio. A moment later, her mike came alive with a voice breaking through the static.

"This is 143 to Unit calling. Go."

Ella depressed the button to transmit and identified herself. "How did it go when you delivered the CB to Naomi Zah? Is she at ease with it?"

"No, not really. While I was trying to teach her how to use it, she hung back, as if she wasn't sure which of us she distrusted most, me or the CB."

Ella swallowed an oath. "As long as you taught her how to use it, she'll reach for it if there's an emergency."

Ella pulled up in front of the hogan an hour later. It was pitch black outside, but at least the moon was starting to come out from behind the clouds.

Naomi came to the entrance and waved at her, inviting her

to come inside. The soft flicker of a kerosene-powered lamp glowed from within.

Ella gathered the mug shot books and went inside. The light was brighter there, but it was still dimmer than she would have preferred. "Can you see those photos clearly? Maybe I can drive you to a café or something."

Naomi laughed. "I can see just fine. If you're hungry, I can heat up some stew and you can have a can of peaches."

"No, I'm okay. I'd rather have you look through these books than fuss over me."

Time seemed to drag as Naomi turned page after page, carefully examining each photo. "None of these faces look right."

"Are you sure?"

"Yes, I am," Naomi said, leafing through the last of the thick volumes.

Ella stood up and stretched her cramped knees. She walked to the doorway and peered out. The moon was bright, and the clouds, at least for now, were gone. The dry plateau looked as if it had been painted in a variety of blue grays.

Naomi Zah was watching her as she turned around. "I could try to use my crystal again. Maybe I'll get something this time that can help you." The old woman picked up a small pouch and pulled out a quartz crystal. "Would you accept this type of help?"

"I'll be grateful for anything that points me in the right direction," Ella said, wondering if perhaps Naomi needed that to jog her own memory. Cursing herself for not having thought of it sooner, she gave Naomi an encouraging smile. "Please try."

"Sometimes it takes a while," Naomi warned, "and sometimes it doesn't happen at all."

"That's okay. Time is not important."

Naomi regarded her for a long moment. "You're restless, though. I don't think I can do this around you. I'll go outside and stand under the stars behind the hogan. Don't interrupt me."

"I won't. I'll be close by though, okay?"

Naomi walked outside and stood facing west, the crystal in her palm. She stared into it as if mesmerized.

Ella watched for several long moments, but Naomi seemed oblivious to everything around her. Ella listened to the chirping of the cicadas, their rhythmic, familiar sound soothing her nerves.

As Ella waited, a flicker of movement to her left caught her eye. She turned her head, studying the area. A shadow was moving between the brambles, heading slowly toward the mesa behind the hogan.

Ella slipped forward far enough out of the glow coming from the hogan's entrance to lose her silhouette. Someone had been watching them! Tension coiled inside her as she realized whoever was there was probably up to no good. There was no reason for hiding, otherwise.

She glanced back at Naomi. As long as the stargazer was concentrating solely on the crystal, she was vulnerable. She did have one thing in her favor, however. In the faint evening light, dressed in earth tones, she would make a difficult target to all but a marksman.

Ella hesitated, not wanting to interrupt Naomi and knowing there was no way to avoid it. Ella approached her and tried not to cringe when Naomi glared at her. "Go back inside the hogan," Ella warned in a whisper, "and wait there with your shotgun. Someone's out here, watching us, and I'm going to find out who it is. I'll whistle when I come back." She saw the expression on Naomi's face change from annoyance to fear. "We'll be okay," Ella assured her.

Ella crept away from the hogan, listening as she went. She suddenly had the feeling she was being led into a trap. He was waiting for her. Ella slowed her progress and listened. It was hard to disguise all sound in a rocky terrain filled with stunted junipers. He was bound to give his position away if she was patient. Scarcely breathing, she remained still. Several seconds elapsed, then she caught a soft padding sound, like someone moving in moccasins or sneakers farther ahead.

Ella continued in the direction of the sound. The route up the low mesa was steep, crisscrossed with narrow gullies that seemed to slice portions out of the mesa itself. Ella was almost all the way to the top when she glanced back toward the hogan.

For a terrifying second she considered the possibility that she'd been led away on purpose.

Ella stepped closer to the sloped edge of the mesa, trying to get a clear view of the ground below. Suddenly an arm snaked out from behind a cluster of thorny brush and pushed her forward, hard. Her feet slid on the rocky footing, and she slipped off the edge, sliding several feet down the cliff face. Ella grasped desperately at the rocks and dirt, slowing her descent as she twisted her lower body toward a narrow ledge.

She fell hard onto the tiny shelf a second later. Hip throbbing, she rolled to a sitting position, pressing her back to the wall. There was no room to stand. To make matters worse, the cliff overhung just enough so she couldn't see the top of the mesa anymore. Ella shifted, assessing her situation and trying not to panic.

Then she felt a vibration above her. The overhang consisted of a large chunk of sandstone, but someone was jumping up and down on it, hoping to dislodge it. If it fell, she'd probably either be crushed beneath the rubble or knocked off the ledge by a two-ton rock. Either way, her chances for survival were slim.

She heard her attacker's labored breathing as he continued to stomp on the overhang. Then he stopped jumping and began scraping at the rock, grunting mightily. She heard the sound of wood creaking, and finally breaking with a loud snap. She realized he was trying to use some form of a pry to force the rock apart. She fought the desperate urge to reach for her gun and fire upward, but the odds of the bullet hitting a rock and ricocheting back on her were too great.

Then abruptly, it was silent, except for the sound of her attacker's labored breath. Ella remained still, waiting to see what his next move would be. If he tried to climb down for her, he'd find himself face-to-face with her nine millimeter, with his back to the sky.

Ella waited. At long last, she heard soft running footsteps. She took several deep breaths. She had to get out of here, for her sake and Naomi's. Ella crawled to the edge of the rock shelf, heart pounding, and reached up. Twice she pulled back, her balance precarious and courage failing her. Finally she managed to gain a handhold and pulled herself up the jagged cliff face. Minutes later, Ella scrambled over the overhang to the mesa's summit, then quickly rolled behind cover.

Tumbleweed branches tore into her long-sleeved blouse, scratching her arms until they drew blood. It hurt, but she consoled herself with the thought that if the vicious plant had drawn her blood, it might have taken a bit of her attacker's flesh or sleeve too. A blood or fabric sample would add pieces to the puzzle that would eventually send him to jail.

Hearing loud, running footsteps moving down the side of the mesa facing away from the hogan, Ella shot forward in pursuit. She scrambled down the west side of the rocky hill, using the boulders for cover until she reached the bottom of the mesa. The figure ahead was barely a shadow that flitted among the pines and scrub brush.

Ella raced gamely after him, but he had quite a head start. Trying to increase her own speed in the dark, she tripped on a root. She went tumbling shoulder first into a clump of sagebrush before she could come to a stop. As she scrambled to her feet, she heard the sound of a vehicle speeding off.

Ella rubbed her shoulder, anger spiraling through her. At least it hadn't been a total failure. If her attacker was the killer, she would now have a good chance of finding tire prints, footprints, and possibly a sample of blood and fabric.

Of course that was a mighty big "if." But it was about time for the tide of events to change. She touched the badger fetish still in her back pocket. Maybe it already had.

SIXTEEN

✖ ✖ ✖

Ella remembered to whistle as she returned to the hogan. It was a good thing, because Naomi was standing just inside the doorway with the shotgun cradled in her arms. Her face was unmarred by worry lines, however. If anything, there seemed to be an air of acceptance about her.

"It was him," she said calmly. "He came back to complete the job he started. Only he's discovering that this old woman isn't the easy target he expected." She patted the shotgun like it was a faithful dog.

"Did you see him when he came down off the mesa, or maybe catch a glimpse of his car?"

"No. But it was him." Naomi's voice was strangely without anger. It was the same tone one might expect from someone simply stating a fact.

Ella stared at Naomi, wondering how she could remain so cool about it. "I wish I had caught him. I would have enjoyed putting my handcuffs on this guy."

Ella used the radio in her unit to call in a report. Though she really hadn't seen enough to afford any leads, she still had some usable information. She also requested that roadblocks be set up immediately in both directions down the highway and kept in place for at least eight hours, providing manpower was available.

She then asked officers to look for anyone resembling the suspect Victor had sketched. She also asked them to take down the names and license numbers of all the men between the ages of eighteen and thirty who passed through the roadblock.

Ella turned and noticed Naomi had come over to join her. "So now he also wants you dead," Naomi said. "You've stopped him from doing what he wanted and he won't forgive you for that." Naomi handed her a dampened washcloth to clean up her scratches.

"His wishes don't concern me in the slightest," Ella said, then smiled. "It's my job to stop him, and I guarantee you, I will."

"I'm sure you will. Everyone knows you're very special."

Ella resisted the urge to sigh and instead focused on wiping the traces of blood and dirt from where her skin had been rubbed raw. It was difficult to accept the People's view of her. She wanted to be known as an excellent cop, not a pseudo-magician. "My mother thinks so," she joked halfheartedly, handing the washcloth back to the old woman.

Naomi shook her head. "You shouldn't make jokes about this."

"Sometimes I have to," Ella replied softly, then shifted her focus to the radio as Big Ed was patched through.

After she finished bringing her boss up to date, she turned back to Naomi. "There'll be a crime scene unit coming by. Justine will be coming too. We may be able to get some information from the land itself."

Naomi shook her head. "Not unless they hurry. Can you smell and feel the moisture in the air? It's going to rain hard soon."

Ella suspected Naomi was right, but she also knew that it was possible it would rain in torrents half a mile away, yet remain dry here. That was often the case in the desert. Clinging to that hope, Ella accompanied Naomi back inside the hogan. "Do you remember how to use the CB?"

Naomi nodded once. "But it won't do any good. If I'm in danger, by the time anyone can respond, it will be too late. I have to continue taking care of myself."

"Can you go away for a while, stay with relatives?"

"I'm waiting for my husband, Raymond, to return."

"How long has he been gone?"

"Six days, but that's his way. He'll be back soon enough. Then we'll leave."

"Do you want me to see if one of our officers can locate him for you?"

Naomi considered it. "No. He'll be back when he's ready. It's better that way."

Ella heard the gusts of wind swirling outside. "I'm going to go back uphill. Maybe I can collect some evidence and preserve it against the weather. Stay here, and keep your shotgun handy, okay?"

Naomi shook her head, concern written on her face. "It isn't wise to go up there when there's going to be lightning."

"There isn't any—" A thundering fork of energy suddenly illuminated the entire mesa like a nuclear strobe light, and two seconds later the ground shook with the shock of expanding air. "Well, there wasn't until now," she conceded with a smile. "But no matter. I still have to go up there. I've got to do what I can to protect the crime scene."

Stopping long to pick up a flashlight and some evidence pouches from her car, Ella hurried up onto the mesa. The winds that usually preceded rain were gusting strong now. She ran toward the bramble that had snagged her clothing. Cutting away several branches that had some cloth fibers and perhaps traces of blood, she quickly placed them inside an evidence pouch.

Ella then hurried downhill to the area where she'd heard the vehicle. Ella studied the tire tracks, quickly stepping off the distance between imprints to determine the wheelbase of the vehicle. From this information, she concluded her assailant had driven a small sedan rather than a pickup. She made a quick sketch of a tire tread pattern, then found a good footprint. It was a Nike cross-trainer. That observation alone made her heart beat faster, and she hoped the guy would try and pass through the roadblocks. Even if he was waved through, she'd still have his name on a list.

Suddenly the skies seemed to open up and sheets of rain began pouring down on her. There was nothing she could do except move fast. The dry wash where the suspect's vehicle had been parked wasn't going to be dry much longer. She scrambled out of the way just as water began to flow down from around the bend in the canyon. Soon it would be ankle deep or higher.

Taking the evidence pouch and holding it close against her, she raced back to the car. The pouch was soaked, and so was she by the time she dove inside her vehicle, but at least she'd preserved the cloth fibers. If the brush had snagged his clothing, or scraped him as it had her, she'd have one more piece of evidence to use against him.

Ella saw the downpour begin to saturate the sand around her vehicle. If she didn't move her car soon, she could be stuck here all night. She drove to the higher ground beside the hogan. As soon as she parked, Ella called in a warning about the weather to the others who were on the way, telling those officers at the roadblocks to watch for a man wearing Nike cross-trainers.

Duty finished, Ella racked the mike. The downpour was making it impossible for her to see more than a foot beyond the windshield. With a resigned sigh, she left the vehicle and raced back to the hogan.

Naomi was sitting inside, a blanket wrapped around her shoulders. She had a small fire going in the little woodstove, and the hogan was cozy. "He won't be back right away. I think your presence surprised him."

"I wish you wouldn't insist on staying out here alone. You should come with me now and leave a note for your husband. Ask him to contact me, and I'll let him know where to meet you."

Naomi shook her head. "I'll wait. My husband is in no danger from this man."

Ella blinked. She also didn't believe that the stargazer's husband was in danger from the killer—it didn't fit the profile—but Naomi's accurate conclusion took her by surprise. "You saw *that* in the crystal?"

The woman smiled, then shook her head. "I know the other two who were killed. We helped the *Dineh* with our own special knowledge. Poor Raymond's only specialty is the bottle."

Ella studied the woman's expression. For the first time she realized just how badly she'd underestimated Naomi. Her abilities went far beyond the services she provided to the tribe.

Ella joined the crime-scene unit when they arrived and turned over the evidence pouch and her sketch. They worked together in the downpour, searching for any remaining scrap of evidence her assailant had left behind. Dedication and tenacity, however, could not compensate for the terrible weather conditions that made any significant discoveries unlikely.

Finally, soaked to the skin, they all met in the van. "If the perp dropped anything," Justine told Ella, "it's buried in a sea of mud. We'll come back out tomorrow and search the area again in daylight, but don't count on us finding much."

As they prepared to leave, Ella left the van and returned to the hogan. She said good-bye to Naomi, amazed at the woman's determination to remain there. "Remember to radio in if you suspect trouble. We'll have a unit patrol the area, just in case."

Naomi's calm smile followed Ella as she returned to her car and headed for the highway. So far the killer had kept the upper hand. Events continued to defy her attempt to reestablish order, but that only challenged her to try even harder. It was part of her nature, part of everything she was, both as a cop and a Navajo.

Ella woke up early the next morning. She'd been exhausted, and had slept almost from the moment her head hit the pillow. Yet after more than eight hours, she still felt weary. Her muscles were sore from yesterday's exertion, but the scratches from the brush had scabbed over. She pulled back the curtains and peered outside. The sun would be up soon. The skies in the east were washed in vivid lavenders and crimsons brought out by the thin layer of atmospheric dust always present in the Southwest.

She dressed slowly, mentally sorting out how she would handle the investigation today, and what she would tell Big Ed.

The roadblocks hadn't resulted in the arrest of a suspect yet. If anyone had been detained, she would have received a call by now. Roadblocks, in Ella's experience, produced results only when the people manning them knew exactly who they were looking for. In this case, her assailant could be waiting somewhere on one of the back roads until the police left. Or it was possible he lived close enough to Naomi's not to have encountered a roadblock at all. By this morning, the roadblocks would be down, and all she'd have would be a list of names to check.

If only she could force the killer into revealing more about himself. Well, maybe the microscope would be able to tell them something about the man's clothing, if the fibers she'd collected belonged to him. So far all she'd confirmed was that the killer and the man who pushed Ella off the ledge both preferred Nike cross-trainers and could be the same person.

By the time she walked into the kitchen, Ella could see her mother outside, offering prayers to the dawn. Releasing a pinch of pollen into the air, she remained still for a moment before returning to the house.

"Good morning," Rose greeted her daughter pleasantly. "I'm glad to see that you're not rushing off today. I wanted to tell you that I invited Wilson Joe to have dinner with us. So what night can I count on your being home?"

"Oh, Mother!" Ella looked away, trying to keep from revealing her impatience. "Wilson and I are good friends. If anything more is going to happen between us, it'll happen naturally. You've got to stop pushing this!"

"He likes you, you like him. You're both Navajo, you're both single. You just don't see each other enough to let nature take its course. You're always too busy with your work. That's why I figured Sunday dinner, if nothing else."

"You know that I'm right in the middle of a case! It's impossible for me to predict when or if I'll be home," Ella protested.

Rose's face was set. "You may pick the day, but I *am* having him over, and you *will* enjoy yourselves."

Ella had heard that tone before. No amount of arguing would do her any good. "I'll see."

Rose went to the stove. "Eggs?"

Ella nodded. "Sure. That'll be fine."

"How are things going with you? Everyone's talking about this killer running around loose."

"I'm getting closer, Mom, but so far luck's been on his side. Sooner or later, though, he'll trip up, and I'm going to be there to catch him."

"You probably know that people are starting to gossip about us again. All the talk about our family bringing trouble."

"Does that bother you? I think there's no way to stop it. The only thing we can do is ride it out, like we did before."

"I'm not worried about myself—"

As the phone began ringing, Ella stood and went to answer it. It was Leroy Johnson at the post office. "What can I do for you, Uncle?"

"I hope you don't mind that I'm calling you at home, but I thought you'd want to know right away. Peterson Yazzie has mailed you a letter. I'm holding it in my hands now. His name and return address are marked clearly on the envelope. That's why I know it's from him. You want it to go out with the regular carrier, or shall I hold on to it?"

"Keep it right there. I'll pick it up in about forty minutes."

"Okay. I'll see you then."

Ella glanced at the eggs her mother was scrambling as she hung up the telephone. Peterson was getting bolder. He didn't care who on the Rez saw his name on the envelope now. "I have to go."

"You'll eat first," Rose said staunchly, adding grated cheese and green chiles to the eggs.

"On the way, then. Just put them in a bowl instead of a plate, and I'll eat in the car."

Rose sighed loudly. "You are an exasperating daughter."

Ella kissed her mother on the cheek. "I know, Mom. I know. What did you expect from a cop?"

Ella picked up the laundry bag she'd put her own work shirt

in for fiber and blood comparison. Justine could exclude them that way when she analyzed the evidence. A moment later she was under way. The highway was nearly deserted so there was no need for her to use the siren or the emergency flasher. The roadblocks she had arranged last night were farther down the highway, so she didn't encounter the one at her end.

Once again, Bruce Cohen hadn't phoned her as they had agreed. She made a mental note to call him later and ask him to explain. She had credited the lawyer with more sense; maybe Peterson had found a way to keep him in line. Either way, she'd call him.

Ella arrived at the post office just as Leroy Johnson was unlocking the lobby doors. He waved as she approached.

"I've got what you came for on my desk in the back. Why don't you come with me?"

Ella followed him inside, then saw he'd placed the letter in one of the sealed plastic bags the post office used for mail that had been damaged in transit.

"Was there a problem with this?" Ella asked, unable to see any damage to the envelope.

"No, but that's what the cops always do on TV when they need to check for fingerprints. I figured I'd help you out."

Ella smiled. "Thanks. I appreciate the effort." There really wasn't much of a worry about fingerprints. She knew who'd written it from the handwriting, and how he'd got it past the staff at the psychiatric facility. But it had been a nice thought on Leroy's part.

"If anything else comes in, I'll let you know."

"Please do."

Ella took the small bag to her car, opened it, and held the envelope up to the light. Assured there was only a note inside and it was safe to open, she tore the envelope carefully.

Ella pulled out Peterson's letter and as she began reading, rage filled her.

You're not aware of how badly you've botched things. Trust me when I tell you that you see only the surface, and it's what lies beneath that will eventually destroy you. Long ago, I offered you the chance to join me and make your dreams come true. Instead of accepting you've turned me into your worst enemy. Sorry I missed you with the bomb in my old T-Bird. But don't get cocky. Eventually, I'll destroy you. I've had a hand in your destiny all along. It's thanks to us that you are who you are today. I know you'll doubt this, so I'll tell you something you don't know. Your husband was killed by a skinwalker. Yes, it's true. How else do you think your father-in-law got his powers?

Ella stared at the words until they seemed to leap out at her. Pain cut through her as she remembered her husband's death. Of course it was just another one of Peterson's lies. Her husband had been killed in an auto accident.

As she turned the letter over, she realized her hands were trembling.

If you still doubt me, why don't you check on your father-in-law's whereabouts the day of the accident? Look at Southern Airways' records, and check for a passenger by the name of Charlie Randall. Your father-in-law was never very imaginative.

Charlie Randall—Randall Clah. It made sense, but it couldn't be. She sat back and slammed her hand against the steering wheel.

No matter how improbable, she'd now have to take the time to follow it up. There was no way she could let this slide. The thought that Peterson had influenced another of the major events in her life made her sick to her stomach.

Ella forced the thought aside. That was precisely what he was trying to do, influence her. He wanted to shatter her concentration on the case and prove her incompetent. She wouldn't give him the satisfaction.

Hearing her call number on the radio, Ella picked up the

mike. Justine was patched through a moment later. "What's going on?" Ella asked.

"Doctor Kring called. Guess what—it seems Yazzie had a visitor, one of the students from the college."

"Who?"

"Betty Lott."

It took her a moment to remember. "Her mother's a nurse at our hospital?"

"Yes, that's the one. It seems that as much as Anna hates traditionalists, Betty is determined to learn all about them."

"Give me an address on her. I want to talk to Betty."

Ella drove directly to a housing community in Shiprock, just on the other side of the new shopping center. Finding the modern tract home, she parked, walked to the front door, and rang the bell. If there was one place she was certain the old ways didn't apply, it was here.

A thin woman in her late forties answered the door. She was wearing jeans and a cotton oxford shirt. "Can I help you?" the woman asked, wiping her hands on a dishtowel that had drawings of ducks all over it.

Ella flashed her badge. "I need to speak with Betty. Is she at home?"

The woman's eyes grew wide. "I'm Anna Lott, her mother. What has she done?"

"She hasn't broken the law," Ella assured the woman quickly. "I just need to get some information from her."

Anna stared at her hard. "What kind of information?"

"I'd rather speak to your daughter first. Is she here?"

A young woman wearing a long, full skirt, a short-sleeved crimson blouse, and fashionable, colorful sandals emerged from the back of the house. A squash blossom necklace hung around her neck. "I'm Betty. Who are you?"

Ella studied the young woman. From her attire, she was neither as traditionalistic as she viewed herself, nor modern. If anything, like so many of their young people, she fell somewhere in the middle. "Can we talk privately?"

"There's nothing you have to say to my daughter that you can't say in front of me," Anna maintained.

Betty turned her head. "I can handle this, Mom. She came to talk to me." Betty pointed to the hallway. "We can talk in my room."

Ella followed the young woman. The tension between mother and daughter was obvious. Justine had been correct in her estimation that the two were at odds over something.

Betty shut the door. "Okay. What do you want?" she asked directly.

"I understand that you've been to see Peterson Yazzie."

She gave Ella a thin smile. "He warned me that you'd find out and come by to hassle me."

"I'm not here to hassle you, just to talk to you. Peterson was at the heart of the trouble that rocked this reservation about a year ago. Now we're facing new problems. I don't want old enemies of the People using this current situation to create even more fear and distrust."

Betty bit her bottom lip. "All I did was go up there to talk to him. I'm doing a psych paper, and they let me talk to him through the door. I wouldn't have been allowed to do *that* if the head nurse hadn't known my mom. Yazzie has already admitted being a killer *and* a skinwalker. I figured he'd make an interesting subject."

"Is that all?"

"Well, sure, what did you expect?" Betty shrugged.

"I'm not sure. What did you talk about?"

"Well, before he would answer any questions, he wanted to know more about me. He knew my mom, but not me. So we talked about my interest in the *Dineh*'s history and our culture. He's a fascinating man."

"He's a killer too—you admitted that yourself," Ella said flatly.

Betty looked hesitant. "He explained that. Yazzie believes that our people need power, and to attain that certain sacrifices have to be made. He said he was trying to help everyone."

"Lives aren't an acceptable sacrifice to gain control over others, and that's what it's all about. It's self-serving, not altruistic."

She shook her head. "I understand what you're saying, but to hear him talk—well, everything sounds so reasonable." She looked down at her hands. "He's intriguing, and is very powerful, in a way."

"He's also evil," Ella said gently. "Be careful."

"He said he only acted in self-defense. He claimed that medicine men attacked him because they didn't understand what he was trying to do. He had to defend himself."

"That wasn't the way it really was. Go to the library and read the newspaper accounts of that time," Ella insisted calmly.

"He said you'd say that. But those accounts aren't necessarily accurate, no more than what they sometimes say about you and your brother. Didn't you see that editorial page the other day?"

Ella looked at the girl, surprised to see that she had discounted the allegations in that. Betty prided herself on logic, it seemed, and that was exactly how Peterson would manipulate her. He would twist arguments to fit whatever point he wanted to make.

"Are you going back to see him again?" Ella asked.

"If I need to for my paper. You can't legally stop me."

"He said that too?"

Betty nodded. "I didn't do anything wrong. You can read my paper when it comes out if you want."

"Be warned, then. He's a danger to you, no matter how harmless he seems. He's spent so much time manipulating people, he's a master at it. Worst of all, in some ways, he's come to depend on it."

"He's not manipulating me. I can think for myself. I'm not a kid anymore."

"You're interested in our past, and in things that speak of power. Do something for your paper, and for yourself. Talk to Clifford, my brother. He's the counterpoise to Peterson Yazzie. He also has power, but it hasn't been corrupted."

"He's the Singer, right?"

"Yes, and Clifford helped put Peterson in jail, where he belongs. That, no matter how you look at it, speaks of a power that's greater than any Peterson possesses."

"Peterson said that your family used trickery, but not real power."

Ella felt anger welling inside her. How dare Peterson accuse her family of what he was guilty of himself! "You must be awfully naive," Ella baited her.

Betty's eyes flashed with anger. "I'm *not* naive. I research things before I decide what to believe."

"That's all I was trying to get you to do."

Betty sat back. "What is that, reverse psychology?"

"No, just the truth," Ella answered, feeling a twinge of guilt. "To take *one* person's word for anything is to shortchange yourself. You know that. I'm asking you to do what you would have done anyway. Confirm your information."

Betty nodded. "Okay, I'll go see the Singer, just as soon as I have time."

Ella stood up, knowing that was the best she was going to get. To push any harder would yield only negative results. "Thanks for talking to me."

Ella opened the bedroom door and practically ran into Betty's mother. Anna's eyes were wide with fear. "What have you done?" she whispered as she walked Ella to the door.

"Tried to get your daughter to start thinking again. She's being brainwashed," Ella answered softly. "The problem started when she went to visit Yazzie."

Anna stepped outside with Ella. "I don't understand this. To even go talk to a man who took so many lives and did incalculable harm to the tribe is just crazy! I can't figure out what Betty is trying to accomplish with this."

"I think she's testing herself, but if you stand in her way now, you may push her in precisely the direction you don't want her to go."

Lines of tension framed Anna's face. "And if I do nothing, that may happen anyway."

"Yes," Ella admitted. "But there's a time when you have to let go and trust that grown children will choose the right paths. There's nothing much you can do to influence her now. Anything you do might backfire."

"Will your brother help her see that man for what he really is?"

"I hope so." Ella forced a thin smile. "I've done all I can. If you need me, or just want to talk, call me. The dispatcher will find me, day or night."

As Ella drove to the station, she tried to figure out a way to keep Peterson from influencing anyone else the way he had Betty. If more kids were allowed to interview him, there was no telling the problems he'd create. She had to put a stop to that even if it took a court order to do it.

As Ella walked through the side doors, Justine came out of her lab and greeted her. "Dispatch got a call from Officer Neskahi. He met Naomi Zah and her husband on the highway. They're going to be at her sister's for a while. And I checked for blood on the brush you collected. Sorry to say that if it was ever there, it isn't anymore. I found several threads, however. They're from a blue cotton chambray work shirt, but any closer analysis will have to wait for the state lab. I don't have the equipment here."

Ella winced. "Chambray shirt? I was wearing that. I meant to bring in a sample sooner. Sorry. I'll get it right now. It's still behind the driver's seat of my car."

"I'll go get it. Then I'll see if it's a match using my own equipment here. It won't be one hundred percent accurate but it'll give us a high degree of probability."

"Okay." Ella handed her the car keys. "I'll be in my office," she said, continuing down the hall.

Ella fished the office keys from the bottom of her purse, unlocked the door, and walked to her desk. No matter how hard she tried to concentrate on the case, her mind continually drifted to that other matter. She needed to check out what Peterson had told her about her father-in-law. She had to prove, if only to herself, that this time Peterson was lying.

Ella picked up the telephone and checked with the airline. As she waited, the thought occurred to her that she was being manipulated just like Betty. Peterson had found her Achilles heel. Eugene's death had devastated her. Since that time, she'd needed to feel in control of herself and her life. By taunting her with this information, Peterson was trying to strip her of that control, which she'd worked so hard to achieve. Clifford had been right in warning her of Yazzie's strategy.

After transferring her repeatedly, the airline finally promised Ella a quick callback. In the meantime, she accessed old records and checked on Randall Clah's whereabouts for that day. The data made her stomach hurt. He'd been away for two days, using some accumulated time off.

Ella paced in her office, hoping the telephone would ring soon. Eugene had been a good man. He'd tried his best to please her, and he'd idolized his father. Surely Peterson couldn't be right.

Fifteen minutes later, the telephone rang. "We did have a passenger by that name registered on the day you requested. He flew from Albuquerque to Columbus, Georgia, with several connecting flights. He returned the following day."

Ella's hands began to shake. Had the skinwalkers truly held the power of life and death over the man closest to her? The implications sent a bolt of fear slamming into her. How much influence could they still exert over those in her life? Fear for her mother and her brother shattered her confidence.

Ella walked directly to Big Ed's office and placed the letter she'd received before him. "I got this a few hours ago."

Big Ed glanced at it, then up at her. "This has nothing to do with the case you're working on."

"It might. There are other players in this who are still at large. If Yazzie wants me to know this now, he must have a reason."

"Yes, he wants to distract you from the investigation. Deep down you know that. You're getting so close now—yesterday you almost got yourself killed."

Ella ran a hand through her hair. "I know what you're saying, and we will catch the killer soon, I hope. But if it's true what

Peterson says about my husband's death, they've affected my entire destiny. I have to know."

"And if it *is* true, what then?"

"I'll find a way to deal with it, but not knowing will gnaw at me until it drives me crazy."

"I can't afford to use department money to send you on a wild-goose chase all the way to Columbus, Georgia."

"I'll pay for the trip myself."

"You've got two days. Try to take less. We need to catch a killer here. I'll call the department in Columbus and ask them to cooperate. I have no official jurisdiction, but it's a courtesy that I think they'll observe."

"Thanks, I really appreciate this."

Big Ed tossed her a set of keys. "Your Jeep's ready, parked behind the station. It's had the tires, windshield, and several body panels replaced, along with a host of mechanical repairs. Try not to destroy it again soon."

Ella caught the keys in midair. "Thanks. Justine has the keys to the car I've been using. I'll get them from her and turn them in."

Ella went down the hall. Hearing footsteps, Justine came out. "I think the threads came from your shirt, but the state lab will have to tell us for sure."

"The way my luck's running on this, you're probably right." Ella motioned for Justine to follow her. "I need to fill you in."

Pausing to drop off the keys to the loaner unit, Ella continued to her office. Behind closed doors, Ella explained about Betty Lott. "See if there's any legal way to prevent Yazzie from having visitors, except relatives and lawyers."

Justine nodded. "That shouldn't be hard, not when he's claimed responsibility for the murders and the bomb in the trunk."

"I've got to go out of town for a couple of days, so I'm counting on you to take care of that. Go to Big Ed for his influence if you have to."

"But how can you go away at a time like this?"

Seeing the puzzled look on Justine's face, Ella explained.

"*Now* he's manipulating you," Justine concluded.

"I'm aware of that, but I've still got to know."

Justine nodded, accepting Ella's decision. "I would feel the same way in your shoes. Do you want me to get you a seat on the next flight?"

"Yes. Make the arrangements through your computer terminal. That would save me time. The sooner I'm out of here, the sooner I can return." Ella gave Justine her credit card information.

"I'll call you at home to let you know your itinerary. I assume you're on the way back there to pack?"

"You bet. Thanks, Justine."

SEVENTEEN

—— ✖ ✖ ✖ ——

Ella packed her weapon inside her small suitcase. She wasn't traveling in an official capacity, so there was no need to go through the paperwork needed to carry it onboard. She then placed her .22 backup derringer and its holster in a drawer for when she returned.

Rose watched her daughter. "This is a very bad idea. The past is over and done with. Your husband, like mine, is gone. Nothing will bring either of them back."

"If Peterson's claim is true, do you realize how much control the skinwalkers have had over my life? Eugene's death led to my becoming a federal cop, and I'm back on the Rez now because of what the skinwalkers did to my father. It may turn out that they've been manipulating me all my adult life."

"And now you're allowing it to continue. Forget what Peterson said. Go on with what you have to do."

"I can't, Mom. I won't be able to concentrate on this case with this hanging over my head. It'll stay right there in the back of my mind, and keep coming up when I need to think about other things."

"I know you loved your husband, but whatever changes his death made in your life have only been for the good. You found yourself and your strengths after his wind breath left his body."

"Yes, and I'll hold on to that if it does turn out that the Navajo witches were responsible. It's ironic, really. Should this prove to be true, all they've done is create an enemy who has the skill to fight and destroy them." Ella glanced at the hunting fetish her brother had given her and set it next to the blazer she'd wear on the flight. She'd need it now more than ever. "Do you understand why I have to go and find the truth?"

Rose nodded. She was about to say more when the telephone rang. Ella picked it up, thinking it would be Justine with her flight information. Instead a man's voice came over the wire.

"Yes, this is Detective Clah," Ella answered.

"This is James Anderson. I'm an attorney. At this hour, FBI headquarters in Los Angeles is being served with a lawsuit. It's my duty to inform you that you, as an individual, are being sued for Wrongful Death. Copies of the documents will be delivered to your office via courier. My clients, Mr. and Mrs. Joseph Campbell, are the parents of the boy you shot to death in the diner in Los Angeles last August."

"Wrongful death? What are you talking about? That case was investigated by both the local police and the FBI. It was judged to be a righteous shooting. The man had taken hostages, and was methodically shooting them. He even had a bomb, for god's sake!"

"My clients' son was mentally ill, and you lost control of the situation."

The accusation, though from a total stranger, came too close to the reality of the hostage incident in Farmington. The chord it struck made Ella's throat tighten, and for a moment she could scarcely breathe. "The bureau's attorney and a tribal attorney will contact you," she said in clipped tones, then took down his name, address, and number.

"Do it soon, Special Investigator Clah."

Ella slammed the phone down. No law enforcement person ever walked away from a shooting unscathed. There was always a lot of second-guessing and sorrow. But she'd done her best and saved lives in every instance. There was no way anyone could blame her for the psycho's death in Los Angeles, even if she did fire the bullets that took him down. How many more people would he have shot if she hadn't stopped him? Her friend Jeremy had been badly wounded, along with several of the customers at the diner. Campbell had planned to finish them all off; he'd said so at the time. His family had no case at all.

The telephone rang again the moment she set it down. She picked it up wondering if it would be Anderson again, but this time it was Justine. Ella jotted down the flight information. "Thanks, Justine. I need you to do something else for me while I'm gone." She explained the call she'd just received. "Get one of the tribal attorneys to call the L.A. FBI office and find out about this lawsuit. They have no case, trust me." Yet even as she said it, she knew many cops sued by the public had lost to smart lawyers playing on the court's sympathy.

"I'll take care of it," Justine said. "You better get going, or you'll miss your connecting flight to Albuquerque."

Ella was reaching for her suitcase when a strong gust of wind slammed against the side of the house, spiraling in through her open window. "Dust devil," Ella said as the curtains fluttered everywhere, brushing papers and a silk flower arrangement onto the floor.

"*Ssssuu!*" Rose whispered the sound used to tell the ill wind it wasn't welcome.

As Ella started to gather up what had been blown to the floor, her mother crouched next to her. "Go. I'll take care of this."

Ella zipped up her small traveling bag, then put on her pressed blazer. "I'll be back in two days," she said, and rushed out the door.

The flight back east took most of the night, with stops and lay-overs in Albuquerque, Dallas, and Atlanta. It was close to one in the morning when Ella finally arrived at her destination. Tired, she checked into the Columbus airport hotel and asked for a seven o'clock wake-up call.

Morning came quickly, and Ella woke up disoriented, look-ing curiously around for a few seconds before she remembered where she was. Away from home, even in a southern city that moved at a pace close to that of the reservation, she felt curiously homesick. The emotion surprised her. She'd spent years away, with not even a twinge of desire to return. She'd obviously changed a lot in the past few months, more than she'd been aware.

Ella reached into the pocket of the jacket she'd worn on the flight, searching for her fetish. That touch of home would soothe her spirit now. Finding the pocket empty, Ella suddenly remembered the dust devil that had cleared everything from her dresser. In the confusion, she'd mislaid the small carving and left it behind. Regretting the oversight, she reluctantly prepared to begin her day.

Ella showered and dressed, then rented a car. She'd drive to the Columbus police department's downtown station to get whatever details were available from them.

Twenty-five minutes later, she parked next to the building and went inside. Ella identified herself at the front desk, and a red-haired sergeant came up from the back of the room.

"We've been expecting you, Investigator Clah. Your police chief called to ask for our cooperation. I've pulled the file you wanted." He offered Ella a cup of coffee and a chair next to his desk, then handed her a manila folder. "Everything we've got is in there, but it's not much. I noticed the victim and you have the same last name. Was this a relative of yours?"

Ella nodded, and looked the sergeant in the eye. "He was my husband."

"I'm sorry, ma'am, er . . . Investigator."

"That's okay," Ella answered, silently agreeing that the accident report inside the file would probably be practically useless to her.

"Can I get you a doughnut?" the sergeant asked, his voice indicating he was trying to somehow make up for the scanty file.

Ella shook her head and began studying the diagrams of the accident scene. Finally the officer's notes at the bottom caught her eye. "I wasn't aware that there had been a hit-and-run aspect to this."

He glanced at the report. "This happened about fifteen years ago, so I've got to tell you I'm not at all familiar with this case." He studied the notes, then shrugged. "I would assume this is accurate. Your husband ran off the road, and head-on into a tree. According to the medical reports he hadn't been drinking or taking any medication. The investigating officer noted sideswipe marks on his vehicle, but they could have been there prior to the accident. Since there weren't any witnesses, and he wasn't able to track down any other driver, the case was closed."

"Can I talk to the officer who made out this report?"

"Only if you talk really loud," the sergeant joked, then his face suddenly reddened as he realized what he'd said. "He's been dead for about eight years."

Ella glanced back at the report.

"Hey, no offense meant," he added hastily.

"None taken." She jotted down the location where the accident had occurred. "Where exactly is this?"

"About a mile west of the base, Fort Benning. I guess he was on his way there."

"Thanks." Ella shook hands with the sergeant, almost out of practice now. On the reservation, one never touched a stranger.

As Ella walked out, she made up her mind to check at the base. Maybe someone there would remember Eugene or his father. If they'd met unexpectedly just before the accident, Eugene wouldn't have had the chance to tell her about it.

Ella showed her ID at the gate, then waited as her request to enter Fort Benning was processed. Twenty minutes later, at ranger headquarters, she was informed that none of the officers her husband had served under was still stationed there.

As a courtesy, the public information officer offered to take her to her husband's grave. Ella hesitated, then shook her head. Seeing the puzzled look on the young man's face, and knowing that he had been trying to be helpful, she explained. "My people don't view death in the same way yours do. My husband's accomplishments and the man he was have nothing to do with the body in that grave."

He seemed to accept that. "Yes, I understand. In my own religion it's much the same way. We believe the spirit goes on. It's just that we still feel the need to visit the gravesites."

"With us, it's the opposite," Ella said, but didn't elaborate.

Ella left the base thinking it hadn't been a wasted trip. She couldn't prove that her father-in-law had played a part in Eugene's death, but she was nearly certain he had. The name, the lack of originality in it, Randall Clah's absence from the station— all made an impressive circumstantial case.

She wondered if Peterson had known beforehand that she wouldn't be able to prove anything. The thought rankled her, and her hatred for the man grew. Even locked up, he continued to play a part in her life.

Ella returned to her hotel room. It wasn't noon yet, but her mission here had been completed. After checking out, she went straight to the airport. Right now her first priority was to get home and get back to work on the murder case.

While she was waiting for reservation information, Ella checked with her office. The initial news from Justine had set her mind at ease. She had managed to get a court order prohibiting Peterson from having visitors. But there were no new leads to the killer. Ella was sorely needed back on the case.

Ella flew standby, unable to get reservations all the way through. By the time she took her seat on the flight from Dallas to Albuquerque, the tension of an uncertain day had taken its toll. She felt exhausted. Finally however, she was well on her way home. She stared outside, but the skies seemed to be filled with clouds, and it was impossible to find any reference point except the lights on the wings. As the ride became bumpy, Ella reached into her pocket, then remembered the fetish was still back home. Air turbulence. She hated it. Taking the headphones from the back of the seat in front of her, she plugged them in and listened to classical music.

When the flight attendant came by offering coffee, Ella opted for one of the little pillows instead. Maybe she could try to catch up on her sleep. She had at least an hour's flight time ahead of her, then another short hop to Farmington. Ella shifted until she found a comfortable position, then closed her eyes. Soon she felt her body become light as tension washed out of her.

"I hate to bother you, but it's time you and I had a chat," she heard a voice whisper near her ear.

Ella blinked her eyes open, wishing she'd been allowed to go to sleep. Her breath caught in her throat as she recognized the face beside her.

Peterson Yazzie smiled at her. "You didn't really think you could elude me, did you?"

Yazzie sat in the seat beside her, leaning close, his back to the other passengers. His hand, shielded from the view of the others in the cabin, held a gleaming blade.

Ella felt it slice through the skin beneath her rib cage. There was no place to escape. She grabbed his hand, hoping to pull it back, but he was too strong. Pain washed over her in waves, sapping her strength. Soon the blade would find its mark and kill her. The roar of the jet's engines filled her ears. She wondered why the last sound she heard couldn't have been music.

"Enough!" A voice cut through her pain, and she felt a pair of strong hands shaking her by the shoulders.

Ella suddenly opened her eyes wide, her lungs sucking in air. For a moment, nothing registered. Blinking, she stared at the stranger who'd taken the seat next to her. He smiled and let go of her.

"Who are you?" she asked. The handsome, gray-eyed Anglo was definitely not Peterson Yazzie.

"I was sitting across the aisle, and I thought for a moment that you were ill. Then I realized you were having a bad dream. I decided to wake you. I hope I did the right thing."

Ella winced as she touched the spot where she'd felt the lethal jab of the blade. It was sore, as if a sharp object had been jammed into her. She ran her hand around the edge of the seat, wondering if something had poked her and she'd incorporated that into her dream. Yet, despite her thoroughness, she found nothing that would explain it.

Ella suddenly realized that the stranger was watching her curiously. She must have looked like someone whose brain cells constantly misfired.

"A vivid dream, nothing more," Ella said for her own benefit as much as his.

He nodded. "I'm Charles Meles," he said.

Ella noticed the trace of an accent. "Thank you for waking
me," she answered. "My name is Ella. Are you from this part of
the country?"

"No, I'm from a little village south of Paris, France. I'm here
on holiday. I'm on my way to Arizona to see your much-talked-
about Grand Canyon."

"I hope you'll find it as breathtaking as I always have."

Meles smiled. "I'll be close by to awaken you again should
you have another disturbing dream."

Ella watched the gentleman return to his seat across the aisle.
For a moment she couldn't figure out if it had really been just a
vivid dream, or some of Peterson's skinwalker magic at work. A
posthypnotic suggestion, perhaps? She felt angry and tired, and
her side was still sore. At least the turbulence had stopped, and
she wasn't going to be jostled around for a while.

She walked to the restroom at the front of the cabin. There, in
the privacy of that closet-sized enclosure, she lifted her blouse
and checked her side. A bright red mark, like a burn, was just beneath her rib cage. Of course, it meant nothing. She'd somehow
injured her side, or been bitten by an insect, and in her dream
state incorporated that into a jumble of her worst fears. Ella clung
to that explanation, needing the safety of logic, as she returned
to her seat.

Ella had just settled in when the flight attendant came by and
asked if she wanted some coffee. Ella nodded. At least that would
keep her awake. She wouldn't sleep anymore on this journey.

Ella reached the Farmington airport shortly after ten, tired and
sore. Her Jeep was still where she'd left it, and she strolled across
the parking lot, enjoying the breeze. It felt good to be home. The
nighttime air was cool, and she felt comfortable in the low humidity of the desert.

Ella wondered if anything more had happened here during
her long flight. She worried about Betty Lott, and the effects of

Peterson's influence on her. It bothered her to think he would try to corrupt someone so young, someone who was obviously no match for him or his games.

As she parked next to her home, Rose came out to greet Ella. "I'm so glad you're back early."

Ella felt the tension within her tighten. "Has something happened?"

"No," Rose answered. "I just didn't like having you so far from the reservation. It reminded me too much of when you used to live away. I guess I was worried that you would remember too."

Ella picked up her overnight case and glanced at her mother, puzzled. "I don't understand."

"I didn't want you to start missing your old life," Rose explained, walking with Ella to her room.

"Actually, I missed my *new* life," she confessed. "I belong here now. Back there in Georgia all I could think of was the work I left here, waiting."

"Ah, it's not the reservation, but your work."

"They're joined now, part of the larger whole."

Rose nodded slowly and smiled. "Well, you do sound more like one of us with each day that passes."

Ella retrieved her badger fetish from the floor, where it had fallen, and slipped it into her pocket. It belonged with her. She wouldn't leave it behind ever again. Ella watched as her mother picked over the clothing she'd dumped out of her traveling bag, adding the few items to the weekly laundry. It was the time of year when running a washer and dryer was best done in the cool evening hours. In their own ways, they were both compulsive. Rose was meticulous about her home, Ella about her work. They should have understood each other years ago and forged the closeness they now shared.

Sometimes, however, it took the passage of years to bring appreciation of what should have been apparent all along. Ella helped her mother carry the load of whites into the kitchen, where the washing machine and dryer were.

"How's Loretta doing?" Ella asked.

"She's being very careful, and not going out much. She went to the doctor yesterday, and they told her to keep doing what she's doing." Rose placed the clothes into the washer, then gestured toward the calendar. "By the way, Wilson Joe is coming for dinner Sunday. I've already invited him."

Ella looked at her mother. She should have expected this. Her mother was not the type to let the matter drop. "Carolyn could use some friendly company right now too. She has the loneliest job on the Rez. Can I ask her to come?"

Rose hesitated. "Is it important to you?"

"I would like her to come here and feel welcome. I know you've never really liked her, but she's a very nice person."

"Women shouldn't do what she does for a living."

"The same could be said for me," Ella pointed out gently.

"It's not the same thing at all. She's older, and has given up on ever having a family, for whatever reason."

"I don't think Carolyn would agree with you. Besides, she lives her life the best way she knows how. I think it hurts her to have people treating her the way they do."

Rose considered it. "Yes, you may be right about that. She is as isolated as you were when you first came, only with her, it's worse. She never left so she has no friends on the outside either." Rose nodded. "Tomorrow's Saturday. You can call her then."

Ella smiled. She knew she could count on Rose's mothering instinct. She'd never been able to withhold comfort or nurturing when she sensed she was needed. "I'll call her from the office. I have to go in early. I'll let you know if she's coming as soon as possible."

Ella poured herself a glass of her mother's tea, then stretched and yawned. "I'll talk to Justine and Big Ed tomorrow. They'll be glad to hear I didn't need the extra time. But for now, I think I'll go to bed."

"Good night, then, daughter. Sleep well."

Ella had just started back to her room when the telephone rang. Beside it already, she answered it.

Justine's voice came through clearly. "I was hoping you'd be home."

"Is something wrong?"

"You could say that. Peterson Yazzie has escaped."

Ella's mouth fell open, but she gathered herself quickly. "When, and how?"

"He must have had help from the inside. Dr. Kring is questioning his staff now. Peterson's door was kept locked, but it was discovered wide open. I was told that only the head nurse and the guard have keys to the room."

"Where are they now?"

"They found the guard who patrols the ward knocked unconscious, and don't have his story yet. They're still searching for the nurse."

"When did this happen?"

"About two and a half hours ago."

Ella felt the blood drain from her face. Just about the time she'd had that dream on the plane.

After arranging to have officers patroling around her home, Ella hung up, her hands shaking. As she dialed Clifford's number, she gave her mother a quick version of the news. Rose said nothing, but the lines around her face became more pronounced.

"We'll be okay," Ella assured her.

"He *won't* touch us here," Rose said firmly, and left the kitchen.

Ella gave her brother the news, then called Wilson Joe. He, too, was in danger, having played a major role in Peterson's capture. Although she tried hard to convince both men to accept police protection, neither accepted. She replaced the phone, still worried.

Male pride was a difficult thing to combat. In her opinion, it often came at the expense of common sense. This time she hoped keeping their egos intact would not come at a price no one wanted to pay.

Ella was up early the following morning. She took the badger fetish from the nightstand and placed it inside her jacket pocket. She had no appetite this morning, but she couldn't face the day ahead on an empty stomach. She went to the kitchen and quickly ate a bowl of cold cereal. As she finished the last spoonful, she knew she couldn't put off what had to be done any longer. She picked up the phone and dialed the station.

Ella checked first with the watch commander. The manhunt was well under way, and other police agencies were manning roadblocks all over San Juan County. Tribal forces had their roadblocks at reservation access points, and that was stretching the police protection planned for potential victims to the bare minimum.

Ella checked with Big Ed next. A nurse at Hilltop Psychiatric Hospital, a young woman by the name of Isabel Fernandez, had been found. She'd been strangled, stripped of her uniform, her body hidden in a trash can. Ella felt sick to her stomach.

Yazzie had somehow lured the nurse into his room, killed her, and assumed her identity. He'd used her lipstick to help his disguise. The guard apparently noticed the ruse, but was knocked unconscious before he could sound the alarm. With Yazzie's long hair and the low lighting of nighttime hours, plus the nurse's pass card to let him through the electronic locks, he'd managed to reach the main entrance. An unknown woman had arrived to pick Peterson up.

Ella asked Big Ed to send an officer over to Naomi Zah's. This would be a very dangerous time for Naomi and she wanted to make sure the stargazer hadn't decided to remain at her hogan after all. Then she requested that someone be sent to check on the whereabouts of Betty Lott. It was possible she was connected to Yazzie's escape. The girl certainly had given the impression she admired Peterson. Ella hoped she wasn't involved in his escape, but it was worth looking into.

Ella sat, trying to figure out what her next move should be. She saw a rolled-up newspaper on the counter. It was too early for the paper to have any news on Peterson's escape, but she needed to keep current on their coverage of her other cases. Opening it, Ella read the headlines. Security preventing the release of specific details pertaining to the murders had been tightened. The reporter, however, had still managed to learn that the killer had left "undisclosed" items at each murder scene and taken other "undisclosed" items belonging to the victims. The reporter had referred to the murderer as the "packrat killer."

The name would probably stick now, and if her experiences with the bureau were any indication, the nickname would only serve to further publicize the killings. On more than one occasion, this had caused a killer who enjoyed publicity to increase the rate of his crimes. She hoped that wouldn't be the case this time.

By seven-thirty she heard her mother coming back inside the house, and Ella turned the paper facedown on the counter. "Mom, you shouldn't go anywhere alone for a while. You know it's dangerous now."

"I pick my herbs in the morning and keep my eyes and my senses attuned to trouble. No one is going to catch me unawares."

"That's not the point. Anytime you're outside in clear view you've placed yourself in danger. No herbs are worth that."

Rose's eyes flashed with anger, and Ella realized that she should have used more tact. "Wait. Let me take that back. What I'm trying to say is that herbs aren't worth risking your life. Wait until someone can be with you and keep watch."

"My herbs help all of us, including Loretta, who needs them now more than ever with her pregnancy. If someone is around when I need to pick them, fine. If not, it's my duty to perform."

Ella knew this wasn't an argument she'd ever win. "Okay. Just be careful. You know that we're all in danger now that our old enemy has escaped. He wants revenge, and he's very good with a rifle. Don't ever forget that, because you can be sure *he* won't."

Hearing a vehicle driving up, Rose went to the window. "We have company. It's your close friend!" she added after a moment.

At first, Ella thought her mother meant Carolyn, and she couldn't figure out what Carolyn would be doing here at this time of day. As she looked over her mother's shoulder, she saw Wilson Joe emerging from his truck. His rifle was in clear view in the gun rack behind the seat.

"He must be worried to come out here this early. I'll go meet him," Ella said, hurrying out.

Wilson walked up to the front porch and met Ella. "Have you heard anything else this morning?" he asked quickly.

"Yazzie's still at large. I just got off the phone a short time ago. Every cop in the county is looking for him, though. He killed a nurse while making his escape, so be on your guard. Have you changed your mind about wanting protection?" Ella added, knowing that she was in no position to offer him much help from the department at the moment.

"No, I was just thinking that we all need to watch over each other now. You'll be at work so you'll have other officers around you. I'm alone at home and so is your mother when you're not here, so I figured she and I could keep each other company when I wasn't at the college."

Ella knew that the carefully worded statement had been for Rose's benefit. They were both aware that she was listening to them through the open window. "You'll have to see what she thinks, but I'm all for it. Our units are stretched very thin right now, so we can't give anyone the kind of protection I'd like."

Rose came outside to the porch. "Come in, Wilson, please. Have you had breakfast? My daughter prefers cold cereal, but I could make you something more substantial."

Wilson smiled at Ella. "I get company *and* good food. You can't beat that."

Rose smiled at him. "Then stay as long as you want. I'll start breakfast for you."

As Rose went back inside, Ella looked pensively at the mesas surrounding her home. "He hasn't been out long, but he's already affecting our lives."

"Surely that doesn't come as a surprise," Wilson said.

"No, but the way things are happening—well, it's just so strange," she whispered, speaking mostly to herself.

"What do you mean?"

"It was just a dream I had," she said, keeping her voice low. Ella definitely didn't want her mother to overhear this. Dreams were sufficient cause to call in a Singer, or, it was believed, what was dreamed might come true.

"Tell me about it," Wilson insisted, coming closer to her and keeping his tone only a hint above a whisper.

Ella was aware of the heat from Wilson's body in the cool of the desert morning. Even thinking of the dream was chilling, and Wilson's closeness was comforting. "It was really a nightmare, probably because I was under so much pressure." Ella recounted the events, remembering how she'd missed her fetish then. "That poor French tourist, Mr. Meles, must have thought I had flipped."

Wilson gave her an odd look. "It's strange that someone would be called that."

"Called what?"

"Meles." He shrugged. "I once wrote a college paper on the weasel family, for a vertebrate zoology class. Meles is the scientific name for a species of badger."

Her fingers coiled around the fetish in her pocket, Ella stared at Wilson in mute shock.

EIGHTEEN

——— ✖ ✖ ✖ ———

Ella spent the rest of the day checking with the officers on the roadblocks, searching for signs of Peterson Yazzie. Betty Lott had been located, and according to witnesses, had not been the woman at the psychiatric hospital. Ella was still trying to track down Steven Nez, however. He was under suspicion for Dodge's murder and remained at large. She was eager for a chance to compare Nez with Victor's sketch, as well as question him. She wondered what kind of alibi he'd be able to give them for the crucial times.

Justine met her in the police station's parking lot. "I got a call from Sally Nez. She says that Steven asked to meet her behind the Totah Café. He's almost out of money, and he's scared. He thinks we're trying to pin both murders on him. He's heard about Peterson's escape, too, and is afraid he'll also get blamed for that. He's desperate to leave the Rez."

"Did Sally agree to meet with him?" Ella asked.

"She told him to call her back after she'd had time to think about it. Then she called me."

Ella smiled. "She's trying to set him up, and I think we can oblige."

Justine shook her head. "Not so simple. I spoke to Big Ed about getting some officers so we could set up a trap for Nez using Sally as bait. He went ballistic. He said that there aren't enough officers available and there's no way he's endangering a young mother on an operation like that. He's taking too much heat on this case as it is."

Ella pursed her lips in thoughtful silence. "Then we'll have to use trickery to reel him in."

"What have you got in mind?"

"You and Cindi look a lot alike. Let's use that."

Justine groaned. "I do *not* look like a teenager."

Ella shrugged. "If he waits for Sally but she doesn't show up, then he sees Cindi having car trouble across the highway . . ."

Justine nodded. "We need to find out what type of car Cindi would be driving."

"We still have Kee Dodge's truck in the impound yard. Someone's bound to have one like it."

"I'll track one down," Justine said. "But I do *not* look like a teenager."

Ella watched her cousin/assistant leave. While Justine was busy working out those details, Ella decided to go talk to Betty Lott. Even if she hadn't been directly involved in Peterson's escape, Betty had visited Peterson recently, and she might have known far more than she'd ever let on about his plans. She cursed herself for not pressing the girl more when they'd first met.

Ella drove quickly across the reservation. She kept her police radio on maximum, hoping yet not expecting to hear that officers at one of the roadblocks had discovered Peterson Yazzie trying to get back on the Rez hiding in the back of a vehicle, or even driving one.

But few calls came in. Even minor traffic accidents were now put on hold, and the involved parties were being instructed to exchange names and license numbers until officers became available again.

Ella arrived at Anna Lott's house and went to the door. Anna answered quickly, her face pale and her eyes red as though she'd been crying.

Ella felt her scalp prickle with unease. "Hello, Anna. Do you know why I'm here?"

"The Yazzie escape, I would imagine. But my daughter had nothing to do with that. Officers have already verified that with witnesses."

"I understand, but she still might know something. Peterson tried his best to influence her, and from what I could tell, did a very good job."

"That he did," Anna conceded. "I hope you catch him and put the man in solitary for the rest of his life."

"We'll get him, sooner or later. In the meantime, I need to speak to Betty. Is she home?"

The young woman came out and stood a few feet behind her mother, leaning against the wall, arms crossed. She was wearing a long skirt and bright orange cotton sleeveless blouse with some cartoon Stone Age characters embroidered on the pocket.

"I'm here, but I can't help you."

Ella walked around Anna. "Can't or won't?" she asked softly.

"I'm sorry he escaped and killed that nurse. But I think he was forced into it."

"Betty!" Anna squealed, then turned to Ella. "She doesn't mean it, really!"

"Yes, I do," Betty assured both women. "That mental hospital would drive anyone over the edge. He may be a disturbed man, but he was being watched and kept there like a wild animal. The fact that doctors and the courts decided he belonged there proves he's not responsible for his actions, not really."

Ella met Betty's gaze and held it. The young woman never looked away. "Your sympathy is misguided. He's not insane, he's just very smart, and a skillful manipulator."

"You're too quick to pass judgment on him. He was right not to trust you."

"And what about the woman he killed? Shouldn't you reserve some compassion for her?"

"She knew the risks when she decided to work there. The mentally ill need to be cured, not shot down by the police."

"So you're saying that you think he belonged where he was and didn't help him in any way?" Ella pressed.

"Of course not." She paused. "But I got the impression he never intended to stay imprisoned there."

"Who *did* help him?"

"I don't know. He did say he was never without friends. He told me that those who'd stood with him had not all been destroyed. You'd only forced them into hiding."

Betty's gaze was unflinching. Instinct told Ella the girl was telling the truth. "Did you speak to my brother?"

"I went by his hogan, but his wife said he was away with a patient. Ask her."

Ella decided to speak in down-to-earth terms. She stood deliberately close to Betty. "I believe you've told me the truth, but if you know *anything* else about Peterson's escape and you don't tell me, you're obstructing justice. Believe me when I tell you I'll take you to jail for that. I'm sworn to uphold the law, and I'll do precisely that."

Betty's eyes grew wide. "You'd put *me* in jail?"

"You bet."

"But I didn't do anything." Betty stopped, then narrowed her gaze. "And I have witnesses who will testify where I was when he escaped."

Ella knew her bluff had been called. "Peterson Yazzie claims responsibility for the two murders that have occurred. Now, with the nurse, that makes three. Keep that firmly in your mind."

"That only supports my claim that he's insane. He's been in that hospital ever since the trial. You know that!"

"The nurse he killed was named Isabel Fernandez. From now on, when you think Yazzie deserves sympathy, think of Isabel Fernandez too. She became a nurse to help people. She deserved better than this." Ella kept her eyes on Betty's until the girl looked away. "If, by any chance, Yazzie happens to contact you, I want you to call me immediately."

Anna took the card from Ella. "*I* will make sure of that. Betty will not be using the telephone or leaving the house without me for the next two weeks. I'll stay home and enforce that."

Delty glared at her mother, turned on her heels, and marched back to her room, slamming the door behind her.

Anna looked at Ella. "I *will* protect my daughter from the likes of him."

The pager at Ella's waist sounded. If she'd been elsewhere, she would have asked to use the telephone, but Betty's contacts with Peterson made her reluctant to discuss anything the girl might overhear. Ella said a quick good-bye to Anna, then hurried to the cellular phone in her vehicle. The dispatcher put Justine through.

"I've got things set up. We have an old Ford like Kee Dodge's, and Sally is ready whenever Steven calls back."

"Any idea when that is going to be?"

"No, but we'll be ready when it happens. You also received a call that sounded important. You should check with your mother as soon as possible. She's at Loretta's."

Ella swallowed back the sinking feeling that gripped her. "Did she say anything more?"

"No, I'm afraid not."

Ella immediately called her brother's house. When Rose answered, Ella's tension increased. "I just got your message," Ella said. "What's going on?"

"Your sister-in-law heard about that man's escape. She became very agitated and started having pains. Your brother was not here, so I came to stay with her until he returns."

"You know, under the circumstances, it would probably be a good idea if you moved in with them, or they moved in with us."

"I'll see," Rose said.

That easy agreement told Ella just how serious things were. "Where's Wilson?"

"He went back to his office at the college to get a few things. He said the college has a security guard there as well as plenty of faculty, so there was no reason for any of us to worry about him."

After Ella said good-bye, she decided to check out her home

and the surrounding area. She had a bad feeling she just couldn't shake, but it wasn't any premonition. It was just that Peterson knew their house very well; he'd been there dozens of times. Experience made her suspect that made her home a prime target.

Ella drove home, intending to see what, if anything, could be done to make it more secure. She was almost certain that her mother would try to get Loretta to move in with them. Rose's herb garden was her most cherished possession, and she wouldn't leave it to the mercy of the summer heat without daily tending. If, by chance, Loretta didn't consent to move in with them, her mother would walk back and forth between their homes, exposing herself to greater danger than the three-digit summer temperatures. But Loretta would know that, too, and would not jeopardize Rose.

As she approached the turnoff, Ella saw white, odd-shaped objects scattered all along the highway, blocking the dirt road that led to their home.

Ella leaned forward, trying to make some sense of the shapes that littered the area. As she drove closer, she realized what they were, and disgust made her breath catch in her throat. Flies were thick in the air, buzzing everywhere. The carcasses of six dead sheep had been dumped near their mailbox. The animals had been gutted and mutilated, exposing bones in several places.

Ella stopped the Jeep beside the highway and then stepped out of her vehicle. She searched the shoulder of the road for tire imprints or anything that would provide her with clues. Unfortunately, all she could see was that someone had deliberately taken a branch to obliterate any marks on the ground.

Unwilling to drive over the carcasses, Ella grabbed the hind legs of the sheep, one at a time, and pulled the mutilated animals off to one side.

Once the path was clear, Ella drove straight through. She wanted animal control to come pick up the carcasses before anyone else could see them. She also wanted Carolyn to take a look at them. If the method used to kill the animals could be linked to the murders, it could provide additional clues to those unsolved crimes.

Ella called the dispatcher and made the necessary arrangements, then carefully went inside her home. After telephoning her mother at Loretta's and letting her know where she was, Ella replaced the receiver. She made a mental note to once again pressure her mother and her brother and his wife to move in together until the case was solved.

Ella was listening to the quiet of the house, deep in thought, when she heard a vehicle drive up. Automatically reaching for her gun, and making sure the snap was unfastened, she went to the edge of the window and peered outside.

Seeing Wilson emerge from his truck, she relaxed, and went outside to greet him. The moment she saw his expression she knew how much the sight of those mutilated animals had angered him. "It's okay. I'm the one who moved them off the road, and I've made arrangements to get them hauled away," Ella said.

"Has your mother returned?"

"No, and she walked to Loretta's, so she'll be coming around through the back when she does come." Ella gestured to her father's old truck, which had been parked in the shade of a tall piñon.

"In case you're wondering why she left . . ."

Ella held up a hand. "I heard about Loretta."

"There's something you should be aware of." He hesitated. "It'll help you understand why Loretta's frightened. We all know the gifts in your family are inherited . . ."

Ella gave him a puzzled look, but slowly understanding dawned over her. "Yazzie wouldn't want the baby to survive, knowing that it carries our line forward."

"Precisely. Clifford knows this too. You can rest assured he'll do his best to guard his wife and make sure she's safe."

Ella led the way inside, glancing around for their old mutt. Not finding him, she went to the kitchen, then opened the back door and whistled.

"If you're looking for Dog, your mother took him with her."

"Thank goodness!" Ella said, relieved. "For a moment . . ."

"No," Wilson said gently. "He's safe, and making sure your mother stays the same way."

Ella dropped down onto one of the chairs at the kitchen table. "There's so much work to be done, and the entire department is spread so thin!"

Wilson went to the refrigerator and brought out a cola for Ella. "Here, you look as if you need it. Do you want me to fix you a sandwich?"

Ella smiled at Wilson and nodded. It felt good to have a friend like him who cared enough to look after her, particularly when she was too tired to do it for herself. Her gaze was gentle as it settled on him. "I don't know why you put up with me."

"Hey, I only see you when you're dead on your feet. It's the only time you sit down! I've got to make the most of the situation, otherwise you'd forget me altogether," he teased.

He placed a peanut butter and jelly sandwich in front of her. "I'm not a master chef, but this will give you some quick energy."

Ella ate slowly, knowing she needed something in her stomach, yet not really hungry. "You realize those animals are Yazzie's calling card?"

Wilson nodded. "Are you any closer to catching him?"

"No, but I do have some leads that I believe will pan out sooner or later. It's the same with our investigation into the murders."

"Are you going to install a security system here at your house?"

"I'm going to try, but you know Mother. She's not going to stand for anything too elaborate. She believes the pollen and the blessings protect better than anything else." Ella exhaled softly. "She may be right, too, when it comes to Peterson, but I doubt this 'packrat killer' would even notice. He's more likely to shy away from lights that are activated by motion. Anyone larger than a rabbit would set those off and advertise their presence. I think Mom will allow that."

"You're just like your mother when it comes to asking for help, but have you considered talking to some of the neighbors?"

Ella smiled, thinking of how different a meaning that would have in the cities where she used to work. A neighbor here could live miles and miles away. "They're too far away to help."

"Herman Cloud would make it his business to keep a watch on this place, even using binoculars, if you asked. He's a loyal friend to your family."

She remembered the elderly man who'd helped them once before. He and his friend Samuel Pete had helped fight the skinwalkers. They'd both stood by her, even during that final battle when all seemed to be lost.

"I'll talk to him."

"I saw him the other day at the Totah Café. He figured you would drop by his place sooner or later."

"I've always meant to go by, but somehow I never quite found the time. Now I have to ask him for a favor." She shook her head. "I hope he understands."

"He will."

Ella heard the sound of vehicles off in the distance. In the wide-open spaces of New Mexico, it was hard to miss the noise from a truck or car. "I better go back to the mailbox. The county's supposed to be coming by, but there's no guarantee they'll arrive before someone else does."

"I'll go with you."

Ella shook her head. "Why don't you stay here in case my mother decides to return? It's probably just tension from the case, but I'd rather not leave the house totally unguarded for any length of time."

Ella drove out toward the main road, and from a distance saw that the vehicle there was not from the animal control people. She increased her speed slightly, straining for a better look.

A moment later, she saw Justine emerge from her car, her face contorted in disgust.

Ella parked on the side of the road. "Animal control is on its way."

"This is Yazzie's doing, isn't it?"

"That's my guess."

"Did your mother see this?"

"No. I'll tell her about it, of course, but at least she was spared the sight." Ella brushed the flies away from her as they buzzed around, landing on her face and clothes. "Is there anything new on the case?"

Justine shook her head. "But I expect to hear from Sally Nez soon, then we'll have a suspect to question."

"If it goes as planned."

Moments later she saw the animal control vehicle approaching. The driver, a tall, thin Anglo, stepped out and surveyed the scene with cold detachment. "My orders say that we're not to dispose of these yet. Just put them in a walk-in cooler. Why? The meat's sure not going to be any good."

"These are part of a chain of evidence. Someone will be by to run some tests on them this afternoon, if possible."

The man smirked. "Okay. Whatever you say."

Wearing long rubber gloves, he tossed the carcasses into the back of the truck effortlessly. Ella was thankful that the dry climate had at least kept the smell from becoming intolerable. The flies were the worst part.

As the man drove away, Ella heard her pager go off. "That'll be Carolyn calling." Ella saw the look on Justine's face and smiled. "No magic intuition. I left a message for her. Follow me home, okay?"

Ella dialed from her cellular unit as she headed back to the home, but reception wasn't good from this stretch of desert. She'd have to place the call from home. The land lines here were usually more reliable than radio waves.

Ella and Justine arrived at Ella's home just as Rose came walking down the hill behind the house. She had taken the back route, as Ella had predicted. Ella quickly joined Justine. "Don't mention the animals until I've had a chance to talk to her, okay?"

"No problem."

By the time Rose came in through the back door, Justine and Ella had joined Wilson in the kitchen. Rose smiled. "This reminds me of old times when your friends would all come over to visit," she said to Ella. "It's a welcome sight."

Ella saw the wistful look in her mother's eyes and realized how much Rose needed her good memories. Although she'd finally accepted the death of her husband and found peace of mind, she was happiest when she was providing for others.

Rose greeted Justine and Wilson with a smile. "It's almost dinnertime. I hope both of you are planning to stay."

Ella glanced at Wilson and Justine who each nodded, then back at her mother. "I have to make one phone call, then I'll be back to help you with the cooking," Ella said.

"No, don't worry. I'll take care of this; you entertain your friends."

Ella glanced at the others and saw the flicker of understanding in their eyes. Wilson and Justine had each sensed her mother needed to pretend, if only for now, that these were just Ella's friends gathered together.

Ella walked to her room and dialed Carolyn's number at the office. Although it was nearly six, Carolyn was still there.

"Hi," Ella greeted her. "What's up?"

"I got your message, and before you ask, the answer is no. I am *not* going to bring six mutilated sheep here to the hospital. The board would hang me up to dry if I did."

"No one expects you to bring those animals to the morgue. Just go over to animal control and take a look at them there. See how they were killed, and if they were shot, try to retrieve a bullet or two."

"I am not a vet," Carolyn clipped out.

"Vets are used to treating live animals, not processing evidence or working with the legal system," Ella insisted. "I need you to do this."

Carolyn said nothing for a moment, then finally agreed. "Okay. I'll take care of it. You going to be home tonight?"

"For several hours at least," Ella answered.

"I'll give you a call there as soon as I can."

"I appreciate it. Listen, if you get a chance, why don't you come over and have some dinner with us? Wilson Joe and Justine are both here."

"Sounds to me like you've got plenty of company," Carolyn said hesitantly.

"Not enough without you. Come on. It'll do you a world of good to take a few hours off and relax."

"What time?"

"It'll take my mother at least an hour and a half to prepare dinner. I figure she'll be making stuffed sopaipillas."

"Are you sure having me there is okay with her?"

"Yes, it's no problem."

"All right, but I may be a little late. I'll stop by and get what I can from the sheep, then come over." She paused. "Maybe I shouldn't have put it that way."

Ella laughed. "Don't give it another thought. I'm the same way, as you know. My work and I are no strangers, but tact and I are."

"Thanks for inviting me to your home. It means a lot to me."

Ella knew that it was Rose's acceptance that Carolyn was referring to. Though Ella hadn't mentioned it, Carolyn knew that the dinner invitation had only come about because of Ella's intervention.

"You're always welcome here," Ella reiterated.

As she hung up the phone, Ella heard laughter from the living room. She joined Justine and Wilson, and saw how quickly they'd taken to each other. She brushed aside a sudden burst of jealousy. There was no place for it in her world, and she had no claim on Wilson other than friendship.

"Your mom suggested that we keep ourselves busy out here. I think that was a polite way of telling us to get out of the kitchen."

Ella smiled. "She's seen what happens when I try to help."

Justine lifted her hair up away from her shoulders. "I hate this time of day. I know everyone says that it's starting to cool off, but I don't feel any difference until the sun goes down." She sipped some of the mint tea Rose had put out on a tray for them.

Ella picked up the one glass still on the tray. "Do you remember when we were kids?" Ella asked, looking at Wilson. "We never worried about things like the weather."

"Of course we did," Wilson answered with a grin, "there were just other more important things to talk about."

"Like guys," Justine said, giving Ella a teasing wink.

"Or basketball," Wilson answered.

Silence fell over them for a moment as they each became temporarily lost in their own memories.

"We've all come a long way," Justine said slowly. "For you two, even further," she grinned.

"Yeah," Ella said with a shrug. "Now we talk shop, or get stuck for a topic."

Wilson laughed. "Are you saying we've become dull?"

Justine looked seriously at her older companions. "No, not dull. It's just that our interests have become totally focused on what we do."

Wilson smiled at Justine. "Well, it may be too late for Ella and me to change, but there's still hope for you."

Justine shook her head. "I see nothing in either of you two or myself that I'd want to change."

Rose came out of the kitchen. "Well, I do," she said. "I was eavesdropping. Why don't you play some music and dance like you used to when you were kids?"

"Mom, it's too hot. The evaporative cooler is working, so it's okay in here, but none of us have the energy to dance," Ella protested weakly. She knew her mother was trying to play matchmaker again, and wished she wasn't quite so dogged about it. Then again, determination was one trait she'd inherited, and it made her a good cop.

Rose sighed and shook her head. "If you youngsters can take the heat for a minute, will you go outside and pick some mint from the garden? I need some for the tea."

"Sure." Ella went outside, and the furnace blast that struck her as she opened the door almost took her breath away. "Wow, I think today's temperature must have beat the record."

"It did," Wilson answered, following her and Justine.

Justine tied her hair back with a piece of yarn she'd grabbed from Rose's knitting basket. "I tried to start a garden over at my place, but all I grew were weeds."

"I have a black thumb," Ella admitted. "Clifford and Loretta have a wonderful garden. He grows melons, corn, green chiles, and squash. I can't even keep a houseplant alive." So much for heredity.

A moment later they stood at the edge of Rose's wagon-wheel-shaped herb garden. Plants were placed in wedge-shaped sections, separated by cedar edging. Although it had been watered that morning, the ground was almost parched again.

Ella noticed out of the corner of her eye that her mother was watching them. "Hey," she whispered to Justine and Wilson. "Mom's watching us. Let's give her a hard time and not find the mint."

"Which one's the mint?" Justine said in a normal tone, scratching her head.

Ella hesitated. "That one." She pointed to a leafy shrub. "No, wait. It might be that one," she said quickly, pointing to a plant that seemed to be made mostly of naked stems. "Oh boy, you know what? I have no idea. She uses both of those in her teas, and chamomile, but which is which?"

Wilson crouched by the leafless plant. "It isn't this one, for sure. I recognize this plant. Locals call it Mormon tea. Doesn't mint have leaves?"

"Maybe it's this one," Justine said enthusiastically, and crouched by a coltsfoot plant with leaves several inches long.

Rose knocked on the window, then pointed. "The one at the end!" she yelled, her tone clearly showing her exasperation. "Use your nose and smell for it."

They returned a moment later, Ella holding a cutting of the fragrant plant.

Rose gave her a hard glare. "I can't believe that you remember every detail of your cases, but you can't figure out what's in the herb garden!"

Ella smiled sheepishly. "I flunked botany, what can I say?"

Justine nodded in agreement, trying to avoid a smile. "We flunked too, right, Wilson?"

He nodded solemnly. "And me a science teacher. How sad."

Rose rolled her eyes, then walked to the pitcher and dropped a few leaves on the surface. "You idiots go clean up. We'll be having dinner in another ten minutes."

Ella washed her hands in the kitchen sink while Justine and Wilson used the bathrooms. "Carolyn's going to be dropping by later."

"Good. It's nice to have people around you when you're not working."

"The same could be said for you, *and* for Loretta. That's why I hope you'll ask her and Clifford to move in with us as soon as possible."

"Do you believe I'm in danger?" Rose asked pointedly.

"You may be," Ella admitted. "I'm going to have an officer checking often, but we don't have the manpower to assign anyone here full-time."

"And your sister-in-law?"

"The same, but Loretta's needs exceed what I can provide her with. How is her health?"

Rose took a deep breath and let it out again. "Her greatest problem is her own fear. She's really very frightened, particularly since your brother was recently asked to give lectures at the college. She knows the other Singer who took the job is now dead."

"Does she believe there's a connection?" Ella asked, wondering how Loretta could have arrived at that conclusion.

Rose shrugged. "She doesn't want her husband following in the steps of one who was murdered. Who can blame her?"

"Well, there's something to that," Ella admitted.

As the others joined them, Ella helped her mother serve the stuffed sopaipillas. The fry bread had been filled with ground beef, beans, and cheese almost to bursting. A red chile sauce with melted cheese covered it liberally.

Ella took a hearty bite of her favorite dish. "This is wonderful!"

Rose smiled. "That's what I like to hear. There are also chocolate chip cookies and ice cream for dessert," she added.

Ella groaned, thinking of her waistline. "I'm going to have to take up jogging again," she said, glancing at Wilson and Justine.

Wilson grinned. "Well, I'm not going to feel guilty. I can't remember the last time someone cooked me a meal like this, and I'm going to enjoy it."

Justine finished her serving and asked for more iced tea. "I'll go jogging with you," she said, glancing at Ella, "but I'm going to have both the cookies and the ice cream."

Ella laughed. "Mother, you're a bad influence."

As Justine and Rose cleared the table, Ella heard a car pull up. "That sounds like Carolyn. I'll go greet her."

Ella walked out quickly, hoping to warn Carolyn not to mention anything about the dead animals within range of her mother's acute hearing. She hadn't had a chance to tell Rose yet, and dinner certainly seemed an inappropriate time.

Ella greeted Carolyn as she parked her vehicle beside Wilson's. "You're just in time for dessert, and Mother saved the fixings for a big stuffed sopaipilla for you too."

Carolyn smiled. "I'll never turn that down," she said cheerfully. "Can't be rude."

"How did things go with the sheep?" Ella asked, keeping her voice low.

"Their throats were slit with big knives, just as if they were being slaughtered," Carolyn answered, matching Ella's soft tone. "Whoever opened up the animals worked like a pro. Probably a Navajo. But the mutilations required an ax."

Ella nodded. She now suspected more than ever that Peterson had engineered the incident. She remembered how he and his skinwalker friends had enjoyed using symbols like these to spread fear. Navajos believed that even looking at a dead animal not intended for food was dangerous.

"My mother doesn't know about this yet, so please be careful what you say around her. I intend to tell her later, but I haven't had a chance, and I didn't want to upset her now. She has enough on her mind worrying about my sister-in-law, who's having a hard time with her pregnancy."

"Yeah, I've heard about that through the gossip mill. Don't worry. I'll keep quiet. I'd offer to keep my mouth shut, but I'm starving."

Ella looked at Carolyn and started laughing. "You know, we've all put on weight."

"I don't know about you, but I'm sick of dieting. I've come to the conclusion that some of us are meant to be rounded, and some of us are meant to be angular. I'm in the rounded category. Besides, at the risk of sounding sorry for myself, it's not as if I have an active social life. The people I see most are way past looking at anything. So I might as well indulge myself."

As they walked into the kitchen, Rose turned her head from what she was frying and smiled at Carolyn. "I'm glad you came to see us. I'm fixing you a stuffed sopaipilla."

"They're *wonderful*," Justine said. "Then we're going to have ice cream and cookies."

To Ella, Justine suddenly sounded as young as she looked. She glanced at Carolyn, who grinned from ear to ear. "There's no generation gap between this child and me. She has her priorities straight."

Even Rose laughed as she placed a large platter of food before Carolyn. "Enjoy," she said. "Now I'll leave you to entertain yourselves. The cookies and ice cream are in the fridge."

As Rose walked down the hall, Ella turned on the Navajo radio station. They finished dinner in easy camaraderie. Country-western music with Navajo-language lyrics might have sounded strange back in L.A., but here it was the rule rather than the exception. Ella loved it.

Wilson watched Carolyn thoughtfully. He started to speak but then reached for his iced tea instead.

Carolyn glanced up as she took her last mouthful of sopaipilla. "What's on your mind, Wilson?"

Wilson glanced away, embarrassed. "I'm trying to figure out how to ask you something. I hope it's not out of line."

"Go ahead. Speak your mind."

Ella stared at Wilson, unable to believe that he would ever purposely hurt Carolyn's feelings. Yet he was obviously leading up to something sensitive.

"You were a family doctor for years, and had a good practice," he said. "You had the respect of everyone. Why did you go into forensics? You must have known how most Navajos would react to that."

Carolyn took a deep breath and leaned back. "Years ago, I

made a deal with myself. The tribe paid for my schooling so, in return, I decided that I'd always make myself as useful as possible. I would place the People's needs at the top of my list. When the position of forensic pathologist became open, no Anglo would take it. The pay was less than they wanted to make, and they didn't like living here. Our own medical staff wouldn't touch it. The need was there and I was qualified, so I stepped in."

Wilson nodded slowly. "You have more courage than I do."

"You don't believe in ghost sickness, do you?" Carolyn asked, surprised.

"Not really, I guess. But I don't think I'd be able to stand the way a lot of people avoid someone in your field."

"I haven't lost all my friends," Carolyn said.

"Like Sadie Morgan?" Wilson smiled.

"Yes, like her."

"That name sounds familiar," Ella said, bringing out the platter of cookies.

"She's on staff at the college. She teaches advanced Navajo to students. Sadie's also working on a special project. She's taping the Navajo language into an audio dictionary, so its sounds will never be lost," Wilson replied.

"She's a tough old gal too," Carolyn said with a half smile. "We suit each other well."

Ella recalled that Sadie Morgan was one of the local experts who had been warned about the Packrat.

Carolyn filled their dishes with big scoops of vanilla ice cream, then began to pass them around. "You know, it's nice to share a meal with friends."

Ella felt the tug at her heart. For a moment she saw herself, years from now, in Carolyn's shoes: a professional woman, busy, but too alone.

"Earth calling," Justine teased, holding out a bowl of ice cream to Ella.

"Thanks," Ella said, her attention back to dessert again.

"Don't tell me. You're thinking about work, right?" Carolyn said with a smile.

Ella was about to side-step an answer when her pager and

Justine's went off almost simultaneously. Ella glanced at her assistant and saw all the playfulness leave Justine's expression. In an instant, she'd switched back to the professional police officer.

Ella stood, and led Justine to the phone in the bedroom. She dialed in first. Sally Nez had called. According to their prearranged plan, she'd agreed to meet Steven behind the Totah Café. "We're on," Ella said, filling Justine in.

Justine dialed in next and found that Sally had left a message for her too. Using the pad beside the phone, she took down the message, then showed it to Ella. "Cindi Dodge's favorite outfit was jeans and a red Shiprock High School T-shirt. I've got jeans, but where am I going to get a T-shirt on short notice?"

"I haven't got one," Ella said, "but I think someone at the station might." She checked her watch. "We've got ninety minutes. Get going, and track down what you need. I'll meet you later. I'll be parked near the Totah Café, using infrared binoculars to keep an eye on you. Once Nez approaches you, detain him for questioning. If he makes a move to get away, arrest him. I'll be there to back you up."

"Got it." Justine followed Ella back into the living room.

Wilson and Carolyn were talking, but quieted immediately when they looked up. Wilson's eyes went to Ella. "You have to leave, right?" he asked morosely.

"Yes," Ella said softly. "I'm sorry to cut the evening short."

Wilson nodded. "I understand." He glanced at Justine. "Take care of Ella. She's not as tough as she'd like to be."

Justine shrugged. "Who is?"

"Am I going to be needed?" Carolyn said, her voice taut.

"I certainly hope not." Ella smiled grimly.

"In that case, it's time I went home too."

Ella said good-bye to Wilson and Carolyn, then went to tell her mother she was leaving. Disapproval came quickly to Rose's eyes, then she relented. "Well, your friends and you have much in common. They probably understand better than I do. Be careful, all right?"

"You too." Ella went through the house, picked up her weapon and jacket, then walked out the front door.

Wilson met her by the Jeep as Justine drove away. "If you don't mind," he said to Ella, "I'm going to install those lights you mentioned tonight. The discount store will still be open, and I think that the sooner it's done, the better."

"I'd really appreciate that." Ella slipped inside her Jeep and turned on the ignition. As she placed the vehicle in gear, she glanced up. "I'm glad we had dinner together."

Wilson smiled, his gaze gentling. "So am I."

As Ella followed Justine's vehicle down the dirt road, she glanced back in the mirror. Her mother had come around to stand beside Wilson. She was glad he was there, but she was also afraid for him as well as her family. None of them would be safe until the killer was caught and Peterson was back in custody.

NINETEEN

———— ✖ ✖ ✖ ————

Ella waited in the dark, behind the cover of an old Dumpster beside the Totah Café. She could see Justine beside the old Ford truck she'd borrowed, parked beneath the light that illuminated the Totah Café's parking area. The hood was up, and she was pretending to work on something in the engine compartment. The Shiprock T-shirt she'd borrowed was a bit too large, making her look even younger than she was.

Ella knew that Steven would show up soon. As she'd suspected, Steven had not said exactly when he would arrive to meet Sally. He probably wanted to check out the parking lot to make sure it was safe to show himself.

They waited another twenty minutes. Ella noted an old sedan cruising past them on the highway. It had already been by three times. This wasn't the vehicle they'd expected. Nez was supposed to have an old beat-up blue truck. But when it went by the fourth time, she knew it was probably him.

Finally she saw the sedan slow down. Justine only allowed him a fleeting glimpse of her face while he was still on the highway. As the man fitting Nez's description stepped out, Ella began moving forward discreetly.

Justine waited until the man was close before turning, identifying herself, and ordering him to remain where he was. Nez immediately spun around and raced for his car.

"Police officers, Nez! Don't do it!" Ella yelled, running forward.

Nez almost made it to the door of his car before Justine tackled him. As he tumbled to the ground, she jumped on his back and grabbed his right arm, twisting it painfully. "Struggling will only prolong the pain, Nez," she snapped, scrambling to her feet. "Get up and lean against the car, hands up and apart, feet back."

Justine handcuffed and frisked Nez quickly while he cursed an endless stream of obscenities, some in Navajo, some in English.

"I've heard them all, and in much more creative phrases, Nez, so do us all a favor and shut up," Ella said pleasantly, and proceeded to read him his rights.

"You've got nothing on me."

"Is that why you ran?" Ella countered.

"I thought I was going to be mugged."

"By a woman half your weight? Where's your pride? You can come up with a better excuse than that."

"I thought my wife was trying to get me arrested for taking the pickup. It's in her name. I want a lawyer."

"You can have one," Ella said.

"You really are making things look bad for yourself," Justine said. "Why have you been hiding out? That just makes you look guilty of murder."

"I'm not! I swear!" he protested as Ella led him to her vehicle. "But I knew I was one of the last to see Dodge alive. I'm on everybody's shit list at the moment. It didn't look good for me, and I knew it. Besides, who says I've been hiding? My wife kicked me out. I've been looking for a place to stay, that's all. I'm not that Packrat guy. Search me."

"You knew we wanted to question you. You just admitted it. If you have nothing to hide, why didn't you come in voluntarily?" Ella demanded.

"I want a lawyer," he said once again.

"Okay. The tribe will provide one for you. But if you're involved with skinwalkers, you're going to need more than a lawyer to keep you in one piece. Our people don't have much sympathy for Navajo witches." Ella wanted to undermine his confidence, and this was one way to do it.

"Skinwalkers! What the hell are you talking about? It's bad enough that everyone around knows I was going out with Cindi Dodge. Where does this bull about skinwalkers come from? Are they back again?"

"Are you joining them?" Ella asked.

"You're crazy! Those guys are on loco weed half the time. I'd have nothing to do with them." He paused. "But I've heard their women sit around naked . . ." He shrugged with a grin.

Ella shook her head. "You've got a one-track mind."

"I want a lawyer. You're out to put somebody away, and it isn't going to be me. Sure I like the ladies, but I'm no killer and no skinwalker. Pin this on someone else."

"By the way, where were you when Dodge was killed?"

"I'm not answering one more thing until I have a tribal lawyer next to me."

Ella transported the suspect, handcuffed in the backseat, while Justine followed close behind. Nez stayed silent the whole way to the station, but Ella could feel his gaze boring holes through the back of her skull.

She wasn't sure whether to believe him. Much would depend on his alibi, but her instincts were telling her that he wasn't the Packrat. His feet seemed too large, for one, and he wore boots. He was also older and heavier than Mrs. Zah's description. He did smell, but that was from a popular aftershave Ella recognized. Of course, these details would have to be checked more definitively later.

All in all, Ella was disappointed. Steven Nez just didn't seem to be the man they were looking for.

Afterward, at the station, Nez met a tribe-appointed lawyer named Chester Manuelito. The young Navajo man spoke briefly with Nez, then approached Ella. "You can't hold him."

"I can for twenty-four hours," Ella replied.

"It would be a waste of time. My client has done nothing illegal," Manuelito argued.

"I want to know where he was on the night of Kee Dodge's murder, and what he's done since then."

"He was at his brother's," the young attorney answered for his client.

Ella estimated Manuelito to be around Justine's age, and just as eager to prove himself at his chosen profession. For a moment, she sized him up as a possible mate for Justine. Suddenly, realizing what she was doing, Ella halted that line of thought. She was doing to her cousin precisely what she hated people doing for her. Maybe she was turning into her mother after all.

"His brother can verify his whereabouts then?" Ella looked from attorney to client.

"Only partially. They weren't together all the time. His brother, for instance, didn't come home until the afternoon after Dodge's murder took place. Same with Haske's."

"So he has no alibi."

"You can't prove my client was at either murder scene. If you can, let's see the evidence."

"We're not revealing any specifics until we go to court. If your client wants to be released before tomorrow, however, he'd better be able to account for his whereabouts for every moment, from the last time he saw Kee Dodge alive to the moment we arrested him tonight. I want the names of anyone who can confirm that too. Is he willing to do that, or do I lock him up?" Ella crossed her arms and waited.

Manuelito glanced over to Steven Nez, who nodded reluctantly. "He'll do it. Then you release him, right?"

"For now. One more thing, Counselor. If your client gets near his wife, she's prepared to file a restraining order. And this department will make darned sure that it's upheld." Ella wanted no reprisals against Sally, and she wanted Nez to realize that she wouldn't stand for it.

Steven gave her a slow, lazy smile. "You've got me all wrong,

Officer. I want my wife back. I wouldn't do anything to drive her away from me."

"You'd better be telling the truth. I've got enough problems on my hands without you harassing the mother of two children. I'll haul you in here so fast you won't know what hit you."

Steven scowled at her. "Have you been turning my wife against me?"

Ella met his gaze without flinching. "No, you've done that all by yourself. Now go to the front desk, get yourself some paper and a pen, and give me a statement."

Anger shone in Steven's eyes, but before he could reply, his attorney shoved him out the door.

Justine appeared in the interview room doorway just as Ella was preparing to go back to her office. "Big Ed wants to see you," she said in a muted voice.

"What's going on?" Ella asked, knowing how fast rumors traveled.

"I think he's worried that we're not making enough progress."

"So a head or two on the chopping block will help him pass the time?" she teased halfheartedly.

Justine shrugged. "Something like that, I suppose."

Ella went down the hall to Big Ed's office. His secretary wasn't at her desk, so she went all the way through the outer office and knocked lightly on her boss's partially open door.

She heard him conclude a telephone conversation, then replace the receiver. "Get in here," he barked.

Ella stepped inside his office and, following the waved invitation to sit down, took the chair closest to his desk.

"I'm getting a lot of pressure from the top to find the 'pack-rat' killer, and to do everything in my power to see that he doesn't strike again."

"I'm doing my best, but he hasn't left us much to go on. We have a profile, which you've seen. But that doesn't point to any particular individual yet. We've finally lured Steven Nez out of hiding, but that's led us nowhere so far. He had the most obvious motive for the Dodge murder, and he doesn't have an alibi, but linking him to Haske is going to be tough, and he doesn't match the description we've compiled."

"What motive can tie him with the second one?"

Ella pressed her lips together. "He could have killed Haske to divert suspicion from the fact he'd killed Dodge. Maybe he thought he could lead us off the trail by staging the Packrat profile."

"That has a certain perverse logic, but is it true?" Big Ed leaned back in his chair and steepled his fingers beneath his chin. His eyes never left Ella's face.

"No," she admitted. "I don't think so. Nez doesn't seem smart enough to come up with a scheme like that, and a lot of the physical clues, like shoe style and size, point in another direction. You can fake a larger shoe size, but not a smaller one."

"I've been empowered to borrow any cops from Farmington who volunteer, to help with the roadblocks. We now have some extra manpower, though it's costing the department a fortune."

"I think Yazzie is on the Rez already. Somebody dumped some freshly mutilated sheep by my mom's mailbox this morning," Ella informed him.

"If that was his work, then we can drop the roadblocks and use the officers to track down other leads." Big Ed shrugged. "You know Yazzie better than I do. What will his next move be?"

"What makes Yazzie such a formidable criminal is that he's part chameleon. He can hide out right under our noses, and we'll still have a problem finding him. I'm not surprised he beat the roadblocks."

"You mean with his skinwalker illusions?"

"Or his skills as an actor and magician. Take your pick."

"Do you think he's behind the killings?"

She took a deep breath then let it out slowly. "I think he would like to be, but I don't think he's as involved as he wants me to believe. It is possible, however, that it's one of his followers, a wannabe, and he knows precisely who it is. That I have no problem believing."

"Do what you have to to find out, but get results. I don't like taking this heat. The whole tribe is on edge about this. And make darned sure no more victims crop up. I'll go ahead and cancel the roadblocks, but I want the extra manpower that becomes freed up to maintain surveillance on potential targets."

"Okay. Any idea how many cops we'll have available for that?"

"We have eight on loan from Farmington, and as far as I'm concerned, you can use all of them on surveillance. I want to prevent any more of our elders from turning up dead. I saw the list of names you compiled in your report, and the short list of locals. All those people are very important to this tribe. If we lose them, we are losing a part of our heritage."

He paused. "I'm not sure I believe that evil is going to destroy us as a tribe, but fear can do untold damage. If one more bad thing happens, it's going to demoralize the tribe. With unemployment high because of the coal mine closings, and the deaths already on record, people may stop believing in us and start taking things into their own hands. And that chaos would be the biggest threat the People have faced in over a century."

"I agree. But protecting those who seem to be the most likely targets for the packrat killer is tricky. They don't want protection," Ella reminded him.

"Tough. We'll watch them from a distance then."

"He could strike elsewhere. This is a big reservation."

"We can guard only against what we know. You may have a personal reason for wanting to find Yazzie, but make sure he takes second place to your search for the murderer. I want this packrat psycho behind bars. I'm hoping everything will fall into place after that."

"I'll do my best."

"Assign cops to watch your brother and your mother too. I haven't seen a report on it yet, but I did hear earlier about those sheep. I want an officer near your family by tonight."

"My brother won't stand for anyone hanging around when he's working, and the tribal council will back him up. But my mother does need protection. I'll have a unit watching from the mesa behind the house, which also covers the access road to my brother's home. They'll be able to see anyone coming or going, and if there's trouble, they'll be there to react."

"Do it then." As the telephone began to ring, he looked at it wearily. "Find answers soon," he said, picking up the receiver.

Ella left Big Ed's office and walked back to her own. Someone was there, standing with his back to her. "Can I help you?" she asked.

As the man turned around, she smiled. Herman Cloud, with his weather-beaten face and white hair, was a welcome sight. "I've been meaning to pay you a visit!" she said. "But tell me, what brings you here today? Are you worried, Uncle?" she asked gently.

"Not for myself. Your family is in more danger than the rest of us if it's true that the Navajo witch has escaped."

"It's true, but why do you believe my family is in greater danger than people like you who fought with us?"

"You and your family stand like a wall between those who would harm the tribe and the rest of us. That means you're the most prominent target, and getting you and those you love out of the picture for good would be a most coveted prize."

Ella bit her bottom lip pensively. "Yes, that's true. But so far, no move has been made directly against us."

"First they must shake your confidence. Afterwards you'll all be easier targets. Don't let that strategy work. Believe in yourself, and in those you love."

"I do. My family and friends are my strength."

"And your weakness. Remember that," Herman Cloud answered. "I will be nearby. When you need me, you won't have to look far."

Ella thanked him, then watched as he walked out. He had remained a staunch family friend throughout all the problems her family had faced. She had no doubt that he'd be there just as he said. Finding comfort in his friendship and loyalty, Ella gathered a few reports, then started toward the door. Somehow she still had to break the news about the carcasses to her mother, and she had to convince her to get Loretta and Clifford to move in.

Ella was in the hall when Justine came by. "I've got a problem. I sent one of our officers, Bradford Atcitty, to talk to Sadie
Morgan, the linguist. She was adamant that she would not alter
her schedule. She records at night, and also sometimes conducts
choir practice at the new church."

"At least she'll be with others during choir practice, and there
will be other members of the congregation on the road. But I've
got to talk to her about those solo recording sessions. That's beg-
ging for trouble. Maybe she'll consent to having one of our tribal
cops with her just at those times."

"I wouldn't count on it. Bradford said that she was having
none of it. She has a rifle, and she'll use it if she's threatened, but
she's not going to have a 'babysitter.' Her words."

Ella sighed. This wasn't going to be easy. If they put un-
wanted surveillance on someone like that, she was just as likely
to shoot them.

"I know she'll be at the church tonight for choir practice. Do
you want me to go talk to her?" Justine asked.

Ella considered it, then shook her head. "No, she's going to
be a problem. I'll take care of this. It's no reflection on you. It's
just that people know about my family. If I tell her that even they
will have protection, it may put things in a different light for her."

"Who's going to guard your family?"

Ella filled Justine in on the way to her car. "So we will have
some extra manpower. That should help. I'll have an officer
watch Sadie's house tonight too. The Packrat seems to prefer
early morning, so she should be covered at that time regardless
of what she says."

"Sounds like a good plan," Justine said, stopping by Ella's vehicle. "If you don't need me anymore tonight, I'm going to meet
Furman. He's been doing his best to keep his ears open for me
and keep a watch out for anyone who might hold a grudge
against our ways." She plucked at the red Chieftains T-shirt she
wore. "He's the one who let me borrow this T-shirt so we could
trap Steven Nez."

"Be careful about giving him details of what we're doing,"

Ella said, concerned not only for Justine but for the investigation. Handling informants was difficult at best.

"I didn't tell him why I needed it. I just mentioned it when I saw him on my way back to the station. He brought it here for me. He didn't have to, you know. He's really pretty decent."

Something nagged at the back of her mind, but Ella reluctantly brushed it aside for now. Justine could be trusted to keep her mouth shut, and she did need a certain amount of autonomy with the sources she cultivated. "Keep me current," Ella said at last, getting into her car.

Ella drove directly home. When she arrived, she saw her mother outside speaking to Clifford. Ella sighed. The last place they should have been hanging around was near a lit porch after nightfall.

"Would you two get into the house? I'd like to speak to you," Ella said, a bit more curtly than she'd intended.

Rose led the way into the living room, then turned to face Ella. Rose's gaze was hard as it rested on her daughter. "I've just heard about the 'message' that was left near our mailbox. Why didn't you tell me? Did you think I didn't have a right to know?"

Ella sighed, then glared at her brother, who just shrugged. "I came home tonight to talk to you about it," Ella said. "There was no chance before."

"Are you telling me that your friends didn't know?"

Ella knew there was no sidestepping the issue. "You had been really looking forward to my having people over. It was enjoyable for us too. The carcasses were being taken care of. I didn't want to bring it up then; it would have ruined your evening."

"So instead, you kept something from me, something that I had every right to know. I'm not an old woman who needs to be sheltered from the truth. I expected more from you." Rose turned and strode down the hall to her room.

"I better go after her," Ella said.

"No, she's too upset to listen to you right now. Give her some time first," Clifford advised.

"Why did you have to tell her?"

"I didn't. Apparently Samuel Pete came by. His visit was unexpected, and she immediately suspected something wasn't right. She finally wormed it out of him."

Ella nodded. "I shouldn't have waited to talk to her about it, but she really was enjoying having company. I didn't want to spoil the evening for her. She's been after me to have people over . . ."

"Not people—*person*," Clifford corrected. "She wanted to fix a quiet dinner for you and Wilson."

"That I can't let her do, but she did enjoy my having Justine, Wilson and Carolyn over."

Clifford's eyebrows shot up. "That doctor was *here?*"

"Yes, and she's a friend of mine," Ella said, stemming any protest he might have made. Clifford nodded once, and she continued. "Now it's time for you and me to have a talk." She gestured to the couch. "All of us are in danger, and the department's manpower is stretched as far as it'll go. It would help matters all the way around if you and Loretta would move in with us until this is over."

He nodded. "I agree. That's why I came over. Loretta's brother is with her now, but she needs someone there almost 'round the clock. I can't be home all the time. There are others who need me as well. I've already asked Mother if we could move in until the baby arrives."

"Did she say yes?"

"Of course," Clifford answered.

Ella glanced back down the hall. Her mother's door was still closed. "Since she doesn't want to talk to me right now, I'll go take care of other business I've got pending. I'll be back in about an hour."

"Good. That'll give her a chance to calm down. You really blew it, you know. Don't ever try to protect her from something like this, even if it's just for a short while. It'll cost you her trust. As it is, it's going to take a long time for you to repair the damage already done."

Ella felt her heart turn to lead. "I know." Without further words, she went back to her vehicle. Sometimes you just couldn't win, no matter what you did.

Ella glanced at her watch. She'd go visit Sadie Morgan and have a talk with her. Maybe she could do some good there.

Pressing down on the accelerator, she headed back to the highway. Right now, speed, and the sense of control it gave her, was exactly what she needed.

Ella shuddered as she made the turn onto the road to the church. How any Navajo, Christian or not, ever managed to go into that place without getting the creeps was beyond her. The blood-soaked tunnels that had once run below and the abominations committed there were still too vivid in Ella's mind. No Blessing rite would ever erase those memories.

Ella watched the moon rise in the night sky. Clouds were massed to the north toward Four Corners, and lightning flashed along the horizon. It was raining, at least somewhere. But near Shiprock, the pale, silver orb washed the ground with a soft, welcoming light. Even that couldn't make Ella relax in this particular spot on the reservation. She opted for a shortcut, anything that would get her to the church and back out as soon as possible.

Taking a much less traveled dirt track, Ella shifted into low gear. She'd barely gone two miles when the ground became really rough. The high winds and summer rains had eroded this section of road. Regretting her decision to take the shortcut, she considered going back to the main road, then decided against it. She'd be fine if she just went slowly; the Jeep would get her there.

Before she reached her destination, she was forced to take two more detours around deep cuts in the road. Her shortcut turned out to be costing her more time than staying on the highway.

Ella expelled her breath in a hiss. That's the way it always was for her near this church. This particular area just brought bad luck, no matter how logically she tried to look at it.

Ella glanced at the digital clock on her dashboard. By now choir practice was over, and people would be getting ready to leave. It was nearly nine-thirty. Cursing her timing, she continued on. At least she'd covered the bases and, whether or not she managed to get to the church on time, a cop would still be watching Sadie's home tonight.

Ella reached the end of the dirt track and bounced the Jeep back onto pavement. As she shifted back into high gear, she saw headlights speeding directly toward her.

Checking her seat belt, Ella reached for the radio and called in. Something was wrong. The car coming her way down the church road was weaving practically all over the road. Ella lifted her foot from the accelerator, slowing down, ready to pursue or fire if she came under attack. Racking the mike, she gripped the steering wheel with both hands, ready to maneuver quickly. Her body was tense, a bead of perspiration running down her brow. The driver of the oncoming car was either running away, or running to, something.

As the car drew near, she recognized it was a VW Bug belonging to old Marie Jim. Ella remembered that Marie had seemed ancient even when Ella had been in high school. The thought of being under attack by old Mrs. Jim was ludicrous.

Mrs. Jim must have finally seen Ella's Jeep approaching because she slammed on the brakes and came to a sliding stop at an angle in the road. Ella stopped just short of the VW.

A few seconds later, Mrs. Jim opened the door and slowly stepped out of the car. Each of her steps was halting, but in the light of their headlights it was clear from her expression that something had upset her terribly.

Ella snapped shut the security strap on her holster and walked to meet the woman, identifying herself as she approached. She glanced automatically at Mrs. Jim's car, but if anyone was hiding in there, they were the size of a gnome. The backseat was filled with books and old cardboard boxes. "Are you all right?" Ella asked softly.

"It's terrible, just terrible!" Mrs. Jim's tone was shrill, nearly incoherent.

"What is?" Ella insisted, forcing her own voice to stay calm.

"They all left, but I had to go back. I forgot my puffer, my asthma inhaler, and I wouldn't have been able to get another one until tomorrow. I'm *always* forgetting it, and then the doctors at the emergency room get angry. On the way back, that's when it must have happened."

"*What* happened?" Ella tried to remain patient. She liked Mrs. Jim. Most people developed a core of hardness that insulated them from the miseries of the world, but Mrs. Jim never had. In many ways, she was like a child trying to act grown-up. Almost as if sensing that she was different, she kept to herself. She seldom went out socially. So finding her out here at this time of night alone was a surprise. "If you tell me what's upset you, maybe I can help," Ella coaxed her.

"I don't know what happened. We had choir practice. I can't sing very well, but no one seems to mind. I do try." Her expression became distant as her thoughts wandered off track.

"You had choir practice, then what? What's the problem?"

Mrs. Jim's expression grew pained. "I *told* you. I had to go back. She was okay when we all left, so I'm not sure what happened! But she is very dead!"

Ella felt her skin prickle. "Who's dead?"

"Sadie Morgan. She's hanging from the choir loft, and there's blood everywhere."

TWENTY

✖ ✖ ✖

Ella felt sick, but she brushed aside the sinking feeling in her stomach. She had to act immediately. Perhaps there was some mistake, or Sadie wasn't dead yet. "Leave your car here, Mrs. Jim. We'll come back for it later. I need you to come with me."

Ella helped Mrs. Jim into the Jeep, brushing aside the old lady's protests as tactfully as possible.

"I really don't want to go with you," Mrs. Jim practically whimpered. "You can see it for yourself. You don't need me."

Ella called for backup and a rescue unit as she sped to the church, her insides knotted. She didn't blame Mrs. Jim for being frightened, but she couldn't leave the other woman alone now either. "You say you went back for your inhaler?"

Mrs. Jim nodded. "I was almost all the way home, but I knew that Sadie usually stays late after everyone's gone. She's been going through all the hymnals, making sure the binding's okay and separating the ones that will need repair. I figured I'd take a chance. There's no phone out there, so I couldn't call, and I wanted to avoid going by the PHS hospital and asking for another puffer. I can barely afford to buy them now. They cost so much."

"And so what happened?"

Mrs. Jim took her inhaler out of her purse, used it, then continued. "The front door was open, so I went down the center aisle and directly upstairs to the choir loft. I found my puffer right by where I'd been sitting and picked it up. Then I heard a squeaking sound."

"Like someone opening a rusty door?"

Mrs. Jim shook her head. "No, more like the sound wood makes when you walk over it, you know?"

Ella nodded. "Then what?"

"I walked to the edge of the loft, thinking it was Sadie coming to see who was there." Mrs. Jim coughed and began to wheeze. She used her inhaler again. "It was her all right, but she was hanging there upside down. I had to bend down and turn my head so I could see her face right-side-up and make sure."

"Did you see or hear anyone else while you were inside?" Ella asked. She was afraid to question Mrs. Jim too long and possibly trigger a severe attack. She needed to be at the crime scene now, not driving someone to the hospital. The old lady shook her head, unable to answer out loud immediately.

Ella pulled to a stop by the main steps. The parking lot was deserted except for an old pickup she assumed belonged to Sadie. Ella turned to Mrs. Jim. "Stay here, and keep the doors locked. If anyone comes up, or your breathing gets worse, honk the horn. I won't be long."

Ella grabbed her flashlight, left the car, and went through the church's front door, which was wide open. A light was on in the foyer, but the rest of the church was in darkness. The moment she stepped inside, she felt her body tense, and she decided to draw her weapon as well as turn on her flashlight. It was more than the murder Mrs. Jim had reported; this place was tainted with evil. No ceremonies to the Christian god could erase that.

Ella felt a gust of wind, then heard the squeaking sound Mrs. Jim had described. As she walked down the center aisle, her flashlight beam illuminated the rope that hung from the choir loft. At the bottom, swaying slowly back and forth like a run-down pendulum bob, was Sadie Morgan.

The woman was hanging by her feet, but her long skirt was

still in place at ankle length, wrapped tightly against her legs with masking tape. The killer had wanted her face to be seen, as well as the wound in her throat.

Ella stared at the trail of blood that had flowed from the victim's neck. It had marked out a crimson path over her chin and face, and lastly dripped down from her long hair onto the floor. The thick pool had not fully coagulated yet. Also covered with blood and dangling from her neck were the remnants of a thin silver chain. A pendant, possibly a cross, had obviously been torn from the chain, breaking it.

Both of the victim's arms dangled almost to the floor, and in the palm of her right hand was another bloody wound. Sticking out of the center, like a nail in Christ's hand, was a white piece of bone. It was the Packrat's M.O. again.

Ella swallowed the bile at the back of her throat and went up to the victim. Once again the crime had been carefully staged, down to the inverted hanging and the application of masking tape. If the killer had kept to his signature style, Sadie Morgan had not been aware of her death, but had been rendered helpless and unconscious first.

As Ella stood near the body she could smell a peculiar scent in the air. It wasn't incense; it had a more acrid, pungent edge. If it was perfume, then Sadie Morgan had used the most distasteful scent she'd ever encountered.

Ella went up the choir loft steps, located the light switch, and looked around. There were a few signs of a struggle. A chair had been knocked over, and hymnals lay scattered all over the floor. Then Ella saw a dirty cloth on the floor, and as she approached, she knew the scent had come from it. She crouched beside it. The smell reminded her of the chemicals at Carolyn's. It was probably chloroform, but she couldn't be sure.

Suddenly hearing the sound of her Jeep's horn echoing through the empty church, Ella jumped to her feet. Reaching for her weapon, she ran down the short flight of stairs and sprinted down the center aisle to the main entrance. It only took a few seconds, but by then the horn had stopped. She stood by the edge of the door for a heartbeat, gun in hand, and peered outside. Seeing the flashing red and blue lights of an approaching police car, Ella sighed with relief. Mrs. Jim had done precisely what she'd been asked to do. She'd seen someone approaching and had honked the horn.

Ella put her weapon away and tried to force her heart rate down. It was going to be a very long night.

Justine was working with Ella in the choir loft as Carolyn did her examination on the victim below. "I'll track down the rope, and check for sources of chloroform," Justine volunteered. That can't be that easy to find on the Rez. I think it might just give us a good solid lead."

"Don't count on it," Ella cautioned. "This guy's crafty. Sick, but smart. For all we know, he drove to Cortez or Farmington for the stuff. Carolyn confirmed my estimate that the victim hadn't been dead long when I arrived. That's why I had Nelson Franklin come in. He and Susan Cohoe are the tribe's best trackers. Franklin prefers his bloodhounds, but Susan works the old way, with her eyes."

"I understand they don't generally like to work with each other, but in this case, they didn't seem to have a problem. Everyone wants this guy caught."

"Do you know if anyone found a set of vehicle tracks leading off by themselves, or in the dirt?" Ella asked. She hoped the killer was still on foot. Franklin and Cohoe were with two well-armed officers.

"Just one set, but Mrs. Jim said that it probably belongs to Reverend Curley's car. He often parks off to the side. They led back to the pavement anyway. But the trackers are following a partially obscured set of footprints now that looks promising."

Ella tried not to get her hopes up, but it was hard not to feel a sense of expectation. The killer had been right where she was standing a short while ago. The trackers were hot on his trail now, and it looked like the thunderstorm she'd noted earlier was passing to the east. No tracks would be erased by rain tonight. The Packrat's luck was starting to run low.

"How's Mrs. Jim breathing? I haven't spoke with her since she confirmed the victim was missing a wooden cross from that chain." With gloved hands, she and Justine finished dusting for fingerprints on the rail from which the body had been suspended.

"The EMT gave her a shot for the asthma," Justine said. "She's calmed down a bit, but she said she wasn't coming into this church again. Strange, considering she's supposed to be Christian. Their view of death is just a passing, I thought. And they stare at that crucifix for hours, forgetting why viewing a dead person is so unpleasant for a traditional Navajo."

"Yes, but the crucifix is just art. It's sanitized, you know? The body, dripping blood—well, that's as real as it gets." Ella saw Justine check around and along the railing for fibers, hair, or anything that would lead to the killer. Later, she knew, the crime team would vacuum the area.

"I've got to confirm everyone on our list has protection tonight, even if they don't want it. I want someone right outside my home too. My brother, my sister-in-law, and my mother will all be there."

Justine stood up. "I'll call that in right now. The watch commander should be able to handle it."

"Go ahead."

Ella searched carefully for a few more minutes, then went downstairs. She joined Carolyn, who was crouched next to the most recent victim. Ella glanced at the corpse, which had been laid on a piece of plastic, then looked at Carolyn. "What can you tell me?"

"This Packrat is one sick puppy. I'm certain he used the chloroform to knock her out, but she struggled for a while before passing out. It looks like she may have scratched him, so I bagged her hands. I'll check for skin, fibers, and hair at the lab."

"The chloroform was necessary to him in more ways than one. He does like them helpless before he kills, but in this case he also needed that in order to be able to tape her skirt around her legs. Had he waited until she was hanging from the rope, it would have been difficult to reach up that high on her ankles to tape. Nobody's found any rolls of masking tape around, so he must have anticipated the problem and brought the tape with him. That means he also knew what she would be wearing. Our Packrat is very organized."

"You've got no argument from me there." Carolyn studied the body before her. "He also has a flair for the dramatic. He strung her from the rail, then slit her throat. She bled to death in a few minutes. He severed her jugular. Hanging her upside down was just for effect. I mean, it served no purpose that I can see. After that, he yanked off the cross pendant. There's a cut on the back of her neck, but no blood around it. I guess he thought it was tacky to take a trophy before completing the kill."

"That fits our guy," Ella said. "Warped all the way."

"You know, since this must have happened right before you got here, Mrs. Jim was lucky to have missed him. Or maybe he just hid from her."

"He's selective about his targets, so who knows? But if he's still nearby, I'll find him. I've got people out there beating the bushes, and roadblocks in place to catch traffic originating from here."

"You've got your investigation under control, so I better get to mine. It's too late for me to begin the autopsy tonight, but I'll get back to you sometime tomorrow."

"Carolyn, you need an assistant."

Carolyn stood up and rubbed her back. "Sure I do, but I don't think I'm likely to find one. Do you?"

Ella gave her a rueful smile. "No, not really. Not a Navajo, at least."

"Don't worry. I may get tired, but I'm good at my work. I don't get sloppy. Not ever."

"I know that," Ella assured her quietly. "I was just looking at the dark circles around your eyes. I have a feeling I have a matching set."

Carolyn smiled. "You do." She glanced around. "I'm going to get Officer Leonard to give me a hand. I've never liked him," she added with a trace of a smile.

Ella sucked in her cheeks to keep from smiling. Officer Leonard seemed to delight in arguing about any subject, but didn't really seem to have any opinions of his own. He simply took the opposite view of whatever was being said, then debated it at length as if it was his most cherished belief. It was annoying after a while. Like most everyone else, she watched what she said around him, tending to snap cryptic orders rather than risk an endless debate.

"Officer Leonard, your help please," Carolyn said brusquely.

He glanced at the body with distaste. "Couldn't you get—"

"Help our medical investigator, Officer," Ella ordered. "If your religious beliefs include ghost sickness, then we'll try to find someone else."

"I do not believe in ghost sickness. That's not founded in logic, although many cultures—"

Ella held up a hand. "Yes or no, Officer? Are you going to help the lady?"

As he reluctantly turned around and walked to the corpse, Carolyn smiled mischievously at Ella, then turned back to the job at hand.

As the body was being wheeled down the center aisle, Ella heard a vehicle's siren start up, and the squeal of tires. Within seconds, the sound of an emergency vehicle had faded into the distance.

Carolyn came in from outside and joined Ella, who was staring at her curiously. "The vehicle that just left was the rescue squad, not a cop car. Apparently some pickup got caught in an arroyo by a wave of water and people were hurt."

"Damn. I was hoping the search team had cornered our killer near the road." Ella shook her head slowly. "I hope there were no deaths. I suppose we'll hear soon enough though. It's so frustrating. We tell kids and adults to stay away from the ditches and arroyos, that they're deadly. Yet every summer someone gets caught in one. You'd think our people would know the land better. Just because it's dry at the moment they go in doesn't mean that in another second a wall of water won't come rushing straight at them. It's the way our terrain is. That's what cut those arroyos in the first place."

"The summer storms have just started. People, particularly kids, forget, or don't listen. I'll let you know as soon as the EMTs make a report if there were fatalities or not."

Ella sucked in a long breath. "If kids have died, the tribe will link it to this latest death here at this ill-fated church."

Carolyn nodded. "They'll say that our new generation is now being threatened. It's going to create a panic."

"And that *will* threaten everyone." Ella felt the crushing weight of responsibility pressing down on her. "Maybe we're borrowing trouble. It's possible no one was seriously hurt." But even as she said it, she could sense it wasn't true. The air itself seemed to vibrate with a fundamental sadness that spoke of tragedies yet to come.

Ella shook free of the feeling, struggling to keep her mind on the crime scene as Carolyn left and Justine approached. "How are the trackers doing?"

"I just spoke to Susan," Justine answered. "There were footprints cutting across the desert toward the college, but then the trail disappeared as he cut through some brush and a rocky canyon. Nelson's dogs couldn't follow it either after that point."

"Anything else I should know about?"

"Mrs. Jim wants to leave. We have her statement, and before the EMT left he said she didn't require further medical treatment, but she's still very upset. I don't think she ought to drive anywhere, but she won't leave Wilma."

"Wilma who?"

"Her car. The VW." Justine smiled and shrugged. "Hey, maybe when you and I get old, we'll name our cars like they're old friends."

"I'm already aging—by the second," Ella answered, glancing at the scene.

Twenty minutes later, Ella found an ATM receipt from the bank in Shiprock in Sadie Morgan's pickup. The date and time indicated she had withdrawn sixty dollars from her account at 6:45 P.M., just a half hour before choir practice.

Walking back into the church, Ella found her assistant sitting on the floor, the contents of the victim's purse spread before her. "Justine, how much money did you find in there?"

"About, let's see, a dollar thirteen in change. I haven't looked in her wallet yet." Justine looked up at Ella curiously. "You think the Packrat took money this time?"

"It really doesn't fit his M.O, but it's worth checking. She should have about sixty-plus dollars with her." Ella held out the ATM receipt for Justine to see. "Packrat's always taken something, but never money, and the cross the victim wore around her neck is missing. Still, sixty bucks is a lot of money and a lot of temptation. Let's see if Packrat succumbed."

Justine opened the old leather billfold carefully by the edges, then whistled softly. Ella leaned over and looked inside. The money compartment was empty except for a small newspaper cartoon of the devil.

"Maybe Packrat left this behind for us in addition to the bone in her palm," Justine said, using a pair of tweezers to pluck the cartoon out.

Ella had two evidence pouches ready, and Justine placed the cartoon in one and the wallet in the other.

"Check everything, including the purse, for prints. We might get lucky," Ella requested. "We'll also have to ask the others who were here tonight if any money changed hands. If not, then it looks like our killer may have taken up theft as well as murder."

"There's a first time for everything," Justine agreed.

"Packrat's not waiting anymore for daylight to strike either," Ella observed grimly.

Two hours later, the crime-scene unit began to pack up. The yellow tape line would remain in place, but for now the work here was finished. A wrecker had already hauled away Sadie's pickup to be impounded.

The trackers and the officers who had responded earlier had cleared out some time go. Their services were needed to help search for victims caught in the flash flood. Ute and Tache had been the next to leave. Justine remained with Ella as she walked around the church, still searching for anything that would point her in the right direction.

"It's getting late," Justine said softly.

"Go home. I can take care of things here."

"No, that's okay. I'll stick around until you're ready to leave."

"Don't you have to drop the evidence pouches off?"

"No, the crime unit took all that in."

Ella stared at the pool of blood that had congealed and now stained the base of the pew. "He's going to make a mistake sooner or later. Then we'll take him down."

Ella glanced at Justine and realized that the young woman was on the brink of exhaustion. "You wanted to work with me. Do you regret that decision now?"

"No," Justine replied softly, too tired to evoke much more emotion than the gentle reply. "This is where I'm needed. That's important to me."

"And to me," Ella admitted. "Come on. Let's call it a night."

They were just locking the side door when they heard a car pulling up. As Ella placed her hand on her pistol butt, she noticed Justine was also reaching for her weapon. Signaling for Justine to remain there, Ella moved noiselessly toward the front of the church.

Suddenly a young Navajo man dressed in black charged inside the church. "This place is a mockery!" he yelled. "It's an insult to every Navajo. This is a place that belongs to us!"

The man was obviously playing to an audience, but the only ones there were Justine and she. Ella called out to him from the shadows. "This is a crime scene. Please step outside *now!*"

"This place *is* a crime, by its very existence!" He reached into his sleeve and pulled out a long black dagger. Turning away from Ella he imbedded the blade in a tapestry depicting the birth of Christ and pulled it down, ripping the fabric.

Justine came out in a Weaver stance, her left foot slightly forward and her pistol in a steady two-handed grip. "Drop the knife. Now!"

The young man did as she ordered, but didn't seem frightened that a pistol was aimed at his chest. "Can't you see that this place is tainted? You should *know* that. No wonder there was a murder here."

Justine handed Ella her weapon, forced the man against the wall, and frisked him.

Ella stood back, gun at the ready. "How do you know about the murder?"

"I was led here. I am a Navajo warlock and skinwalker."

"A *whaaat?*" Ella resisted the impulse to laugh. It was like claiming to be a Baptist druid.

"I am in league with Satan and his demons. They brought me here tonight. They told me about the murder."

"I don't know how to break it to you," Justine said, cuffing him, "but warlocks, devils, and the Christian god have nothing to do with skinwalkers."

"I use all the entities that give me aid. Our own skinwalkers haven't even dreamed of the power I hold."

Justine glanced back at Ella, keeping her hand on the suspect leaning against the wall, and rolled her eyes. "What's your name?"

"How can you *not* know who I am?"

"Humor me," Justine snapped.

"I'm Anton Lewis." The man was indignant. "You better release me right now. You don't want the kind of trouble I can bring you."

Ella moved forward, replacing her gun in the holster now that the suspect was cuffed. She handed Justine her own weapon since there was no longer a risk of Lewis's making a grab for it. "Are you threatening a police officer at a crime scene?"

"I'm stating a fact. I am a powerful Navajo warlock, the first of my kind, but not the last. There will be more like me."

Ella shook her head. "I'm going to radio for backup and let a uniform take him."

Justine took the prisoner and followed Ella outside. As they waited for a unit to arrive, Justine made Lewis sit on the ground. Finally a patrol car approached, and Officer Leonard emerged. "I just came on duty. It's a good thing too. All available officers

from the evening shift are still at that drowning accident." He
looked at the cuffed suspect with obvious distaste. "Not *you*
again, Lewis. I thought I told you to stay away from this church."

"You know him?" Ella asked.

"He shows up on Sundays and Wednesdays once in a while
and harasses the Christian worshipers. It's his *mission*."

Leonard grabbed Lewis's arm. "Come on. I tried to tell you.
Nobody's interested in your smorgasbord religious doctrine."

"I am who and what I am. That alone should refute your
skepticism," Lewis countered angrily.

"I'm me and you're not. How do you like that?" Officer
Leonard shot back.

Ella watched cop and prisoner argue all the way back to the
squad car, grateful she wasn't going to be riding with them. As
they drove away, she and Justine walked to Lewis's car, which
not surprisingly was an old black hearse. "Get this impounded
and taken to the station," she told Justine, peering inside. "So
much for the devil connection. He's got a police scanner in here,
and a list of 10- codes. He knew what was going on here."

"What a nut case!" Justine said. Picking up her portable radio,
she called in the request for a tow.

Ella rubbed her eyes, then stifled a yawn. "I've got to get
some sleep." She glanced at Justine and smiled. "And so do you."

"Yeah. I think it's time to wrap up for the night. Lewis will
wait until tomorrow. Besides the obvious, what do you make of
him?"

"I don't know yet. But it is interesting how he scrambles skinwalker beliefs with the Christian counterpart, devil worship.
That could account for the ash painting at the first crime scene
not being quite right, and the medicine pouch full of weeds. It's
also interesting to note that the latest victim belongs to this
church, whose members he's harassed on a regular basis."

"Sadie Morgan was a devout Christian, all right. But she was
keeping our past alive, too, by teaching and preserving our language. If he wanted to kill cultural experts, and hates Christians,
she was a perfect target."

Ella shook her head. "But why kill cultural experts? So no-

body can argue the illogic of what he claims to be? I don't know."
Ella said finally, "We'll dig up everything we can on Lewis tomorrow. Right now I've got to go check on my family."

"Do you want me to go with you?"

"No, but thanks for the offer. Who's assigned to watch them, do you know?"

"I think Officer Michael Cloud volunteered."

"My family couldn't be in better hands," Ella said with a tiny smile. "He's Herman Cloud's nephew."

"I figured you'd approve." Justine walked to her car. "See you tomorrow."

Ella drove home quickly, wondering how her family had reacted to Officer Cloud's presence. Since Herman Cloud was a longtime family friend, she didn't really expect much trouble.

Ella arrived home some time later and saw the patrol unit parked by the side of the house. She could barely make out the car's shadow within the shadow of the house, but instinct told her that Officer Cloud was right there, watching over those Ella loved.

As Ella walked up to the front porch, lights came on, illuminating the front and backyards. Wilson had installed the motion detectors.

"I'm here," Officer Cloud said, stepping out to meet her, "and I'll be here until morning. Another officer will relieve me then, but I'll be back in the evening. Your family will have 'round-the-clock protection."

"Who will relieve you?"

"There were plenty of volunteers, but my brother Philip will be the one who takes over for me here during the day."

Ella smiled. "How did you two manage that?"

Michael smiled. "We weren't allowed to guard our own uncle, like we'd planned, so we traded with Norman Bitsillie and Irwin Nakai for this post."

Ella nodded. "I'm glad you two will be here," she said, then walked inside her home.

Rose came out of the kitchen as soon as she came in. "I've been very worried about you. Something else has happened, right?"

"Yes." Ella looked around. "Where's Loretta?"

Clifford came into the living room from the hall. "She's finally asleep. You can talk freely."

Ella told them about the murder without mentioning Sadie except by references out of respect for their beliefs. To avoid summoning his or her *chindi* it was unwise to name the dead until four days had passed. "I know she was a friend of Wilson's. I really don't look forward to giving him the news, but I will do it tomorrow morning. I'd like him to hear it from me first."

"I think he would appreciate that very much," Rose answered. "But this is terrible," she said, slipping down into one of the chairs. "The *Dineh* is losing its greatest treasures. Those who possess knowledge of old are disappearing. When is it going to end?"

Ella thought about the incident at the arroyo, but decided against mentioning it until she knew more. If children had died, then it would be said that along with the old and the knowledge they possessed, evil was robbing them of the very lifeblood of the future. She suppressed the shudder that touched her spine.

"Do you have a suspect?" Clifford asked.

"Yes, but I'll have to check him out more thoroughly before I can be sure." Ella told them about Anton Lewis. "Have you heard anything about this guy?"

Clifford nodded. "Some. He likes attention, that much I've learned, and he drives an old hearse, probably for that reason. I know he's harassed Reverend Williamson, but he's really singled out Reverend Curley. He's the new church's minister."

"Is this Reverend Curley a Navajo?"

"Sort of," Clifford answered with a trace of a smile.

"What do you mean by that?" Ella asked.

"By race he's Navajo, but he was raised in a California city and knows absolutely nothing about his heritage and our customs."

"Anything else you can tell me about Anton Lewis?"

Clifford considered it, his gaze fixing on something across the room. "Most just avoid him, but I do believe he has a small band of followers. Supposedly they look up to him and do what he asks."

"Which says something about their intelligence." Ella blinked the haze out of her vision. Her eyelids felt like sandpaper. "I need to get some sleep." She glanced at her mother. "I assume you put our visitors in my room, right?"

Rose shook her head. "No. Your brother and his wife have my room. It's larger than yours, and I figured they would be more comfortable in there. I'll sleep on the sofa bed in your father's study."

Ella shook her head. "No, let me take that." Ella suspected that her mother would feel restless in a room that had retained so much of her father's personality. "You can use my room."

Rose shook her head stubbornly. "You need uninterrupted, comfortable sleep time. Stay in your own room. I'll stay in the den. Your brother did a Blessingway on everything after your father's death. There's nothing in there that can bother me."

"Are you sure?" Ella saw her mom nod, so she continued. "In that case, I'm off to bed. I have to be up early, but I'll try not to wake anyone."

"I'll be up at dawn," Clifford said.

"I hope you're not planning to go anywhere. You're needed here," Ella said.

"I'll be around. Things are too critical. With Peterson at large, I won't trust my family to anyone else. I know Michael and Philip Cloud, and I'm sure they'll do their best, but this is primarily my responsibility."

Ella walked slowly to her room. So many were counting on her! She needed to make progress soon. Her mother was right. The tribe couldn't afford any more tragedies.

The following morning, Ella went to work early. By then she had the details of the other disaster that had taken place the night before. The newspaper reported the Packrat's killing of Sadie Morgan, but most of the front page detailed the drowning deaths of almost an entire Navajo family. It coincided with a report Carolyn had given her.

Their pickup had become stuck in a deep arroyo and a wave of water from the thunderstorm had swept away five small children riding in the open bed and two teenagers in the cab. One small boy had survived somehow by clinging to a wheel of the overturned truck, but six were dead. The Tribal Council had called an emergency meeting to discuss ways of coping with the recent tragedy.

Ella's mother and brother had read the accounts. Although a touch of fear had shone in their eyes, the only audible comment they'd made was their decision to keep the paper out of Loretta's hands for now.

Shortly after nine, Justine walked into Ella's office, folder in hand. "I've got the book on Lewis. He has no real record. He's disrupted Sunday services, but Reverend Curley wouldn't press charges."

"Why not?"

"You'll have to ask him," Justine said.

"Let's talk to Lewis first. We'll have to release him soon, anyway, because the knife he had doesn't check out as the murder weapon. Carolyn verified that it's much too big and dull to have made the throat wounds. There is no physical evidence at all linking him to the crime, either. The church isn't even going to make him pay for the damage to the tapestry. Did he ever ask for an attorney?"

"No, Lewis says he has nothing to hide, so he doesn't need one."

"Then let's go ask our questions before he changes his mind," Ella said, reaching for the phone.

Ella made a call to have Lewis escorted from the holding cell to one of the small interview rooms they used to question suspects. Ella met their prisoner there, then nodded to the officer who had brought him in handcuffed.

After Lewis's hands were free, Ella asked him to sit down. Lewis stared at her suspiciously, then glanced at Justine, who stood leaning against the wall. "If you two think this is going to put you on my good side and I'll make some dramatic confession, you're wrong."

"You're in a lot of trouble, Lewis," Ella warned, "and you'd be doing yourself a favor if you talked to us. There was a murder committed in that church a short time before you arrived."

"But that's the key, isn't it?" Lewis baited her. "I wasn't there *when* the murder was committed. There's no way you can place me there at the time of the murder."

"You were sure there soon enough afterwards. You could have been hiding nearby, parked in some arroyo, waiting for our people to clear," Justine challenged.

"Then why wouldn't I have waited until all of you were gone?" he countered smoothly. "I heard all your calls on the scanner. I knew who was coming and going. You're grasping at straws. Don't underestimate my intelligence. I'm a lot smarter than, say, those idiots who drowned last night." The smile he gave Justine never reached his eyes.

"You may have wanted to taunt us," Ella suggested, ignoring his crude comment. "By coming out and putting on a show, you were doing what you do best—getting attention for yourself."

His eyes flashed with anger. "I have certain powers and I offer them to our People. It's what I do for them."

"Oh, please! Cut the crap. Nobody has boots high enough to wade through that much manure." Ella's tone was harsh.

"Don't insult me. You don't want to turn me into an enemy." His voice was monotone, lending it even more menace.

"You said that already, last night. Are you threatening me again?" Ella countered.

"It's just a matter of logic," Lewis answered with a shrug. "You need information from me. You're going to lose all hope of getting it if you piss me off."

Ella felt her temper rising. With effort, she kept it from showing in her expression. "If you have information pertinent to the crime, tell it to me now. You don't want to be charged with obstructing justice, do you?"

"Some justice," Lewis spat out. "You're picking on me because I had the guts to try and shut down that church. It's a place that no one without powers can approach with impunity. What happened there just proves my point."

"But you can go there without endangering yourself, right?" Justine asked.

"You bet I can. I can control the forces there, even more so than those who rely only on their abilities as skinwalkers. I command the demons that fight the cross as well. They help me whenever I ask."

"Why are you trying to run the Christians off from that site? What difference could it possibly make to you? You live off the reservation in Farmington," Ella insisted.

"I'm trying to show Navajos a better way. Skinwalkers, Christianity—it's all a search for power. I can show them how to get it."

"There have been three murders on this reservation recently. After the way you acted at the church, and particularly in view of your beliefs and goals, tell me why we shouldn't consider you a suspect."

"I've read about the murders. I have no alibi that you would value. Kee Dodge was killed right before one of his classes, according to what I read. I'm usually in bed until noon. I don't like mornings," he added with a shrug. "Haske was killed in the early morning too."

"Can anyone corroborate that you were in bed?"

He laughed. "You mean did I have one of my followers there to keep me warm?" He shook his head. "I don't play those games."

Ella watched him carefully. "What kind of games *do* you play?"

"You're starting to bore me. I know you can only hold me for twenty-four hours without filing charges. Do you have anything to charge me with? If not, then I'm close to walking out of here."

Ella met the challenge in his gaze with one of her own. "Oh, we'll eventually let you go. We want you to have enough rope to hang yourself if you *did* murder those people."

"I haven't killed anyone," Lewis answered with a thin smile. "But by all means, waste your time looking for evidence against me while the real killer runs free. Then people will see your incompetence. When people lose faith in their leaders, they look elsewhere for their salvation. I intend to be there to offer them a choice. With all these people dying lately, it may be sooner than you think."

The words were so reminiscent of Peterson Yazzie's that Ella regarded him bitterly. "That's enough for now, Lewis." She glanced at Justine. "Take him back to his cell until his twenty-four hours are up."

He was playing with her, much like Peterson would have. She watched Justine handcuff and lead him out to return him to holding. Before the end of the day, however, she intended to know everything about Anton Lewis. If he was Peterson's stooge, then Peterson had made a crucial mistake, and she intended to exploit it for all it was worth.

Big Ed came into the interview room and sat across the desk from her. "Is that our man?"

"Maybe. He fits the profile, and his shoe size matches. But the knife he had wasn't the murder weapon."

"If Peterson Yazzie is using Lewis, then that could be another of Peterson's mind games."

"That's very true, but I can only work with the evidence I uncover. For now I'll just have to continue gathering facts. Eventually the pieces will all start to fit together, then the weave of the pattern will be clear." She stared at a spiderweb that filled the far corner of the room. "I've learned one thing over the years: To restore order, or harmony as my brother would say, one needs patience most of all."

TWENTY-ONE

———— ✖ ✖ ✖ ————

Shortly after ten-thirty that morning, Justine walked into Ella's office. "I got the bureau report on the paint chips recovered from Haske's clothing. It's a factory finish on the more inexpensive Ford fleet vehicles, both sedans and trucks."

"At least we can exclude trucks, based on the evidence we already have. But that doesn't narrow our search much. Several tribal agencies use fleet vehicles from the interagency motor pool."

"We can call around first to see if any vehicles have been damaged recently. If there's no record, then we'll have to go and check every single one," Justine said with a shrug. "Shall I get on that?"

"Please. I've been trying to get hold of Peterson's lawyer, Bruce Cohen, but I can't get him either at the office or at home. I may end up having to go over there."

Ella made one more call to Cohen's office and finally a stranger answered. It was another attorney, a man named Bob Carpenter. According to him, Bruce Cohen had asked for police protection the moment Yazzie escaped. Within hours, Cohen had taken a leave of absence and left town, headed somewhere back east with his family. He wasn't planning on returning until Yazzie was returned to confinement.

As her telephone began to ring, Ella picked it up and identified herself. Leroy Johnson, from the post office in Shiprock, was on the other end. "Can you stop by my office? I think you'll want to see a letter we intercepted that's addressed to you. Since it has no return address I kept it here like you asked, but it was mailed from inside the reservation."

"I can be there in about forty-five minutes. Is that soon enough?"

"No problem. I'll be here."

Ella hung up the phone. "I think something's up. Leroy just called from the post office. There's a letter for me that might be from Peterson."

Justine nodded. "What would you like me to do first, then?"

"Start on the fleet vehicles. I should be back in about two hours, then I'll work with you. It'll go faster with both of us checking things out," Ella said.

"Great!"

Her relief was so obvious, Ella laughed. "I wasn't going to abandon you to it," she said.

"Good. Tracking down individual fleet cars in search of one in particular is going to be like searching for the proverbial needle in a haystack."

"Maybe we'll get lucky. We're about due for a change."

When Ella arrived at the post office, she found Leroy behind the counter sorting packages.

Seeing her come through the door, he gave her a worried smile. "I hope I haven't wasted your time."

"Don't give that another thought. I'm grateful that you telephoned me rather than just sending the letter out for delivery."

Leonard led the way back to his desk, then reached into the bottom drawer to withdraw a plastic sack that held a legal-sized envelope. He handled it gingerly, as if it were tainted. "I wish none of us had ever heard of skinwalkers. Many people are coming here with fear in their eyes now that those youngsters are dead and Yazzie is still on the loose. People are wondering what will happen next."

Ella reached inside her purse and pulled out surgical gloves. It was a slim hope, but maybe if they could lift another fingerprint besides Yazzie's, she'd be able to track him down through whoever was helping him. Ella removed the envelope, slit it open carefully with her pocketknife, then pulled the letter out.

It took all her training not to let the vileness of the comments within show in her expression, but she didn't want to alarm Leroy.

> Ella
> I hope you are sleeping well. You looked so tired last time we spoke. I want you to be rested when I come for you and put my hands around your neck. Speaking of strangulation, I could just feel my strength growing when I squeezed the life out of that pretty nurse—Isabel, was that her name? Maybe that's the way I'll kill you. Or do you prefer a knife to the heart? Perhaps I'll let you choose, if you're nice to me.
>
> I believe the work of my novice student has attracted some of your attention, too. I had a good laugh when he described how he killed that quack Haske. I only wish I could have been there myself. He gave me all the details when he helped me escape that jail they call a hospital.
>
> He wanted me there next time one of your friends dies. I told him I'd be delighted. You're invited too, only I know you'll be late, as usual. Ella, you're getting too old and stupid to put a stop to us. Give up, and just wait there in your home. We'll get around to you sooner or later. Just how soon will be our surprise.
>
> Yours in every way imaginable—Peterson

Ella folded the letter slowly, taking care not to reveal her thoughts.

"It was from Yazzie, right?"

Ella nodded. "I appreciate your help. I wouldn't have wanted this delivered to my home."

"I heard this morning that you've caught the Packrat," Leroy said.

Ella smiled, knowing the futility of trying to keep gossip from spreading. "We have a suspect, that's all, but we can't charge him at this point."

"I don't understand. I thought you'd arrested Anton Lewis."

"How did you hear that?"

Leroy smiled, but shook his head. "I don't want to get any-one in trouble. But for every police officer, there are mothers and fathers, and uncles and . . . Well, we all talk."

Ella nodded. "Anton Lewis is a strange one, but I don't have enough evidence to hold him at this point."

"He's one crazy Navajo. He should have stayed in Nevada with his father."

"What can you tell me about him?"

"I know that his mother is Navajo and his father is an Anglo card dealer at some casino in Lake Tahoe or Reno. His mother and father divorced a few years back, when Anton was in his twenties. Some say Anton's been on his own since he was seven. His parents never paid any attention to him unless he got into trouble."

"Have you met Lewis?"

"Nah, the only ones who come into contact with him are his followers and the people who attend that Christian church on the Rez. Lewis gets his rabble to stand in the road or in front of the doors and block the way to the church services. He makes a big pain out of himself."

"Thanks for the information. I appreciate it."

Ella checked in with the dispatcher on the way back to the sta-tion, then was patched through to Justine. "What progress have you made?" Ella asked.

"I've narrowed it down some. My calls to the tribal govern-ment led to a few cars that had come in for servicing. I went to the garage, but none had front-end damage like we're looking for. I then arranged for several departments to have their supervisors check each car for exterior damage as it's driven in tomorrow. They'll call us if they find anything. Last of all, I finally received permission to check the fleet vehicles the college uses. The campus is going to be my next stop."

"I'll meet you there."

Justine gave her directions to the assigned area where the vehicles were parked. "Just drive up to the fence behind the library. I'll be there by the time you arrive."

"Expect me in thirty," Ella said and increased her speed. The transit times were starting to wear on her. With Peterson on the loose, she knew there was little time to lose. Somehow she felt certain that the promise he'd made in his letter of another murder was not part of a mind game, but rather a very real possibility.

Ella stayed on the paved roads. It was after lunchtime, and the heat was oppressive enough to have made the roads almost deserted. People had a tendency to stay indoors when it was in the one-hundred-degree range.

Ella saw the distortions of objects nearby as heat seemed to shimmer off the pavement and rise up in curling waves. Poor Justine was probably cursing the investigation and Peterson Yazzie by now. Extremes in heat did little to improve anyone's mood.

Ella drummed her fingers on the wheel, reviewing the case and listening to radio calls as she drove. She had to get a lead to Peterson soon. She had a feeling he was frantically trying to locate his remaining followers. The murders might have all been intended to keep her distracted while he escaped and regrouped his people.

That thought sent a shudder up her spine. She was no coward, but a fight with skinwalkers would always involve the trickery and illusion that were so much a part of their arsenal. As much as she hated to admit it, those things unnerved her deeply. She preferred cleaner fights, where toughness and skill determined the winner.

As she arrived at the college, Ella followed Justine's directions and met her at the parking lot.

Justine opened the gate for her and led her to the cars. "I've got the first row done. The secretary couldn't remember any vehicles reported as being in an accident, but their computer is down. Since there aren't that many, I figured that I'd go through these one at a time and search for damage or attempts to fix or cover up something."

"I'll take the second row while you take the third, and we'll finish the lot twice as quickly," Ella said.

"I've also got some other news," Justine said as they worked. "There was nothing particularly relevant about the rope used on Morgan, or the knots, or anything along those lines, but I did find one interesting thing about the chloroform. I suppose one could mail order it, but I found out that there are a couple of places that keep it on hand around here.

"One is the high school science lab. They've had one bottle for years. They don't tend to use it very much anymore. The teacher checked, and no one's tampered with it. Then I went by the Math and Science building here on campus, but I couldn't get hold of anyone. I figured I'd try again later."

"Wilson's the chairperson of the math and science department. I'll be happy to pay him a visit once we finish here."

Justine smiled.

"What's that grin for?" Ella asked.

"He really likes you. And if any civilian understands the demands of our job, he does. You should give him a break."

Ella rolled her eyes. "I socialize with him more than with anyone else."

"Which isn't saying much, from what I've heard," she teased.

"When was *your* last date?"

"I came across Furman Brownhat about an hour ago, and we had some iced tea in the student center. We talked about the case a little. He didn't have much to say, except that he'd seen you here the other day."

"That was when I visited Wilson Joe." Ella lapsed into a thoughtful silence.

After several quiet moments, Justine glanced over at Ella. "By the way, don't worry about my relationship with Furman, okay?

I'm friendly with him, but it's not like we're dating. I try to make sure he feels comfortable around me, but that's just part of the job."

"It's a hard line to walk," Ella observed.

"Yes, but I can handle it."

"Out of curiosity, when was your last real date, Justine?"

Justine considered Ella's question. "I can't remember. Gee, boss, thanks for depressing me."

"If you say that around my mother, she'll fix you up before you can blink an eye." Ella bent over the front of one of the cars in her row, searching for damage.

"Remind me not to," Justine said with a wry smile.

Ella walked down to a white sedan parked two empty spaces away from the others, next to the fence. She edged against the fence, studying the front end. "Bingo. I've got something here."

Justine joined her and noted the extensive damage to the right front of the vehicle. The hood and front fender had been dented, and half the plastic grille on that side was broken away. The signal light cover and headlamp trim were missing as well. "This car certainly hit something, and it wasn't another car, or we'd see smudges of the other car's paint somewhere."

"Have it towed in and find out who drives it," Ella said. "Also, see if any of the front-end fragments we recovered match the damage here. If it turns out to be the wrong car, we'll return it, but I don't want to leave it here unguarded another second."

Justine nodded. "I'll get on this right away. It shouldn't take me too long to get a comparison done on the paint from this car and the chips from Haske's clothing. If you okay it, I can have a courier get on a flight out of Farmington to Albuquerque."

"Have Blalock put a rush on it like before. They'll give it top priority then."

Ella watched as Justine called the information in, then glanced at her watch. "I'll meet you back at our office later. I've got several people to see."

Ella took a few steps, then turned and came back to look at

the damage closely. After a moment, she stood up and waved to Justine, who was still at her car.

Justine ran back to join her. "What did you find?"

Ella pointed to the damaged bumper. "See those circles where water droplets dried up? It hasn't rained in this area since the murder."

"Maybe the car was driven past a sprinkler," Justine speculated.

"Or washed off with a hose." Ella got down on her hands and knees and looked up under the front of the damaged area. "Here it is," she exclaimed.

"What are you looking at?" Justine got down beside her and peered up.

Ella pointed to several dark drops that had been washed down from above but had not fallen off the car completely. "These look like blood that the Packrat hastily tried to wash off the car. Make sure you get a good sample of this to check before the vehicle is towed. I don't want to lose it in a scrape or a puddle." Ella stood and brushed the grit off her slacks. "I have a feeling this is Haske's blood."

While Justine stayed behind to collect the dried droplets into an evidence container, Ella drove to Wilson Joe's office. Although lab science wasn't one of his courses, he would be able to get the information they needed faster than if she went through channels. She found him walking down the hall as she went around a curve.

"Coming from or going to class?" she asked.

"Coming from," Wilson said. "It's good to see you. But am I ever going to get to see you when we're both alone?"

Ella glanced in both directions. "We're alone now."

"I mean really alone, for more than twelve seconds," he answered as another member of the staff strode quickly past them. "One of these days, I'd like to take you to dinner or a movie."

"And one of these days I'd love to have a chance to go," she answered with a wistful smile.

"But right now, you're in a rush for something," he observed. "What's going on?"

"I need you to check and see if you have chloroform in the lab or storeroom. If you do, I want you to verify that all your bottles are accounted for."

"You need this right away?"

"It would help. Can you manage it?"

"Sure. Let's go. I have a key to the storage room."

A few moments later, after a walk around the circular hall to the other side of the building, they reached a room the size of a large walk-in closet, blocked off by a half door. CHEMICAL STORAGE read the sign overhead, and there were various other warning signs as required by the fire marshal.

Wilson flipped on the lights, then glanced around. "Here is the inventory list," he said. He stopped to check it, then walked along the metal shelves stocked with reagent bottles until he reached the end of one row. "We're supposed to have five bottles on hand, but there are only three."

Ella glanced at the shelf below. "Here's another one, misplaced. That's four, so you're still one short."

Ella and Wilson searched all the shelves. Fifteen minutes later, they hadn't turned up the missing bottle.

"I'm afraid it's not here. Of course, it could just be an error on the inventory, but we're all usually quite precise about this. It's an occupational trait, you know," Wilson added with a tiny smile.

"You asked about the murders before. Now let me ask you a question. Is there any kind of professional jealousy among the staff?"

Wilson looked shocked. "I'm surprised at your question. I've never encountered a more pleasant work environment than this one. The competition that's so prevalent in most colleges is totally absent here. There's a spirit of cooperation that is so—well, Navajo."

"It's not a reflection on the staff. I'm simply trying to determine who might have had something against the victims."

"Professor Morgan was well liked by everyone here. I've never even heard students complain about her. She went out of her way to be fair to everyone. Those who flunked her classes did so because they didn't work. She was always available to anyone, staff or student, who needed her," Wilson replied staunchly.

"That piece in the tribal paper this morning, have you seen it?" Wilson added.

Ella tried not to cringe. "Which one are you referring to?"

"The editorial. They're really pushing the common denominator, that all the victims were experts in Navajo culture, and that the People are under attack. Groups are getting together, ready to fight. Many feel that this is the biggest threat to our people in a hundred and fifty years."

"Vigilantes are the last thing I need. An article like that could incite people to go off half-cocked, and maybe spur the killer to find another quick victim. When the press starts putting their speculations in print, it always causes trouble."

"Is it speculation?" Wilson asked. "I'd say it's a sound hypothesis."

"The crimes have been carefully staged. That's not general knowledge, but it's true. Roughly what that means is that someone is trying very hard to manipulate people's thinking."

Wilson gave Ella a long, thoughtful look. "I've seen the response to that article. You're right about major trouble brewing. People are starting to lose faith in the police and are thinking that they have to defend themselves."

"You're in a unique position to help the college and the community as a leader. Ask people to stay cool and levelheaded and to avoid undue speculation. Encourage your students to really think about their actions and not to go off half-cocked."

"I can try," Wilson answered carefully, "but young people aren't known for their infinite patience. The only answer is for your department to solve the case quickly."

"We're bringing all our resources to bear on this case. I expect to have a break very soon. Remember, my own family is on the line."

Wilson walked Ella back to her car. "I've heard about the guards posted around people considered to be at risk. Some of them really resent it, are you aware of that?" He didn't wait for a reply. "Old Samuel Pete and Herman Cloud took it as a personal affront, a verification that you believe they're too old to take care of themselves."

"They'll calm down, and when they think about it they'll see it has nothing to do with their age. I also have one on Victor Charlie, and he's younger than I am."

"So that's how Jaime Beyale of the tribal paper knew about it. Victor works for her. She said in one of her editorials that there's got to be a better way for the police to handle this crisis than imprisoning innocent people in their homes and letting the criminals go free."

Ella rolled her eyes. "Oh, terrific. Just what I needed. Peterson Yazzie is probably laughing his fool head off."

"And there are other letters in there, too, that essentially say what's on most people's minds. Every time one of our cultural leaders is killed, it triggers more casualties of some kind."

Wilson paused thoughtfully, then continued. "It doesn't matter if there really is a connection or not, you know. If the Navajo people lose their culture through this attrition, we really will cease to exist as a tribe. All we'll have is a lost history, and fading memories that cannot be restored."

Ella slipped behind the wheel. "That's why catching this packrat killer is so important. I better get going. I've got some people to interview this afternoon." Ella checked with the dispatcher and got the address of Reverend Curley's home. She wasn't surprised to find that the preacher lived in the center of Shiprock, where more amenities were available, rather than on the outskirts.

Ella found the man outside watering his vegetable garden, and he smiled and waved as she approached. He was a well-proportioned man in his early forties, with well-groomed, wavy black hair.

"I expected you earlier," Reverend Curley said. "I heard what happened last night, and my prayers are with Sister Morgan." He put the hose down and dried his hands on his jeans. "I knew you'd want to talk to me, but I really know nothing of this."

"Tell me about Anton Lewis," she suggested.

"I always thought the man needed serious help—not just religious, but psychological. I believe anyone can find himself through Christ, but to Lewis, Christ was nothing more than a word he used as a curse, or to emphasize a point. Then again, most of what Anton does is simply for effect. I really don't believe he's a murderer."

"Were you at the church last night?"

"Only for an hour or so. My presence wasn't necessary at choir practice. Sadie handled everything. Since many of the hymns had been translated into Navajo, she devoted quite a bit of her time to the chorus. She was a good Christian woman. I have no doubt that she's found her place in Heaven."

Ella said nothing, but noted that the reverend was watching her speculatively. He must have known her father had been the last preacher of his congregation. Perhaps he was wondering why she wasn't a member too. "Did Sadie have any enemies that you know of?"

"Not at all. She was a good Christian, and very well liked. She never married, you know. Teaching her native tongue and working for the church were her world. She led a fulfilling, though I suspect lonely, life."

Ella wondered if that had been meant as a special message for her, but then decided it hadn't been. "Thanks for your help, Reverend."

"How soon will it be before we are allowed to go back into the church? I would like to resume services there as soon as possible."

Ella paused. "Are you sure people will come?"

Doubt flickered in the man's eyes. "I don't know, but I've got to try, for Our Lord's sake. With all the trouble and the deaths recently, we've got a lot of praying to do."

Ella met his eyes, and saw the sadness there. He was as alone here on the Rez as she'd ever been on the outside. Her father, too, had found his religious convictions cut him off, but at least he'd had his family. Reverend Curley was alone. Perhaps that explained his comment about Sadie's lifestyle. He also knew the cost of an all-consuming job. Without glancing back, Ella got into her vehicle and drove away.

TWENTY-TWO

———— ✖ ✖ ✖ ————

Ella arrived at the station a short time later. It was already midafternoon, and she still hadn't eaten lunch. Her stomach growled in protest.

As she walked down the hall, Justine stepped out of her small lab. "I've got some news. I've confirmed your suspicions that the vehicle used to hit Haske was the one we found on campus. If you'll come outside, I'll show you what else I've discovered."

Justine led the way to the fenced-in area where the towed vehicle had been placed. This impound area was kept under padlock twenty-four hours a day. Ella followed her assistant up to the car.

Justine crouched by the turn signal light and brought out a taped-together section of plastic pieces they'd found on the road at the crime scene. Ella's assistant held it up to the car, and the edges fit exactly, except in the spots where a few pieces were still missing.

"You see this?" Justine asked. "It fits perfectly. The paint chips also match, and the dried-up drops you found on the underneath of the bumper are blood, the same type as Haske's. Further results that could cinch the identification are still pending. I need the crime lab to process those."

Ella nodded. "Good job. Did you find any fingerprints inside?"

"Too many; almost all are smudged or degraded to nothing from the heat inside the car. That was a dead end. But I did find two other things that are noteworthy. On the front seat I found a long, reddish yellow thread that I'm almost certain comes from an expensive brand of designer jeans. Those cost a bundle, and the color is distinctive. The crime lab is verifying that. I asked Blalock for a priority, and they've given it to us."

"Most of the students and the faculty wear Levi's, Lee's, or Wranglers. Nobody I know is exactly rich around here. How sure are you of your findings?"

"I'd bet on it. I only asked the state lab in order to confirm it. They have comparison samples of thousands of fibers."

"Maybe the thread was left by a college official—what do you think?" Ella speculated. "Somebody who makes the big bucks."

"Well, that would explain the use of the fleet car. But how does that fit the profile? It would have to be a pretty young executive," Justine said. "I asked around, but the administration couldn't tell me who used that car last. They said they'd have to have a secretary check the records and leave a message at the station."

"I think we should go back to the college tomorrow if we haven't heard by then and knock on doors until we get an answer," Ella said. "You're right about the profile. I find it hard to believe that the Packrat would use his own job car to kill Haske, then simply return it when he was done. We should learn how the college assigns and uses their vehicles. If the last person to legally use this car is not our killer, then we need to learn how the Packrat got hold of the key."

"That's an important point." Justine nodded. "I do know that there's a garage near campus that services the vehicles. It's a small operation, but the owner gave the college the best bid, and so he got the contract."

"I'll go over there and talk to the owner. What do you know about him?"

"His name is John Begay. He doesn't have any record, except for a few speeding tickets. But I remember something interesting. Several years back John and Daniel Tsosie got drunk and decided to get even with old Henrietta Johnson for something or another. They broke into Henrietta's home, smashed her things, and scattered ashes over everything. The charges were dropped, because the boys' parents made restitution. Nowadays, though, John is a good citizen. He's really too busy with work to have much free time. The garage is a two-man operation. It's just Darrell Begay and his son John. Darrell has been sick for a long time, so John runs the operation practically by himself. In fact, he lives over the garage. John's in his mid-twenties, and single."

"Does he have any other connection to the college?"

"I checked and found out that he used to be a student. I spoke to Furman earlier, and he said he remembered John from one of Kee Dodge's classes, but that he flunked out."

"Keep digging. In the meantime, I'm going to pay him a visit."

"I'll talk to Furman and try to track down a few of Begay's professors."

"Good. I'm on my way."

"Before you go—" Justine cleared her throat. "There's something you should know. It seems that Anton Lewis went from jail to the press. He claimed we're persecuting him because of his religious beliefs."

"That's a crock of—"

"I know, but he was quoted as saying that he's no different from others who have special powers, like you and your brother."

"You're not serious. They printed that?"

"Yeah. I've pretty much covered the gist of what they wrote, but I can get you the paper if you want to see for yourself. It's still in my lab, I think."

"I better read the whole article, but I'll buy my own copy. Don't worry about it." Ella walked to the newspaper box at the front of the station, dropped in two quarters, and retrieved the latest issue. At a glance she could see that the murders were the top story of the day. Unfortunately the crimes had been linked by the author to the accidents and coal mine closings under the headline "NAVAJO TRIBE UNDER SIEGE."

Ella returned to her car and dropped the paper on the seat next to her. As she drove away, she couldn't resist snatching quick glances. Sadie Morgan's death had started an outcry about the police department's inability to catch the perp. Ella, in particular, was under fire because of the prediction that the *Dineh* would continue to suffer heavily until the killer was stopped.

Ella thought of Begay. Here at least was a lead she could follow up right now. Ella drove down the highway, exceeding the speed limit by a good fifteen miles per hour. She still hadn't had anything to eat. After she finished with Begay, she'd stop someplace and grab a quick meal.

A short while later, Ella pulled up beside a newly painted auto repair shop about three miles down the road from the college. She recognized the place. A long time ago, before it had been within miles of anything, men would meet there to shoot craps and drink beer, both illegal on the Rez. Then Shiprock had expanded outward from the river, and now a modernized building with a two-service-bay garage had replaced the ramshackle tarpaper shack.

Ella left the Jeep and approached the office, where a man sat behind a desk reading a newspaper. As she walked inside the small air-conditioned office, Ella braced herself, determined not to let the article undermine her in any way. "I need to see John Begay."

The young man glanced up and gave her a wary look. "Who are you?"

Ella flashed her badge. "You're John Begay?" she asked, already suspecting the answer.

"Yeah. What do you want?"

Ella noticed his shoes. He wore dirty cross-trainers, and they appeared to be about the right size. "I'd like to ask you about the fleet cars you service. Who brings them in and keeps track of their maintenance records?"

"I do. Is there a problem?"

Ella ignored the question. "How do you decide which cars to service? I'd like you to tell me the process you follow."

"Did one of the cars I repaired break down again?" he demanded. "I swear, the college gets me for peanuts, but holds me responsible for every little thing. I do all my work to factory specs."

"Just tell me the process you follow."

"It's no big deal. I keep track of each car's mileage, and I go by there at least twice a week to check them out. When they need oil changes, or tune-ups, I bring them here."

"What if the car needs body repair work?"

"If it's minor, I bring in someone, like my cousin who works in Farmington. Otherwise it's not part of what they contract me for."

Ella was wondering why the car's damage had not been discovered by Begay. "Do you do a walk-around to check the body every time you record mileage on the vehicles?"

"Sure."

"When was the last time you went up there to check?"

"Is that what this interrogation is all about? I admit my crime. I didn't go over there last Friday. I was busy, and car use is always down in the summer."

"I don't work for the college," Ella said brusquely. "Now answer my question." Ella thought she knew the answer anyway. "Do you inspect each car for damage when you're there?"

"No, it's not in my contract. If the college wants me to do that, they better let me know."

"Okay, forget that for now. Who can access the keys to these cars?"

The mechanic looked at her speculatively. "I've got a set for every one of them, if that's what you're really asking. Also, administration normally gives out keys to their office people, recruiters, and visiting dignitaries. The college maintenance people have cars assigned to them full-time too. You'd have to ask the head honcho there about the details."

"Have you ever noticed any of *your* keys missing?"

"Look, I don't know what you're leading up to, but there's no way you're going to pin anything on me. My keys are right here in this office where they always are." He opened the padlock on a metal locker and pulled a box from the lower shelf.

Ella watched him carefully. He was wearing inexpensive jeans, probably from a discount store. But, then again, he wouldn't wear his expensive ones to work around cars.

"Here they are," he said, opening the cigar box. "They're all tagged and marked. There should be thirty. Take a minute and count them yourself."

She did. "You still haven't answered my question. Have you ever noticed any of them missing, even for a short while?"

He slammed the lid of the box shut. "No."

Begay wore the right size shoe, she was almost positive about that. And if *he* was responsible for the murders, no keys would have been missing. "Have you ever gone in to pick up a vehicle for maintenance and found it wasn't there?"

"No."

Ella watched Begay. He was getting nervous about something. "Going someplace tonight?"

"Not in particular."

"You seem in a rush."

"I want you to hurry up and leave so I can close up for the day. You're annoying. I've read about you in the papers, you know. You've been running around in circles since you got that Navajo man shot in Farmington. I knew him. All he wanted was his little girl. Now you're screwing up this murder investigation, trying to find this Packrat guy, while the whole reservation goes down the toilet. Well, go look someplace else. I'm not your man."

Ella felt her temper boil dangerously close to the surface. "You're not making matters any easier on yourself, you know."

"I take care of those fleet cars, that's all. If you have a problem with any of them, take it up with the college. I'm here every day except Sunday. My place opens at seven, and stays open until seven at night."

"Where were you on Monday morning, two weeks ago?"

"I just told you. Here. Like every other day. I haven't been on vacation for the last eighteen months. Since my dad got sick, I haven't been out of this stinking garage."

Ella suddenly remembered Naomi Zah telling her about the man's peculiar smell. A definite odor of oil and solvents clung to his clothing. "Can anyone support your story?"

"I have no idea. You'll have to ask around. There's nothing around here except the college, but it's possible some student driving by saw me. Or maybe not. Who knows? Either way, it's your job to find out, not mine."

"Before I'm through, I'll know what you had for breakfast that day. Count on it." Ella stared at him until he looked away. Wordlessly she turned and walked back out to her car.

As she drove on to the college, she had the dispatcher put her through to Big Ed. She gave him a thorough verbal report, then waited for his reaction. For several moments all she heard was static.

"You've got a good candidate there," Big Ed said at last. "If he works alone, he could take off at any time and not be missed. You want to bring him in for questioning? We can let him sweat it here for a while. You never know what you'll get."

"Not yet. Let me do a little more digging first."

"We're having a problem with Naomi Zah. Have you heard?"

"I thought she'd left to stay with relatives."

"She came back. One of my men found out, and we sent someone to keep an eye on her. But she's furious. She doesn't want anyone around, thinks it may scare off people who come to her for help."

"I'll try to stop by there soon. Maybe I can explain things and help her see the necessity."

"She's a stubborn old woman, but give it a try. Either way, Neskahi and Duran will alternate shifts and stay close by."

"Have the stepped-up patrols turned up anything?"

"Not a thing, and between the heat and the tension everyone is feeling nowadays, our officers are starting to get extremely restless."

"Something will break soon on the case. I'm sure of it."

"I sure as hell hope so. Casualties are getting way too high. Keep me posted." Big Ed signed off.

Ella headed down toward the main highway. So much was changing on the Rez. She saw areas filling with new houses and businesses, while others went downhill, time and neglect taking their toll. Changes were continually woven into the pattern of life. Despite the opposition change received, nothing ever remained the same, not even here on the reservation, where the old ways still commanded respect if not acceptance, from all.

Ella used her radio to contact Justine. They agreed to meet at the Totah Café.

Twenty minutes later, Ella and Justine were waiting to be served. Ella stirred her iced tea absently, not taking a sip.

Justine finally spoke. "That constant *chinkachink* is driving me crazy, boss. What's bothering you?"

"The case, what else? We need to make progress, but for every answer we uncover, we end up with ten more questions."

"Does this have to do with John Begay?"

Ella briefed her assistant on what she'd learned from her interview with the mechanic. "He seems to meet some of our criteria, and he was defensive, very much so."

"Maybe if we keep probing, the answer will come," Justine suggested.

Ella started to reply when she noticed someone outside reaching into Justine's open car window. "Trouble." Ella stood, just as the man started pouring something from a plastic bucket onto Justine's windshield.

"My car!" Justine leaped up, but Ella was already at the door.

Running outside, Ella saw a man dart around the rear of Justine's car and tackle the man with the bucket. As she drew closer, Ella recognized them instantly. It was Furman Brownhat, and the man with the bucket he had knocked to the ground was Anton Lewis.

The two men rolled back and forth on the pavement, wrestling, each trying to end up on top.

"Enough!" Ella yelled, grabbing Lewis's wrist in a hold designed to produce enough pain to immobilize him. Lewis let out one long yell, then curled up into a ball, Ella still retaining her grip on his hand.

Justine grabbed Furman by the arm. "Furman, it's me, Justine. Let him go and get up. Ella has him under control."

Furman finally noticed Justine was there and with dark anger in his eyes relented and stood up.

Ella glanced at Justine's car. "What the hell is that stuff?"

"It's blood, you bitch," Lewis managed, trying to remain defiant despite the fact that Ella held him immobile, his nose pressed against the asphalt.

"Why would you do that, you sick jerk?" Justine demanded, moving over to cuff Lewis.

"I was walking over for a bite to eat when I saw this sicko pouring that gunk onto your car, Justine. I ran over, but I couldn't stop him in time," Furman put in, his words coming rapidly as he tried to even his breathing.

Justine nodded, then took a look inside her open window. "Damn. That pervert put a dead dog on my car seat too." Opening the door, Justine reached in and grabbed the carcass carefully, lifting it out and onto the pavement. The animal had obviously been run over several hours ago. Flies covered it liberally.

"Call it in, Justine," Ella ordered. "Let's get this 'monk' a cell of his own to meditate in. This time, Lewis, you have somebody who *will* be pressing charges."

"I wish I'd poured the blood inside the car instead. And in yours too!" Lewis growled, turning his head toward Ella. "You're both bitches. You all deserve to die."

"Watch your mouth, asshole!" Furman stepped up close, but Justine had returned from making the call and put a hand on his arm, pulling him away gently.

"He's not worth it, Furman. But thanks for stepping in before he did anything else to the car." Justine smiled at the young man, then looked back at her vehicle. The windshield and front were dripping blood heavily, and some was running down inside the engine compartment from around the wipers.

"You can take that to Allison's Car Wash, Justine." Ella noted a police car approaching from up the road. "Meanwhile, start the paperwork on this idiot. I want him out of here, ASAP. Then, afterwards, maybe we can have an early dinner."

"Sounds like a plan. Want to join us, Furman?" Justine suggested.

"Okay. I sure worked up an appetite in a hurry."

Ella noted that Furman's eyes lighted up as they came to rest on Justine.

Later, as they had their meal, Ella watched Furman. Justine didn't pay much attention to it, but Furman was genuinely interested in her. Although it was obvious that Justine considered him just a source, Furman appeared to interpret her interest much differently.

After they finished their meal and walked out to the parking area, Ella waited until Furman was out of earshot. "You may have a problem," she warned Justine.

"I know he likes me, boss. I like him, but it's nothing. Really. See you tomorrow?"

"Bright and early." As Ella walked to her own car, she glanced back at Justine, unable to shake her uneasiness. She trusted her assistant, but the budding friendship—and that's what it was even if Justine didn't admit it—worried her.

TWENTY-THREE

✗ ✗ ✗

The following morning Ella arrived at her office early. As she sat down, she patted her pocket one more time to confirm that her badger fetish was with her. It was getting to be a habit. Things at home were going as well as could be expected, although the constant tension was beginning to take its toll. Her mother worried about everyone, from Clifford and Loretta to the cops outside. Loretta's moods, now that she was in her last trimester, were also beginning to take their toll on everyone, including Clifford. Her heart went out to her brother, who never seemed to know what to do when Loretta would burst into tears without the slightest provocation.

Ella had just finished a report for Big Ed, including the episode with Anton Lewis, when Justine walked into her office.

"I'm going over to check with my contact in administration at the college. I'm trying to find out who was last assigned the car we've connected to the murders. So far all I'm getting is the run around, and I'm getting tired of playing phone tag."

"If you can cut through the red tape, so much the better. We need a name, and then we have to find out what that person was doing when Haske and Dodge were killed."

"I've also been trying to find out which stores, if any, in this area carry Kevin Jordan designer jeans, the brand indicated by the thread we found in the vehicle we impounded. So far I've got zip," Justine said. "But I haven't gone down the entire list of outlets that carry jeans yet. I should be able to finish that in another ten minutes, then I'm going to see Ritamae over at the college. I'll let you know as soon as I come up with anything useful." Justine left the office, her stride filled with purpose.

Ella sat behind the computer, searching the records for the name of Anton Lewis's mother. If she was Navajo, then Ella would be able to find her, with or without an address. There were few people her brother didn't know, and he was only one phone call away.

It took her another hour, but with Clifford's help, she found Therma Lewis. The woman lived a few miles from the high school. She worked as part of the janitorial staff there.

It took Ella less than twenty minutes to drive there, and the relatively quick trip was a welcome change. Ella walked up to the trailer home that had been placed next to a ditch bank. The place looked small and well worn by time, but the bright sunflowers by the entrance attested to someone who cared about details yet was perpetually short of money.

Ella waited near the car, staying in the shade of a tall pine. Finally she saw an elderly woman come to the door, give her a quizzical look, then wave for her to come in. By the time Ella walked through the door, the woman had pulled out a chair for her to sit in.

"I think I recognize you. You're that woman detective, right?"

Ella nodded, and flashed her badge. "I came to talk to you about your son."

Mrs. Lewis nodded slowly. "I heard what he's been up to, and about last night. It doesn't surprise me, you know. He was always in trouble, even as a boy. I couldn't handle him. He lived with his father, but then those two didn't get along either. He eventually came back, but I couldn't let him stay here. Not after that night when—" She stopped abruptly and shook her head.

"I need to know everything about him. He may be in a great deal more trouble than you realize."

"And you want me to help you keep him in jail?" She shook

her head. "No matter what else, he's still my son."

"Anton needs help. He's very troubled. Letting him go on his own isn't the answer."

Mrs. Lewis hesitated. "You're not trying to help him," she said at last. "You just want to see him behind bars. He's not guilty of anything, except maybe trying to get attention."

"Why attention?"

"My son wants to be accepted. He wants others to notice him so he'll finally get some respect. He says he's a skinwalker, but he isn't. He doesn't know the first thing about our ways. What he's doing is trying to be a leader of other people. He needs them to need him. Do you understand?"

"Anton's very troubled, Mrs. Lewis. It's possible he may hurt others as well as himself if he continues this way."

"No, you're wrong about him. He may not like animals—" She stopped short, then turned away. "Please leave, I've already said too much."

Ella stood up slowly. "You can help Anton by talking to me," she said, and placed her card on the table. "You can reach me anytime, day or night, if you change your mind."

Ella was just pulling back out onto the road when an elderly woman who lived in an old but well-maintained house about fifty yards away came out and stood watching.

Ella saw her in the rearview mirror and, reversing direction, drove up to the house. "Is something wrong?" Ella asked, stepping out of her vehicle.

The woman looked at her for a moment as if trying to make up her mind. She made little plucking motions at her long skirts. "I saw you there at my neighbor's. Were you asking about her son?"

Ella nodded. "Is there something you wanted to tell me?"

The woman gestured for Ella to follow her inside. "You don't remember me, do you?" she observed.

Ella looked at the woman. Her bright turquoise blouse made her light gray hair look even paler by contrast. A network of lines framed her face. "I'm sorry. I don't."

The woman's gentle smile seemed to be filled with memories

she alone held. "You're Ella. I taught you back in junior high school many, many years ago. I taught your brother Clifford too. I'm Mrs. Keyonnie."

Remembering the name, Ella smiled. "I remember you! English, right?"

The woman chuckled. "I know, I've changed. A few more pounds, more years."

"Well, the same can be said about me, but you remembered," Ella answered.

"I read about Anton in the papers. That boy was always in trouble. Most of our kids here were friendly and liked the dances and get-togethers. Not Anton. He always went out of his way to make it unpleasant for everyone."

"What happened that made his mother kick him out of the house?"

Mrs. Keyonnie took a deep breath then let it out slowly. "He liked killing little animals he found, like birds, lizards, and such. He said he was going to be a skinwalker. His mother argued that he didn't know what he was talking about, that killing animals would accomplish nothing. But then one night, he was trying to do some kind of strange ritual. I have no idea what he thought he was doing. I was returning with his mother from a fundraiser at the school, when she found him outside. The animals"—she shuddered—"a kitten and a puppy. They'd been killed, and skinned. It was awful."

"Did you know him well?"

She shook her head. "Not really. I never taught him, but I know others who did. He had the IQ of a genius, but he was always unstable. He would fly off the handle for no reason and no one could ever predict what he was going to do. Something else—I remember that the one subject he excelled at in high school was drama. He was really good at playing a role, and wearing disguises and all. That's the only class he ever got A's in."

"Where does Anton work?"

"He doesn't; that's one of the things his mother and I have talked about. She doesn't send him any money, and neither does his father. I have no idea how he makes ends meet. Of course, he's always trying to get followers. Maybe he gets donations from them."

"Do you know the names of any of his followers?"

She shook her head. "They're young kids, most just out of high school, I know that. But they come and go, particularly during the summer. They're from outside the reservation. Nobody takes him seriously here." She paused, then added, "Though maybe they should."

After thanking her, Ella returned to her vehicle, lost in thought. John Begay was a possible suspect, but Anton Lewis was also fitting the profile. Fortunately he was still in jail, having refused to post bail after being charged with vandalism of a tribal vehicle.

As she headed back to the office, the dispatcher put through a call from Justine. "I've found a store that carries the jeans we're trying to track down. It's not on the Rez, but just outside it, at that big factory outlet shopping center between Kirtland and Farmington. I've checked with Big Ed and called the county sheriff. There's no problem if we go in and ask a few questions."

Ella felt her heart begin to race as it always did when the trail was getting warm. "Good job! Tell me exactly where it is. I've never been there—who has time for shopping?" Ella wrote down the directions. "You're at the office now?"

"Yeah, I'm on my way out. I can meet you there, if you want."

"I do, but I'm going to need you to locate a photo of John Begay, and get a copy of the photo taken when we booked Anton Lewis. Then find five other photos of guys who fit the same general description. Let's see if the salesclerk can pick out either of our suspects."

"I'll see you there," Justine answered.

After leaving the reservation, Ella made her way to Kirtland, a growing community between Shiprock and Farmington. Kirtland had many Navajo residents, and there had been a great rivalry between the Kirtland Broncos and the Shiprock Chieftains for years.

As Ella was getting out of her Jeep beside the store Justine had mentioned, Ella saw Justine's car turn off the highway and into the lot. She waited as Justine pulled into the parking space next to hers.

Justine left the vehicle quickly. "I've got the photos. The college had a recent one of Begay, and I had them fax me a copy. I've made fax copies of every photo, so we won't influence witnesses with different quality images. Except the sketch, of course. You ready?"

Ella nodded once. "Let's get to work."

Ella led the way inside the large factory outlet. From what she could tell, the store specialized in casual clothes, but carried only exclusive name brands. She picked up the tag from a denim jacket and expelled her breath in a rush. *Expensive* name brands. Even at outlet prices, if the Packrat had bought his jeans here, he'd left a great deal poorer.

Ella walked up to the counter, identified herself, and asked to see the manager. A young man who appeared to be in his early twenties came out of a back room and gave her the slightly patronizing smile of a salesman.

"I need your help," Ella said, deciding the direct approach would save them all time and effort. "Do you normally sell a lot of Kevin Jordan jeans?"

The manager shrugged. "Not many. That's the most exclusive line of men's wear in the Southwest. Most Kevin Jordan jeans are purchased by out-of-state tourists with their charge cards. I'd say we sell a pair or two a week. Most of the local trade buy those less expensive cotton and polyester boot-cut brands."

"Could you ask your staff if they remember selling a pair recently to a Navajo man, young, medium height, and perhaps of slender build?"

A young woman clerk who had been straightening the jeans approached hesitantly. "I did, about three weeks ago. I remember, because it was one of the few times I've seen any local people willing to shell out the cash for something like that instead of using a charge card."

Ella gestured for Justine to produce the photos, and Justine laid them out on the glass counter. She'd selected half a dozen shots, including the sketch Victor had made.

The young woman looked at all of them carefully, then finally shook her head. "I'm sorry. I know he was Navajo, but that's all I can tell you for sure. I have a problem remembering faces. Some of the men customers, if you look them in the eye, think you're flirting with them. You know what I mean?" She looked at Justine for verification, which Ella found slightly annoying. Justine nodded solemnly.

The clerk smiled hopefully. "But if he walked back in here, I think I could recognize him. It works that way for me."

"If he does, will you call me?" Ella asked, producing her card.

"Sure. No problem. All these faces look about right though, except that drawing. This guy was clean-shaven and his hair was short. I think in one of those shaved styles high school boys are wearing nowadays. He was young looking. I remember thinking that he looked too young to be making that kind of money, unless he saved a lot."

After a few more fruitless questions, Ella walked back to the parking lot with Justine. "This is very aggravating," she commented.

"I saw your reaction when the clerk mentioned guys flirting, then looked at me instead of you for approval. Is that what aggravated you?" Justine teased.

"Do you like your job in the department?" Ella grumbled. Then she grinned, unable to keep a straight face.

Justine chuckled. "I'm sorry. I shouldn't have interrupted your chain of thought. I do know what you mean. People don't *look* at people anymore. Half of them don't care, and the other half are afraid to."

"Only cops are perpetually nosy," Ella answered.

"So now what?" Justine asked.

"Something's bugging me about this whole thing. What do you say we walk to that coffee shop across the parking lot, have something quick to eat, and talk it over? I'd like to bounce some ideas around."

"Sure." Justine fell into step beside Ella as they crossed the shopping center parking area. When they entered the coffee shop, she waited as Ella picked out a rear table that faced the room.

After ordering two iced teas, Ella stared pensively at the shopping center traffic just outside the large window. "It's the motives that just don't add up. I can believe that Lewis might be crazy enough to kill the old ones so he could proclaim himself an authority. He threatened our lives last night, which is consistent with the notion he's unbalanced. Yet, that blood and dead dog was more malicious than deadly.

"Begay is a whole different can of worms." She told Justine about her meeting. "He's the most likely suspect based on circumstantial evidence, at least with the *hataalii* who was his teacher, but I can't see him caring about Navajo culture one way or the other." She paused, then added, "Unless, of course, the murders stem from a personal grudge. He *is* supposed to have flunked out, and now I get the impression that he feels overworked and underpaid."

Justine shook her head, unconvinced. "No, that doesn't sound right. I spoke to Furman about Begay earlier this morning. He says that the only trouble with him was he just didn't care about anything. He flunked out because he never did any work. Furman could never figure out why he'd taken any classes at all. Maybe he went just to please his parents or something."

Ella toyed with her spoon. "I can't figure out how either of these men fit in with Peterson either. Lewis is too unpredictable; I don't think even Peterson could ever really control him. Begay, on the other hand, doesn't seem the idealistic type. He works hard to make a living, and his concerns are down to earth. The garage, in fact, seems to be the focal point of his life."

"Or that's the impression he wants you to have of him."

"True enough. He does have opportunity, and just because we haven't figured out a motive doesn't mean there isn't one," Ella conceded.

"Oh, one interesting fact. I checked with members of the church choir about the money missing from the victim's purse. Mrs. Jim said that Sadie mentioned she'd be going to the flea markets the next day. She always carried plenty of cash for those. She loved shopping for bargains."

"Neither of the other two murders had a robbery linked with it," Ella reminded her.

"There was a lot of blood at Sadie's murder site. Maybe the killer got some on his clothes and felt that the victim should 'buy' him new ones," Justine suggested.

"That money would have bought him a new pair of designer jeans," Ella theorized. "Barely."

"There are so many questions. We never seem to run out of them," Justine mused.

"We better get back to the office. I need to work on a report, and you have your leads to follow up."

Two hours later, back at the police station, Ella stared at the form she'd been filling out. Paperwork had to be the worst part of a cop's job. Hearing footsteps and eager for a diversion, she glanced up.

Justine knocked on her open door, then walked inside, Furman Brownhat half a step behind her. "I think there's something you should hear for yourself." Justine gave Furman a nod.

Furman shifted nervously, as if about to give a speech before a big audience. "I don't know if this makes any difference," he said hesitantly, "but I heard some more gossip about Anton Lewis. I thought you might want to know that he's spent several mornings recently on campus passing out leaflets. Whenever anyone questioned him about his so-called religion, he came completely unglued and started arguing as loudly as possible. It's as if he wanted to make sure everyone could hear him." He handed Ella a leaflet. "Here. I brought you one I found tacked to a bulletin board. Figured you'd want to see it."

Ella looked at the sheet proclaiming power for any who followed him and extolling the values of merging Navajo gods with the Anglo world's devils. "This doesn't make any sense," she said at last. "Skinwalkers aren't devil worshipers. The two are incompatible."

"Well, apparently someone else brought that up, and Lewis

tried to punch him out. It took six guys to pull the two of them apart. Lewis was finally kicked off the campus by security."

Ella glanced at Furman, looking him over carefully for the first time and wondering why she hadn't paid that much attention to him before. His hair was cut short, in a current off-reservation trend where the lower half was almost shaven. He was wearing baggy tan slacks and a colorful Hawaiian print shirt. On his feet were Nike cross-trainers that were about the right size. "Thanks for bringing this to us, Furman. We'll check it out."

"I just wanted to help," he affirmed. "If there's anything else I can do, just ask, okay? I don't like how these murders are changing people."

"How do you mean?"

"Nobody trusts anybody else. It feels like there's a war brewing." He shrugged. "But you two are cops. You know what I mean."

Ella nodded. "Thanks again," she said.

Justine walked out with Furman and returned several moments later. "I saw you looking at his cross-trainers. I had seen them before, but I've also noticed he usually wears brown loafers. He's also within our size profile. But he's not our man."

"How do you know?"

"I know him. He's a hard worker, trying to make something out of his life and himself. He's a good student, and he's valued at his job. He works part-time, but he's been offered a full-time position."

"Is this what he's told you?"

Justine's eyes flashed with anger. "Yes, but I also checked it all out. I have a friend who works at that bank. I called in a favor."

Ella nodded. Something was still bothering her about Furman. He had been conveniently on hand last night. It was possible he'd been following Justine. Ella did know he was interested romantically in her, but there could be more to him than that. His coming to the station, and his apprehension, sparked a memory of something she'd heard at the bureau. Serial killers liked to play games with the police to prove they were smarter. They were always pushing to test themselves, and their courage. Furman's attitude had reminded her of that. On the other hand, it was also true that many people who came to the station felt intimidated by the armed police officers. Furman was still searching for identity, and this could have been the case with him.

"Well, I better get back to the lab. I'm still going through the suspect's vehicle, and waiting to hear from Ritamae. She promised to get me the name of the person who was assigned that car one way or another. We also need to find out if he, or she, wears Kevin Jordan jeans. If the person does, that will corroborate the other evidence we've already gathered. I'm hoping to have something before the end of today."

"Getting the name of the staff member who uses that vehicle shouldn't be this complicated. What's the hold-up?"

"The list is in the office of the administrative supervisor, but no one's been able to find it. The guy's been out of town, and not scheduled back until today."

"Get what we need, but make sure you don't give out any more information than you absolutely have to. We don't want to alert the Packrat that we're tightening the net."

"Already done, boss. I've passed the story around that the fleet car we towed had been tracked to a batch stolen from a dealer in Albuquerque. But that'll buy us a few days at most. You know how it is around here."

Ella watched Justine leave. It was clear to her that Justine was far more involved with Furman than she was admitting. She'd definitely risen to his defense. Still, Ella wasn't sure if it was a matter of pride with her because Furman was a contact she'd found on her own, or an indication that her involvement with him transcended business.

Ella sat back for a moment, considering the problem. Finally she stood up and walked to Big Ed's office. It was time she checked out Furman for herself. Although she wanted to keep her plan under wraps, Big Ed would have to know, just in case of trouble.

Ella drove east again, off the reservation and back to Farmington. She'd made a cursory background check on Furman before leaving. He wasn't scheduled at the bank today, but he did have two classes. One started at five in the evening and the other at seven. From the information Wilson had given her, she knew Furman never missed class. Ella intended to take full advantage of the opportunity to do a more thorough check on this man.

First she'd find out more about where he lived. That often told a great deal about a person. If possible, she'd speak to a neighbor or two, and maybe dig up something useful.

Ella drove down a tree-lined street in an older, established Farmington neighborhood. She had no doubt that even part-time, Furman's computer expertise enabled him to command a decent salary. From the neighborhood, it was clear that although he wasn't wealthy, he certainly lived more comfortably than most Navajos.

She parked across the street from the small apartment building. It was the kind of place young people moved into as their last step before buying a home. There was a communal lawn maintained by management, short driveways in front of each unit, and a pool where a few residents were sunbathing. It was a pleasant-looking place and blended well with the private homes in the neighborhood.

Ella parked at the curb, then walked along the sidewalk until she came to the apartment listed as Furman's. It must have been trash day, because almost every apartment had one or two green plastic trash bags out by the curb.

She glanced up and down the street. There was no one outside in the ninety-degree heat except the people by the pool. From the drawn curtains, she figured that most either worked, or holed up during this part of the day.

Ella walked back to her car, then drove farther down until she was directly in front of Furman's apartment. Stepping out quickly, she grabbed the trash bag and shoved it on the floorboard in the back of the Jeep.

Ella was about to close the door when Furman's neighbor came out. The woman, a slightly overweight blonde in her mid-twenties, came toward her. For a second Ella wondered if she was going to have to explain about stealing trash. Ella closed the Jeep door quickly and walked up to meet the woman halfway.

The neighbor gave Ella a hesitant smile. "Are you a friend of Mr. Brownhat's? I've been trying to catch him all week!"

"Yes I am, but it turns out he's not home right now."

"Well, I'm about to go to Colorado on vacation, but I wanted to thank him for acting so quickly on our complaint. We'd left a note on his door about his cat. It was digging up our bulbs and really making a mess. And he took care of the problem right away. We haven't even seen the cat since then. When you talk to Mr. Brownhat, will you tell him that we really do appreciate it?"

"Sure. No problem. I'll catch up to him soon," Ella assured the woman.

A second later, Ella was on her way. She hadn't gone more than a block when a putrid smell began to fill the air-conditioned car.

A missing cat, and now the trash with this suffocating odor. She rolled down the windows and headed back to the station. That was the only place she could conduct a search without having to look over her shoulder constantly and guard against an ambush. With Peterson on the loose, she couldn't afford to take anything for granted.

She sped down the highway, trying to breathe only through her mouth. Before long she'd know exactly what Furman Brownhat considered garbage.

TWENTY-FOUR

————— ✖ ✖ ✖ —————

Ella parked behind the station, near their Dumpster. Placing several evidence pouches beside her, and wearing rubber gloves, she began to work. The moment she opened the tie on the bag, an awful, heavy smell rose up into the air, engulfing her. Something wrapped in another plastic bag within caught her attention. She pulled it out carefully, dreading having to check whatever was hidden inside.

She felt a small leg beneath the white plastic, then another. It was an animal carcass, she was certain of it. She tried not to cringe as she unwound the metal tie and reached inside the bag. It was bony, like something that had been stripped of its skin.

The smell made her gag. As she pulled a leg out, she realized it wasn't the right type of carcass for a cat. A second later she was staring at the remains of a baked chicken.

Hearing someone clearing their throat, Ella snapped her head around. Justine was standing there, a hand pressed over her nose. "If you're that hungry, I can suggest several restaurants."

"Don't bother. There's still some meat on this!" Ella held out a leg as she cracked a smile, trying to remember to breathe through her mouth only. "How did you know I was here?"

"Officer Nez saw you here when he pulled in. What on earth are you doing?"

Ella stood up and turned her head away from the bag, breathing deeply. "Go back inside. I'll explain later. No reason for you to have to breathe this stench too."

"I can help you," Justine said, then pulled rubber gloves out of her back pocket. "Is this what I think it is? Furman's garbage?"

"How did you know?"

"I was walking past Big Ed's office when you went to talk to him. I overheard enough to figure out what you were doing."

Ella shrugged. "Don't take it personally. I was just following a hunch."

"No problem. How did you get a search warrant? We didn't have enough evidence."

"I didn't need one for this," Ella answered, explaining where she'd found the sack. "But nothing we find in here would be considered conclusive evidence. Any defense attorney would argue that whatever we found in the bag could have been planted there by someone else *after* Furman brought it out of his house."

"So what's the point?"

"It might help us build circumstantial evidence, and with luck, it could give us another clue we can follow up on."

"Have you found anything yet?"

"No, but I just got started," Ella answered.

Justine crouched next to her and began sorting through a gooey mess of leftover salsa that had smeared several utility bills. "I want you to know I'm not personally involved with Furman," Justine said softly. "I just didn't want to admit, even to myself, that I might have misjudged the man. I thought you'd lose all faith in me if my informant turned out to be the Packrat. Not that I'd blame you," she added.

"I suspected that might be it."

"But after you left, I did some more checking on my own. Furman has only one living relative on the Rez, his grandmother, Lena Brownhat. She lives about fifteen miles from the mouth of Dry Wash. Maybe we should go talk to her."

As Ella neared the bottom of the sack, she pulled out a small piece of foiled paper, then unfolded it. "I've got something. Chewed gum."

"We can check it against the piece we found at the Dodge crime scene."

"It's still circumstantial, but it might help us build a case. I want you to take it in to Albuquerque yourself. Fly over there, and tell them that we must have results as quickly as possible."

"It might take a couple of weeks for a complete work-up, although we could get some info within twenty-four hours."

"The sooner you get there, the better then," Ella said.

"I'll take care of it right away." Justine took the gum from Ella, placed it in an evidence pouch, and strode back inside the building.

Ella placed the rest of the trash back inside the bag, then tossed it in the Dumpster. The flies were pleased.

Removing her gloves and tossing them into the Dumpster too, she went inside to give Big Ed a report. The moment she walked into his office, she saw him recoil.

"Cripes, what is that smell?"

Ella explained what she'd done and what she had found. "I'm going to have Justine fly it over. In the meantime, I'm going to go talk to Brownhat's grandmother. Justine tracked her down."

"That's fine, but do us all a favor. Take a shower and change clothes before you go. You can't subject an old woman to this smell. No one deserves *that*."

As she left Shiprock, Ella checked in with the dispatcher, to give a full report of her route and destination. Once she drove down into the canyon, she was sure the terrain would block the signal.

She glanced at the map one of the patrolmen at the station had made for her. It started with an easy drive along the Teece Nos Pos highway, but as she left the highway and turned north, there were suddenly fewer obvious landmarks except the mountains to the west. Weaving along the badly rutted dirt road, she finally reached Dry Wash, a large, meandering arroyo that eventually fed into the San Juan. Two small hills flanked it like silent sentinels.

Ella drove slowly down into the wash, a vague feeling of unease filling her. The shack where the skinwalkers' tunnels had originated from was only about five miles south, and the sun was going down.

She chided herself for allowing memories to disturb her, but her uneasiness grew. Ella continued on through the canyon, then the road left the winding wash and she saw a wide valley opening up ahead. She could just about make out Lena Brownhat's shack in the distance, up against a hill.

Ella went over a small ridge and had started down the slope when a gunshot blasted through the air. The bullet took out her right front tire, and the Jeep swerved abruptly to the right. As Ella fought to keep control, two more shots whined overhead, forcing her to swerve in the opposite direction. There was no cover on the slope, but there were some large boulders at the bottom. Ella swerved the Jeep back and forth to throw off her attacker's aim and tried to radio in. As she'd suspected, the terrain was blocking the signal.

A round smashed through the windshield, leaving a spiderweb pattern. It had missed Ella's head by inches. There were at least two gunmen, firing from two different directions. More gunfire erupted, forcing her to keep her head down. She could barely see where she was going.

She could smell gasoline, so a bullet must have hit the gas tank or fuel line. At least there was no sign of fire yet. She slammed on the brakes at the bottom of the hill and spun the vehicle sideways. Grabbing her shotgun and its ammo sling, she crawled out of the car, radio at her waist. Behind her was a boulder about the size of a refrigerator. It was the only thing in sight that would give her cover for now, but with that advantage came a disadvantage: it would block her vision too.

Ella racked a shell into the shotgun's chamber then checked the clip on her pistol. It was full, and she had two spare clips in her pocket. She had plenty of firepower, though it was short-ranged. If they approached, she'd take them out. Providing she held out until morning, her absence would be noticed and someone would start looking for her. Her mother and brother would make sure of that by calling the station.

It took awhile, but as darkness descended, she began to hear the cautious movement of those who were trying to force her out from cover. She remained still, hardly breathing, then detected someone moving to her right. In the darkness before moonrise, it was impossible for her to discern a shape.

Ella concentrated, aligning the faintly glowing tritium dots on her pistol sights. When she heard the noise again, she aimed in the direction of the sound and fired two quick shots. She heard a gasp, and the thud of a body striking the ground. Soon there was another scrape, like clothing brushing against a branch, but this time to her left.

As she waited, listening, it seemed that the darkness was filled with whispers. She touched the fetish in her pocket and remained quiet. There were more than two others out there now, yet they were holding back. They had seen that she wouldn't be frightened into doing something stupid and that her training was excellent. If they approached, the first two or three would be killed, regardless of what happened to her. Her enemies had lost their advantage.

Ella heard the sound of something being dragged away somewhere off to her right. She fired two shots in that direction and shifted her position slightly in case the brief flashes had been noted. There was a moment of utter silence, then suddenly the wailing cry of coyotes rose high in the air. Her flesh prickled, and she shuddered. Skinwalkers. It was Peterson Yazzie's friends, and probably he as well.

They hadn't followed her, she was sure. At least two had been in position, waiting for her to go by. That meant that they must have known where she was going. Searching for an answer, she tried to put herself in Peterson's head and think like he did. Suddenly she knew precisely what had happened. Peterson had come after her not as a common criminal intent on revenge, but as an ex-cop turned bad. Needing an edge, he'd undoubtedly purchased, or had someone purchase, a police scanner. She'd given him the information he'd needed to ambush her by reporting in.

Hours passed, expanding into lifetimes. Silence settled over the land. She suspected she was alone now, but she still couldn't venture out into the open. If she came out of the shadows, she'd be completely vulnerable. It was important to remain close to her car. The vehicle and the boulder provided her only cover.

Ella stayed awake and alert all through the night. The hum of the insects seemed like a song that reverberated with promise to anyone who could survive the dangers hidden in the darkness. Although weary, her nerves were so taut it was easy to keep watch. As a law enforcement officer she'd faced death and cheated it many times. Those narrow escapes had made her more attuned to life and appreciative of what it held. What didn't kill you made you stronger, so a great philosopher had said. He must have had some Navajo in him.

It was close to sunrise when Ella heard vehicles in the distance. Darkness lingered only in the lengthy shadows that still hid from the predawn light. Ella, still cautious, came out slowly. Peterson might have left someone behind to strike her down just as she began to feel safe. Catching a glimpse of red and blue lights in the distance and hearing the sirens speeding toward her, she breathed a sigh of relief.

Ella pulled out her handheld radio and got Justine almost immediately. For now at least, it was over.

Ella accompanied Justine back uphill to the position where the gunfire had begun. They collected and tagged blood discovered in a large, dried-out splotch on the ground.

"This won't give us much without a suspect to link it to though. And I doubt they'll check the guy into a hospital," Justine said.

"I agree, but follow it up anyway," Ella answered.

They searched the ground carefully for spent shells, footprints, or anything else that might give them a clue.

"They were skinwalkers, I'm certain of that," Ella said softly.

"If you never got a clear look, how do you know?" Justine challenged quietly.

"I've dealt with them before. The howls of rage and frustration . . ." Ella shook her head slowly. "It's a half-human, half-animal sound. You don't soon forget it."

Justine nodded, accepting her explanation. "I was afraid for you," she admitted. "When I came back from Albuquerque, it was four in the morning. Mechanical problems kept us from taking off for hours. Then I learned your mother had left several messages for me. She and your brother were worried because you hadn't come home or called. They felt that you were in danger and needed help. But they didn't know where you were. I asked the dispatcher to give me your last ten-twenty and started out this way as quickly as possible."

Ella nodded. She had no doubt her mother and Clifford had sensed something was terribly wrong. It was part of that special ability the three had always shared, the legacy passed down through their ancestors that had always made them unique. "You need to go over this scene, but I have to get going to Lena Brownhat's. I'm taking your vehicle, since mine's out of commission. You can ride back with the other officers if you finish before I'm done." Ella paused, then added, "I'm worried about Mrs. Brownhat. The gunfire must have frightened her."

"Maybe. Depends how sharp her hearing is, and the direction the wind was blowing last night. She's in her seventies."

"I'll go check on her. In the meantime, make sure you issue an alert that our calls are being monitored. From now on, if you need to talk to me about something important, switch frequencies. Use Tac two. The ordinary scanners can't pick up our tactical channels."

Justine nodded. "I'll also let Big Ed know. He wants me to report back as soon as possible."

"I'll catch up to you later."

Ella drove across the grassy knoll to the wooden shack nestled against the hillside. She parked fifty feet or so in front of the door and waited. Time stretched out, but no one came to the doorway. Ella felt her muscles tighten as she looked farther up the hill, then down toward the river at a half dozen or so sheep grazing on the tall grass. What if the old woman had come out to see what was happening last night and been shot? She wasn't sure how discriminating Peterson and his allies had been prepared to be.

Ella glanced at the clock on the dashboard. She'd wait another two minutes, then she was going inside, invited or not. A breath later, Lena Brownhat appeared in the doorway. The elderly woman was dressed in a traditional long skirt and a faded yellow blouse. She wore a brightly colored scarf around her head. Mrs. Brownhat studied the car for a moment, then waved for Ella to come inside.

With a sigh of relief, Ella got out of her car and walked to the door. The shack had a peculiar dusty, decaying smell. It was as if the dwelling had enveloped the scent of something that had outlived its time and usefulness. Ella glanced around, letting her eyes adjust to the semidarkness, and took a seat in an old folding chair that was offered to her.

"The plastic on the seat is torn, but it's still good," Mrs. Brownhat said in the loud voice those who couldn't hear often adopted.

"Are you Furman's grandmother?" Ella asked in an equally loud tone, though keeping her expression gentle.

"That is my grandson's Anglo name," Lena Brownhat said. "Is there some trouble?"

Ella noted her surroundings without making any obvious glances that might be considered rude. Mrs. Brownhat had an old iron bed, and few possessions. Her food was mostly canned goods, but there were plenty lining the wooden boxes that served as cupboards against the plywood wall. A big plastic garbage can probably held flour or cornmeal. Everything attested to the poverty and the marginal living found throughout the reservation. For those from big clans, there was always a circle of family members or relatives around them. This woman, Ella knew, had outlived her contemporaries. Furman should have seen to her welfare, but that now seemed as likely to happen as the sun rising in the west.

Ella measured her words carefully. Lena Brownhat had enough to handle living out here. "I need to know about him, that's all."

Lena's eyes sparkled with intelligence. "My grandson has done something bad, I can tell. I can tell," she repeated.

"You sound as if you were expecting that."

"I have been," she admitted, practically shouting the words, and oblivious to the fact. "He was never the same after his mother died. They lived way out on the reservation, even further than this place. They were not close to Shiprock or any town at all. My son preferred it that way. He made a good life because he was a hard worker, even though he never went to the tribe's school. I'd brought him up to speak Navajo only. He appreciated our ways."

Ella nodded, wanting the woman to go on at her own pace.

"Then one winter my daughter-in-law grew ill with a fever. They waited, thinking that she would improve, then a *hataalii* was called in. But she got worse, not better. Finally my son decided to take her to a medical doctor at one of the clinics. But their car was old, and it was winter. It wouldn't start, no matter how hard he tried. He had sold his horses just that fall. My son ran miles to the highway to get a car to stop. The one that did held an Anglo man and his woman, but they couldn't understand him. They didn't let him into their car."

"Did your daughter-in-law die?"

Lena Brownhat nodded. "By the time a Navajo man in a pickup came by to help, it was too late. Even the Anglo doctors with all their medicine and machines couldn't stop the fever. She died. My grandson was only twelve at the time, but he blamed his father. Furman said that if they'd been just like everyone else, and turned their backs on the old ways, his mother would have still been alive. Eventually my son couldn't stand seeing the hatred in his own son's eyes. He went out one winter night and just sat down in the snow and froze," she said, her voice fading.

"Does your grandson ever come to see you?"

Mrs. Brownhat shook her head. "I took him in after his parents were gone, but he kept running away to the town. He wanted nothing to do with our ways. He couldn't stand living out here, following our rituals. He hated everything Navajo. He said that useless people like me were dying out, and that those who continued to teach the old ways were hurting the young people." Her voice broke, and she lapsed into a short silence.

"I tried, but I couldn't make him understand," she continued. "One day the people at the tribal welfare office came and took him away. They said he needed proper schooling. They put him in a boarding school at Chinle. I didn't try to stop them. I thought maybe he would be better off there."

"How would he feel about enemies of the tribe, like Peterson Yazzie?"

The old woman's eyes grew wide. "You mean the skin-walker?" Her voice was still loud, but much more muted than her normal speaking level. Seeing Ella nod, she sighed. "I can tell you for sure that he hates them just as much as he hates *hataaliis*. I saw my grandson last year when I went to Shiprock to trade some wool for supplies. He told me he was glad that you had killed so many skinwalkers. He said they were like vultures on the modern world."

"Do you think he would ever join with them, if only to destroy those who teach the *Dineh* the old ways?"

The woman considered it, then shook her head. "I know Yazzie escaped," she said. "Every so often, my friend's daughter comes by in her car. She brings me food, and reads the newspaper to me." Lena gave Ella a long, thoughtful look. "My grandson would never help a skinwalker. He would try to destroy him. They're part of the old ways, too, you see. What he might do is learn all he could about them, then use that knowledge to hunt them down."

"Your grandson has enrolled in the community college. He's a good student. Maybe he's changed."

Lena closed her eyes slowly, then opened them again. The gesture spoke of weariness and sorrow. "He is very smart, and when he puts on his act he can fool almost anyone. Don't let him trick you too. He believes it is his mission to destroy the old ways. He would never give up on that."

Ella stood up. "Is there someplace I can take you? Anything you need?"

Lena smiled. "I've lived out here most of my life. Where would I go? This is home. I have my sheep and a good dog watching them now. This is where I'll stay until I go join my ancestors."

Ella looked at her for a long time. She really didn't want to leave Lena all alone here. If something happened to her . . .

"Go now," Lena said, as if sensing her conflict. "I have plenty of food, my cupboards are full. I have friends. I lack nothing. If I moved into town I would lack my home and peace. This is where I belong."

Ella walked out of the ramshackle home. If it had been up to her, she would have taken Lena back to Shiprock and arranged for one of the agencies to find suitable housing for her. But to take away her right to be where she wanted to be was wrong too. That was a lesson she'd learned from history. Sometimes irreparable harm was done by those who tried to do what they thought was best for others.

Ella picked Justine up on the way back and filled her in. Justine took the news with remarkable poise, even when Ella put out an APB on Furman, along with orders to tail rather than apprehend him.

"I know this is hard on you," Ella added as they walked inside the station. "And I want you to be extra careful. Furman has paid you a lot of attention."

"I feel as if I've failed at the one thing I wanted to do well," Justine answered quietly.

"You haven't failed, not if you're learning from what happened. There's a difference."

Justine nodded. "Big Ed should be happy that we found shell casings, drops of blood, and some clothing fibers at the ambush site. We also have plaster-cast prints of the tires and footprints."

"Good. Anything easily traceable on the shells?"

"Easy to trace? Only if we find the actual weapons. These are .30-30 Winchester shell casings, the most common caliber and brand around here. But we have other things, and there are people out there trying to follow the tracks. I expect they'll lead to the highway, but if I can identify the vehicle, or type of vehicle from the tracks, and identify the fibers, we may be able to ask some pointed questions of gas station owners and convenience food places that line the main road."

Ella stopped a few steps from Big Ed's door. "Let's just hope we manage to locate Furman quickly." She took a deep breath to brace herself before going inside. "I'll see you in a little while."

Big Ed's face was expressionless as Ella gave him a detailed report.

"The dispatcher checked with me on the APB that involved the Farmington police," Big Ed said at last. "I called their chief myself. He assured me his men would take care of things from their end." Big Ed sat back. "I also heard from the public defender's office. It appears that Bruce Cohen has resigned. He and his wife are staying back east with an old school friend of his. They won't even go outside the front door alone."

"I expected something like that. Peterson scared him half to death. Cohen wasn't prepared mentally to deal with someone like him," Ella answered.

"What's the connection between Furman Brownhat and Peterson Yazzie?"

"I don't think there is a direct link. In my opinion, Peterson used the murders to get attention for himself, though he wasn't actually involved in them. He has his own agenda. If Furman and Peterson ever meet, I believe one will kill the other."

"Is there a chance they've combined forces, if only for a short time?" Big Ed persisted.

Ella considered it. "Peterson would have used anyone and anything to escape. Furman, I also believe, would use anything he could to accomplish what he feels is his mission. A partnership between the two seems unlikely, but stranger things have happened."

"Watch yourself. I don't like the way this is shaping up," Big Ed warned. "Peterson hates you most of all."

As Ella left Big Ed's office, Justine came up to her. "No one with a gunshot wound was taken to the hospital either last night or this morning. No big surprise there. Also, this arrived in the mail for you. It's from the PD in Columbus, Georgia."

Ella took the package and tore it open. There was a folder inside, with a letter clipped to the outside of it.

"I'm going to go to that store that has the designer jeans and show them Furman's college photo," Justine said. "I'll pick up a copy at the college records office."

"Excellent idea," Ella said.

Ella read the letter in her office. The officer in Georgia had looked up some news photos taken just after her husband's accident. He'd sent them to her as a professional courtesy. As she studied the prints, her eyes fell on a familiar face in the background. Taking out a small magnifying glass from her desk, Ella looked closely. Her eyes clouded with tears as she recognized her father-in-law in the crowd staring at the wreckage, his expression filled with mixed emotions.

Ella felt the bitterness that rose inside her, and she began to pace. Swallowing hard, she willed back the tears that threatened to come spilling down her face. Peterson hadn't lied. Her father-in-law *had* caused her husband's death. With that one act, he'd set himself on the path that had killed him, and her on the path she now followed.

Ella felt her hatred for Peterson and everything he represented boiling inside her. He had thought to disable her with this piece of information. Yet all he'd done was turn her into an enemy who would not give up until she brought him to his knees. Her body trembled with anger, and the need for revenge filled her heart. Without thinking, she took her pistol out of its holster and checked to verify the clip was full.

As she walked past the window, Ella caught a reflection of her face. Contorted with hatred and rage, it scarcely looked like her at all.

She had to bring her emotions under control. If she allowed hatred to rule her, it would cloud her thinking and give Yazzie the advantage he had planned upon. She had to fight him harder than ever now, because the battleground he'd chosen was within herself.

A silent figure crawled along the arroyo, then stopped behind a clump of high desert grasses. Parting the stalks slightly, he angled his body, wanting a clearer view of the house below. Two cops were guarding the old woman. He'd seen the one at night on the mesa, and now this one, probably his brother. They were never far, and their eyes were constantly watching.

He saw the woman's son, the Singer, come out, and glance around as if he sensed the threat to her. Another would die soon. He would bring a new order once they were all dead, even the one who used powers he'd never dreamed existed. But the ultimate power was his. He chose who was to live and who was to die.

He'd learned from the others who used superstition against the People. He had powers of his own, too, greater than theirs because tradition hadn't shackled him. He would use the freedom his intellect gave him to bring in all the good things the modern world had to offer. No more lack, no more poverty, just power, as raw and vital as the land that surrounded them.

He knew that he was losing himself bit by bit, but it seemed such a small price to pay now. He was being transformed, just like he would transform others in the time to come.

Ella drove home in Justine's car. Justine would use an available patrol unit until Ella's Jeep was repaired a second time.

Ella noticed her mother hanging laundry on the clothesline in the back as she pulled up. Clifford was with her, but his gaze moved constantly everywhere else. The expression on his face was one she hadn't seen in a long time. As Ella stepped out of the vehicle, she suddenly understood why. Something had got their attention. Perhaps a skinwalker, or even Furman, was close by.

She saw the police officer walking around the mesa above the house. His binoculars were on their surroundings, checking for trouble, though nothing seemed amiss.

Then Ella noticed Dog. He was sitting a few feet to the side of Rose, his head up, sniffing the air. There was an alertness about him, as if he, too, were waiting for a threat he sensed, but couldn't see.

TWENTY-FIVE

——— ✕ ✕ ✕ ———

Ella spent a long time searching the area, then finally showered and slept for a while from sheer exhaustion. After a few hours, the phone woke her up. Ella picked up the receiver before the second ring and identified herself.

"I'm sorry to wake you," Justine said, "but I thought you'd want to know. I found the man who drove the fleet car used in Haske's murder, and spoke to him a few hours ago. He just returned from vacation. He said the car was intact when he left. He doesn't know anything about its being damaged. Unfortunately he's in the habit of leaving the car keys in the ignition. Thefts aren't normally a problem on the Rez."

"So Furman could have walked right up and driven it away, then returned the car to where we found it when he was finished. Disposing of the keys with his prints, he also made sure he muddled up any trail that could lead us back to him."

Ella paused thoughtfully. "It's time we brought Furman in."

"I've got bad news. No one's been able to find him. I've got people out looking as we speak."

"Let's get a warrant to search his home," Ella said.

"Find the judge. I'll get the Farmington cops to stake out his home until we can get there."

Ella got up and dressed quickly. She had just put on her boots when Rose walked in her room.

"I thought I heard the phone ring. You haven't had enough sleep!"

"I have to go to work."

Rose nodded. "I know that. I can feel the danger pressing in on all of us now. It's not as strong as it was before, but it's still here."

Ella looked at her mother and saw the worry on her face. "There's an officer outside, and Clifford is here with you. If *anything* at all happens, call the station. Other cops will get out here immediately. There's a patrol unit in the neighborhood too."

Rose said nothing.

Ella gave her mother a quick hug. "I have to go. I'll check in with you often, though."

"Good."

Ella jumped into the car, switched frequencies as arranged, then had the dispatcher put her through to Justine. "What's the progress on that court order?"

"I got Judge Barelas to start putting the paperwork through. She understands the urgency. Someone from the Farmington police will meet you at Furman's with the warrant. I figured it would save time rather than having to stop by the courthouse."

"Good job! Meet me at Furman's," she added, knowing Justine needed to be in on this. Now more than ever, Ella had to show her that one mistake in judgment did not mean she was any less of a cop—just human.

Ella and Justine parked behind the patrol car that had been watching Furman's apartment. The officer reported there was still no sign of the owner. Justine left the tribal police vehicle and joined Ella in what had been Justine's unmarked unit.

"The court order should be here soon," Justine said. "The cop bringing it to us must have decided to walk here. I checked in transit, and the paperwork was completed."

"It hasn't been as long as it seems," Ella said, nevertheless feeling each second drag.

After what seemed to be an eternity, a patrol car finally pulled up and a young uniformed cop stepped out. Ella walked over to meet him. Taking the court order, she motioned for Justine, and together they walked toward the apartment manager's office.

Ella used the manager's passkey to open the front door, then walked inside cautiously. More than one criminal had been known to booby-trap his home, or wait inside, undetected for hours. Justine stood just behind her to the right, ready in case of unexpected trouble, but the house was dark, quiet, and cool.

Ella and Justine both slipped on medical latex gloves to preserve any evidence they might find as they studied the area around them. The two-bedroom furnished apartment was small, and there were only a few pieces of furniture.

"It looks like a simple search," Ella said, "but don't take anything for granted. We'll go through each and every room with a fine-toothed comb. I want something on this guy that I can use to put him behind bars."

Ella started in the smaller bedroom used as a study, while Justine worked the living room. They searched each room methodically, but even after an hour, they'd found nothing.

Justine met Ella in the kitchen. Ella had emptied all the drawers and even checked beneath them, searching for anything that had been taped to the underneath or to the sides.

"This was a waste of time. He must have hidden anything important or incriminating somewhere else."

Ella shook her head. "No, it's here. Think about it. This is where he *lives*. Everyone has things that would be considered private, but we haven't found *anything* at all like that. This place has been sanitized, don't you see? There must be a hiding place where he keeps whatever he values and considers personal."

"Where? We've searched everywhere! Even the freezer!"

Ella glanced around the room. "He's probably fashioned something to serve as his vault."

"It can't be a light fixture; they all work. I checked that while I was searching. I'd read someplace that dope was often hidden in light fixtures."

"A vent, then," Ella said, staring thoughtfully at the heating and cooling grates above the door where cool air was currently originating. "Look for one that doesn't belong. There should be a vent above the door in each room, and a long one in the hall, below the furnace. Anything else is a phony."

They began their search again, both eager to pursue this new possibility. After five minutes, Ella walked back to the living room. One look at Justine told her she'd found nothing either.

Ella dropped down onto the couch. They'd have to abandon the search, yet something continued to nag at her. "There's something here we're not seeing. I just *feel* it."

Justine gave her a guarded look. "There's no place else to look. I even moved the few pieces of furniture in the bedrooms, and the appliances in the kitchen. And beneath this tile and carpeting is a concrete floor, so it's not buried here."

Ella went to the doorway and glanced back into the room. "I guess it's time to go," she said wearily, ignoring the feeling that continued to nag at her. "Let's turn out the lights— Wait a second."

"I checked the light fixtures, remember?" Justine said.

"I know, but did you check the outlets?" She pointed directly ahead. Two were above the baseboard, about three feet apart from each other. A desk lamp had been plugged into one; the other was empty.

"Wait, if you want to start messing with electrical outlets, I think—"

Ella was already crouched by the outlet, using her pocketknife blade on the center screw.

"Be careful!." Justine protested. "You'll electrocute yourself."

Ella finished removing the white cover plate, then stared at the empty hole behind it. "Bingo."

"Don't stick your hand in there until I get a flashlight," Justine said. "I saw one in a kitchen drawer. I'll be right back."

Ella peered into the darkened crevice. She had no intention of sticking her hand anywhere she couldn't see.

Justine returned a minute later. "Okay. I unscrewed the flashlight first to look inside. Just batteries." She crouched behind Ella and aimed the beam for her.

The opening in the wall was a little less than six inches deep, and a foot and a half or so wide. Inside were several loose pieces of newspaper and some other smaller items wedged between two boards used in the framing. Ella put her gloves back on, then reached in and carefully extracted the papers first.

Using the carpet below the phony outlet as backing, she flattened out newspaper clippings about each of the murders. There were several, from local and state papers. Next came a piece of notebook paper. "This is the page that was missing from Kee Dodge's lesson plans," she said, reading the precisely written notations concerning Navajo historical events.

Reaching into the opening again, she brought out a piece of abalone shell and a small wooden crucifix. "The items missing from two of the crime scenes."

"His trophies, taken from Haske's medicine bundle and from Sadie Morgan's necklace," Justine said in a hushed tone. "I guess we can eliminate Lewis and Begay as suspects on this case."

Ella unfolded a small sheet of notebook paper that had been placed beneath the stolen items. "And this is even more than what we hoped for."

Ella showed Justine a list of the murder victims, their names checked off neatly with a red pen. First on the list, but not checked, was Naomi Zah. At the bottom, below Sadie Morgan's name, was Rose Destea's.

A chill crept over Ella, and she shuddered. Her mother had told her only hours before that she felt herself in danger. Rose's feelings never lied.

As Ella raced back to the reservation, she picked up her cellular phone and arranged for added security to be placed around her mother. She then contacted Big Ed, who insisted on a strategy meeting at her home, since he wanted to oversee security there at the same time. Officers had still failed to locate Brownhat or Yazzie.

Ella arrived home twenty-five minutes later. Big Ed and three more patrol cars were parked around the house. Ella went to greet the officers stationed there. As she approached the porch, she passed two of the force's best sharpshooters. She silently noted their extra clips of ammo, and the rifles they each carried. One rifle had a special starlight scope for use at night.

Big Ed came out of the house and went to meet her. "I've got the best here. No one is going to even get close to your family."

"I've been thinking about this. I feel like a sitting duck, waiting for Yazzie or Brownhat to make a move before we can act."

"What choice do we have? We have no idea where they are."

"We could set up a trap, one guaranteed to flush them out."

"I hope you're not suggesting we make your mother a target," Big Ed said, looking at Ella through narrowed eyes.

"Of course not. But you are thinking along the same lines I am. If we use the right bait, they'll come out of hiding, and we'll be right there to make them choke on it."

"Tell me what you have in mind."

It was nearly ten P.M. when Ella stood in the police station's largest interview room, surrounded by press and TV cameras. Even the Albuquerque media would carry this story. Wherever Peterson and Furman were, they wouldn't be likely to miss this. By morning, it would hit every paper and radio and TV station in the state.

Ella briefed the reporters, using her carefully prepared statement. "A Navajo woman named Naomi Zah, one of our stargazers, was the first intended victim, but she really outsmarted her killer. Her cunning and bravery got him so rattled he couldn't quite pull it off," Ella said. "He has been incredibly lucky to pull off the crimes he's committed since then. In fact, from Naomi's description of his behavior, we have reason to believe that he's needed constant guidance from someone else. It's the reason he's been able to kill at all."

"So you're saying that the killer is acting under someone else's direction?" a woman in the front asked.

"Yes, the fact that an old woman was able to outthink and outfight him demonstrated his need to seek help from someone smarter than he is. Our web is closing now, though, and we hope to make an arrest very soon."

"So you know the identity of the Packrat?"

Ella had expected the question. She didn't want Furman to bolt—she wanted him angry and susceptible to the bait. "We don't know *who* he is, but we do know *what* he is. We have a carefully constructed profile based on clues we've collected from each of the murders. We believe he's in his mid-twenties. He's got a limited education and is probably unemployed. According to what Naomi's told us, we also know he's sloppy and disorganized about everything. He's ineffectual, unattractive or at least unappealing. Naomi has corroborated that for us. She is almost certain she can identify him if they ever come face-to-face again. All we need is the right person in a lineup."

Ella answered a few more questions, always careful to avoid giving a name and trying to profile Brownhat in a way that would enrage him and build up Naomi Zah at the same time. The angrier he got with Naomi, the more likely he'd be to take the bait and try to finish her off.

Peterson, of course, was another matter. But if things went Ella's way, and she was confident they would, she'd nail both of them.

When the reporter for the Farmington paper spoke, he brought the room to complete silence. "Every time one of the tribe's special teachers has been murdered by the Packrat, something else really bad has also happened, almost immediately. The last time, after Sadie Morgan's death, Navajo children died. The two events were only an hour or so apart according to reports. Do *you* think there's a connection? Are some journalists correct in calling this a curse?"

All eyes were on Ella. She looked around the room and took a drink of water, considering silently what she should say. The belief that the events were related was a common one now, and many were losing hope, just as Big Ed and others had predicted. She had to restore their faith somehow. "We are taught that good and evil live side by side, and that for harmony to be maintained in the world, some kind of balance must be achieved. There have been many unhappy events lately, and sadly, lives have been lost. But we must work together to restore that balance between light and dark. Bringing the Packrat to justice will be a step in that direction, I believe."

A Navajo reporter had the last question. "The ex-cop, Peterson Yazzie, has killed several of our people, and recently murdered a nurse while escaping from a mental hospital. Do you have any hope of catching *him* before he kills again?"

Ella had already planned her answer, anticipating at least one question about Yazzie. "We hope to find him soon, of course, but he's not our top priority. His power and influence are all but gone from the reservation. He killed an innocent health worker while escaping, but our people are too well protected to make easy prey. All he's managed to do since his escape is kill a few sheep."

With the conference ended, the reporters left quickly to file their stories. Big Ed stood beside her.

"Are you sure about this? You're provoking an attack." The police chief crossed his arms, waiting for her answer.

"Yes, and it's going to work too." Ella gave him a quick half smile. "It's our best shot. Peterson is going to see this for exactly what it is. He'll know we're setting up Furman, and provoking him to go after Naomi Zah. We'll make sure our radio traffic, which he's listening in on, supports this impression. Yazzie also knows that there's no way we'd allow Naomi to put herself in the line of fire. He'll conclude that *I'll* be the one posing as Naomi, or that I'll be close by, ready to spring the trap. Peterson knows where we'll be, and he'll make his move while we're setting things up. It's imperative that he see *me* getting into my disguise as Naomi. That's going to draw him in close, and we've got to give him the opportunity. Then we'll seal the trap. I've already assigned two officers to remain at the Zah hogan. They're in position now. Even if he still has sources within the department, he won't be able to get there ahead of us."

"Good idea. Now, what about Furman?"

"He'll wait until the area is clear. His pattern so far is to watch first, learn the pattern, then strike. He's not professionally trained, but he is smart. He's not going to stick around if he sees lots of cops. He'll think we're trying to trap him, so he'll leave and bide his time. We'll have to draw him in whenever we're ready by announcing an arrest, then seeming to have the cops pull out. When he thinks Naomi is alone, he'll make his move, and we'll be there to catch him. And who knows?" Ella tried to sound optimistic. "Maybe we won't have to go through all this trouble with Brownhat. If he shows up at any of the places we have staked out, our officers will nab him."

"I have a real bad feeling about this, Ella. Peterson, from the reports I've read, could alter his appearance and make people believe he was someone else. If he slips through our net . . ."

"I'm going to ask my brother for his help. Clifford knows the tricks Peterson would use and how to counter them. Maybe he can give our team some support and tell us how to tip the scales in our favor."

"Good idea. I like it." Big Ed finally smiled.

Justine walked inside, holding a long-haired gray wig. "It's mostly talcum powder," she explained, "but it'll complete your disguise. You can tie it into a bun like Naomi does. I've also got a long skirt and a colorful blouse like she wears. From a distance, with a little padding around the hips, no one will be the wiser."

"I'll have to try and learn the way she walks, and what her routine is."

"Naomi's on the way here now. One of our uniforms picked her and her husband Raymond up before the press conference. They'll be here shortly."

"The news story will be everywhere by tomorrow morning, so I figure our people have to sneak in and be in place not too long after dawn. We'll make a show of getting ready later, but that'll be for Peterson's benefit. Peterson will want to strike in the early morning, as soon after he hears the news as possible. Furman's M.O. is to strike either late at night or just after dawn, so he will need more time to get ready. If he learned one thing from his first attack on Naomi, *and* from his second, it was to be prepared for the unexpected. The earliest he will show up should be tomorrow evening."

"I'll have men placed all over the area of the Zah hogan. If Yazzie comes with an army, we'll still be ready," Justine said.

"He won't," Ella assured her. "This is personal. He wants me dead by his own hand, not one of his people's. He'll come for me himself."

Ella spent the rest of the evening talking to Naomi, familiarizing herself with her routines, and trying to talk and walk like the woman while wearing a cumbersome disguise. Naomi enjoyed the activity immensely. She laughed at Ella's efforts as if she were one of the Navajo clowns who impersonate dancers during ceremonies, becoming caricatures of the real thing.

Ella continued her efforts until she was confident that she could fool Furman when the time came. Naomi, too, seemed pleased with the transformation.

"We're done for tonight," Ella finally told Naomi. "Thanks for helping. We'll put you and your husband under protective custody until this is over. Don't worry about anything. You won't be in any danger. You have my word."

Naomi nodded slowly. "And you?"

"I'll be doing my job," Ella assured the stargazer. "I know what I'm doing."

"You're a strong woman, but remember that like all of us, you bleed too. Is there another, less dangerous way?"

Her genuine concern touched Ella deeply. Slowly but surely she was gaining acceptance among the tribe. "This is the way I serve," Ella said softly, knowing that Naomi would understand.

The elderly woman nodded somberly. "Then look after yourself as well as you do those you protect, and you will be fine."

Ella saw Naomi and Raymond leave, escorted by two plainclothesmen. She was glad that the elderly couple would be safely out of the way. It would be one less thing to worry about.

Ella changed out of her disguise and drove home quickly, placing the bubble on top of her car and breaking the speed limits on the deserted roads. She wanted to get a few hours' sleep at home, but she had no illusions. Even her mother's special herbs wouldn't help her relax tonight.

When she arrived, she expected the household to be asleep;

it was almost midnight. Instead she heard her mother and Loretta moving around in the back room, and saw Clifford place a suitcase near the front door.

"What's going on?"

"Loretta's gone into labor. With Peterson and his friends on the loose, I have to take her to the hospital and stay by her side."

Rose came out of the back bedroom and placed an overnight suitcase of her own next to Loretta's. "I'm going too. She needs a woman with her, and her relatives live too far away to come quickly."

"No, you can't, Mom," Ella said softly. "You're a target. I can't risk—"

Rose cut her off with a wave of her hand. "I will not allow our enemies to keep me from helping my family. My unborn grandson is also in danger, and I will be there to do all I can."

"The doctors . . ." Ella saw the look in her mother's eye and knew any further argument was useless. "All right, but the officers outside will have to go with you."

"Do whatever you feel is necessary," Rose answered with a shrug, then returned to Loretta's side.

Ella stood alone with Clifford. "I was hoping you'd help me. We're laying a trap for Peterson, but his abilities to disguise himself are going to make things difficult."

"My wife and my son need me now," he said. "I have to be with them."

"It could be a daughter," Ella teased halfheartedly.

"No, it is a son," he said with perfect assurance.

Clifford reached into his medicine pouch. "Close your eyes," he said firmly.

Ella did as he asked, then felt her brother touch both her eyelids, muttering a prayer she'd never heard before.

"Now open them." He met Ella's gaze. "That will help you see the truth. Remember to use your intuition, and you won't be wrong."

Ella ordered one of the officers to transport her family in his own patrol unit while two others followed close behind. She remained on the porch until the cars disappeared from view, then returned inside. One officer remained nearby, guarding her. Big Ed had insisted on that.

Ella walked around the empty living room. The house felt odd now, so empty. She sat in her mother's chair and, as the silence encompassed her, she wondered what tomorrow would hold. She was under siege from all sides now. Instinct assured her that she would either emerge victorious, or find death.

Ella retired to her room soon afterward, but spent a restless night. She heard every creak and groan the old house made, listening and wishing she could sleep.

Ella rose shortly after four, turning off the alarm before it rang. She felt tense and in need of action.

She had just finished dressing when an officer came to the door. Ella recognized Philip Cloud. "Is something wrong?"

"No," Philip answered quickly. "I just wanted you to know that Officer Frank will be watching the house today. I've been reassigned."

"To do what?"

"Well, for starters, I'm to follow you to the station," he said, evading her question. "Big Ed called me personally, but he also told me not to discuss it with anyone." He glanced at Officer Frank then back at Ella. "You can check with the boss, if you want."

If there was one family she knew she could trust, it was the Clouds. "No need. Let's go."

"My replacement, Michael, is back again. He'll be watching the house now."

Ella nodded. "All right. Let's go."

"I'm ready."

He stayed no more than two car lengths behind her as they drove down the highway. Ella's stomach growled and she was suddenly very aware that she hadn't eaten anything in the last sixteen hours. Unwilling to stop, she decided to grab a sandwich from the machine at the station. Even one of those cardboard-tasting specials would be fine about now.

A short time later Ella walked inside the station and turned to smile at Philip Cloud. "You're relieved, Officer."

He shook his head, and keeping his voice low, explained. "I'm part of the team that's guarding you today. It's a good thing too. If I wasn't, my uncle would have my head on a platter."

Ella smiled, thinking of Herman and how he'd always been there to help. If he couldn't be there now, it was a foregone conclusion that he'd want one of his family in his stead. "You're right. Your uncle *would* want you there. But what about you?"

"I'm a cop. It's all part of my job."

Ella smiled. His simple answer, so close to what her own would have been, said it all. "Let's get to it then."

Ella arrived at her office and saw Justine already there. A plate covered with tinfoil had been placed on Ella's desk. The aroma of eggs and bread filled her nostrils, making her mouth water. "Is that for me?" Ella asked, hoping for a positive response.

"I had a feeling that you wouldn't have stopped for breakfast, and I knew you'd need it. There's no telling how long things will take out there today, and our breaks will be few. When I made breakfast this morning, I decided to make enough for both of us."

After thanking Justine, Ella ate greedily and quickly. The eggs, scrambled with chiles and spices, with thick slices of toast on the side, were filling and renewed her energy.

Big Ed came into her office carrying two armor vests just as she was getting her disguise together. "Add this to your outfit, Ella, one inside the other. And come on. We want to be there while the papers are still being tossed, and before the morning TV newscasts."

"I'll be ready in a few minutes," she said, tying the wig's hair into a bun and fastening it while it was still on the Styrofoam head.

"I know we discussed this before, but I think you should keep in mind that there's still a chance Furman and Peterson are working together," Big Ed said.

"It's not that likely. That's not the profile of most serial killers. They rarely work with anyone else. Do you think Peterson would trust someone like Furman, or take him into his hiding places, or let him know who any of his followers are? Peterson is too smart to deal with a psycho. According to his grandmother, Furman would eventually target Yazzie anyway. Peterson would have figured that out too."

"You're right. Peterson is an ex-cop, and that stays with a person. He might have been judged crazy by the courts, but he's certainly not stupid." Big Ed glanced at the clothing that lay on Ella's desk. "I wonder how soon Peterson will show up. I hope we won't have to wait long. I'd like him in custody and out of the way as soon as possible."

"The morning news will broadcast at six-thirty, an hour and a half from now, and the papers will hit the stands shortly after that. Depending on how close he is to Naomi's hogan, I expect him to strike soon afterwards. He knows the terrain around there like the back of his hand, and he's taken tactical training. Providing he has adequate transportation and weapons, and I think he probably has both, we shouldn't have too long a wait."

"He won't expect you to be alone. I wonder how he plans to get around that."

"He'll undoubtedly use trickery to get through my screen of officers, and count on striking before we're ready for Brownhat."

"You'll have the best team with you."

"Then let's get moving. I'll park behind good cover and carry my disguise in. I want Peterson to know for sure that it's me impersonating Naomi, so I won't be changing clothes until after I'm there. Just one more thing. Remind the others that it's possible Peterson got early word about the press release and is already in position, ready to strike. Having two of our officers out there all night doesn't necessarily mean he didn't manage to circumnavigate them."

Ella picked up her disguise, patted her pocket to verify the badger fetish was with her, then went to the parking lot. The time had come to confront her enemies. Fear made her mouth feel as dry as the sand that surrounded her. She had no wish to die, but the possibility was inescapable. Forcing herself to concentrate on the details of their plan, she placed her key in the ignition and began the journey.

TWENTY-SIX

—————— ✗ ✗ ✗ ——————

Ella made no effort to hide her arrival at Naomi Zah's hogan, and everyone had been briefed. Peterson's ability to alter his appearance had been explained to each officer. The last time Ella had faced him in a deadly confrontation, when she'd arrested and sent him to jail, he'd almost managed to fool even her by appearing as an elderly woman.

Today, despite the care taken to make her appear a good target for Peterson, she wouldn't be alone. She took comfort in that. The majority of the police officers would be "hiding" where an experienced hunter like Peterson could spot them. They were to allow Peterson to evade them, maintaining radio silence unless they came under individual attack. The key was to make it hard, but not impossible, for Peterson to get through. The frightening thing, Ella realized, was that Yazzie probably would have been able to elude them anyway.

Only Justine and Big Ed would maintain surveillance on the hogan from carefully selected places of concealment nearby. Just to make sure she'd get some advance warning, Ella had ordered hidden video cameras set up, covering the area around the hogan for fifty yards. If anyone approached, the cameras would record them. Peterson's skinwalker powers of illusion and misdirection might confuse a human being's senses; the camera, however, could not be tricked as easily. It was a totally objective adversary that had a greater chance of remaining unseen while it continued its relentless monitoring.

Ella walked around the hogan several times, performing Naomi's routine chores. Although she made sure she was visible, she always stayed close to cover. The time she spent waiting inside the hogan was the more difficult. The morning was cool, but curiously silent. She tried to let her fear work for her, attuning her senses. She had the battery-powered camera monitors there inside the small hogan and kept her eyes on them, searching, vigilant.

Minutes ticked by. Three hours passed. She had expected Peterson to act by now, or at least to show some sign of his approach. The stillness grated on her nerves. Suddenly, as she watched the monitors, she caught a flicker of a shadow. For a moment she wasn't sure if she'd really seen it at all.

Her muscles tensed and she scarcely breathed. The next camera would be only yards from the hogan. She kept her eyes on the monitor and saw Peterson pass by, his body blending in well against the junipers and sagebrush.

Yazzie had selected his clothing with the precision of a soldier going on an assault, and would be hard to spot even out in the open. She checked the clip on her nine-millimeter pistol, reached down to touch the fetish in her pocket, then set a pot on the stove loudly, the clanking metal a warning sign for Big Ed and Justine.

Ella pressed her back to the thick log wall as she stood beside the entrance. An explosion, a short distance to the north, shook the hogan, loosing dust into the air and tossing Ella to the dirt floor.

Chaos erupted all around, and she heard loud voices everywhere. As she tried to scramble to her feet, the opening of the hogan went dark for a second, then Peterson slipped inside. He spun around in the semidarkness as if sensing her presence behind him and threw a cloud of fine white dust into the air.

Ella rolled behind the stove and held her breath, but she reacted a second too late. Everything in the hogan started to slant as if she were on a boat during a storm. She wanted to fire her pistol, but her finger was suddenly frozen in place.

Peterson's laugh was low and deadly. "Now, it's time."

Through a slow-motion haze, she saw Peterson approach. He reached for the long dagger at his waist. "For you, Ella, the end will be quick. Your family won't be so lucky. First will come their capture, then, eventually, their deaths."

Before he could take another step, she saw the outline of a small figure in the doorway.

"Stop!" Justine's voice cracked in the hogan like a whip.

"Okay. Relax. You've won." Peterson turned around slowly, then with a flick of his wrist sent the dagger flying. It struck Justine just above her armored vest, near the collarbone. Crying out in pain, she fell to her knees, the pistol dropping out of her hands.

Ella felt as if her body was frozen. Yet seeing the attack on Justine allowed her to summon strength beyond the power of Yazzie's drug. Swinging her pistol around, she fired three times.

Peterson stared at her in surprise as he crumpled to his knees. "I misjudged you. You are strong . . ." His voice faded, and he fell facedown.

Blood stained the packed sand, flowing quickly into a growing pool that coated the parched floor. Ella stumbled to where Justine was. Her cousin sat leaning against the hogan wall. She'd pulled out the dagger and was holding one bloody hand over the wound, her recovered pistol in the other. Big Ed rushed into the small room, pistol in hand. Surveying the scene in a glance, he quickly pulled out his radio. He called for paramedics and notified his officers to verify each other's safety, then assemble near the hogan.

Crouching next to Justine, Big Ed lifted the handkerchief Ella had given her and studied the wound. "You'll be okay, young lady. You were quick to react, and lucky as well. The knife missed your artery, thank God!" He glanced up at Ella, who was standing unsteadily behind him. "What the heck happened here, and what's that strange odor?"

"I don't know," Ella admitted. At least the room had stopped spinning like a child's wind-up toy. "He threw some powder in the air, then everything went crazy."

Big Ed nodded, understanding. "Go outside. I'll stay with Justine."

Giving Justine an encouraging smile, Ella stepped out into the open. She took several deep gulps of the cool morning air. Although it helped, her legs still felt rubbery. As she leaned against the side of the hogan, Peterson's last threat echoed in her mind.

Ella hurried back inside the hogan, and Big Ed looked up, startled. "Send more people to the hospital." She quickly explained what Peterson had said would happen.

"All right. We're also going to have to release the press statement now, to announce an arrest. The news has to reach Furman soon if we're going to try to enact phase two of your plan. If we don't act now, we'll lose our advantage. Are you up to it?" Big Ed stepped out of the hogan and allowed Officer Philip Cloud to enter with a first-aid kit.

Ella forced herself to focus on the job that remained to be done. "Yes. Let's finish this. We'll clear out as soon as the paramedics take Justine in. Then I'll release the story that the Packrat, our serial killer, has been caught, but withhold news of any death, or he'll know that Naomi would never return here. We'll also withhold any ID on the suspect, saying that we're awaiting final confirmation of the Packrat's identity."

"The big headlines and TV program interruptions should enrage Furman," Big Ed said. "It's obvious from the newspaper clippings he had hidden in his apartment that he wants all the attention he can get. He won't want to share it with some impostor. Hopefully he'll come here and try to strike tonight or tomorrow morning. It'll get really tough if he remains calm enough to wait."

"His ego won't let him wait long," Ella said. "He'll have to prove to us again how clever he is, and how stupid we are. He needs that as much as you and I need air to breathe."

Ella looked down at her youthful partner. Officer Cloud had

Justine's bandage in place and had convinced her to lie down on his jacket.

"Justine won't be here to back us up," Big Ed said, pointing out the obvious. "Who do you want here instead?"

"Officer Neskahi knows this area better than all of us. I think he'll want this opportunity."

As the paramedics arrived, Ella and Big Ed moved farther away, letting them get on with their work. Ella saw Officer Cloud move as far away from the hogan as he could while remaining within sight of Ella and Big Ed. Now that Peterson had died here, Naomi would not be returning to the hogan. Everyone else would stay away too once word got around. Peterson's *chindi* would be feared far more than Peterson's abilities as a skinwalker ever had been.

Ten minutes later, certain Justine was stabilized, the paramedics lifted her onto a stretcher and carried her to the ambulance.

Before they could place her inside, Justine reached for Ella's hand. "I did okay, right?"

Ella smiled. "You saved my life. I don't think it gets more okay than that. Get that shoulder healed and get back on the job soon. I need you."

Ella, now out of her disguise, weathered the pandemonium at the press conference with Big Ed by her side. The details they gave the reporters fueled a frenzy of questions that left her exhausted by the time it was finally over.

Afterward, Big Ed led her down the hall to her office. "I think I'd rather face an armed opponent."

"Funny. I was just thinking the same thing." Ella dropped wearily into her desk chair.

"I spoke to Officer Neskahi. He'll back us up. I'll have patrol units in the vicinity, but no one close. We don't want to spook Brownhat."

"The three of us will be able to handle this. Furman will want to approach and catch me unawares, so he can follow through on his usual style of killing."

"The monitors are still there, and the cameras. Their batteries are being recharged now. They served us well before, so I figured they could do so again."

"Naomi Zah goes outside her hogan each night to do her stargazing. I'm going to follow her usual pattern. I'm not as worried about a high-powered rifle with Furman as I was with Peterson."

"Once he gets close, he'll recognize you."

"True, but by then, he's ours."

Big Ed nodded once. "We'll go out there separately and sneak our way in from different directions. Just remember that we're in this together. We'll take him down as a team."

Ella watched Big Ed leave her office. The reporters were already long gone, hurrying off to get their stories into print. Ella called the hospital and asked for her mom. After several minutes, Rose picked up the phone.

"Are you all okay?" Ella asked.

"There's been no trouble. We have extra men here now," her mother answered noncommittally. "And your cousin is here in the next hall, right by the children's ward, with an officer by her door. She's asleep now, but she'll be fine."

Ella breathed a sigh of relief. "Good. Take care of everyone. I'll be there as soon as I can."

"Remember what I warned you about?" Rose's voice was whisper soft.

"About the danger to all of us?" Ella asked.

"It still exists," Rose answered.

Ella felt her skin prickle. "Keep the officers right there, and Clifford. No one can strike in such a public place when you're under such tight guard." She knew her mother's predictions were invariably true, but logic dictated that for now it would be all right. "Tell no one but Clifford that our old enemy is finally dead. My work isn't over yet."

"I understand."

Ella hung up the phone as Big Ed came in. "It's time."

Ella nodded, and followed him out to the parking lot. Big Ed drove away first and she followed five minutes later.

The late afternoon heat set her nerves on edge. She was tired. Despite several cups of coffee, lack of sleep and tension were catching up to her, and at the worst possible time. She aimed the air-conditioner vent directly at her face. The blast of icy air helped.

By the time she reached the rough juniper and piñon plateau, it was the hottest part of the day. She parked her vehicle a few hundred yards off the highway, got into her disguise, then began the mile walk to the hogan. Heat blazed against the rocks and sand, and the body armor beneath her blouse accentuated every degree.

Ella arrived at the hogan twenty minutes later, glanced around outside, then went in. The hogan was cooler, but not by much. She reached beneath her skirt and pulled out her portable radio. "I'm here," she said, using the same tactical frequency as before.

"So are we," came Big Ed's reply.

Ella drank some water from the plastic barrel that Naomi kept on hand, but it wasn't much help. She forced herself to wait patiently, but her thoughts kept drifting to her family and to Justine.

Finally the sun disappeared behind the clouds, and twilight began to descend over the desert. Ella heard the night insects begin their incessant humming. Most times the monotony of the sound soothed, but tonight it got on her nerves as it obscured other sounds.

Ella studied the low-light monitors for an hour through bleary eyes. There was still no sign of anyone outside. Once the stars were out, she hunched over to hide her height and went outside holding one of Naomi's crystals. With methodical precision, she repeated the pattern the stargazer had taught her. Everything remained quiet.

After a while, she walked back to the hogan. Maybe Brownhat had decided to wait. By now he might have become complacent, certain that he'd outwitted the police. Ella sat there, watching the monitors as the hours passed uneventfully. Toward dawn, she wrapped herself in a blanket to ward off the chill. The officers keeping watch had no such luxury, but Ella knew they were all wearing jackets.

Just toward dawn, the tension rose again, and Ella started pacing. She built a fire in the stove and started heating water, just like Naomi would do under normal circumstances. Sitting there, bleary eyes on the monitors, Ella tried to analyze the situation.

If Furman didn't come within the next hour or so, he would probably not take action until the next evening. It would be hard for any of the cops to maintain their sharp edge if they had to sit up another night. It would also be harder to maintain security on the deception the longer time went by.

Ella reached down into her pocket and took out the badger fetish. It was cool to the touch, and her intuition told her that Furman wasn't buying the trap. Still, she had to wait it out a little longer. Bored, she made herself some coffee. The men outside, around her, would have to wait for theirs.

Finally, at eight o'clock in the morning, Ella decided to call it off for the day. She pulled out her radio. "He's not showing. Let's stand down for a while."

"I agree," Big Ed answered back. Looking as discouraged and tired as she felt, he met Ella by the entrance to the hogan. "I'll have our team report in, then work their way here, checking the area as they proceed."

By the time he'd radioed his instructions over the tactical frequency, Ella had poured a cup of coffee for the chief. He took it gratefully.

"Thank you, Mrs. Zah. What do you think Brownhat is up to?" Big Ed wondered aloud, looking around the edge of the trees as he spoke. Some of the closer-positioned officers were now visible.

"Frankly, I'm surprised. Our security was pretty good, and I don't think we tipped ourselves off during the night. Let's see what the rest of the team has to say."

Fifteen minutes later, all the officers made their reports. No one had seen any sign of Furman, or any other human, for that matter. The closest call any of them had was Officer Neskahi. A skunk had walked right past him, and it had been difficult to keep his position and not gag at the smell.

Ella removed her disguise while others collected the monitor batteries for recharging. They had to be ready for the next evening.

Anxious to check on her family and Justine, Ella went to her car while Big Ed briefed two new officers who had arrived. They would be watching the place during the day.

Ella reached the vehicle and picked up the cellular phone as she drove out to the highway. She got her mother within two minutes.

"Hello, Mother," Ella said nervously. "How is everyone? Has Loretta had the baby yet?"

Her mother's worried voice came through the air clearly. "Loretta is delivering the child now. The time has come."

Ella drove with the bubble on top of her vehicle and the siren screaming. She thought of the last stillbirth. If anything happened to this child, she wasn't sure how her brother and sister-in-law would weather it.

Forty minutes later, Ella raced into the hospital, flashing her badge at each checkpoint from the entrance doors to the elevator. Finally reaching Loretta's room, Ella peered inside. Rose placed a finger to her lips.

Loretta was sleeping and Clifford sat by her bed. Her brother gave her a tired, proud smile. "Go see the baby. He's perfect," he whispered.

Rose led Ella down to the nursery. "Labor was short and difficult, but the child is healthy and strong," she assured Ella. "For now, he must stay in a special incubator because he's not full-term, but in a short time he'll be home."

Ella went inside the small room with her mother. Two nurses walked around, tending the infants.

Rose stopped by the small unit near the door and looked down at her grandchild. "Your nephew," she said.

Ella looked down at the baby. A tiny silver chain hung around his neck, holding a thick silver square that rested on the child's breast. "Is that a gift from you?"

Rose shook her head. She reached for the nurse, who was passing by. "What is that chain on the child?"

"It might be a gift, but it doesn't belong inside that incubator," the nurse snapped. "I'll have to remove it."

Ella watched as the nurse took the chain off the baby. "May I have that?"

"Certainly, but no one is to put any jewelry on that child until he leaves this unit."

Ella took the chain from her hand and studied it. "The ornament isn't a medal of any kind. It looks like it came from a watchband." Ella twisted the chain, so she could study the back without handling it. As Rose came to stand beside her, Ella saw that the initials *R.C.* had been carved into it.

Rose gasped. "That belonged to your father-in-law! It's an invitation for his *chindi* to enter the child." Rose's voice was a horrified whisper.

Ella faced the nurse. "I want a list of everyone who came near this child."

"Our staff goes in and out, and parents are allowed too." The nurse shook her head slowly. "I'm sorry, but your request is impossible to fulfill."

Clifford came into the room. Seeing the look on his mother's face, he quickly turned to Ella. "What's happened?"

"This was on the baby," Ella said, holding the pendant up for Clifford to see.

Clifford grabbed it from her hand and threw it onto the floor. "My child will not be harmed by this. I *will* see to it." His voice shook with emotion.

The nurse picked the chain up and handed it back to Ella. "You're disturbing the other infants. Please take your problems outside."

Ella took the chain. Fingerprints would be useless now. She'd known that Peterson's allies would make some move against them, but she hadn't expected this.

Clifford stood by his child and, reaching into his medicine

pouch, began to chant in a soft voice. The nurse started to order him out again, but then, after one look from Clifford, changed her mind. She went over to check another tiny patient in her care.

Rose walked out with Ella. "My grandson will be fine. There are ways to counter this. He will grow to be strong and healthy," she assured Ella.

"How is Justine, Mother? I haven't gone to see her yet."

"She was recovering well last I heard. I haven't had a chance to stop by her room since just before you called." Rose patted her daughter's hand. "Don't worry. She's not been neglected. She may even have company right now. A young man called just a while ago asking about her. I took the call for her because the nurse had taken her to X-ray."

Ella stopped suddenly. "What young man? Nobody besides immediate family is supposed to know she's even here."

Rose paled. "He didn't give his name. It couldn't be . . ."

"What's her room number, Mom? Quickly."

"It's 328. Go past the children's ward and turn left."

Ella was already halfway down the hall, checking numbers on the doors as she ran. Pulling out her radio, she ordered all officers to keep an eye out for Furman Brownhat and gave a description. Then she made a specific call. "Report in, whoever is assigned to watch Officer Justine Goodluck's room. Report in now!"

Ella entered the stairwell and ran up the stairs. She'd been on the second floor, but she didn't have time for the elevator. A call came through while she was climbing, but the message was garbled, probably because of the metal stairs.

Bursting out the heavy door, Ella looked at the number of the closest door. It was 312. "Repeat your message, I didn't copy," she yelled.

The radio crackled. "This is Officer Lujan. I'm just outside Goodluck's door. Everything looks clear."

Ella heaved a sigh of relief and slowed to a jog. "Stay in position, no matter what. I'm almost at your 20." Ella placed the radio back on her hip and slowed to a walk as a young couple came her way. She saw them stare at her, but they glanced away as soon as she met their gazes. Ella felt as if she'd been running a marathon, and guessing from their expressions, probably looked it too.

As she passed the hall door leading into the children's ward, Ella had the sensation that someone was watching her. She stopped, placed her hand on the butt of her pistol, and turned back to look through the window in the door. Several beds in the ward had children in them, but only one adult was present, bending over, talking to a child. Her heart stopped as the adult turned around and she saw Furman look directly at her.

Before she could even respond, he ran out the door at the other end of the ward. Ella hurried after him, radio in hand, reporting Furman's position and direction of travel to all the officers within range. As she passed one small child, Ella looked to see if she had been hurt. The little girl smiled, and said hi.

"Hi," Ella said, and managed a smile. Increasing her speed, she slipped out the same doors Furman had just exited, then looked around. There was only one way to go. Another stairwell was at the end of the hall.

Calling out her position over the radio, Ella reached the stairwell door and peeked through the window. She couldn't see anyone, but she could hear footsteps going down the metal steps. Without hesitation, she followed.

Taking three steps at a time, Ella flew down the stairs. She passed the second-floor landing, then the first, following the running footsteps just ahead of her. Finally she burst through the door to the basement and ran right into Carolyn Roanhorse.

"What's going on? First somebody runs past my office full speed, then you almost knock me down," Carolyn complained.

"I'm after a killer, a young man. How many ways are there out of here?" Ella was breathing hard, but thinking clearly.

"There are only two ways to leave: up the stairs you came down, and the elevator." Carolyn waved her hand in the direction of the elevator, less than ten feet away.

"Did the guy take the elevator?"

"No, he went toward the morgue." Carolyn looked down the hall anxiously.

"Do you have keys to the stairwell?" Ella took her pistol in hand.

Carolyn nodded. "Sure, they're right here in my pocket."

"Give them to me, then take the elevator up and switch it off, so nobody can use it. Tell the officers you find to come back down in the elevator, armed and ready. I'm locking myself, and him, in."

Carolyn handed her the keys and ran to the elevator as Ella locked the door leading to the stairs. "You shouldn't do this alone," Carolyn called back.

"Go, and don't worry. This is what I do."

Ella, watching the hallway closely, radioed instructions to the other officers in the building. She would have help coming down soon, but meanwhile, Furman could not leave the floor.

Carolyn got on the elevator, and in a few seconds the doors began to close. "Be careful," Carolyn called out.

Placing her radio back on her belt, Ella walked slowly and silently down the hall. The first room was Carolyn's office, and Ella could tell at a glance it was empty. Moving cautiously, Ella reached in, locked the door, and pulled it shut. Then she proceeded toward the morgue itself.

The floor was completely silent. She suppressed a shudder. Walking wide to the right so Furman could not grab her as she entered the room, Ella peered to her left toward the place where the bodies were stored. Three gleaming chrome and steel gurneys in front of it were empty, white sheets fresh and ready, but two carts on the other side of the room held covered bodies. Although it was customary to leave the feet dangling out from under the white sheets so the toe tags could be read, both bodies were completely hidden.

Ella watched the bodies for a second. They were completely still; she couldn't detect even the slightest breathing motion. She decided to bypass the bodies for now. If she was lucky, she'd find Furman some other place first. Walking so both bodies were within her field of view, Ella edged over to the door of the autopsy room. She glanced quickly through the window, but the tile and metal room seemed empty. Bringing the keys in her pocket out with her left hand, Ella glanced up at the autopsy room number and down at the keys. Finding the right key, she quickly locked the door. If Furman was inside, he would stay there until help arrived.

Standing back from the covered bodies, Ella put the keys into her pocket and retrieved her radio. Quickly she reported her actions, and learned that four officers would soon be coming down in the elevator.

Reattaching the radio to her belt, Ella tried to decide if she wanted to peek under the sheets now or wait for the other officers to arrive. Circling around the gurneys with the bodies, Ella waited patiently. If he was underneath one of the sheets, Furman was being very still.

A quick glance around revealed there were no other hiding places. Either Furman was locked in the autopsy room or he was masquerading as a corpse. Then she noticed a smudge mark on one of the sheets. It was near the edge, on the far side. She brought her pistol up, ready, and moved closer. "Okay, Furman. It's time to stop the game. You have nowhere to run anymore. Come out with your hands where I can see them."

Her only response was the same eerie, lifeless silence that had encompassed her since Carolyn had left the floor. Ella stepped to within three feet of the gurney. The mark on the sheet was a footprint. She stared at it for a moment. Slowly, comprehension dawned on her. Ella looked up quickly just as Furman came crashing down through the ceiling tiles from above.

He collided hard against her, the full force of the blow slamming her in the middle of her back. Ella fell heavily to the floor, losing her pistol in the process. Furman spotted it and moved toward the weapon, but Ella grabbed at his leg and twisted his ankle as he kicked out.

Furman groaned in pain. "Let go, you bitch!"

With both hands on his ankle, Ella rolled over, gaining enough leverage in the move to roll Furman with her, farther away from the pistol. "Give it up, you little asshole." Furman would never be able to defeat her in a hand-to-hand fight. All she needed was to get a little closer to him, and she could put him down for good.

Suddenly there was a flash of silver, and instant recognition caused Ella to jerk her hands back from Furman's leg. The scalpel missed her hands completely, but sank into Furman's own calf at least halfway. He screamed and scrambled to a sitting position, leaving the blade in place. Ella quickly reached for the backup pistol in her boot, but the fight had gone out of Furman. He arched his back and cried like a child as blood gushed from the jagged wound. Ella stared, almost feeling sorry for him.

The other officers arrived a minute later. By then, Ella had the Packrat in cuffs and was trying to stem the flow of blood.

A half hour later, Ella was back with her mother, standing outside the room where her brother and his wife were both asleep. Ella was beyond sleep at the moment, but she knew that when it finally came she would be out for a whole day.

Ella glanced at her mother. "Our family, and our tribe, have been through so much the last few weeks. Has the danger finally passed?"

Rose shut her eyes for several moments, then opened them again. "Yes, for now, we are safe. You can rest, daughter," she answered softly, then smiled. "Maybe you should call Wilson. Spending a quiet evening together would do you both worlds of good."

"Rest? Quiet evening?" Ella chuckled and shook her head. "No way. I've finished the fieldwork, true, and the Packrat is locked up and under guard. But now I've got to face the real scourge of every cop's life."

"I don't understand. What can be worse than what you've already confronted?"

"Paperwork," Ella answered. Giving her mother a quick hug, she headed for the exit.